THE SECRET
IN HIS HEART

BY
CAROLINE ANDERSON

THE ER'S
NEWEST DAD

BY
JANICE LYNN

MILLS
BOON

3 8014 05166 6722

Caroline Anderson has the mind of a butterfly. She's been a nurse, a secretary, a teacher, run her own soft furnishing business, and now she's settled on writing. She says, 'I was looking for that elusive something. I finally realised it was variety, and now I have it in abundance. Every book brings new horizons and new friends, and in between books I have learned to be a juggler. My teacher husband John and I have two beautiful and talented daughters, Sarah and Hannah, umpteen pets, and several acres of Suffolk that nature tries to reclaim every time we turn our backs!' Caroline also writes for the Mills & Boon® Cherish™ series.

Janice Lynn has a Masters in Nursing from Vanderbilt University, and works as a nurse practitioner in a family practice. She lives in the southern United States with her husband, their four children, their Jack Russell—appropriately named Trouble—and a lot of unnamed dust bunnies that have moved in since she started her writing career.

To find out more about Janice and her writing visit www.janicelynn.com

THE SECRET
IN HIS HEART

BY
CAROLINE ANDERSON

First published in Great Britain 2013
by Mills & Boon, an imprint of Harlequin (UK) Limited.
Harlequin (UK) Limited, Eton House, 18-24 Paradise Road,
Richmond, Surrey TW9 1SR

© Caroline Anderson 2013

ISBN: 978 0 263 89897 2

Harlequin (UK) policy is to use papers that are natural, renewable and recyclable products and made from wood grown in sustainable forests. The logging and manufacturing process conform to the legal environmental regulations of the country of origin.

Printed and bound in Spain
by Blackprint CPI, Barcelona

Dear Reader,

Writing can be an accidental process. The book that preceded this one, *From Christmas to Eternity*, had a clinical lead called James. That was all I knew about him, until I wrote the words, 'Why not just take the time and enjoy your family? God knows you're lucky enough to have one.' And just like that, James became a person. A widower with a tragic past and no future other than work. Enter Connie, widow of his best friend, ex-colleague—and an attraction he's spent years denying. But Connie has a problem, and James could help her solve it, if he could defeat his own demons.

Now, you'd think that'd be enough complication, but, no, I gave them a dog. Not just any dog. I was fascinated when I first learned that Penn Farthing, an ex-serviceman, had 'adopted' starving, feral dogs in Helmand and set up a charity to rescue them, so of course when Connie's husband and James' friend Joe was killed in Afghanistan, the dog he'd planned to rescue had to come home—the last thing she could do for him. And where Connie goes, Saffy has to go, too, causing havoc and ultimately bringing Connie and James together.

You can find more about the work of Penn Farthing at www.nowzad.com, and to find out how Saffy helps James and Connie find the love they both deserve, read on...!

Caroline x

**Praise for
Caroline Anderson:**

'From one of category romance's most accomplished voices comes a beautifully told, intensely emotional and wonderfully uplifting tale of second chances, new beginnings, hope, triumph and everlasting love. Caroline Anderson's WEDDING OF THE YEAR is an engrossing, enthralling and highly enjoyable tale that will move you to tears and keep you riveted from the first page until the very last sentence. Moving, heartbreaking and absolutely fantastic, with WEDDING OF THE YEAR Caroline Anderson is at her mesmerising best!'
—*www.cataromance.com* on
ST PIRAN'S: WEDDING OF THE YEAR

'Photojournalist Maisie Douglas and businessman Robert Mackenzie have been more or less amicably divorced for almost two decades, but the upcoming marriage of their daughter, Jenni, stirs up old emotions on both sides. Very young when she married him, Maisie—pregnant and disowned by her family— was miserable living in Scotland with Rob's judgmental parents, and left after little more than a year. Maisie hasn't found another partner and neither has Rob. Can they find a way to trust each other again, after all this time? This lovely reunion romance is rich with emotion and humour, and all of the characters are exquisitely rendered.'
—*RT Book Reviews* on
MOTHER OF THE BRIDE

CHAPTER ONE

SILENCE.

No bleeps, no clipped instructions or clattering instruments, no hasty footsteps. Just a blissful, short-lived hush.

James stretched out his shoulders and felt the tension drain away. The relief was incredible. He savoured it for a moment before breaking the silence.

'Great teamwork, guys. Thank you. You did a good job.'

Someone chuckled. 'Would you accept anything less?'

He grinned. Fair cop, but it worked. Their critically injured patient was stabilised and on her way to Theatre, and for what seemed like the first time that day the red phone was quiet. Time to grab a break.

He glanced up at the clock. Ten to four? No wonder he was feeling light-headed. And his phone was jiggling again in his pocket.

'Right, this time I'm *really* going for lunch,' he said drily. 'Anything less than a MAJAX, you're on your own.'

There was a ripple of laughter as he tore off the thin plastic apron, dropped it in the bin with his gloves and walked out of Resus, leaving the rest of the team to clear up the chaos and restock ready for the next emergency. One of the perks of being clinical lead, he thought wryly as the door dropped shut behind him. God knows there were few enough.

He took the shortcut to the coffee shop, bought a coffee and a soft wholegrain roll stuffed with ham and salad, added a chocolate bar to boost his blood sugar and headed outside, drawing the fresh summer air deep into his lungs.

One of the best things about Yoxburgh Park Hospital was its setting. Behind the elaborate facade of the old Victorian building a modern general hospital had been created, providing the community not only with much needed medical facilities, but also a beautiful recreational area. It was green and quiet and peaceful, and he took his breaks out here whenever he could.

Not nearly often enough.

He found an empty bench under the trees and settled down to eat his lunch, pulling his phone out simultaneously to check for messages. It had jiggled in his pocket more than once in the last hour, but there were no messages, just two missed calls.

From Connie?

He frowned slightly. He hadn't heard from her in ages, and now two missed calls in the space of an hour? He felt his heart rate pick up and he called her back, drumming his fingers impatiently as he waited for the phone to connect.

She answered almost instantly, and to his relief she sounded fine.

'James, hi. Sorry, I didn't mean to disturb you. Are you at work?'

'Yeah—doesn't matter, I'm on a break now. How are you, Connie? You've been very quiet recently.' Well, not even that recently. Apart from the odd email saying nothing significant and a couple of ridiculously brief phone calls, she hadn't really contacted him since she'd got back from Afghanistan after Christmas. It wasn't just her fault. He hadn't contacted her, either, and now he felt a flicker of guilt.

She laughed, the soft musical sound making him ache a little inside. There'd been a time not so long ago when she'd never laughed...

'What, you mean I've left you in peace, Slater?'

'Something like that,' he said mildly. 'So, how are you?'

'Fine. Good. Great, really. Ready to move on.' The silence stretched out for a heartbeat, and then she said, 'Actually, I need to talk to you about that.'

She sounded oddly hesitant, and his radar started beeping.

'Fire away.'

That troubling silence again. 'I don't think it's something we can do over the phone,' she said eventually. 'I'd thought you might be off today as it's Sunday, and I thought maybe we could get together, it's been a while, but obviously not if you're working. Have you got any days off coming up?'

'Tomorrow? I'm off then for a couple of days. I don't get many weekends at the moment—crazy staffing issues—but I can always come over and see you tomorrow evening after you've finished work if it's urgent.'

'No, don't do that, I'll come to you. I'm not working at the moment so I've got plenty of time. And it isn't really urgent, I just—I wanted to talk to you. Can I pop over in the morning?'

Pop? From a hundred and thirty odd miles away? And why wasn't she working? 'Sure. Why don't you

stay over till Tuesday, if you're free? We can catch up.'
*And I can find out what the hell's going on that's so
'not urgent' that you have to come tomorrow morning.*

'Are you sure? It would be lovely but I've got the dog,
don't forget. Can you cope with that? She's very good
now—housetrained and all that, but I can't put her in
kennels at such short notice.'

Had she mentioned a dog? Possibly, but it didn't matter. He had a secure garden. She'd be fine. The dog was
the least of his worries.

'I'm sure we'll cope,' he said. 'Come. It'll be lovely
to see you.'

'Thanks. When do you want me?'

Always...

He crushed the inappropriate thought. 'Whenever
you're ready,' he said. 'Give me a call when you're an
hour away, so I can be sure I'm at home. I'll see you
tomorrow some time.'

'Great. Thanks, James.'

'No worries. Drive carefully.'

Ending the call, he ate the soft, squishy roll, drank
his coffee and tasted neither. All he could think about
was Connie and her non-urgent topic of conversation.
He ripped the wrapper off the chocolate bar and bit
into it absently.

What the hell did she want to talk to him about? He
had no idea, but he was beginning to regret his invitation. He must have been crazy. His place was a mess,
he had a zillion and one things to do, and catching up
with Connie just wasn't on his agenda—especially not
like this. The prospect of being alone with her for thirty-
six hours was going to test him to the limit. Not that he
wasn't looking forward to seeing her. Not at all.

Just—maybe a little too much...

Crushing the cup in his hand, he headed off back to the department, his thoughts and emotions tumbling.

Connie. His old friend, his ex-colleague, and his best friend's wife.

No. His best friend's *widow*. The woman he'd promised to take care of.

'When it happens, James—'

'If it happens—'

'When it happens—promise me you'll take care of her.'

'Of course I will, you daft bastard. It won't happen. It's your last tour. You'll be fine.'

Famous last words.

The ache of loss, still raw after two years, put everything back in perspective and gave him a timely reminder of his duties and responsibilities. It didn't matter what else he'd had planned, whatever his personal feelings for her, his duty to Connie came first and right now she needed him.

But apparently not urgently. Tomorrow would do.

Sheesh.

Savagely tossing the crushed cup into a bin, he strode through the door and headed back to work.

'Well. We're going to see James. What do you think of that, Saffy? Do you think he'll understand?'

Saffy thumped her tail once, head on Connie's foot, eyes alert as she peered up at her. Connie reached down a hand and stroked her gently, and Saffy groaned and rolled over, one leg lifted to reveal the vulnerable underside she was offering for a tickle.

'Hussy,' she crooned, rubbing the scarred tummy, and the dog's tail wagged again. She licked Connie's ankle, the contact of her warm, moist tongue cement-

ing the already close bond between them. Almost as if
she understood. No, of course she didn't, Connie told
herself. How could she, even though Connie had told
her everything there was to tell about it all in excruci-
ating detail.

'Sorry, sweetheart,' she murmured, straightening up
and getting to her feet. 'No time for cuddles, I've got
too much to do.'

If she was going to see James tomorrow, she needed
to pull herself together and get ready. Do some washing
so she had something other than jeans and a ratty old
T shirt to wear. Pack. Make sure the house was clean
and tidy before they left.

Not that it was dirty or untidy, but now the decision
was made and she was going to see him, to ask him the
most monumental and massive favour, she needed to
do something to keep herself busy or she'd go crazy.

She'd rehearsed her speech over and over again, gone
through what she was going to say until she'd worn it
out. There was nothing left to do but clean the house,
so she cleaned it until it squeaked, and then she fell into
bed and slept restlessly until dawn.

God, the place was a tip.

He'd been going to tackle it last night, but as usual
he'd been held up by admin and hadn't got home until
ten, so he'd left it till this morning. Now, looking round
it, he realised that had probably been a massive mistake.

He blitzed the worst of it, made up a bed for her and
went back downstairs.

Better. Slightly. If he ever had any regular time off
he might stand a chance, but right now that was just a
distant dream. He glanced at his watch. Ten to ten. Supermarket now, or later, after she'd arrived? She was

an early riser but the journey would take her a good two hours.

Now, he decided, if he was quick, and ten minutes later he was standing there in the aisles and trying to remember what she liked. Was she a vegetarian?

No, of course she wasn't. He recalled watching her eating a bun crammed with roast pork and apple sauce at the Suffolk Show, the memory still vivid. It must have been the first year he'd been in Yoxburgh, and Joe had been on leave.

And he'd been watching her eat, his body throbbing with need as she'd flicked out her tongue and scooped up a dribble of apple sauce on her chin. He'd dragged his eyes away and found Joe staring at him, an odd expression on his face.

'Food envy,' he'd explained hastily, and Joe had laughed and bought him another roll from the hog roast stand.

He'd had to force himself to eat it, because he hadn't had food envy at all, just plain old envy. He was jealous of Joe, jealous of his best friend for being so ridiculously happy with his lovely wife. How sick was that? How lonely and empty and barren— Whatever. She wasn't vegetarian, so he picked up a nice piece of fillet steak from the butchery counter, threw some other stuff into the trolley and headed home, wondering for the hundredth time what she wanted to say to him. She'd said she was ready to move on, and now it was in his head a disturbing possibility wouldn't go away.

Was there someone new in her life?

Why not? It was perfectly plausible. She was a beautiful woman, she was alone, she was free to do whatever she liked—but even the thought of her replacing the best friend a man could wish for, the kindest and most courageous man he'd ever known, made him feel sick.

Dismissing the pointless speculation, he drove down Ferry Road towards the little community grouped around the harbour mouth, turned onto the gravel track that led past a little string of houses to his cottage and pulled up on the drive next to a four-wheel drive he'd never seen before, just as his phone pinged.

Damn. He'd meant to be here, but she hadn't rung— or had she, while he'd been vacuuming the house?

Yup. There was a missed call from her, and a voice-mail.

'I've arrived. Couldn't get you on the phone earlier, but I'm here now so I'm walking the dog. Call me when you get home.'

He dialled her number as he carried the bags into the kitchen and dumped them on the worktop, and she answered on the second ring, sounding breathless.

'Hi—did you get my message?'

'Yeah. Sorry I wasn't here, I went food shopping. I'm back now. Where are you?'

'On the sea wall. I'll be two ticks, I can see the cottage from here,' she told him, so he opened the front door and stood on the porch step scanning the path, and there she was, blonde hair flying in the breeze, a huge sandy-coloured dog loping by her side as she ran towards him, her long limbs moving smoothly as she covered the ground with an effortless stride.

God, she was lovely.

Lovelier than ever, and that took some doing. His heart lurched, and he dredged up what he hoped was a civilised smile as he went to meet her.

She looked amazing, fit and well and bursting with energy. Her pale gold hair was gleaming, her blue eyes bright, her cheeks flushed with the sea breeze and the exertion as she ran up, her smile as wide as her arms, and threw herself at him. Her body slammed into his and knocked the breath from him in every way, and he nearly staggered at the impact.

'Hey, Slater!'

'Hey yourself, Princess,' he said on a slight laugh as his arms wrapped round her and caught her tight against him. 'Good to see you.'

'You, too.'

She hugged him hard, her body warm and firm against his for the brief duration of the embrace, and he hugged her back, ridiculously pleased to see her, because he'd missed her, this woman of Joe's. Missed her warmth and her humour, missed the laughter she carried with her everywhere she went. Or had, until she'd lost Joe.

Don't tell me you're getting married again—please, don't tell me that...

Swearing silently, he dropped his arms and stepped back, looking down at the great rangy hound standing panting at Connie's side, tongue lolling as it watched him alertly.

'So—I take it this is your rescued dog? I'd pictured some little terrier or spaniel.'

Connie winced ruefully. 'Sorry. Teensy bit bigger. This is Saffy—Safiya. It means best friend. Joe sort of adopted her in Afghanistan on his last tour. He was going to bring her home, but—well, he didn't make it, so I brought her back.'

Typical Joe, he thought with a lump in his throat. Big tough guy, soft as lights. And he'd just bet she'd been his best friend, in the harsh and desolate desert, thousands of miles from home. A touch of humanity in the inhumanity of war.

He held out his hand for Saffy to sniff. She did more than sniff it. She licked it. Gently, tentatively, coming closer to press her head against his shoulder as he crouched down to her level and stroked her long, floppy ears. A gentle giant of a dog. No wonder Joe had fallen for her.

He laughed softly, a little taken aback by the trusting gesture, and straightened up again. 'She's a sweetie,' he said, his voice slightly choked, and Connie nodded.

'She is. I had to bring her home.'

Of course she'd had to, because Saffy was her last link to Joe. If Joe had been soft, Connie was softer, but there was a core of steel in there, too. He'd seen plenty of evidence of that in the past few years.

He'd seen her holding herself together when Joe was deployed to Afghanistan for what was meant to be his final tour, and then again, just months later, when he came home for the last time in a flag-draped coffin—

'So, this is the new house, then,' she said, yanking him back to the present as he opened the gate and ushered her and Saffy through it.

He hauled in a breath and put the memories away. 'Hardly new. I've been here over two years. I'd forgotten you hadn't seen it.'

'No, well, things got in the way. I can't believe it's that long,' she said. She looked slightly bemused, as if the time had somehow passed and she'd been suspended in an emotional void. He supposed she might well have been. He had, for years. Still was in many ways, and it was a lonely place.

Take care of Connie.

Guilt ate at him. He should have been there more for

her, should have looked out for her, emailed her more often, rung her. It had been months, and he'd just let it drift by. Too busy, as usual, for the things that really mattered.

There didn't seem to be anything else to say, so he took her into the house, looking at it with the critical eyes of a stranger and finding it wanting. Not the house, but his treatment of it. The house was lovely and deserved better than a quick once-over as and when.

'Sorry, it's a bit of a mess. I haven't done a great deal to it, but the people I bought it from left it in great condition so I just moved in and got on with other things. I've been so busy I haven't even unpacked the books yet.'

She looked around and smiled. 'I can see that. You haven't put any pictures up, either.'

'I've got the sea. I don't need pictures,' he said simply, and she turned and looked out of the window, feeling the calming effect of the breakers rolling slowly in, the quiet suck of the surf on the shingle curiously soothing.

'No, I suppose you don't,' she said. She glanced around again. The living space was all open, the seating area at the front of the house facing the sea, the full-width dining and kitchen area at the back overlooking the marshes and the meandering river beyond. There was an unspoilt beauty about the area, and she could absolutely see why he'd bought the cottage.

'It's lovely, James. Really gorgeous. I was expecting something tiny from the name.'

'Thrift Cottage? There's a plant called sea thrift—*Armeria maritima*. The garden's full of it. I don't know which came first but I imagine that's the connection. It was certainly nothing to do with the price,' he said drily. 'Coffee?'

She chuckled. 'Love one. I haven't had my caffeine fix yet today.'

'Espresso, cappuccino, latte, Americano?'

She blinked. 'Wow, you must have a fancy coffee machine.'

He grinned. 'Some things have to be taken seriously.'

'So do me a flat white,' she challenged, her eyes sparkling with laughter.

Typical Connie, he thought. Never take the easy route or expect anyone else to. He rolled his eyes, took the milk out of the carrier bag he'd just brought home and started work while she and the dog watched his every move, Connie from the other side of the room, Saffy from her position on the floor just close enough to reach anything he might drop. Hope personified, he thought with a smile.

'You do know I was a *barista* while I was at uni?' he offered over his shoulder, the mischievous grin dimpling his lean cheek again and making her mouth tug in response.

'I didn't, but it doesn't surprise me.'

She watched him as he stuck a cup under the spout of the coffee machine, his broad shoulders and wide stance reminding her of Joe, and yet not. Joe had been shorter, stockier, his hair a lighter brown, and his eyes had been a muted green, unlike James's, which were a striking, brilliant ice-blue rimmed with navy. She noticed the touch of grey at his temples and frowned slightly. That was new. Or had she just not noticed before?

'So how long did the drive take you?' he asked, turning to look at her with those piercing eyes.

'Just over two hours—about two fifteen? I had a good run but I had to stop to let Saffy out for a minute.'

She stepped over the dog and perched on a high stool

beside him, and the light drift of her perfume teased his nostrils. He could feel her eyes on him as he foamed the milk, tapping the jug, swirling the espresso round the warmed cup before he poured the milk into it in a carefully controlled stream, wiggling the jug to create a perfect rosetta of microfoamed milk on top of the crema.

'Here,' he said, sliding the cup towards her with a flourish, pleased to see he hadn't lost his touch despite the audience.

'Latte art? Show-off,' she said, but she looked impressed and he couldn't resist a slightly smug chuckle.

He tore open a packet of freshly baked cookies from the supermarket, the really wicked ones oozing with calories. He wouldn't normally have bought them, but he knew Connie was a sucker for gooey cookies. He slid them towards her as Saffy watched hopefully.

'Here. Don't eat them all.'

'Whatever gave you that idea?' she said innocently, her smile teasing, and he felt his heart lurch dangerously.

'I've never yet met a woman who could resist triple choc chip cookies still warm from the oven.'

Her eyes lit up. 'Are they still warm?' she said, diving in, and he watched in fascination as she closed her eyes and sank her teeth into one.

He nearly groaned out loud. How could eating a cookie be so sexy?

'Murgh,' she said, eyes still closed, and he gave a strained chuckle and trashed his own rosetta as his hand jerked.

'That good?' he asked, his voice sounding rusty, and she nodded.

'Oh, yes,' she said, a little more intelligibly, and he laughed again, set his own coffee down on the breakfast bar and joined her on the other stool, shifting it away from her a little after he'd taken a cookie from the bag.

Her eyes were open again, and she was pulling another one apart, dissecting it slowly and savouring every bit, and he almost whimpered.

He *did* whimper. Did he? *Really?*

'Saffy, don't beg,' she said through a mouthful of cookie, and he realised it was the dog. He heaved a quiet sigh of relief and grabbed the last cookie, as much as anything so he wouldn't have to watch her eat it.

And then, just because they had to talk about something and anyway, the suspense was killing him, he asked, 'So, what did you want to talk to me about?'

Connie felt her heart thump.

This was it, her chance to ask him, and yet now she was here she had no idea—*no* idea—how to do it. Her carefully rehearsed speech had deserted her, and her mind flailed. *Start at the beginning*, she told herself, and took a deep breath.

'Um—did you realise Joe and I were having problems?' she asked tentatively.

'Problems?'

James stared at her, stunned by that. Problems were the last thing he would have associated with them. They'd always seemed really happy together, and Joe, certainly, had loved Connie to bits. Had it not been mutual? No, Joe would have said—wouldn't he? Maybe not.

'What sort of problems?' he asked warily, not at all sure he wanted to know.

'Only one—well, two, if you count the fact that I spent our entire marriage waiting for the doorbell to ring and someone in uniform to tell me he was dead.'

'I'd count that,' he said gruffly. He'd felt it himself, every time Joe had been deployed on active service—and it didn't get much more active than being a bomb disposal officer. But still, he'd never really expected it to happen. Maybe Connie had been more realistic.

'And the other problem?'

She looked away, her expression suddenly bleak. 'We couldn't have children.'

He frowned, speechless for a second as it sank in. He set his cup down carefully and closed his eyes. When he opened them she was watching him again, her bottom lip caught between her teeth, waiting for him to say the right thing.

Whatever the hell that was. He let out a long, slow sigh and shook his head.

'Ah, Connie. I'm so sorry. I didn't realise there was anything wrong. I always thought it was by choice, something you'd get round to when he'd finished that last tour.'

...except he never had...

'It was.' She smiled a little unsteadily, and looked away again. 'Actually, he was going to come and see you about it when he got home.'

'Me?' he asked, puzzled by that. 'I don't know anything about infertility. You're a doctor, you probably know as much about it as I do, if not more. You needed to see a specialist.'

'We had. It wasn't for that. We'd had the tests, and he was the one with the problem. Firing blanks, as he put it.' She grimaced a little awkwardly, uncomfortable revealing what Joe had considered a weakness, a failure, something to be ashamed of. 'I wanted him to tell you, but he wouldn't, not for ages. He was psyching himself up to do it when he got home, but it was so hard for him, even though you were so close.'

'We were, but—guys don't talk about that kind of thing, Connie, especially when they're like Joe.'

'I know. It's stupid, I feel so disloyal telling you because he just wouldn't talk about it. I would have told you ages ago, but he couldn't, and so nor could I because it wasn't my secret to tell.'

He sighed and reached out a hand, laying it over her arm and squeezing gently. 'Don't feel disloyal. I loved him, too, remember. You can tell me anything you need to, and you know it won't go any further.'

She nodded. 'I know. I just wish he'd felt he could tell you.'

'Me, too.' He sighed again and withdrew his hand. 'I'm really sorry, Connie. That must have been so tough to deal with.'

She looked down at her coffee, poking at the foam with the teaspoon, drawing little trails absently through the rosetta, and he noticed her cheeks had coloured a little.

She sucked in a slightly shaky breath. 'He was going to tell you, as soon as he got back. He wanted to ask you...' *Oh, just spit it out, woman! He can only say no!*

She sat up straighter and made herself look him in the eye, her heart pounding. 'He was going to ask you if you'd consider being a sperm donor for us.'

He stared at her blankly, the shock robbing him of his breath for a moment. He hauled it back in and frowned. 'Me?'

They'd wanted him to give them a child?

'Why me?' he asked, his voice sounding strangely distant. *Of all the people in the world, why me?*

She shrugged. 'Why not? I would have thought it

was obvious. He doesn't have a brother, you were his best friend, he loved and respected you. Plus you're not exactly ugly or stupid. Who better?' She paused for a second, fiddled with her spoon, then met his eyes again, her own a little wary. 'Would you have said yes?'

He shook his head to clear it, still reeling a little from the shock.

'Hell, I don't know, Connie. I have no idea.'

'But—possibly?'

He shrugged. 'Maybe.'

A baby? Maybe not. Most likely not.

'Definitely maybe? Like, probably?'

Would he? He tried to think, but he was still trying to come to terms with it and thinking seemed too hard right then.

'I don't know. I really don't know. I might have considered it, I suppose, but it's irrelevant now, so it's hard to know how I would have reacted. But you would have been brilliant parents. I'm just so sorry you never had the chance. That really sucks.'

She'd shifted her attention to the cookie crumbs on the breakfast bar, pushing them around with her fingertip, and he saw her swallow. Then she lifted her head and met his eyes. Her whole body seemed to go still, as if every cell was holding its breath. And then she spoke.

'What if it wasn't irrelevant now?'

CHAPTER TWO

WAS THIS WHY she'd wanted to see him? To ask him *this*?

He searched her eyes, and they didn't waver.

'What are you saying, Connie?' he asked quietly, but he knew already, could feel the cold reality of it curling around him like freezing fog.

He saw her swallow again. 'I wondered—I don't know how you'll feel about it, and I know Joe's not here now, but—James, I still really want a baby.'

He stared at her, saw the pleading in her eyes, and he felt suddenly drenched with icy sweat. She meant it. She really, really meant it—

He shoved the stool back abruptly and stood up, taking a step away on legs that felt like rubber. 'No. I'm sorry, Connie. I can't do it.'

He walked away, going out onto the veranda and curling his fingers round the rail, his hands gripping it so hard his knuckles were bleached white while the memories poured through him.

Cathy, coming into their bedroom, her eyes bright with joy in her pale face, a little white wand in her hand.

'I might've worked out why I've been feeling rough...'

He heard Connie's footsteps on the boards behind him, could feel her just inches away, feel her warmth, hear the soft sigh of her breath. Her voice, when she spoke, was hesitant.

'James? I'm sorry. I know it's a bit weird, coming out of the blue like that, but please don't just say no without considering it—'

Her voice cracked slightly, and she broke off. Her hand was light on his shoulder, tentative, trembling slightly. It burned him all the way through to his soul.

'James? Talk to me?'

'There's nothing to talk about,' he said, his voice hollow. 'Joe's dead, Connie. He's gone.' *They're all gone...*

Her breath sucked in softly. 'Do you think I don't know that? Do you really think that in the last two years I haven't noticed? But I'm still here, and I'm alive, and I'm trying to move on with my life, to rescue something from the wreckage. And you could help me do that. Give me something to live for. Please. At least think about it.'

He turned his head slightly and stared at her, then looked away again. 'Hell, Connie, you know how to push a guy's buttons.' His voice was raw now, rasping, and he swallowed hard, shaking his head again to clear it, but it didn't work this time any more than it had the last.

'I'm sorry. I know it's a bit sudden and unexpected, but—you said you would have considered it.'

'No, I said I *might* have considered it, for you and Joe. Not just for you! I can't do that, Connie! I can't just hand you a little pot of my genetic material and walk away and leave you on your own. What kind of person would that make me?'

'Generous? I'd still be the mother, still be the primary carer, whatever. What's the difference?'

'The difference? The *difference* is that you're on your

own, and children need two parents. There's no way I could be responsible for a child coming into the world that I wasn't involved with on a daily basis—'

'So—what? You want to be involved? You can be involved—'

'What? No! Connie, no. Absolutely not. I don't want to be a father! It's not anywhere, anyhow, on my agenda.'

Not any more.

'Joe said you might say that. I mean, if you'd wanted kids you would have got married again, wouldn't you? But he said you'd always said you wouldn't, and he thought that might be the very reason you'd agree, because you might see it as the only way you'd ever have a child...'

She trailed off, as if she knew she'd gone too far, and he stared down at his stark white knuckles, his fingers burning with the tension. One by one he made them relax so that he could let go of the rail and walk away. Away from Connie, away from the memories that were breaking through his carefully erected defences and flaying him to shreds.

Cathy's face, her eyes alight with joy. The first scan, that amazing picture of their baby. And then, just weeks later...

'No, Connie. I'm sorry, but—no. You don't know what you're asking. I can't. I just can't...'

The last finger peeled away from the railing and he spun on his heel and walked off, down the steps, across the garden, out of the gate.

She watched him go, her eyes filling, her last hope of having the child she and Joe had longed for so desperately fading with every step he took, and she put her hand over her mouth to hold in the sob and went back to the kitchen to a scene of utter chaos.

'Oh, Saffy, no!' she wailed as the dog shot past her, a slab of meat dangling from her jaws.

It was the last straw. Sinking down on the floor next to the ravaged shopping bags, Connie pulled up her knees, rested her head on them and sobbed her heart out as all the hopes and dreams she and Joe had cherished crumbled into dust.

It took him a while to realise the dog was at his side.

He was sitting on the sea wall, hugging one knee and staring blindly out over the water. He couldn't see anything but Connie.

Not the boats, not the sea—not even the face of the wife he'd loved and lost. He struggled to pull up the image, but he couldn't, not now, when he wanted to. All he could see was Connie's face, the hope and pleading in her eyes as she'd asked him the impossible, the agonising disappointment when he'd turned her down, and it was tearing him apart.

Finally aware of Saffy's presence, he turned his head and met her eyes. She was sitting beside him, the tip of her tail flickering tentatively, and he lifted his hand and stroked her.

'I can't do it, Saffy,' he said, his voice scraping like the shingle on the beach. 'I want to help her, I promised to look after her, but I can't do that, I just can't. She doesn't know what she's asking, and I can't tell her. I can't explain. I can't say it out loud.'

Saffy shifted slightly, leaning on him, and he put his arm over her back and rested his hand on her chest, rubbing it gently; after a moment she sank down to the ground with a soft grunt and laid her head on her paws, her weight against him somehow comforting and reassuring.

How many times had Joe sat like this with her, in the heat and dust and horror of Helmand? He stroked her side, and she shifted again, so that his hand fell naturally onto the soft, unguarded belly, offered with such trust.

He ran his fingers over it and stilled, feeling the ridges of scars under his fingertips. It shocked him out of his grief.

'Oh, Saffy, what happened to you, sweetheart?' he murmured. He turned his head to study the scars, and saw feet.

Two feet, long and slim, slightly dusty, clad in sandals, the nails painted fire-engine-red. He hadn't heard her approaching over the sound of the sea, but there she was, and he couldn't help staring at those nails. They seemed so cheerful and jolly, so totally out of kilter with his despair.

He glanced up at her and saw that she'd been crying, her eyes red-rimmed and bloodshot, her cheeks smudged with tears. His throat closed a little, but he said nothing, and after a second she sat down on the other side of the dog, her legs dangling over the wall as she stared out to sea.

'She was injured when he found her,' she said softly, answering his question. 'They did a controlled explosion of an IED, and Saffy must have got caught in the blast. She had wounds all over her. He should have shot her, really, but he was racked with guilt and felt responsible, and the wounds were only superficial, so he fed her and put antiseptic on them, and bit by bit she got better, and she adored him. I've got photos of them together with his arm round her in the compound. His commanding officer would have flayed the skin off him if he'd known, especially as Joe was the officer in charge of the little outpost, but he couldn't have done anything else. He broke all the rules for her, and nobody ever said a word.'

'And you brought her home for him.'

She tried to smile. 'I had to. I owed it to her, and anyway, he'd already arranged it. There's a charity run by an ex-serviceman to help soldiers bring home the dogs that they've adopted over there, and it was all set up, but when Joe died the arrangements ground to a halt. Then a year later, just before I went out to Afghanistan, someone from the charity contacted me and said the dog was still hanging around the compound and did I still want to go ahead.'

'And of course you did.' He smiled at her, his eyes creasing with a gentle understanding that brought a lump to her throat. She swallowed.

'Yeah. Well. Anyway, they were so helpful. The money wasn't the issue because Joe had already paid them, it was the red tape, and they knew just how to cut through it, and she was flown home a month later, just after I left for Afghanistan. She was waiting for me in the quarantine kennels when I got home at the end of December, and she's been with me ever since, but it hasn't been easy.'

'No, I'm sure it hasn't. Poor Saffy,' he said, his hand gentle on her side, and Connie reached out and put her hand over his, stilling it.

'James, I'm really sorry. I didn't mean to upset you. I just—it was the last piece of the puzzle, really, the last thing we'd planned apart from bringing Saffy home. We'd talked about it for so long, and he was so excited about the idea that maybe at last we could have a baby.

He didn't know what you'd say, which way you'd go, but he was hoping he could talk you into it.'

And maybe he could have done, she thought, if James had meant what he'd said about considering it. But now, because Joe was dead, James had flatly refused to help her because she'd be alone and that was different, apparently.

'You know,' she said softly, going on because she couldn't just give up on this at the first hurdle, 'if you'd said yes to him and then he'd been killed in some accident, for instance, I would still have had to bring the baby up alone. What would you have done then, if I'd already had a child?'

'I would have looked after you both,' he said instantly, 'but you haven't had a child, and Joe's gone, and I don't want that responsibility.'

'There is no responsibility.'

He stared at her. 'Of course there is, Connie. I can't just give you a child and let you walk off into the sunset with it and forget about it. Get real. This is my flesh and blood you're talking about. My child. I could never forget my child.'

Ever...

'But you would have done it for us?'

He shook his head slowly. 'I don't know. Maybe, maybe not, but Joe's not here any more, and a stable, happily married couple who desperately want a baby isn't the same as a grieving widow clinging to the remnants of a dream.'

'But that's not what I'm doing, not what this is about.'

'Are you sure? Have you really analysed your motives, Connie? I don't think so. And what if you meet someone?' he asked her, that nagging fear suddenly rising again unbidden and sickening him. 'What if, a couple of years down the line, another man comes into your life? What then? Would you expect me to sit back and watch a total stranger bringing up my child, with no say in how they do it?'

She shook her head vehemently. 'That won't happen—and anyway, I'm getting older. I'm thirty-six now. Time's ebbing away. I don't know if I'll ever be truly over Joe, and by the time I am, and I've met someone and trust him enough to fall in love, it'll be too late for me and I really, really want this. It's now or never, James.'

It was. He could see that, knew that her fertility was declining with every year that passed, but that wasn't his problem. Nothing about this was his problem. Until she spoke again.

'I don't want to put pressure on you, and I respect your decision. I just—I would much rather it was someone Joe had loved and respected, someone I loved and respected, than an anonymous donor.'

'Anonymous donor?' he said, his voice sounding rough and gritty to his ears.

'Well, what else? If it can't be you, I don't know who else it would be. There's nobody else I could ask, but if I go for a donor how do I know what they're like? How do I know if they've got a sense of humour, or any brains or integrity—I might as well go and pull someone in a nightclub and have a random—'

'Connie, for God's sake!'

She gave a wry, twisted little smile.

'Don't worry, James. It's OK. I'm not *that* crazy. I won't do anything stupid.'

'Good,' he said tautly. 'And for the record, I don't like emotional blackmail.'

'It wasn't!' she protested, her eyes filling with tears.

'Really, James, it wasn't, I wouldn't do that to you. I wasn't serious. I'm really not that nuts.'

He wasn't sure. Not nuts, maybe, but—desperate?

'When it happens—promise me you'll take care of her.'

'Of course I will, you daft bastard. It won't happen. It's your last tour. You'll be fine.'

But he hadn't been fine, and now Connie was here, making hideous jokes about doing something utterly repugnant, and he felt the weight of responsibility crush him.

'Promise me you won't do anything stupid,' he said gruffly.

'I won't.'

'Nothing. Don't do anything. Not yet.'

She tilted her head and searched his eyes, her brows pleating together thoughtfully. 'Not yet?'

Not ever, because I can't bear the thought of you giving your body to a total stranger in some random, drunken encounter, and because if anybody's going to give you a baby, it's me—

The thought shocked him rigid. He jack-knifed to his feet and strode back to the house, his heart pounding, and after a few moments he heard the crunch of gravel behind him on the path.

Saffy was already there at his side, glued to his leg, and as he walked into the kitchen and stared at the wreckage of his shopping bags, she wagged her tail sheepishly, guilt written all over her.

A shadow fell across the room.

'Ah. Sorry. I was coming to tell you—she stole the steak.'

He gave a soft, slightly unsteady laugh and shook his head. 'Oh, Saffy. You are such a bad dog,' he murmured, with so much affection in his voice it brought a lump to her throat. He seemed to be doing that a lot today.

'She was starving when Joe found her. She steals because it's all she knows, the only way she could survive. And it really is her only vice. I'll replace the steak—'

'To hell with the steak,' he said gruffly. 'She's welcome to it. We'll just have to go to the pub tonight.'

Better that way than sitting alone together in his house trying to have a civilised conversation over dinner and picking their way through this minefield. Perhaps Saffy had inadvertently done them both a favour.

'Well, I could have handled that better, couldn't I, Saff?'

Saffy just wagged her tail lazily and stretched. James had gone shopping again because it turned out it was more than just the steak that needed replacing, so Connie was sitting on a bench in the garden basking in the lovely warm June sunshine and contemplating the mess she'd made of all this.

He'd refused her offer of company, saying the dog had spent long enough in the car, and to be honest she was glad he'd gone without her because it had all become really awkward and uncomfortable, and if it hadn't mattered so much she would have packed up the dog and her luggage and left.

But then he'd said 'yet'.

Don't do anything yet.

She dropped her head back against the wall of the cabin behind her and closed her eyes and wondered what he'd really meant by 'yet'.

She had no idea.

None that she dared to contemplate, anyway, in case a ray of hope sneaked back in and she had to face having it dashed all over again, but he'd had a strange look about him, and then he'd stalked off.

Run away?

'No! Stop it! Stop thinking about it. He didn't mean anything, it was just a turn of phrase.'

Maybe…

She opened her eyes and looked up at the house, trying to distract herself. It was set up slightly above the level of the garden, possibly because of the threat of flooding before the sea wall had been built, but the result was that even from the ground floor there were lovely views out to sea across the mouth of the estuary and across the marshes behind, and from the bedrooms the views would be even better.

She wondered where she'd be sleeping. He hadn't shown her to her room yet, but it wasn't a big house so she wouldn't be far away from him, and she felt suddenly, ridiculously uneasy about being alone in the house with him for the night.

Crazy. There was nothing to feel uneasy about. He'd stayed with them loads of times, and he'd stayed the night after Joe's funeral, too, refusing to leave her until he was sure she was all right.

And anyway, what was he going to do, jump her bones? Hardly, James just wasn't like that. He'd never so much as looked at her sideways, never mind made her feel uncomfortable like some of Joe's other friends had.

If he had, there was no way she would have broached the sperm donor subject. Way too intimate. It had been hard enough as it was, and maybe that was why she felt uneasy. The whole subject was necessarily very personal and intimate, and she'd gone wading in there without any warning and shocked his socks off.

It dawned on her belatedly that she hadn't even asked

if there was anyone else who might have been a consideration in this, but that was so stupid. He was a fit, healthy and presumably sexual active man who was entitled to have a relationship with anyone he chose. She'd just assumed he wasn't in a relationship, assumed that just because he'd never mentioned anyone, there wasn't anyone.

OK, so he probably wasn't getting married to her, whoever she might be, but that didn't stop him having a lover. Several, if he chose. Did he bring them back here?

She realised she was staring up at the house and wondering which was his bedroom, wondering where in the house he made love to the *femme du jour*, and it stopped her in her tracks.

What was she *doing*, even *thinking* about his private life? Why the hell was she here at all? How had she had the nerve to ask him to do this?

But he'd said 'yet'…

She sighed and stopped staring up at the house. Thinking about James and sex in the same breath was so not the way forward, not if she wanted to keep this clinical and uninvolved. And she did. She had to, because it was complicated enough. She looked around her instead, her eye drawn again to the cabin behind her. It was painted in a lovely muted grey-green, set up slightly on stilts so it was raised above the level of the garden like the house, with steps up to the doors.

She wondered what he used it for. It might be a store room, but it seemed far too good to use as a glory-hole. That would be such a waste.

Home gym? Possibly, although he didn't have the sort of muscles that came from working out. He looked like more of a runner, or maybe a tennis player. Not that she'd studied his body, she thought, frowning at herself. Why would she? But she'd noticed, of course she had.

She dragged herself back to the subject. Hobbies room? She wasn't aware that he had any. James had never mentioned it, and she realised that for all she'd known him for years, she hardly *knew* him. Not really. Not deep down. She'd met him nine years ago, worked with him for a year as his SHO, seen him umpteen times since then while she'd been with Joe, but he didn't give a lot away, at least not to her. Never had.

Maybe that was how she'd felt able to come down here and ask him this? Although if she'd known more about how he ticked she could have engineered her argument to target his weak spot. Or had she inadvertently done that? His reaction had been instant and unmistakeable. He'd recoiled from the idea as if it was unthinkable, but then he'd begun to relent—hadn't he?

She wasn't sure. It would have helped if Joe had paved the way, but he hadn't, and so she'd had to go in cold and blunder about in what was obviously a very sensitive area. Pushing his buttons, as he'd put it. And he'd said no, so she'd upset him for nothing.

Except he hadn't given her a flat-out no in the end, had he? He'd said don't do anything *yet*. Whatever yet meant.

She sighed. Back to that again.

He didn't really need another trip to the supermarket. They could have managed. He'd just needed space to think, to work out what, if anything, he could do to stop Connie from making the biggest mistake of her life.

Or his.

He swore softly under his breath, swung the car into a parking space and did a quick raid of the bacon and sausage aisle to replace all the breakfast ingredients Saffy had pinched, then he drove back home, lecturing himself every inch of the way on how his responsibility to Connie did *not* mean he had to do this.

He just had to stop her doing something utterly crazy. The very thought of her with a total stranger made him gag, but he wasn't much more thrilled by the idea of her conceiving a child from a nameless donor courtesy of a turkey baster.

Hell, it could be anybody! They could have some inherited disease, some genetic disorder that would be passed on to a child—a predisposition to cancer, heart disease, all manner of things. Rationally, of course, he knew that no reputable clinic would use unscreened donors, and the checks were rigorous. Very rigorous. He *knew* that, but even so...

What would Joe have thought about it? If he'd refused, what would Joe and Connie have done next? Asked another friend? Gone to a clinic?

It was irrelevant, he told himself again. That was then, this was now, this was Connie on her own, fulfilling a lost dream. God knows what her motives were, but he was pretty sure she hadn't examined them in enough detail or thought through the ramifications. Somehow or other he had to talk her out of it, or at the very least try. He owed it to Joe. He'd promised to take care of her, and he would, because he kept his promises, and he'd keep this one if it killed him.

Assuming she'd let him, because her biological clock was obviously ticking so loud it was deafening her to reason. And as for his crazy reaction, that absurd urge to give her his baby—and without the benefit of any damn turkey baster—

Swearing viciously under his breath, he pulled up in

a slew of gravel, and immediately he could hear Saffy yipping and scrabbling at the gate.

'Do you reckon she can smell the shopping?' Connie asked, smiling tentatively at him over the top, and he laughed briefly and turned his attention to the shopping bags, wondering yet again how on earth he was in this position. Why she hadn't warned him over the phone, said something, anything, some little hint so he hadn't been quite so unprepared when she'd just come out with it, though quite how she would have warned him—

'Probably,' he said drily. 'I think I'd better put this lot away in the fridge pronto. I take it she can't open the fridge?'

'She hasn't ever done it yet.'

'Don't start now,' he said, giving the dog a level stare immediately cancelled out by a head-rub that had her shadowing him into the kitchen.

Connie followed him, too, hesitating on the threshold. 'James, I'm really sorry. I didn't mean to put you in a difficult position.'

He paused, his hand on the fridge door, and looked at her over his shoulder. 'You didn't,' he said honestly. 'Joe did. It was his idea. You were just following up on it.'

'I could have let it go.'

'So why didn't you?'

Her smile was wry and touched with sadness. 'Because I couldn't,' she answered softly, 'not while there was any hope,' and he straightened up and shut the fridge and hugged her, because she just looked so damned unhappy and there was nothing he could do to make it better.

No amount of taking care of her was going to sort this out, short of doing what she'd asked, and he wasn't sure he would ever be able to do that, despite that visceral urge which had caught him off guard. Or because of it? Just the thought of her pregnant with his child...

He let her go, easing her gently away with his hands on her shoulders and creating some much-needed distance between them, because his thoughts were suddenly wildly inappropriate, and the graphic images shocked him.

'Why don't you stick the kettle on and we'll have a cup of tea, and then we can take Saffy for a walk and go to the pub for supper.'

'Are we still going? I thought you'd just been shopping.'

He shrugged. 'I didn't bother to get anything for tonight. The pub seemed like a good idea—unless—is Saffy all right to leave here while we eat?'

She stared at him for a second, as if she was regrouping.

'Yes, she's fine. I've got a big wire travelling crate I use for her—it's a sort of retreat. I leave the door open all day so she can go in there to sleep or get away from it all, and I put her in there at night.'

'Because you don't trust her?'

'Not entirely,' she said drily. 'Still early days, and she did pinch the steak and the sausages.'

'The crate it is, then.' He smiled wryly, then glanced at his watch. 'Why don't we bring your luggage in and put it in your room while the kettle boils? I would have done it before but things ran away with us a little.'

Didn't they just? she thought.

He carried the dog's crate, she carried her overnight bag and the bag of stuff for Saffy—food, toys, blanket. Well, not a blanket, really, just an old jumper of Joe's she'd been unable to part with, and then when Saffy had come home she'd found a justification for her sentimental idiocy.

'Can we leave the crate down here?' she asked. 'She'll be fine in the kitchen, she's used to it.'

'Sure. Come on up, I'll give you a guided tour. It'll take about ten seconds. The house isn't exactly enormous.'

It wasn't, but it was lovely. There were doors from the entrance hall into the ground floor living space, essentially one big L-shaped room, with a cloakroom off the hallway under the stairs, and the landing above led into three bedrooms, two doubles and a single, and a small but well-equipped and surprisingly luxurious bathroom.

He showed her into the large bedroom at the front, simply furnished with a double bed, wardrobe and chest of drawers. There was a pale blue and white rug on the bare boards between the bed and the window, and on the edge of it was a comfy armchair, just right for reading in. And the bed, made up in crisp white linen, sat squarely opposite the window—perfect for lying there drinking early morning tea and gazing out to sea.

She crossed to the window and looked left, over the river mouth, the current rippling the water. The window was open and she could hear the suck of the sea on the shingle, the keening of the gulls overhead, and if she breathed in she could smell the salt in the air.

'Oh, James, it's lovely,' she sighed.

'Everyone likes this room.' He put her bag down and took a step towards the door. 'I'll leave you to settle in.'

'No need. I travel light. It'll take me three seconds to unpack.'

She followed him back out onto the landing and noticed another flight of stairs leading up.

'So what's up there?' she asked.

'My room.'

He didn't volunteer anything else, didn't offer to show it to her, and she didn't ask. She didn't want to enter his personal space. Not under the circumstances. Not after her earlier speculation about his love life. The last thing she needed was to see the bed he slept in. So she didn't ask, just followed him downstairs, got her walking boots out of the car and put them on.

'In your own time, Slater,' she said lightly, and he gave her one of those wry smiles of his and got off the steps and led her and Saffy out of the gate.

CHAPTER THREE

SHE PUT SAFFY on a lead because she didn't really want to spend half the evening looking for her if she ran off, but the dog attached herself to James like glue and trotted by his side, the lead hanging rather pointlessly across the gap between her and Connie.

Faithless hound.

'So, where are we going?' she asked, falling in beside them.

'I thought we could go along by the river, then cut inland on the other side of the marshes and pick up the lane. It'll bring us out on the sea wall from the other direction. It's about three miles. Is that OK?'

'Sounds good.'

The path narrowed on top of the river wall, and she dropped back behind him, Saffy still glued to his heels, and in the end she gave him the lead.

'You seem to have a new friend,' she said drily, and he glanced down at the dog and threw her a grin over his shoulder.

'Looks like it. Is that a problem?'

'No, of course not,' she said promptly. 'I'm glad she likes you. She does seem to like men, I expect because she's been used to them looking after her out in Helmand, but she'll have to get over it when we go home tomorrow. I hope it won't unsettle her.'

'Do you think it might?'

'I don't know. I hope not. She's doing so well.'

'Apart from the thieving,' he said drily, and she gave a guilty chuckle.

'Yeah, well. Apart from that.'

They walked in silence for a while by the muddy shallows at the edge of the river, and then as they turned inland and headed uphill, he dropped back beside her and said, 'So, how was Afghanistan? You haven't really told me anything about it.'

'No. It was a bit strange really. A bit surreal, but I'm glad I went. The facilities at Camp Bastion are fantastic. The things they do, what they achieve—for a field hospital it's unbelievable. Did you know it's got the busiest trauma unit in the world?'

'I'm not surprised. Most of them aren't in an area that has conflict.'

'No. No, they aren't. And I found that aspect really difficult.'

'Because of Joe?'

She nodded. 'Sort of. Because of all of them, really. I had second thoughts about going, after he died. I didn't know how I'd feel facing the stark reality of it, but I realised when the first wave of grief receded that I still wanted to go. There was so much I wanted to try and understand, such as why it was necessary, why he'd gone in the first place, what he'd been trying to achieve.'

'And did you?'

'No. No, I still don't understand, not really. I don't think I ever will and I'm not sure I want to. People killing each other, maiming each other—it all seems so pointless and destructive. There must be a better way than all this senseless violence.'

'It must have been really hard for you, Connie,' he said, his voice gentle. 'Very close to home.'

She nodded slowly, remembering the shock of seeing the first casualties come in, the realisation that this was it, this was what really happened out there. 'It was. I'd seen videos, had training, but I hadn't really understood what it was like for him until then. Seeing the injured lads there, though, fighting so hard to save them—it brought it all home to me, what he'd gone through, the threat he'd faced every day, never knowing when or if it might happen to him. That was tough.'

'I'm sure. He mentioned you were talking about going. I got the feeling he didn't like it much.'

'No, he didn't. I don't think he wanted to be worrying about me while he was trying to do his job, and he'd tried to put me off when I joined the Territorial Army as a volunteer doctor four years ago, but I thought, if Joe can do it, so can I. Not in the same way, but to do something, to do some good—and I'm glad I did, even though it was tough, because it's an incredible experience as a doctor.'

They fell silent for a while, then she went on, 'It's amazing what they can do there, you know, saving people that in civilian medicine we simply couldn't save because we just don't get to them fast enough or treat them aggressively enough when we do.'

He followed her lead and switched the conversation to practical medical aspects. 'So what would you change about the way we do things here?'

'Speed. Blood loss. That's the real killer out there, so stopping that fast is key, and transfusions. Massive transfusions. We gave one guy a hundred and fifty units of whole blood, plasma, platelets—you name it. No mucking about with saline and colloids, it's straight in with the blood products. And total body scans, the second they're stable enough to go, so they can see exactly what's wrong and treat it. We should really be doing that with multiple trauma, because it's so easy to miss something when there's loads going on.'

He nodded. 'If only we could, but we just don't have the resources. And as for the time issue—we lose people so often because they just get to us too slowly.'

'Oh, they do. We have the golden hour. They have the platinum ten minutes—they fly out a consultant-led team, scoop them up and bring them back and they're treating them aggressively before the helicopter's even airborne. Every soldier carries a tourniquet and is trained to use it in an emergency, and it's made so much difference. They save ninety per cent of multiple trauma patients, where in the rest of the world we save about twenty per cent. And I realised that if Joe died despite everything they were able to throw at him, it was because he was unsaveable. That was quite cathartic.'

He nodded slowly. 'I can imagine it would be. So, will you go again?'

'No,' she said softly. 'I'm glad I went, because it helped me let go of Joe, but I've done it now, and I've said goodbye and I've left the TA. I need to move on. I have other goals now.'

A baby, for one.

He went quiet for a while, then turned his head and looked at her searchingly.

'So how come you aren't working at the moment?'

She gave him a fleeting smile and looked away again. 'I wondered if you'd ask that. I could blame it on Saffy, say she'd taken a lot of time, a lot of training, and in a way it's true, but really she's just an excuse. I guess I was—I don't know... Taking time out to regroup, maybe? I worked solidly for the first year after he died, and I didn't give myself time to think, and then I went off to Afghanistan and put even more pressure on myself. That was a mistake, and by the time I got back after Christmas I was wiped. I needed time just to breathe a bit and work out where I go from here. A bit of a gap year, in a way. So I took it—or a few months, anyway. Just to try and make some sense of it.'

She made herself meet his eyes again, and found a gentle understanding in them.'Yeah. I did that after Cathy died. Took a gap year and grabbed the world by the throat, trying to make sense of it.'

'Did it help?'

He thought back to the aching emptiness, the people he'd met who'd scarcely registered in the haze of grief that had surrounded him. 'No. I don't know. Maybe. Maybe not. It took me away from it, but when I came back it was still there, lurking in wait. The grief, the loneliness.'

It was the closest he'd ever got to talking about Cathy, so she pushed a little more, to see if he'd open up further.

'She had cancer, didn't she?'

The shadows in his eyes darkened. 'Yes. One minute she was fine, the next she was dying.'

Connie felt her heart ache for him. 'Oh, James. It must have been dreadful watching that.'

He could see her now, the image crystal clear, pale as a ghost against the crisp white sheets, trying to smile at him, the small, neat curve of her doomed pregnancy so prominent in that thin frame.

'It was,' he said simply.

They reached the lane then, and he led the way, walking in single file for a while, facing the oncoming traffic.

Convenient, she thought, since it meant they couldn't talk. Far from opening up, he'd shut down again, so she left him alone, just following on behind until they reached the sea wall again and turned left towards the harbour and the little community clustered around the river mouth.

As they drew nearer they passed a house, a sprawling, ultra-modern house clad in cedar that had faded to silver. It was set in a wonderful garden on the end of the little string of properties, and there were children playing outside on the lawn, running in and out of a sprinkler and shrieking happily, and a woman with a baby on her hip waved to him.

He waved back, and turned to Connie as they walked on. 'That's Molly. She and her husband used to own my house. They outgrew it.'

'I should think they did. There were a lot of children there.'

'Oh, they're not all hers,' he said with a fleeting smile. 'The baby's theirs and she's got a son of about twelve, I think, and they've got another little one. The others will be her sister-in-law's. They didn't want to move away from here, but with two children and room for her painting they were struggling for space, as you can imagine, and then that house came on the market and David pounced on it.'

'It's an amazing house. They must have had a stash of cash somewhere or a lottery win.'

He chuckled, the sombre mood seeming to slip away. 'Oh, it didn't look like that when they bought it, but I don't think they're exactly strapped. David's a property developer and he part-owns a chain of boutique hotels in Australia. His father's a local building contractor, and they extended the house massively. She's got a great studio space and gallery there, and they've done a lovely job of it. They're nice people. Good neighbours.'

She wondered what it must be like to live in one place long enough to get to know your neighbours. She'd moved so much with Joe, shifting from one base to another, never putting down roots, and it hadn't been much better in her childhood. She envied James the stability of his life, even if he was alone. Not that she knew that for sure, she reminded herself.

He cut down off the sea wall to his garden gate and held it for her. 'Right, I need a shower, and then shall we go over to the pub? I haven't had anything but those cookies since breakfast and I'm starving.'

'Me, too, but I need to feed the dog. You take the bathroom first.'

'No need. I've got my own upstairs.'

She felt the tension she'd been unaware of leave her. So, no sharing a bathroom, no awkward moments of him tapping on the door or her being caught in the hall with dripping hair.

Heavens, what was wrong with her? This was *James*!

'Half an hour?' he suggested.

'That's fine. I'll feed Saffy first.'

He disappeared up the stairs, and she fed the dog and put her in the crate, not taking any chances while she was getting ready to go out. This would *not* be the diplomatic time to find out that Saffy could, indeed, open the door of the fridge.

She put her hair up in a knot and showered quickly, then contemplated her clothes. She hadn't really brought anything for going out, it hadn't occurred to her, but it was only the pub and she'd got a pretty top that would do. She put it on over her cropped jeans, let her hair down and then put on some makeup. Not much, just a touch of neutral eyeshadow, a swipe of mascara and a clear, shimmery lipgloss. Just enough to hide behind.

'Stupid woman,' she muttered. They were going to the local pub for a quick meal to make up for the fact that Saffy had stolen the steak. It wasn't an interview, and it sure as hell wasn't a date.

Not even remotely!

So why did she feel so nervous?

She looked gorgeous.

She wasn't dressed up, but she'd put on a little bit of makeup and a fine, soft jersey top that draped enticingly over her subtle curves.

She wasn't over-endowed, but she was in proportion, and when she leant forward to pick up her drink the low neckline fell away slightly, just enough to give him a tantalising glimpse of the firm swell of her breasts cradled in lace.

Fine, delicate lace, the colour of ripe raspberries.

He hauled his eyes away from her underwear and sat back, propping an ankle on the other knee to give his unruly body a little privacy. God, what was *wrong* with him?

'So, what are you going to eat?' he asked, studying the menu even though he knew it by heart.

'I don't know. What's good?'

'All of it. I eat here fairly often, and there's always something new on. The specials are worth a punt, but if you don't fancy anything on the board there's a good menu.'

She swivelled round to look at the board, arching

backwards so she could get a better view, and the top pulled tight over those lace-clad breasts.

Raspberry lace, the fruit inside them ripe and soft and full, he thought, and almost groaned out loud.

'Do they do good puds?'

An image of her eating the cookies with such relish popped into his head, and gave a slightly strangled chuckle. 'Yes,' he said, feeling doomed. 'They do brilliant puds. Save room.'

'Just what I was thinking.'

'Yeah. It wasn't hard to read your mind. I can hear it from here.'

She turned back, the top sliding back into place and settling down, and he breathed a tiny sigh of relief.

Regret?

Hell, Slater, pull yourself together!

'I think I'll have the shell-on prawns.'

He might have known. Now he'd have to spend the whole meal watching her sucking her fingers while the juice ran down her chin. He was beginning to think the steak at home might have been easier...

'That was amazing. Thank you. I wish you'd let me pay.'

'Why? I invited you to stay.'

'And you bought steak,' she pointed out, still feeling guilty, 'and my dog ate it.'

He gave a wry smile. 'And I should have put it in the fridge.'

'OK, I give up, have it your way, I'll pay next time,' she said with a laugh, and they headed up the gravel track away from the pub, cut across to the sea wall and went back along the top. She paused for a moment, looking out over the estuary, absorbing the scene. It felt oddly romantic, standing there with him as the evening sun slanted across the marshes behind them and turned everything to gold. Absurdly romantic. Crazy. This was James—

'Slack water. The tide's just on the turn. Look—the boats are swinging at anchor.'

He pointed back upriver, and she nodded, watching the fishing boats and little cabin cruisers trying to make up their minds which way to point. 'It's so peaceful. Joe said it was lovely here. No wonder you bought the cottage.'

'It was just lucky it came up when I was looking. Properties down here are pretty rarely on the market, and they have a ridiculous premium, but I fell in love with it.'

'I'm sure. I can see why. Was the cabin there?'

'Oh, yes. I wouldn't have added it, I simply don't need it. Molly used to use it for paying guests. That was how she met David, apparently, and then after they were married she used it as her studio. I just sling the garden furniture in it for the winter, which seems a wicked waste. I put a bed in there in case I ever needed to use it, and there's even a small shower room, but I'm hardly short of guest rooms,' he said drily, 'and anyway, I don't seem to have time for entertaining these days. Life is more than a tad hectic at work.'

'So what's this staffing problem?' she asked.

'Oh, one of the ED consultants had a brain tumour last autumn and he's been off for months. He's only recently come back part time, and he's decided he wants to keep it like that, which would be bad enough without him going off on paternity leave any minute now, but that's just the usual ongoing nightmare. Finding someone to cover the other half of his rota permanently is much more of a problem. Decent well-qualified trauma

specialists are hard to find; they aren't usually kicking
about without a job, and even if they are, they don't
want to work part time, and we're on a bit of limb here
out in the back end of Suffolk.'

'Really?' she said, surprised. 'But it's gorgeous here,
and anyway, you wanted to do it so why not other people?'

'It was a golden opportunity for me. I'd had a consultancy, it was a chance at a clinical lead job in a small
department, a brilliant rung on the ladder—it was perfect for me, so perfect I might just stay here forever.'

And she guessed he didn't care where he lived because he had no ties. Fewer, even, than her, because she
at least had a dog now. James had nothing.

They got back to the cottage and she took Saffy out
for a little walk along the sea wall to stretch her legs,
then settled down with the dog on the veranda, soaking up the last rays of the evening sun while James
made the coffee.

He came out, slid the tray onto the table as he sat
down and eyed her thoughtfully. 'You OK?'

'Mmm. Just basking in the sun. It's lovely here. I
could stay forever just chilling out.'

'Well, if you haven't got any ties, why don't you
stay on for a bit, have a break? God knows I've got the
space.'

'A break from what? I'm not doing anything. Anyway, I can't. I've got to go back to my friend's house
and pack it up because she's home in a couple of weeks
and I need to find myself a job and another house to
live in. It's time to get back to reality and frankly I'm
running out of money.'

He eyed her thoughtfully. He'd already told her
that people of her calibre were hard to find, especially

ones who would work part time. Would she consider it? Locum for him part time, and chill out the rest?

'Are you sure you're ready to work?'

'Yes. Absolutely.'

I am, she realised suddenly, and she felt as if a weight had been lifted off her. *I'm ready now, more than ready. Ready to move on, to start my life again in every way.*

'In which case, do you want the locum job?'

She sat bolt upright and turned to stare at him. 'What?'

'The locum job—the other half of Andy's job. Just for a while, to ease yourself back in. You could stay here, in the cabin if you wanted, if I give it a bit of a scrub. It would be perfect for you and Saffy, and when you felt ready or we got someone else, you could move on. It would give you time to work out what you're going to do, to look for a job properly without any haste, no strings, no rent, no notice period. Well, a week or two might be nice, but not if it compromised an opportunity, and you could have the cabin for as long as you want.'

She searched his face for clues, but there were none. 'Why are you doing this?' she asked, perplexed.

He laughed. 'Why? *Why?* Haven't you been listening? I can't get a locum for love or money. Andy's about to go off on paternity leave, and I'm already pretty much covering half his workload already. I can't do the other half. I need you, Connie, I genuinely need you. This isn't charity, we're desperate, and if you're really ready to start again, you'd be saving my life.'

She thought about it, considering it carefully. It would be so easy—too easy?

'Decent pay?'

'Yes, absolutely. It's a consultant's post. This is a

straightforward offer, Connie, I'm not just being nice
to you. There is just one condition, though.'

She searched his eyes, and they were serious, not a
hint of a smile.

'Which is?'

He looked away. 'I can't do the baby thing,' he said,
his voice oddly expressionless. 'I would help you if I
could, but I can't, so please don't ask me again.'

She nodded slowly. No. She'd realised that. Just not
why.

'Can you tell me why?' she asked softly. 'Just so I
can understand? Because plenty of women have babies
on their own and manage fine, so that just doesn't make
sense to me that that's the reason.'

'It does to me,' he said firmly.

'Why? I would have been bringing up the baby
mostly anyway, even if Joe was still alive. Is it because
you don't trust *me*?'

'Oh, Connie, of course I trust you, but you couldn't
just hand your baby over to me and let me get on with it,
could you? So how can you expect me to do it for you?'

'Because you don't want a baby,' she said, as if it was
obvious. 'You've said that. You said you don't want a
child, that it's never going to be on your agenda. You
don't want to be involved, but that's fine, because it
would be *my* baby! All you'd have to do is—well, you
know what you'd have to do,' she said, blushing furi-
ously and looking away. 'I'd be the one to carry it, to
give birth to it, to bring it up—'

'No. It would be *our* baby, my son or daughter,' he
told her, the words twisting his insides. 'I would insist
on being involved right from the beginning, whether
I wanted to or not, and I can't do that. Please, Connie,
try and understand. It's not that I don't trust you, I just

don't want the emotional involvement and the logistics of it are a nightmare. We'd have to live near each other, which probably means I couldn't stay here, and I like it here. I'm settled. It's taken me a long time to reach this point, and I don't want that to change. I just want peace.'

She nodded slowly, her eyes filling. 'No—no, I can see that. I'm sorry. It's a lot to ask, to be that involved with me, I see that.'

He sighed. 'It isn't that. And anyway, there's still the possibility that another man will come along and snap you up. Look at you, Connie—you're gorgeous. You'll find someone, someday, and I don't know how I'd feel about another man being involved with bringing up my child if you got married again.'

'We've had this conversation. I won't get married again.'

'You don't know that.'

She gave him a keen look that seemed to slash right to the heart of him. 'You seem to.'

He looked away. 'That's different.'

'Is it? You don't seem to have moved on in the nine years I've known you, James. You're still single, still shut down, still alone, and it's not because you're hideous or a lousy catch. You're not. Women must be throwing themselves at you. Don't tell me you don't notice. Or is there someone? A woman in your life? I didn't even think of that before, but is that why? Because there's some woman lurking in the wings who might not like it?'

'There's no woman in my life, Connie,' he said quietly, feeling curiously sad about it all of a sudden. 'I don't do relationships. They get demanding. People have expectations, they want more than I'm prepared to give, and I can't and won't meet them. So, no, there's nobody who's got any right to have an opinion. It's entirely my decision and that's the way it's staying. I'm not interested in dating.'

'Why?'

Because they're not you.

He closed his eyes briefly. 'This is irrelevant. The point is, there's more to bringing up children than I've got time to commit to, and I don't want to go there. I don't know if we'll feel the same way about things, and we have to be able to compromise when we disagree, trust each other's judgement. We have to like each other, even when the chips are down and the gloves are off, and I don't know if we can do that.'

That shocked her. 'You don't like me?' she asked, feeling gutted, because it was the one thing that had never occurred to her, but he shook his head instantly.

'Connie, don't be ridiculous, of course I like you. I've always liked you. It's just such a significant thing, so monumental, and I just don't think I can do it. And I don't want you building your hopes up, allowing yourself to imagine that this is all going to work out in the end, because it's not. So, there you have it. You wanted to know why I can't help you. That's why.'

She lifted her shoulders slightly. 'So that's it, then. I go down the anonymous donor route,' she told him simply.

He held her eyes for a moment, then looked away, hating the idea, unwilling to confront the reality of her doing what she'd said. Watching another man's child grow inside her, knowing it could have been his.

No. That was never going to happen. The immediate future was bad enough, though, the prospect of being close to Connie for weeks or maybe even months with this ridiculous longing for her, this burning need occupying his every waking thought. Could he do it without losing his mind?

'Fair enough. It's your decision. So, will you still take the job?'

He could feel her eyes on him, and he turned his head and searched them.

'Yes. Yes, I will. Why not? I need a job and some-where to live. You need a locum, I'm certainly qualified enough, and the cabin would be brilliant. It would be great for Saffy, and it would give us both privacy and enough space to retreat if we get on top of each other. It would be perfect.'

He didn't want to think about them getting on top of each other; the images it brought to mind were enough to blow his mind. But she was right, it would be per-fect for her and the dog, and it would solve his staff-ing crisis. And despite him telling her he wouldn't talk about it and couldn't do it, it would give him a chance to get to know her, to understand her motivations for wanting a baby.

So he could give her the child she so desperately wanted?

Panic clawed at him. Hell, what on earth was he get-ting himself into? The very thought of his child grow-ing in her body made his chest tighten with long-buried emotions that he really didn't want to analyse or con-front. But...

'So?' she prompted. 'Do we have a deal?'

He met her eyes, and she saw the tension in his face, the reluctance, the hesitation, and something else she didn't really understand, some powerful emotion that scared her slightly because it was the closest she'd ever come to seeing inside his soul. It was so raw, so ele-mental, and she was about to tell him to forget it when he nodded his head.

Just once, slowly.

'OK. Do the locum thing, but I don't want to hear another word about this baby idea. OK?'

'OK. So—can I look at this cabin?'

He gave a short huff of laughter. 'Um—yeah, but it's not exactly pristine. I haven't even opened the door for months.'

'Well, no time like the present,' she said cheerfully, putting her mug down. 'Come on. Where's the key?'

'Right here.'

He unhooked it from the back of the kitchen door and went down the steps and across the lawn, put it in the lock and swung the door open, flicking on the light to dispel the gathering dusk.

'Wow.'

He looked around and winced. Maybe he should have left the light off. 'I'll clear it out and give it a good clean. It's a tip.'

'No, it's fine. OK, it's a bit dusty, but it's lovely! Oh, James, it'll be perfect!'

He studied it, trying to see it through her eyes, but all he could see was the garden furniture stacked up against the wall and the amount of work he'd have to do to clean it up.

'I don't know about perfect, but you're right, it would be ideal for you and the dog. We could easily rig up a small kitchen area, a kettle and toaster, something like that. I can get you a small fridge, too.'

'Are you sure?'

Was he? Probably not, but he'd said he'd do it now so how could he change his mind and let her down? The enthusiasm in her eyes was enough to cripple him.

'Yes, I'm sure,' he said gruffly. 'When do you want to start?'

* * *

Well, she wasn't getting what she'd come for, but he'd taken a lot of the stress and worry out of the next few weeks at a stroke, and she supposed she should be thankful for that.

And she'd be working with James again, after all this time. She'd never thought she'd do that again, and the prospect was oddly exciting.

She'd loved working with him nine years ago. He'd been a brilliant doctor and a skilful and patient mentor and she couldn't wait to work with him again. And she was looking forward to getting back to normality, to real life. Not the strange and somehow dislocated life of an army wife trying to keep her career going despite the constant moves, or the empty and fruitless life of a woman widowed far too young and unfulfilled, but real life where she could make her own decisions.

She'd thought about it all night, lying awake in that beautiful bedroom listening to the sound of the sea sucking on the shingle, the rhythm curiously soothing. She'd had to go down and let Saffy out in the middle of the night, and once she'd settled her she'd curled up in the chair in the bedroom window staring out over the moonlit sea and hoping she wouldn't let him down.

Not that there was any reason why she should, of course. She was a good doctor, too, and she had confidence in herself. And if he didn't want to give her a child, felt he couldn't do it—well, he had the right to do that. It was a shame, though, because he was perfect for the job. Intelligent, good looking, funny, kind to animals, he could make amazing coffee...

He'd make someone a perfect husband, if only he wasn't so set against it. What a waste. But that was his business, his decision, his choice to make. And when it came to the baby thing, there were other ways, other avenues to explore.

Except maybe, of course, if she was working along-side him, he might change his mind—

She'd stopped that train of thought right there, gone back to bed and tried to sleep, but it had been pointless and she'd got dressed and come downstairs shortly before six, let Saffy out again and made herself a cup of tea, taking it out onto the veranda and huddling up on the bench waiting for James to wake up.

She'd agreed to come back down to Yoxburgh in two weeks, when Andy was due off on paternity leave, and all she had to do was go back to Angie's house and pack her things and come back. She didn't have much to pack. Most of her stuff was in store, flung there in haste after Joe died when she'd had to move out of the married quarters; she still had to go through it prop-erly, but that task would keep until she had somewhere permanent.

Somewhere for her and a baby?

She pressed a hand to her chest and sucked in a breath, and Saffy got to her feet and came and put her nose against her arm, nuzzling her.

'Oh, Saffy. I wonder where we'll end up?' she mur-mured, and then she heard sounds behind her and James appeared in a pair of jeans and bare feet, looking tou-sled and sleepy and more sexy than a man of forty-two had any right to look.

Sheesh. She yanked her eyes away from his bare chest and swallowed hard.

'Morning,' she managed, and he grunted.

'Coffee?'

'Please. Just a straight, normal coffee.'

'That's all you get at this time of day. It's too early for party tricks.'

He walked off again, going back into the house and leaving her on the veranda, and she let out the breath she'd been holding and stared up at the sky. Wow. How had she never *noticed* before?

Because you were in love with Joe. Why would you notice another man? You had a husband who was more than man enough for you!

But—James was every bit as much a man as Joe had been, in his own way, and anyway, she had noticed him, all those years ago when she'd first met him. She'd asked about him hopefully, and been told about Cathy. Not that anyone knew very much, just that his wife had died and he didn't talk about it.

Didn't talk about anything except work, really, and didn't date as far as anyone knew, but then one weekend she'd been out with friends and bumped into him in a bar, and he'd introduced her to Joe.

And that was that. Joe with his wicked smile and irrepressible sense of humour had swept her off her feet, and she'd fallen hook, line and sinker. Now she was back to square one, noticing a man who still wasn't interested, who was still shut down, closed off from life and love and anything apart from his work.

A man she'd tried to talk into agreeing to something that he was obviously deeply reluctant about—

'Hey, what's up?'

He set the coffee down on the table in front of her and she looked up at him, searching his eyes for the reticence that had been there last night, but there was none, just gentle concern, so she smiled at him and reached for her coffee, telling herself she was relieved that he'd pulled a shirt on.

'Nothing,' she lied. 'I'm fine—just a bit tired. I didn't sleep very well—it was too quiet and all I could hear was the sound of the sea.'

'I can't sleep without it now,' he said wryly, dropping down beside her on the bench and fondling Saffy's ears. 'So, how was your night, Saffy? Find anything naughty to do in the cage?'

'She was fine. I came down at three and let her out because I could hear her whining, but I think she just wanted reassurance.'

'I heard you get up.'

So he hadn't slept, either. Wondering what he'd let himself in for?

Nothing, she reminded herself. They were just going to work together, and the baby conversation—well, it was as if it had never happened. They'd just opened the door on the subject, that was all, and he'd shut it again.

Only, maybe, it would never be the same again. Whatever happened now, that door had been opened, and she sensed that it would have changed something in the dynamic of their relationship.

'Connie? I'm sorry I can't help you.'

How did he know what she was thinking? Could he read her mind? Or perhaps, like her, it was the only thing *on* his mind?

She nodded, and he reached out a hand—a large, square hand with strong, blunt fingers—and laid it gently over her wrist.

'Whatever happens, whatever you decide to do, I'll always be here for you,' he said quietly. 'I promised Joe I'd take care of you if anything happened to him, and I will, and if you decide to take the clinic route and have a baby, I'll still be here, I'll still support you in your decision even if I don't agree with it. You won't ever be alone. Just—please, don't be hasty.'

'Oh, James…'

Her eyes filled with tears, and she put her coffee down and sucked in a shaky breath.

He stared at her in dismay. Hell. Now he'd made her cry.

'Hush, Connie, hush,' he murmured, gathering her against his chest. 'It's OK. I didn't mean to make you cry. Come on, now. It's all right. It'll be OK.'

'Why are you so damn nice?' she said unsteadily, swiping tears out of her eyes and wondering why his chest felt so good to rest her head against. She could stay there all day in his arms, resting her face against the soft cotton of his shirt, inhaling the scent of his body and listening to the steady thud of his heart while he held her. It had been such a long time since anyone had held her, and it had been him then, too, after Joe's funeral.

He'd held her for ages, letting her cry, crying with her, and nobody had held her since. Not really. She'd had the odd hug but nothing like this, this silent support that meant more than any words.

But she couldn't stay there all day, no matter how tempting, so she pulled herself together, swiped the tears away again and sat up.

'So what about this breakfast then?' she asked, her voice uneven, and he gave a soft laugh and leant back, his arm along the bench behind her.

'Drink your coffee and let me have mine. I can't function this early, I need a minute. And don't talk. Just sit and relax and stop worrying. I can hear your mind from here.'

Sound advice. She didn't think it had a hope in hell of working, but she was wrong. The distant sound of the shingle sighing on the beach, the drone of bees in the honeysuckle, the whisper of the wind in the tall grass beyond the garden—all of it soothed her, taking away the tension and leaving her calm and relaxed.

Or was that the touch of his hand on her back, the slow, gentle circling sweep of his thumb back and forth over her shoulder blade? She closed her eyes and rested her head back against the wall of the house, and felt something that had been coiled tight inside her for so long slowly give way.

CHAPTER FOUR

HE WATCHED HER sleep, his arm trapped behind her, unable to move in case he disturbed her.

And he didn't want to disturb her, because as long as she was sleeping he could watch her.

Watch the slight fluttering of her eyelashes against her faintly flushed cheeks, still streaked with the dried remnants of her tears. Watch the soft rise and fall of her chest with every breath, and hear the gentle sigh of air as she exhaled through parted lips that were pink and moist and so damn kissable it was killing him.

He looked away, unable to watch her any longer, unable to sit there with his arm around Joe's wife and lust after her when she'd been entrusted to his care.

And he'd actually agreed to let her come and live with him and locum in the department? He must have been mad. He'd have to sort the rota so that they worked opposing shifts—not that that would help much, but at least she was living in the cabin rather than the house. And that was essential because if he didn't keep his distance, he wasn't sure he could keep these deeply inappropriate feelings under wraps.

And he needed to start now.

He shifted his hand a fraction, turning his thumb out

to take it off her shoulder blade, and she rolled her head towards him, those smoky blue eyes clear and unglazed.

She hadn't been asleep at all, apparently, just resting her eyes, but now they were open and she smiled at him.

'Can I speak yet?' she asked cheekily, her mouth twitching, and he laughed and pulled his arm out from behind her, shifting slightly away to give himself some much-needed space.

'If you can manage not to say anything contentious.'

'I don't know what you mean.'

That taunting smile playing around her mouth, she sat up straighter, moving away from him a little more, and he had to remind himself that that was good.

'I was going to say, if I'm going to be working with you here, it might be an idea if I knew what I was signing up for.'

He nodded, knowing exactly what kind of exquisite torture *he* was signing up for, but the exit door on that had slammed firmly shut already so analysing why he'd done it was purely academic. He was already committed to the emotional chaos and physical torment that was bound to come his way with having her underfoot day in, day out. He must have been mad to suggest it.

'Sure. Want a guided tour of the hospital?'

'That would be good. Can we have breakfast first? I'm starving.'

He gave a soft huff of laughter and stood up, taking the empty coffee cup from her and walking back inside, and she watched him go and let out an almost silent groan.

How could she be so *aware* of him? OK, it had been a while, but—James? Really? Not that there was anything wrong with him, far from it, but there was more than good looks and raw sex appeal in this. There was

his relationship with Joe—*her* relationship with Joe—
and she knew for him that would be a massive issue.

And Joe had made him promise to take care of her?
Trust him. Trust Joe to pile that kind of responsibility
on his friend, but she reckoned he would have become
her self-appointed guardian anyway regardless of what
Joe might have said, because he was just like that, so
she'd just have to learn to live with it and make very,
very sure he got no hint of her feelings.

Not that she knew what they were, exactly.

A flicker of interest?

OK, more than a flicker, then, a lot more, but of
what? Lust?

No. More than that. More than a flicker, of more
than lust. And that was deeply scary. This situation
was complicated enough without this crazy magnetic
attraction rearing its head.

She got to her feet and stuck her head round the
kitchen door. 'Want a hand?'

'No, I'm fine.'

'Right. I'll take Saffy for a quick run. Ten minutes?'

'Barely. Don't be longer.'

'I won't.'

She shoved her feet into her abandoned trainers,
put Saffy's lead on and escaped from the confines of
James's garden. She ran along the river wall this time,
retracing their footsteps of the day before beside the
remains of the old rotting hulks, their ribs sticking up
like skeletons out of the mud of the little natural inlets
in the marshy river bank.

The smell was amazing—salt and mud and fish, all
mingled together in that incredible mix that reminded
her of holidays in Cornish fishing villages and sailing
in the Solent in her childhood.

Wonderful, evocative smells that brought back so many happy memories. And the sounds—amazing sounds. The clink of halliards, the slap of wavelets on the undersides of the moored boats, the squeak of oars in rowlocks, the putter of an outboard engine.

And the gulls. Always the gulls, wheeling overhead, keening their sad, mournful cry.

The sunlight was dancing on the water, and the tide had just turned, the boats swinging round so they faced downriver as the water began surging up the estuary with the rising tide. She stood and watched for a moment as the last of the boats swung round and settled on their moorings.

Just twelve hours, she thought, since they'd watched this happen together. Twelve hours ago, she'd had no idea of what her future held, just a flat no to her request for a baby and a massive question mark hanging over her next job, next home, all of it. Yet in the past twelve hours all that had become clearer, her immediate future settled and secure if not in the way she'd hoped.

Unless he changed his mind? Unlikely, but just in case, she'd make sure she kept a lid on her feelings and kept them to herself, and then maybe...

She glanced at her watch, and yelped. She was going to be late for breakfast, and he'd told her not to be longer than ten minutes. She had three to get back, and she made it with seconds to spare.

He was propped up in the doorway, arms folded, legs crossed at the ankle, and his lips twitched.

'Close,' he said, glancing at his watch, and she smiled, hands propped on her knees, her breath sawing in and out.

'Sorry. I was watching the tide turn. I could watch it all day.'

'Well, four times, anyway. Scrambled or fried?'

She straightened up, chest heaving, and grinned, oblivious of the effect she was having on him. 'Scrambled.'

Like his brains, he thought desperately, watching her chest rise and fall, the wild tangle of blonde hair spilling over her shoulders, the faint sheen of moisture gilding her glowing skin—

'Can I do anything?'

'Yes,' he said blandly. 'Get the dog out of the kitchen. She's eyeing up the sausages.'

They left, and he braced his hands on the worktop, breathed in and counted to ten, then let the air out of his lungs on a whoosh and turned his attention to the eggs.

Working with her, all day, every day, and having her here at home? For months?

It was going to kill him.

'This is such an amazing building.'

'Isn't it? It's all a front, of course, all this beauty, and it hid a hideous truth. Apparently it used to be the pauper lunatic asylum.'

'How frightfully politically correct.'

He grinned wryly. 'Not my words. That's the Victorians for you. Actually it was a workhouse taking advantage of the inmates, and I'd like to be able to say it's moved on, but in the last few months I've wondered.'

'Ah, poor baby. That'll teach you to be clinical lead.'

He rolled his eyes and punched her arm lightly. 'Do you want this job or not?'

'Is this a formal interview?'

He laughed. 'Hardly. Any qualified doctor with a pulse would get my vote at the moment. The fact that you've got all the necessary and appropriate qualifications and outstanding experience to back them up is just the cherry on top. Trust me, the job's yours.'

'I'm not sure I'm flattered.'

'Be flattered. I'm fussy who I work with. That's why there isn't anyone. We're round here in the new wing.'

He drove round the corner of the old building and pulled up in a marked parking bay close to the ED, and her eyes widened.

'Wow. That's a bit sharper. I did wonder if we'd be working by gas light.'

'Hardly,' he said with a chuckle. 'We're very proud of it—of the whole hospital. It was necessary. People living on the coast were having to travel long distances for emergency treatment, and they were dying—back to your platinum ten minutes, I guess. We can treat them much quicker here, and if we have to we can then refer them on once they're stable. That said we can do most stuff here, but it's not like Camp Bastion.'

'Hopefully it doesn't need to be,' she said quietly, and he glanced down and saw a flicker of something wounded and vulnerable in her eyes and could have kicked himself.

'Sorry. I didn't mean to drag it all up.'

'It's OK, it's never far away.' She gave him a too bright and very fleeting smile. 'So, talk me round your department, Mr Clinic Lead Slater.'

He took her in via Reception so she could see the triage area where the walking wounded were graded according to severity, and then went through into the back, to the row of cubicles where the ambulance cases were brought directly.

'We've got four high dependency beds where we can keep people under constant observation, and we can accommodate three patients in Resus at any time. It's not often idle.'

They stood at the doors of Resus and watched a team working on a patient. It looked calm and measured. A man looked up and smiled at James through the glass, waggling his fingers, and he waved back and turned to her. 'That's Andy. He's been damn lucky. He had an awake craniotomy and had to talk through it to make sure his speech centre wasn't damaged when they removed the meningioma, but the post-op swelling gave him aphasia. He lost his speech—nothing else. He could understand everything, all the words were on the tip of his tongue, he just couldn't find them, but of course he couldn't work until he got his speech back, and he was tearing his hair out for weeks.' He grinned wryly. 'So was I, because there was no guarantee he ever would recover completely.'

'You still are, aren't you? Tearing your hair out, trying to replace half of him?'

He shrugged. 'Pretty much. It's a bit frustrating trying to get anyone decent all the way out here, but he's brilliant and getting anyone as good as him is just not possible on a part-time contract. And no,' he said with a smile, holding a finger up to silence her, 'before you say it, that's not a criticism of you, because I know you've got bigger fish to fry and you aren't here for the long haul. I wish to God you were. You'd solve all my problems at a stroke.'

Well, not quite all. Not the one of having enough distance between them so that he wasn't being constantly reminded of just how damned lovely she was and how very, very inaccessible.

Not to mention asking the impossible of him…

The door to Resus opened and Andy came out, his smile a little strained. 'Hi. Did you get my text?'

'Your text?' he said, getting a bad feeling.

'Yes. Lucy rang. She says she's in labour and she doesn't hang about. I'm just about to bail, I'm afraid.'

He swore silently, closed his eyes for a moment and then opened them to find Connie smiling knowingly.

'Yes,' she said.

He let out something halfway between a laugh and a sigh and introduced them. 'Connie, this is Andy Gallagher. Andy, this is Connie Murray. I worked with her several years ago, and she was obviously so inspired by me she became a trauma specialist.'

Andy eyed her hopefully. 'Tell me she's our new locum.'

'She is, indeed, as of—well, virtually now. Say hello to her very, very nicely. She wasn't due to start for a fortnight.'

'Oh, Connie—I'm so pleased to meet you,' Andy said fervently, his shoulders dropping as a smile lit up his face. 'I thought I was about to dump a whole world of stuff on James, so to know you're here is such a relief. Thank you. From the bottom of my heart. And his,' he added with a grin. 'Probably especially his.'

This time James gave a genuine laugh. 'Too right. You'll be out of here in ten seconds, if you've got any sense, and utterly oblivious to the chaos you're leaving in your wake, which is exactly how it should be. Go. Shoo. And let us know the minute it's born!'

'I will!' Andy yelled over his shoulder, heading out of the department at a run.

James let his breath out on a low whistle and pushed open the door of Resus. 'You guys OK in here, or do you need me?'

'No, we're all done. He's on his way to ICU. They're just coming down for him.'

'OK, Andy's gone but I'm around, page me if you need me. Pete's on later, and I'll be in tomorrow morning first thing. Oh, and this is Connie Murray. She's our new locum, starting tomorrow. Be really, really nice to her.'

They all grinned. 'You bet, Boss,' one of them said, and they all laughed.

He let the door shut, turned to Connie and searched her eyes, still not quite able to believe his luck.

'Are you really OK with this?'

'I'm fine,' she said, mentally running through the logistics and counting on her fingers. 'Look, it's eleven o'clock. I can get home, grab my stuff and be back here by eight tonight at the latest. That'll give me three hours to pack and clean the house, and it won't take that long.' She hoped. 'Can you cope with Saffy if I leave her? I can't get her and all my stuff in the car.'

'Sure. She can help me scrub out the cabin.'

'Yeah, right. Just don't let her run off,' she warned as they walked briskly back to the car.

'I won't. Don't worry, Connie, the dog's the least of my problems. You saw that cabin.'

She ignored him. 'Put her in the crate if you have to go back to the hospital,' she said as she put on her seat belt. 'She's used to it. And she has a scoop of the dry food twice a day, morning and evening, so you might need to feed her if I'm held up in traffic—'

He stopped her, his hand over her mouth, his eyes laughing. 'Connie, I can manage the dog. If all else fails, I'll bribe her with fillet steak.'

She left almost immediately when they got back to the cottage, and as she was getting in the car he gave in to impulse and pulled her into his arms and hugged her.

'Thank you, Connie. Thank you so much. I'm so, so grateful.'

'I'll remind you of that when I'm driving you crazy,' she said with a cheeky grin, and slamming the door, she dropped the clutch, spraying gravel in all directions. 'See you later!'

'Drive carefully,' he called after her, but she was gone, and he watched her car until she'd turned out onto the road and headed away, the imprint of her body still burned onto his.

'Well, Saffy,' he said softly as he went back into the garden and shut the gate firmly. 'It's just you and me, old thing, so no running off. Shall we go and have a look at this cabin?'

It was worse than he'd thought.

Dirtier, dustier, mustier. Oh, well, he could do with a bit of hard physical graft. It might settle his raging libido down a bit after that innocent hug.

He snorted. Apparently there was no such thing as far as his body was concerned.

He threw open all the windows and the doors, took everything including the bed outside and blitzed it. He vacuumed the curtains, washed the windows, mopped the walls and floors, slung the rug over the veranda rail and bashed it with a broom to knock the dust out before he vacuumed it and returned it to the now dry floor, and finally he reassembled it all, stripped the bedding off the bed upstairs and brought it all down and made up the bed.

And through it all Saffy lay there and watched him as if butter wouldn't melt in her mouth. He trusted her about as far as he could throw her, but she seemed content to be with him, and once it was all tidy and ready for Connie's return, he took her out for a walk, picking up his phone on the way.

And he had a message, a text with a picture of a new baby. Very new, a mere two hours old, the caption reading, 'Daniel, eight pounds three ounces, both well'.

He felt something twist inside him.

'Congratulations!' he texted back, and put the phone in his pocket. Saffy was watching him closely, head cocked on one side, eyes like molten amber searching his face.

'It's OK, Saffy,' he said, rubbing her head, but he wasn't sure it was. Over the years countless colleagues had had babies, and he'd been happy for them. For some reason this baby, this time, felt different. Because the possibility was being dangled in front of his nose, tantalising him?

The possibility of being a father, something he'd thought for the past eleven years that he'd never be? He'd said no to Connie, and he'd meant it, but what if he'd said yes? What if he'd agreed to give her a child?

A well of emotion came up and lodged in his chest, making it hard to breathe, and he hauled in a lungful of sea air and set off, Saffy trotting happily at his side as he broke into a jog.

He ran for miles, round the walk he'd taken Connie on yesterday, but with a detour to make it longer, and Saffy loped easily along at his side. He guessed she ran with Connie—another thing they had in common, apart from medicine? Maybe.

He wondered what else he'd find. Art? Music? Food he knew they agreed on, but these were irrelevancies. If he'd agreed to her suggestion, then she'd be bringing up his child, so he would have needed to be more concerned with her politics, her attitude to education, her ability to compromise. It didn't matter a damn if they both liked the same pictures or the same songs. It mattered if she thought kids could be taken out of school in the term time to go on holiday, something he thought was out of the question. How could you be sure they wouldn't miss some vital building block that could affect their entire future?

And what on *earth* was he doing worrying about that? He'd said no, and he'd meant it! He had! And anyway, there were bigger things to worry about. Things like his ability to deal with the emotional minefield that he'd find himself in the moment her pregnancy started to manifest itself—

'What pregnancy?' he growled, startling Saffy so that she missed her stride, and he ruffled her head and picked up the pace, driving on harder to banish the images that flooded his mind.

Not images of Cathy, for once, but of Connie, radiant, glowing, her body blooming with health and vitality, the proud swell of her pregnancy—

He closed his eyes and stumbled. Idiot.

He stopped running, standing with one hand on a fence post, chest heaving with emotion as much as exertion. This was madness. It was hypothetical. He'd said no, and she was going to a clinic if she did anything, so nothing was going to happen to her that involved him.

Ever.

But that just left him feeling empty and frustrated, and he turned for home, jogging slowly now, cooling down, dropping back to a walk as they hit the sea wall and the row of houses. And then there was Molly, out in the garden again with David and their children, and he waved to them and Molly straightened up with a handful of weeds and walked over.

'So who's your friend?' she asked, openly curious as well she might be, because he hardly ever had anyone to stay, and certainly never anyone single, female and as blatantly gorgeous as Connie.

'Connie Murray. She's a doctor. I've known her for years, she was married to a friend of mine.'

'The one who died? Joe?'

He nodded. 'She's going to be here for a while—she's taking the locum job I've been trying to fill, and she'll be living in the cabin.' He got that one in quick, before Molly got any matchmaking ideas, because frankly there was enough going on without that.

But it didn't stop the little hint of speculation in her eyes.

'I'm glad you've got someone. I know you've been working crazy hours, we hardly ever see you these days.' She dropped the weeds in a bucket and looked up at him again. 'You should bring her to my private view on Friday.'

'That would be nice, thanks,' he said, fully intending to be busy. 'I'll have to check the rota, though.'

'Do that. And change it if necessary. No excuses. You've had plenty of warning. We told you weeks ago.'

He gave a quiet mental sigh and smiled. 'So you did.'

She laughed and waved him away. 'Go on, go away. We'll see you on Friday at seven. Tell her to wear something pretty.'

He nodded and turned away, walked the short distance to his house while he contemplated that sentence, and let Saffy off the lead in the garden.

She found her water bowl on the veranda while he was doing some stretches, drank noisily for a moment and then flopped down in the shade under the bench and went to sleep, so while she was happy he ran upstairs and showered, then on the way down he gathered up Connie's things from her bedroom, Molly's words still echoing in his head.

Tell her to wear something pretty.

Like the top she'd worn last night which was lying on the chair, together with the raspberry red lace bra and matching lace shorts that sent his blood pressure into orbit? Or then there were her pyjamas. Thin cotton trousers and a little jersey vest trimmed with lace. They were pretty, but nothing like substantial enough to call pyjamas, he thought, and bundling them up with the other things, he grabbed her wash bag out of the bathroom and took them all down to the cabin.

Saffy was still snoozing innocently, so he topped up her water bowl, filled a glass for himself and drained it, then put the kettle on to make tea and sat down with the paper and chilled out.

Or tried to, but it seemed he couldn't.

Connie would be back in a very few hours, and from then on his space would be invaded. He wasn't used to sharing it, and having her around was altogether too disturbing. That lace underwear, for example. And the pyjamas. If he had to see them every morning—

He got up, prowling round the garden restlessly, and then he saw the roses and remembered he'd been going to put flowers in her room yesterday, but he'd run out of time.

So he cut a handful and put them in a vase on the chest of drawers and went back to reading the paper, but it didn't hold his attention. The only thing that seemed to be able to do that was Connie.

And going to Molly's private view with her just sounded altogether too cosy. And dangerous. He wondered what pretty actually meant, and how Connie would interpret it. He was rather afraid to find out.

But how the hell could he get out of it?

It didn't take long to pack up her things.

Much less than the three hours she'd allowed, and because she'd cleaned the house so thoroughly on Sunday there was nothing much to do, so she was back on the road by three-thirty and back in Yoxburgh before six.

She wondered if James would be around, but he was there, sitting on the veranda in a pair of long cargo shorts with Saffy at his feet, reading a newspaper in the early evening sun.

He folded it and came down to the gate, leaning on it and smiling as she clambered out of the car and stretched.

'You must drive like a lunatic.'

She laughed softly and shook her head. 'That was Joe. I'm not an adrenaline junkie. There was practically nothing to do.'

And not that much in the way of possessions, he thought, looking at the back of her small SUV. Sure, it was packed, but only vaguely. She handed him a cool box out of the front footwell. 'Here, find room for that lot in the fridge,' she said, locking the car and coming through the gate to give Saffy a hug. 'Hello, gorgeous. Have you been a good girl?'

Saffy wagged her tail and leaned against her.

'She's been fine. We went for a run.'

'Oh, she will have enjoyed that! Thank you. She loves it when we run.'

'She seemed to know the drill.'

'What, don't stop in front of you to sniff something so you fall over her? Yeah. We both learned that one the hard way.'

He laughed and carried the cool box up to the kitchen, shocked at the lightness in his heart now she was back, with her lovely smile and sassy sense of humour.

'So how did you get on with the cabin?' she asked, following him up the steps to the kitchen.

'OK, I suppose. It's clean now, but I'm sure you'll want to do something to it to make it home.'

He turned his head as he said that, catching a flicker of something slightly lost and puzzled in her expression, and could have kicked himself.

Home? Who was he kidding? She hadn't had a proper home for ages now, not since she'd met Joe. They'd moved around constantly from one base to another, and she'd had to move out of the married quarters pretty smartly after he'd died. By all accounts she'd been on the move ever since, living in hospital accommodation in the year after Joe died, then out in Afghanistan, then staying with a friend. It was only one step up from sofa-surfing, and the thought of her being so lost and unsettled gutted him.

But the look was gone now, banished by a smile. 'Can I put my stuff straight in there?'

'Sure. I'll put Saffy in her crate, so she doesn't run off while the gate's open. The door's not locked.'

Connie opened the cabin door, and blinked. The dust was gone, as was the stack of garden furniture, and it was immaculate. He'd made the bed up with the linen she'd had last night, and her pyjamas were folded neatly on the pillow, her overnight bag on the bed. She stuck her head round the bathroom door and found her wash things on the side, and when she came back out she noticed the flowers on the chest of drawers.

Roses from the garden, she realised, and a lump formed in her throat. He hadn't needed to cut the roses, but he had, to make her welcome, and the room was filled with the scent of them.

It was the attention to detail that got to her. The careful way he'd folded her pyjamas. The fact that he'd brought her things down at all when it would have been so easy to leave them there.

'I hope you don't mind, I moved your stuff in case you were really late back, so you didn't have to bother.'

'Mind? Why should I mind?'

And then she remembered she'd left yesterday's clothes on the chair—her top, her underwear. Yikes. The red lace.

Don't be silly. He knows what underwear looks like.

But she felt the heat crawl up her neck anyway. 'It looks lovely,' she said, turning away so he wouldn't see. 'You've even put flowers in here.'

'I always put flowers in a guest room,' he lied, kicking himself for doing it in case she misinterpreted the gesture. Or, rather, rumbled him? 'I would have done it yesterday but I ran out of time. Give me your car keys, I'll bring your stuff in.'

She handed them over without argument, grateful for a moment alone to draw breath, because suddenly, with him standing there beside her and the spectre of her underwear floating in the air between them, the cabin had seemed suddenly airless.

How on earth was she going to deal with this? Thank God they'd be busy at work, because there was no way she could be trusted around him without him guessing where her feelings were going, and there was no way she was going to act on them. He was a friend, and his friendship was too important to her to compromise for something as fleeting and trivial as lust.

'So where do you want this lot?'

He was standing in the doorway, his arms full, and she groped for common sense.

'Just put everything down on the floor, I'll sort it out later.'

She walked past him, her arm brushing his as he turned, and she felt a streak of heat race through her like lightning.

Really? *Really?*

This was beginning to look like a thoroughly bad idea…

CHAPTER FIVE

'SUPPER AT the pub?'

She straightened up from one of the boxes and tried to read his eyes, but they were just looking at her normally. Odd, because for a second there—

'That would be great. Just give me a moment to sort out some work clothes for tomorrow and I'll be with you.'

'Do you want the iron?'

She laughed. 'What, so I make a good impression on the boss?'

He propped himself up on the doorframe and grinned mischievously. 'Doesn't hurt.'

'I think I'll pass. I'll just hang them up for now and do it when we've eaten—if I really have to. Have you fed Saffy?'

'Yes, just before you got back. She seemed to think it was appropriate.'

'I'll bet,' she said with a chuckle, and pulling out a pair of trousers and a top that didn't cling or gape or otherwise reveal too much, she draped them over the bed and gave up. 'Right, that'll do for tomorrow. Let's go. I'm starving, it's a long time since breakfast.'

'You haven't eaten since breakfast? You're mad.'

'I just sort of forgot.'

'You emptied the fridge. There was food in your hands. How could you forget?'

Because she'd been utterly distracted by the thought of what she was doing? Because all she could think about was that she was coming back here to James, taking the first step towards the rest of her life?

'Just call me dozy,' she said, and slinging a cardi round her shoulders in case it got cold, she headed for the door.

They took Saffy with them and sat outside in the pub garden, with the lead firmly anchored to the leg of the picnic bench in case a cat strolled past, and he went in to order and came back with drinks.

'So, what time are we starting tomorrow?' she asked, to distract herself from the sight of those muscular, hairy legs sticking out of the bottom of his shorts. Definitely a runner—

'Eight, technically, but I'd like to be in by seven. You can bring your car and come later if you like. I'll sort you out a parking permit.'

'I can do seven,' she said. 'I'll have to walk Saffy first, and I'll need to come back at lunchtime to let her out and give her a bit of a run so I'll need my car anyway, if you can sort a permit for me that soon. Will that be all right?'

'That's fine. I don't expect you to work full time, Connie. I know you've got the dog, I know you haven't worked since you got her and I know you can't leave her indefinitely. I expect HR will want to check all sorts of stuff with you before they let you loose on a patient anyway, so there's no point in being too early. I take it you've brought the necessary paperwork?'

'Oh, sure. I've got everything I need to show them. So, did you hear from Andy? Is there any news?'

'Ah. Yes. He sent me a text.'

'And?'

'It's a boy,' he said, the words somehow sticking in his throat and choking him. 'Daniel. Eight pounds three ounces. Mother and baby both doing well.'

'Did he send a picture?'

'Of course.' And she would want to see it, wouldn't she? He pulled his phone out of his pocket and found the text, then slid it across to her. 'There.'

'Oh—oh, James, he's gorgeous. What are the others?'

'Girls. Three girls. Emily, Megan and Lottie.'

'And now they've got their boy. Oh, that's amazing. They must be so thrilled.'

'Yeah.' He couldn't bring himself to speculate on their delight, or debate the merits of boys or girls. It was all too close to home, too close to the reason she was here—and the very reason he didn't want her here at all.

No, that was a lie. He did want her here. Just—not like this. Not for why she'd come, and not feeling the way he did, so that he had to be so damn guarded all the time in case he gave away how he felt about her. And if he could work *that* one out for himself he'd be doing well, because frankly at the moment it was as clear as mud.

'So, tell me about this friend you've been staying with,' he said, changing the subject without any pretence at subtlety, and after a second of startled silence, she cleared her throat.

'Um. Yeah. Angie. Long-time friend. We worked together a couple of times. She's been in Spain for a few months visiting family but she's back in a week or so—I really ought to write to her and thank her for lending me the house. It's been a lifesaver. Getting a rented place with a dog is really hard, especially a dog like Saffy.'

She pricked up her ears at her name, and James reached down and rubbed her head. She shifted it, putting her chin on his foot and sighing, and he gave a wry chuckle.

'I can imagine. I thought you and Joe had bought somewhere?'

'We had. It's rented out, on a long lease. The tenant's great and it pays the mortgage.'

'So why not live there?'

She shrugged. 'It was where we were going when he came out of the army. It was going to be our family home, where we brought up our children.'

And just like that, the subject reared its head again. James opened his mouth, shut it again and exhaled softly.

'Don't say it, James. I know we aren't talking about it, I was just stating a fact.'

'I wasn't going to.'

'Weren't you?'

He shrugged. The truth was he hadn't known what to say, so he'd said nothing.

'Two sea bass?'

He sat back, smiled at the waitress and sighed with relief.

'Saved by the bass,' Connie said drily, and picking up her knife and fork, she attacked her supper and let the subject drop.

HR wanted all manner of forms filled in, and it was driving her mad.

She was itching to get to work now, if only to settle her nerves. She'd been away from it too long, she told

herself, that was all. She'd be fine once she started. And
then finally the forms were done.

'Right, that's it. Thank you, Connie. Welcome to
Yoxburgh Park Hospital. I hope you enjoy your time
with us.'

'Thanks.'

She picked up her bag and legged it, almost but not
quite running, and made her way to the ED. She found
James up to his eyes in Resus, and he glanced up.

'Cleared for takeoff?' he asked, and she nodded.

'Good. We've got an RTC coming in, nineteen year
old male pedestrian versus van, query head, chest and
pelvic injuries and I haven't got anyone I can spare. Do
you feel ready to take it?'

She nodded, used to being flung in at the deep end as
a locum. 'Sure. Where will you be, just in case I need
to check protocol?'

'Right here. Don't worry, Connie, I won't abandon
you. I won't be much longer here.'

She nodded again, and he pointed her in the direction of the ambulance bay. She met the ambulance, took
the history and handover from the paramedics, and by
the time they were in Resus she was right back in the
swing of it.

'Hi, there, Steve,' she said to the patient, holding
her face above his so he could see her without moving.
'I'm Connie Murray, and I'm the doctor who's going to
be looking after you. Can you tell me where you are?'

'Hospital,' he said, but his voice was slurred—from
the head injury, or the morphine the paramedics had
given him? She wasn't sure, but at this stage it was irrelevant because until she was sure he wasn't going to
bleed out in the next few minutes the head injury was
secondary.

'OK. Can you tell me where it hurts?'

'Everywhere,' he mumbled. 'Legs, back—everything.'

'OK. We'll soon have you more comfortable. Can we have an orthopaedic consultant down here, please? This pelvic fracture needs stabilising, and can we do a FAST scan, please? We need a full trauma series—do we have a radiographer available? And a total body CT scan. I need to know what's going on here.'

She delegated rapidly, and the team working with her slipped smoothly into action, but throughout she was conscious of James at the other end of the room keeping an ear open in case she needed backup.

The X-rays showed multiple fractures in his pelvis, and the FAST scan had shown free fluid in his abdomen.

She glanced up and he raised an eyebrow.

'Do we have access to a catheter lab? I think he's got significant vascular damage to the pelvic vessels and I don't want to wait for CT.'

'Yes, if you think it's necessary. What are his stats like?'

'Awful. He's hypotensive and shocky and the ultrasound is showing free fluids in the abdomen. He's had two units of packed cells and his systolic's eighty-five and falling. We need to stop this bleed.'

'OK. Order whatever you need. I won't be a tick.'

He wasn't. Moments later, he was standing opposite her across the bed, quietly taking his cues from her and nodding to confirm her decisions.

And when they'd got him stable and shipped him off to the catheter lab for urgent vascular surgery prior to a CT scan to check for other injuries, he just smiled at her and nodded. 'You've learned a lot since I last saw you in action.'

'I'd hope so. It's been more than eight years.' Years in which she met, married and lost his best friend.

'I always said you had promise. It's nice to see you fulfilling your potential.'

Crazy that his praise should make her feel ten feet tall. She knew she was good. She'd worked with some of the best trauma surgeons in the world, she didn't need James to tell her.

And yet somehow, those few words meant everything to her.

'Want me to talk to the relatives?' he asked, but she shook her head.

'No, I'm fine with it. Come with me, though. I might need to direct them to where they can wait.'

'OK.'

They spoke to the relatives together; she explained the situation, and James filled in the details she'd missed—the name of the orthopaedic surgeon, where the ward was, how long it might take, what would happen next—and then as they left the room he looked up at the clock and grinned.

'Coffee?'

'I've only just started work!'

'You can still have coffee. I'm the boss, remember? Anyway, it's quiet now and it won't last. Come on. I reckon we've got ten seconds before the red phone rings.'

'How far can we get?'

'Out of earshot,' he said with a chuckle, and all but dragged her out of the department.

They ended up outside in the park, sitting on a bench under a tree, and she leant back and peeled the lid off her cappuccino and sighed. 'Bliss. I'm going to like working here.'

He snorted rudely. 'Don't run away with the idea that it's always like this. Usually we don't have time to stop.'

'The gods must be smiling on us.'

James laughed and stretched out his legs in front of him, ankles crossed. 'Don't push your luck. How did you get on with HR?'

'I've got writer's cramp.'

He laughed again and took a long pull on his coffee. 'That good, eh?'

'At least. I hate paperwork.'

'So don't ever, ever find yourself winding up as clinical lead,' he said drily, just as his pager bleeped. He glanced at it, sighed and drained his cup. 'Duty calls.'

'Really?' She sighed, took a swallow of her coffee and burnt her tongue.

'That's why I never have a cappuccino at work,' he said, getting to his feet. 'It takes too long to cool down. Bring it with you. I can hear a siren.'

And just to punctuate that, his bleep went off again.

She followed him, coffee in hand, and she almost—almost—got to finish it by the time it all kicked off again.

He sent her home at one to let Saffy out, and she walked back in to the news that the pedestrian had died of his head injury.

'You're kidding me,' she said, the colour draining from her face. 'Oh, damn it. Damn it.'

And she walked off, back rigid, her face like stone. He couldn't follow her. He was up to his eyes, about to see a relative, but as soon as he was free he went to look for her.

He found her under the tree where they'd had their coffee, staring blindly out across the grass with the drying tracks of tears down her cheeks.

'Why did he have to die?' she asked angrily. 'My first patient. Why? What did I do wrong, James?'

He sat down next to her and took her hand in his. It was rigid, her body vibrating with tension.

'You didn't do anything wrong. You know that.'

'Do I?' she said bitterly. 'I'm not so sure.'

'Yes, you are. We can't save everyone.'

'But he died of a head injury. All I was worried about was stopping him bleeding out, and all the time it was his head I should have been thinking about.'

'No. His pelvic injury was horrific. If you'd sent him for CT before he was stable, he would have bled out and died anyway. You did what you had to do, in the order you had to do it, and he didn't make it. It was a no-win situation. Not your fault. I wouldn't have done anything different, and neither would Andy.'

'But he was nineteen,' she said, her voice cracking. 'Only nineteen, James! All that wasted potential—all the effort and time put into bringing him up, turning him into a young man, wiped out like that by some idiot—'

'He had headphones in his ears. He wasn't listening to the traffic. It wasn't the van driver's fault, and he's distraught that he hit him. He's been hanging around waiting for news, apparently, and he's devastated.'

Connie turned her head and searched his eyes. 'It was Steve's fault? Are you sure?'

'Apparently so, according to the police. And it certainly wasn't your fault he died.'

She looked away again, but not before he saw the

bleakness in her eyes. 'It feels like it. It feels like I let him down.'

'You didn't, Connie. You did your best with what you were given, that's all any of us can do.' He pressed her hand between his, stroked the back of it with his thumb. 'Are you OK to go back in there, or do you need some time?'

'No. I'm fine,' she said, even though she wasn't, and tugging her hand back she got to her feet and walked away.

He followed slowly, letting out his breath on a long sigh, and found her picking up a case in cubicles. He said nothing, just laid a hand on her shoulder briefly and left her to it, and at five he found her and told her to go home.

'James, I'm fine.'

'I don't doubt it, but you're supposed to be part-time and Saffy's been in the cage long enough. Go home, Connie,' he said gently. 'I'll be back at seven.'

She went, reluctantly, because she didn't want to be alone, didn't want to go back to the empty house and think about the boy she'd allowed to die.

Instead she worried about Saffy, because the cabin was in full sun and she should have thought of that. Another layer of guilt. What if the dog was too hot? What if she'd collapsed and died?

She hadn't. She let her out of the crate the moment she got home, and Saffy went out to the garden, sniffed around for a few minutes, had a drink and flopped down under a tree in the shade.

Connie poured herself a drink and joined her, fondling her ears and thinking about her day.

She was still angry with herself for losing Steve, but she knew James was right. She'd done everything she could, and you couldn't save everyone. She knew that, too. She'd had plenty of evidence.

She went into the cabin and changed into shorts and a sleeveless vest, slid her feet into her trainers and took Saffy for a run. Anything to get away from the inside of her head.

She went the other way this time, up the sea wall, along the lane and back along the river, and as she reached the beginning of the river wall she saw another runner up ahead of her.

It stopped her in her tracks for a moment, because he'd lost one leg below the knee and was running on a blade. Ex-military? Possibly. Probably. So many of them ended up injured in that way.

Or worse. She'd spoken to the surgeon who'd gone out to Joe in the helicopter, and he'd told her about his injuries. And she'd been glad, then, for Joe, that he'd died. He would have hated it.

The man veered off at the end of the path, and she carried on at a slower pace, cooling down, then dropped to a steady jog, then down to a walk as they reached the end of the path.

Molly was there with the children, the baby in a buggy, a little girl of three or four running giggling round the grass chasing a leggy boy of twelve or so. Happy families, Connie thought as Molly smiled at her.

'Hi there. You're Connie, aren't you? It's nice to meet you properly. So, are you coming on Friday to my private view?'

She stared blankly, and Molly rolled her eyes.

'He hasn't mentioned it, has he?' Connie shook her head, and she tutted and smiled. 'Men. He probably hasn't even told you I'm an artist. Seven o'clock, Friday night, our house. We'd love to see you.'

'Thanks. I'd love to come. I love art exhibitions, even though I can hardly hold a pencil. I haven't seen the rota yet, but if I'm not on, it would be great. Thank you.'

'I told James to change the rota. He'd better have done it. And I also told him to tell you to wear something pretty.'

She blinked. 'Pretty? How pretty?'

'As pretty as you like,' Molly said, deadpan, but there was a subtext there Connie could read a mile away, and she wondered if Molly was matchmaking. She could have saved her the trouble. James wasn't interested in her. He wasn't interested in anything except work. He certainly wasn't interested in babies.

'I'll see what I've got,' she said, and towed Saffy away from the little girl who'd given up chasing her brother and was pulling Saffy's ears gently and giggling when she licked her. 'I'd better get back, I need to feed the dog, but I'll see you on Friday and I'll make sure James changes the rota.'

'Brilliant. We'll see you then.'

She walked away, glancing back in time to see the runner with the blade join them. David? Really? He swept the little girl up in his arms and plonked her on his shoulders, and her giggle followed Connie up the path, causing an ache in her heart.

They looked so happy together, all of them, but it obviously hadn't been all plain sailing. Was it ever? And would she find that happiness, or a version of it, before it was too late?

Maybe not, unless James changed his mind, and frankly she couldn't really see that happening. She trudged up the steps to the veranda and took Saffy in to feed her.

* * *

'So how was the cabin last night?' he asked as she plonked the salad bowl down on the newly evicted garden table. 'You haven't mentioned it so I imagine it wasn't too dreadful. Unless it was so awful you can't talk about it?'

'No, not at all, it was fine. Very nice, actually. It's good to have direct access to the garden for Saffy, although I have to admit she slept on the bed last night. I'm sorry about that.'

'I should think so. Shocking,' he said, his eyes crinkling with amusement.

Connie frowned. 'She's not supposed to,' she said sternly. 'She's supposed to have manners.'

The crinkles turned to laughter as he helped himself to the salad. 'Yeah. I'm sure she is. She's not supposed to steal, either, but I wouldn't beat yourself up over it. The family dog slept on my bed his entire life, and then his successor took over.'

'Well, I don't want Saffy doing that. She's too big and she hogs the bed.'

'She can't be worse than Joe. I remember sharing a tent with him in our teens. Nightmare.' And then he looked at her, rammed a hand through his hair and sighed sharply. 'Sorry. That was tactless.'

'True, though. He did hog the bed. At least the dog doesn't snore.' She twiddled her spaghetti for a moment, then glanced up at him. 'James, about earlier. I know it wasn't my fault Steve died. I was just raw. It was just— so wrong.'

'It's always wrong. Stuff happens, Connie. You know that.'

She held his gaze for a long time, then turned slowly away. 'I know. I'm sorry I got all wet on you.'

'Don't be. You can always talk to me.'

'You can talk to me, too,' she pointed out, and he looked up from his plate and met her eyes. His smile was rueful.

'I'm not good at talking.'

'I know. You weren't nine years ago, and you haven't got better.'

'I have. Just not at the talking.'

'I rest my case.'

'Physician, heal thyself?'

She held his eyes. 'Maybe we can heal each other.'

His gaze remained steady for an age, and then he smiled sadly.

'I wish.'

'Will you tell me about her?' she asked gently. 'About how she died?'

Could he? Could he find the words to tell her? Maybe. And maybe it was time he talked about it. Told someone, at least, what had happened.

But not yet. He wasn't ready yet.

'Maybe one day,' he said gruffly, then he got up and cleared the table, and she watched him go.

Would he tell her? Could he trust her enough to share something so painful with her?

It was a nice idea. Something from cloud cuckoo land, probably. There was no way James would have let anyone in in the past, and she wasn't sure he'd changed that much.

He stuck his head back out of the kitchen door.

'Coffee?'

'Lovely. I'll have a flat white, since you're offering.'

She heard the snort as his head disappeared back into the kitchen, and she smiled sadly. She could hear him working, hear the tap of the jug, the sound of the frother, the sound of Saffy's bowl skidding round the floor as he fed her something. Probably the leftover spaghetti. She'd like that. She'd be his slave for life if she got the chance.

The light was fading, and he paused on the veranda, mugs in hand. 'Why don't you put Saffy on a lead and we'll take our coffee up on the sea wall? It's lovely up there at night.'

It was. The seagulls were silent at last, and all they could hear was the gentle wash of the waves on the shingle. The sea was almost flat calm, and the air was still.

Saffy lay down beside him, her nose over the edge of the wall, and they sat there side by side in the gathering dusk drinking their coffee and listening to the sound of the sea and just being quiet.

Inevitably her mind went back over the events of the day, and sadness came to the fore again.

'How are Steve's parents going to feel, James?' she asked softly. 'How will they get over it?'

'They won't. You don't ever get over the loss of a child. You just learn to live with it.'

It was too dark to read his expression but his voice sounded bleak, and she frowned.

He'd never had a child. She knew that. And yet—he sounded as if he understood—really understood, in the way you only could if you'd been through it. Or perhaps he knew someone who had.

And maybe he was just empathetic and she was being ridiculous.

She was about to change the subject and tell him she'd seen David and Molly when he started to speak again.

'It's probably time I told you about Cathy.'

She sucked in a quiet breath. 'Only if you want to.'

He made a sound that could have been a laugh if it hadn't been so close to despair, but he didn't speak again, just sat there for so long that she really thought he'd changed his mind, but then he started to talk, his voice low, hesitant as he dug out the words from deep inside.

'She wasn't well. She felt sick, tired, her breasts were tender—classic symptoms of early pregnancy, so she did a test and it was positive.'

'She was pregnant?' she whispered, and felt sick with horror. 'Joe never told me that—!'

'He didn't know. He was away at the time and I didn't tell anyone. Anyway, there wasn't really time. She was nearly twelve weeks by the time she realised she was pregnant, and she was delighted, we both were, but she felt dreadful. By sixteen weeks I thought she ought to be feeling better. She'd been to see the doctor, seen the midwife, been checked for all the normal pregnancy things, but she was getting worse, if anything. So she went back to the doctor, and he referred her to the hospital for tests, and they discovered she'd got cancer. They never found the primary, but she was riddled with it, and over the next six weeks I watched her fade away. She was twenty-two weeks pregnant when she died.'

Too soon for the baby to be viable. She closed her eyes, unable to look at him, but she could hear the pain in his voice, in every word he spoke, as raw as the day it had happened, and the tears cascaded down her cheeks.

His voice was so bleak, and she could have kicked herself. He'd lost a child, albeit an unborn one, and she felt sure he still grieved for it. No wonder he hadn't wanted to help her have a baby. How must he have felt when she'd blundered in and asked him to help her?

Awful.

He must have been plunged straight back there into that dreadful time. Not that it was ever far away, she knew from experience, but even so.

She shook her head, fresh tears scalding her eyes. 'I'm sorry,' she said softly, 'so, so sorry. I should never have asked you about the baby thing. If I'd known about Cathy, if I'd had the slightest idea that she was pregnant, I would never have asked you—never—'

His hand reached out in the darkness, wiping the tears from her cheeks, and he pulled her into his arms and held her.

'It's OK. You weren't to know, and I'm used to it, Connie. I live in a world filled with children. I can't avoid the subject, try as I might.'

'No. I guess not, but I'm still sorry I hurt you so much by bringing it up.'

'But you did bring it up, and because of that you're here, and maybe you're right, even if I can't make that dream come true for you, maybe we can help each other heal.'

'Do you think so?' she asked sadly, wondering if anything could take away a pain that great.

'Well, I'm talking to you now. That's a first. I didn't tell anyone. I didn't want their pity. I didn't want anything. I lost everything on that day. My wife, my child, my future—all at once, everything was gone and I wanted to die, too. There was no way I could talk about it, no way I could stay there. I had nothing to live for, but I was alive, and so I packed up the house, sold it, gave everything away and went travelling, but it didn't really help. It just passed the time, gave me a bit of distance from it geographically and emotionally, and I worked and partied my way around the world. And all the time

I felt nothing. A bit of me's still numb, I think. I guess you can understand that.'

She nodded. 'Oh, yes. Yes, I can understand that. It's how I felt after Joe died—just—nothing. Empty. Just a huge void. But at least you had the chance to say goodbye. That must have been a comfort.'

'No. Not really,' he said softly, surprising her. 'I didn't even have the chance to say hello to our baby, never mind goodbye, and with Cathy—well, you can't ever really say goodbye I don't think, not in any meaningful way, because even though you know it's happening, you still hope they might be wrong, that there's been a mistake, that there'll be a miracle cure. You just have to say the things you need to say over and over, until they can't understand any more because the drugs have stolen them from you, and then you wait until someone comes and tells you they've gone, and even then you don't believe it, even though you were sitting there watching it happen and you knew it was coming.'

She nodded. 'I did that with Joe,' she told him softly. 'I didn't watch him die, but from the moment I met him I waited for it, knowing it was coming, unable to say goodbye because I kept hoping it wouldn't be necessary, that it wouldn't happen, and in the end it took almost seven years. I always knew I'd lose him, just not when, so I never did say goodbye.'

He sighed and took her hands with his free one, folding them in his, warming them as they lay in her lap. 'I should never have introduced you. You could have been happily married to someone else, have half a dozen kids by now, not be here like this trying to convince me to give you the child you wanted with Joe.'

'I won't ask you again. I feel dreadful—'

'Shh.' He pressed a finger to her lips, then took it

away and kissed her, just lightly, the slightest brush of his lips on hers. 'It's OK, Connie. Truly. I'd rather you'd come to me like that than call me one day and tell me you'd been to a clinic and you were pregnant. At least this way I'm forewarned that it's on the cards.'

'I'm sorry you don't approve.'

'It's not that I don't approve, Connie. I just don't want you to make a mistake, to rush into it.'

'It's hardly a rush. We started trying four years ago. That's a lot of time to think about it.'

'I wish I'd known.'

'I wish you'd known. I wish we'd known about Cathy. Maybe we could have helped you.'

'We'll have to look after each other, then, won't we?'

Could they? Maybe. She sucked in a breath and let it go, letting it take some of the pain away.

'Sounds like a plan. I saw Molly's husband today, by the way, out on a run,' she went on, after a long and pensive silence. 'I didn't know he'd lost his leg. Is he ex-army?'

'No. He got in a muddle with a propeller in Australia.'

'Ouch. Some muddle.'

'Evidently. He doesn't let it hold him up much, though. I run with him sometimes and believe me, he's pretty fit. Oh, and incidentally, Molly's having a private view on Friday. She wants us to go.'

'Yes, she mentioned it. She said she'd told you to tell me.'

'Sorry. Slipped my mind,' he said, but she had a feeling he was lying.

'So, how's the rota looking for Friday?' she asked lightly.

He turned his head, the moon coming out from behind the clouds just long enough for her to see the wry grin. 'Don't worry, I'll be there and so will you. And Molly said wear something pretty, by the way.'

She grinned back at him, feeling the sombre mood slip gently from her shoulders, taking the shadows of the past with it. 'Is that you or me?' she teased.

He chuckled, his laugh warm, wrapping round her in the darkness of the night just like the arm that was still draped round her shoulders, holding her close. 'Oh, I think you do pretty rather better than me,' he said softly, and she joined in the laughter, but something in his voice made her laugh slightly breathless.

She looked up at him, their eyes meeting in the pale light of the moon, and for an endless moment she thought he was going to kiss her again, but then he turned away and she forced herself to breathe again.

Of course he hadn't been going to kiss her! Not like that. Why on earth would he do that? He didn't have anything to do with women, he'd told her that, and certainly not her.

'I'll try not to let you down,' she said, her voice unsteady, and his wry chuckle teased her senses.

'Oh, you won't let me down, Connie,' he said softly, and she swallowed hard.

Was he flirting with her? Was she with him? Surely not. Or were they? Both of them?

She gave up talking after that in case it got her into any more trouble, just closed her eyes and listened to the sea, her fingers still linked with his, his other arm still round her, taking the moment at face value.

One day at a time. One hour at a time.

Or even just a stolen ten minutes on a dark, romantic night with an old friend. Maybe more than an old friend.

Right now, tonight, she'd settle for that.

CHAPTER SIX

HE FELT SLIGHTLY shell-shocked.

He'd come home that evening uncertain of what he'd find after the rough start she'd had, and he'd walked into a warm welcome, food ready for the table, and company.

Good company. Utterly gorgeous company, if he was honest. She'd been for a run, she said, and she'd obviously showered because she smelled amazing. Her hair had drifted against him at one point, and he'd caught the scent of apples. Such a simple thing, but it made his gut tighten inexplicably.

It had been so long since anyone other than his mother or the wife of a friend had cooked for him—except, of course, that Connie *was* the wife of a friend.

Only this evening it hadn't felt like it, not really. It had felt more like two old friends who were oddly drawn to each other, sharing a companionable evening that had touched in turn on trivia and tragedy and somehow, at points, on—romance? Innuendo? A little light flirtation?

The food had been simple but really tasty, and they'd sat there over it and talked about all sorts of things. Friendship, and Joe's sleeping habits and the dog's, and how he ought to talk more. How they could help each other heal.

He still wasn't sure about the possibility of that. Some wounds, surely, never truly healed. Acceptance, he'd discovered after a while, was the new happy, and that had seemed enough—until now. And suddenly, because of Connie, he was wondering if there might be more out there for him than just this endless void.

With her?

No. That was just fantasy. Wasn't it? He didn't know, but he'd felt comfortable with her in a way he hadn't felt comfortable with anyone for years, possibly ever, and it wasn't because the subjects were comfortable, because they weren't.

They'd talked about Steve and how his parents would be feeling, and then somehow he'd found himself able to tell her about Cathy and the baby. He still couldn't quite believe that, couldn't believe he'd let her in, shared it so easily.

And it had been easy, in a way. Easier than he'd thought, although it had made her feel guilty. Still, at least now perhaps she'd understand his reluctance to discuss the baby thing, the emotional minefield that it meant for him, and it would help her understand his refusal.

Then they'd talked about Molly's private view, and her looking pretty, and he'd flirted with her. What had he been thinking about? He must have been mad, and he'd come so close to kissing her. Not the light brush of his lips on hers. That didn't count, although it had nearly killed him to pull away. But properly.

He let his breath out on a short sigh and closed his eyes. Too close. Thankfully it had been dark, just a sliver of moonlight, so maybe he'd got away with it, but Friday was going to be a trial, with her all dressed up.

He was actually looking forward to it—not to the

art, he'd meant what he'd said about not needing pictures, but to seeing Connie wearing whatever she'd decided was 'pretty'.

Hell, she'd look pretty in a bin bag. She couldn't help it. The anticipation kept him on edge all night, humming away in the background like a tune stuck in his head, and when he slept, she haunted his dreams, floating through them in some gauzy confection that left nothing to the imagination.

He got up at six, had a cold shower to dowse his raging hormones and met her in the kitchen. In her pyjamas, if you could call them that, which totally negated the effects of the shower.

'You're up early,' he said, noticing the kettle was already on.

'I've been up for ages. I couldn't sleep.'

'Worrying about work?'

'No. Saffy snoring on the bed. I take back what I said about Joe, she's much worse. She really has no manners.'

He laughed then, glancing down at Saffy who was lying on the floor and watching him hopefully. Better than studying Connie in her pyjamas. It was going to kill him, having this encounter every morning.

'I haven't done anything about getting you a kettle and toaster,' he said, changing the subject abruptly. 'I'll order them today.'

'Don't do that, I've got both of them in storage. I've got all sorts of things in storage, I just haven't dealt with them. They don't give you long to move out of married quarters, and I just packed everything up and got it out of the way.'

He eyed her thoughtfully. 'Maybe you need to deal with it.'

She nodded. 'Probably. I would, if I had anywhere to put the stuff.'

'You could bring it here. Put it in a spare room. I have three, after all. You're welcome to at least two.'

'Are you sure?'

'Why not?'

'I don't know. It just seems an imposition.'

'It's no imposition. How much is there? Is it furniture as well?'

'Oh, no, I put the decent stuff into our own house and gave the rest away. It's just personal stuff, really.' She looked troubled, and he wondered whose stuff. Joe's?

'Think about it,' he said, reaching for a pair of mugs and sticking them in front of the kettle. 'Tea or coffee?'

'Oh—tea. It's way too early for coffee. Are you going to work already?'

'Might as well. Why don't you come in at nine? There's always a rush then in Minors. I could do with someone reliable in there if you wouldn't mind.'

She gave him a wry smile. 'Is this because you feel you can't use me on the front line after Steve?'

He rolled his eyes. 'Connie, I *know* I can use you on the front line, but I need someone I can trust in Minors. And I can call you if I need to. And I will, believe me.'

'Promise?'

He met her eyes, saw the challenge in them and smiled. 'Promise.'

'Thank you. Have you made that tea yet?'

She thought she'd be bored, but actually working in Minors was busy, varied and interesting, and she found herself enjoying it.

And then he rang her, just when she was beginning to think he'd lied.

'We've got an RTC, two vehicles, mother and child in a car, and a van driver, all trapped. They need a team on site and we need to leave now. I'm in the ambulance bay.'

Her heart skipped. 'I'm on my way.'

She passed the fracture case she was dealing with to the SHO and met James in the ambulance bay. He handed her a coat that said 'DOCTOR' on the back in big letters, and they ran for the door.

'So what do we know?' she asked as the rapid response car pulled away, sirens blaring.

'Not a lot. Three casualties, one's a small child. It's not far away.'

It wasn't, ten minutes, tops, but it was a white knuckle ride and she was glad when they got there. The police were already in attendance, and an officer came over as they pulled up and got out.

'The woman in the car might have chest injuries, she's complaining of shortness of breath and pain, and we can't get to the child but it's screaming so it's alive. The car's rolled a couple of times but it's on its wheels. She swerved to avoid a cyclist and hit the van and it flipped her over into a field.'

'And the van driver?' James asked briskly. She could see him eyeing the scene and weighing up their priorities, and they could hear the child crying already.

'He's conscious, breathing, trapped by one leg but not complaining. She was clearly on the wrong side of the road and going too fast. Oh, and she's pregnant.'

Connie saw the blood drain from his face.

'Right. Connie, come with me,' he said tautly. 'The van driver'll keep till the ambulance gets here. Let's look at the mother and child. Can we get in the car?'

'Not yet. The fire crew's on its way.'

'Right.'

He wasn't impressed by what they found. It was a mess. All the windows were shattered, and the roof was bent and twisted. It wasn't going to be quick or easy to open the doors, but they could probably get in if they had to.

He crouched down and peered through the shattered glass of the driver's door, and his heart rate kicked up another notch.

The woman was pale, very distressed and covered in blood from superficial glass injuries, and he reached a hand in and touched her shoulder, smiling reassuringly—he hoped—as she turned back to face him.

'Hi there. I'm James Slater, I'm a doctor. Can you tell me your name?'

'Judith. Judith Meyers.'

'OK, Judith. Can you tell me how you're feeling? Any pain, shortness of breath, numbness, tingling?'

'Can't breathe. Banged my knee. Please, look after my little boy. Get him out—please, get him out!' She pressed her hand to her chest and gave a little wail of distress, and then tried to open the door.

'I can't get out,' she sobbed, her breath catching, and there was a blue tinge to her lips.

Damn. He straightened up and tugged the door. Nothing.

'Right, I need this door open now. Where the hell is the fire crew?' he growled.

'I can see them, they'll be here in seconds,' the police officer told him.

'Good.' He tried the handle again, tugged the door harder but it wouldn't give, and he glanced across the dented roof and saw Connie leaning in the back window.

'How does it look your end?' he called, and she pulled her head back out and shrugged.

'He's still restrained by the car seat, seems OK, moving well but I can't really assess him without getting in there. He's yelling well, though.'

He smiled thinly. 'I can hear that. Just hang on, the fire crew'll be here in a tick. Do what you can. OK, Judith, we're going to get the door open soon so we can get a better look at you, and we'll get your baby out as soon as we can, but yelling's good. What's his name?'

'Zak,' she said unevenly, her breathing worsening, and he frowned and checked her air entry again.

'OK, Connie, we've got a— Connie? What are you doing?' he asked, pointlessly, because he could see exactly what she was doing. She'd crawled into the car through the broken window and she was running her hands over Zak's limbs, oblivious to the broken glass and shattered debris on the back seat. She was going to be cut to ribbons.

'Checking the baby. He seems fine. Hey, Zak, you're all right, Mummy's just there.'

'Can you get him out?'

'Yes. He's moving well, no obvious signs of injury. Frankly I think he just needs a cuddle more than anything at the moment. He's fighting to get out but I'll need someone to take him from me. How's mum?'

'Reduced air entry on the left. Query pneumothorax. I need to fit a chest drain. Can you help me from there?'

'Not easily. Can you do it on your own?'

'I can if you can hold stuff.'

'Sure. I can do that. I'm going deaf but hey.'

By that time the fire crew was there and managed to wrench the driver's door open so he had better access, and Connie was leaning through the gap between the seats to help him when someone yelled.

'Clear the vehicle, Doc,' the fire officer in charge said quietly in his ear. 'Fuel leak.'

His heart rate went into hyperdrive, and he felt sick. He turned his head so Judith couldn't lipread. 'I can't move her yet. I need to secure her airway, get a spinal board on her and lift her out.'

'Not before we've made it safe.'

He ducked out of the car for a second. 'I can't leave her, she'll die. They'll both die, her and her unborn baby, and the baby'll die in the next few minutes if I can't secure that airway,' he said bluntly. 'Just do what you have to do and leave me to do the same.'

He stuck his head back in and met Connie's challenging eyes. 'Out,' he said, but she just shook her head.

'I'll get Zak out. Here, someone, take the baby carefully, please!' she said, and freeing little Zak, she lifted him up to the window and handed him over, then with a wriggle she was next to him on the passenger seat, sitting on another load of broken glass and debris.

'Right, what can I do?'

'You need to get out—'

'Shut up, Slater. You're wasting time. Where's the cannula?'

He was going to kill her.

Right after he'd hugged her for staying to help him save Judith's baby. He hoped.

They'd got Judith out in the nick of time, and just moments after they'd loaded her into the ambulance the car had gone up. If it had happened sooner—

'Hey, Slater, why the long face?'

He just stared at her expressionlessly. 'Your cuts need attention.'

'Later. I'm not finished with Judith. How's Zak?'

'He's fine. Check her over, make sure the baby's all right and get an X-ray of those ribs if you can.'

'James, I can manage,' she said firmly, and turned her attention to Judith as they wheeled her into Resus.

'Hi, Judith, remember me? Connie? I'm taking you over now from James Slater, the clinical lead, because he's looking after Zak, OK? You don't need to worry about him, he seems fine but James just wants to check him out.'

'I want to see him!' she sobbed hysterically. 'Please, let me see Zak. I need to know he's all right.'

'He's all right,' James said from behind her. 'Don't worry, Judith, I'll just look at him and do a few tests and then I'll bring him over to you. You just lie still and let Connie check you over.'

Fat chance. She stopped fighting the restraints, but moved on to another worry that was obviously eating holes in her, her hand grabbing at Connie and hanging on for dear life. 'How's the baby?' she asked, her eyes fixed on Connie's. 'Tell me it's all right, please. It has to be all right.'

'I'm going to do an ultrasound now. Cold gel coming.' She swept the head of the ultrasound over Judith's bump, and the sound of the baby's strong, steady heartbeat filled Resus.

Judith sobbed with relief, and behind her Connie heard James let out a ragged sigh.

'There you are,' Connie said with more confidence than she felt, her legs suddenly like jelly. 'Good and solid. Let me just get a look at the placenta—it's fine, no obvious signs of bleeding. How many weeks are you?'

'Thirty-one tomorrow.'

'So even if you did go into labour the baby's viable now. We just need to make sure that you don't if possible, so I want you to lie here and relax as much as you can, and I'll get an obstetrician to come down and look at you.'

She checked her thoroughly, did a full set of neuro

obs, and the neck X-rays came back clear and so did the ribs.

'Any back ache? Leg pain?'

'No. Only from lying flat, and no leg pain.'

'We'll log-roll her to check and then she can come off the spinal board,' James said, appearing at her side with the little boy in his arms. 'Here, Judith, have a cuddle with your little man for a moment. He's fine.'

'Mumum,' he said, reaching out to her, and James laid him carefully down in his mother's arms.

Then he glanced up and met Connie's eyes, and she smiled at him, searching his face.

'OK?' she said softly, and his mouth twisted in a cynical smile.

'Apart from being ready to kill you,' he said, so softly that only she could hear, but it didn't faze her, it was exactly how Joe would have reacted.

She held his eyes for a moment, just long enough to say she understood, and he frowned and looked down at the mother and child snuggled up together.

'I don't want to break up the party, but could I have Zak, Judith? We need to take you off the board and check your back.'

'Oh—yes, of course. Sorry, I'm being so pathetic but I just can't believe we're all all right.'

'Don't worry, I'd expect you to be concerned. I'd worry much more if you weren't.'

Her back was fine, and apart from a few cuts and bruises and the pneumothorax, so was the rest of her. More or less.

'There's a bruise on her temple,' Connie told James, and he knew instantly that she was thinking of Steve and his head injury.

* * *

'I think we'll keep her here under observation overnight, check her head injury, keep an eye on the baby, unless you want to do it in Maternity?'

He glanced past her with a smile, and she looked up as a man in scrubs approached.

'Do what in Maternity?'

'Observe a pregnant patient overnight. Minor head injury, pneumothorax from seat belt injury, a few cuts and bruises, thirty-one weeks tomorrow, rolled the car. We've just got back from freeing her.'

'Yikes. OK. Shall I take a look at her?'

'Please. Connie, this is Ben Walker. Ben, Connie. Want to talk him through it?'

She shook his hand, introduced him to Judith and filled him in on her findings. He was gentle, reassuring and happy to have her for the night.

'Just to be on the safe side,' he said with a smile. 'I'll make sure we've got an antenatal bed for you when they're ready to transfer you.'

He turned back to James with a grin. 'So, met little Daniel Gallagher yet?'

James ignored the odd sensation in his chest. 'No. How is he?'

'Fine. Gorgeous. Lovely healthy baby. Fighting fit. They're still here—he was a little bit jaundiced so we've kept them in till this afternoon. You ought to pop up and say hello.'

He could feel that his smile was strained, but there was nothing he could do about it. 'I think we're probably a bit busy. I'm sure I'll see him soon enough. We'll send Judith up as soon as we're done with her.'

'Do that. Cheers. Nice to meet you, Connie.'

'You, too.'

Connie watched him go out of the corner of her eye, most of her attention on James. Wall to wall babies today, or so it seemed, and he wasn't enjoying it one bit. It was right what he'd said last night, he couldn't avoid it, he was surrounded by children in one way or another, and so was she. They just had to deal with it, but it didn't make it easy.

She did the paperwork for Judith's transfer, handed little Zak over to the woman's harassed husband when he arrived and then went over to James.

'Anything else I can do?'

He shook his head. 'Just get your cuts seen to,' he said tightly.

'You're welcome.'

He sighed. 'Thank you, Connie. Really, thank you. Now, please, get your cuts seen to.'

She did. They were worse than she'd realised, little nicks all over her legs and bottom from the car seats, but she wasn't worried about herself. She'd seen his face in the car, seen the tension in his shoulders in Resus until they'd heard the baby's heartbeat. He wasn't alone, everyone in there had been worried for them, and if she hadn't known about Cathy she probably wouldn't have thought anything of it, but there was just something else, another element to his concern that underlined his lingering grief.

And Andy's baby. He'd definitely not wanted to go up and see it. OK, so they probably were busy, but even if they hadn't been he wouldn't have gone. Because it hurt too much?

She changed into scrubs, because her trousers were ruined, and went back to work to carry on with her fractures and squashed fingers and foreign bodies up the noses of small children, but he was at the back of her mind for the rest of the day.

'How are the cuts?'

'I'll live.'

He snorted. 'Not for want of trying, you crazy woman. You should have got out when I told you.'

'What, and leave a pregnant woman stuck in a car that was about to blow? Not to mention you. No way was I going anywhere without both of you, so save your breath, Slater.'

'Damn you, Connie,' he growled, and with a ragged sigh he hauled her into his arms and hugged her hard. 'Don't ever do that to me again.'

'What, stand up to you?'

'Put your life in danger.'

'Don't get carried away, I didn't do it for you,' she said, leaning on him because it felt so good and she'd been worried sick about him underneath the calm.

'I know that.'

He rested his head against hers and let out a long, slow sigh. 'Thanks for staying. You were good with her. She was pretty hysterical.'

'She was scared. All I did was reassure her and try and keep her calm.'

'And you did it well. You were really good. Calm, methodical, systematic—and you didn't waste any time.'

'Well, I wonder who I got that from?' she teased, and he gave a soft huff of laughter. 'It's true,' she protested. 'I modelled myself on you. I always loved watching you work. You're funny, warm, gentle, cool as a cucumber—and terrifyingly efficient.'

He lifted his head and stared down into her eyes. 'Terrifyingly?'

'Absolutely. You were a brilliant role model, though.'

'You were a pretty good student.'

'Then I guess we're both pretty marvellous.'

He laughed softly, then the laughter died and he stared down at her mouth.

It was the lightest kiss. Fleeting. Tender, like the kiss of the night before.

The kiss of a friend?

Probably not, but it was over so soon she couldn't really assess it. She just knew it was too short.

He stepped back, dropping his arms and moving away from her, and she swayed slightly without his support.

He frowned at her. 'Have you eaten?'

'Um—no. I wasn't really hungry. I had some chocolate.'

'Nice balanced diet. Good one, Connie.'

'What about you? It's late, James. Surely you've eaten something at work?'

He shook his head. 'I'll have some cheese on toast. Want some?'

'Yeah. Just a slice.'

She followed him into the kitchen, Saffy following hopefully at her heels, and perched on the stool and watched him as he made bubbly cheese on toast, and then afterwards he found some ice cream and dished it up, and they all ate it in silence.

Too tired to talk? Or was the kiss troubling him as much as it was troubling her?

'Is there any more of that ice cream left?'

'A scraping.' He opened the freezer and handed her the plastic container. 'Here. Be my guest. Coffee?'

'Mmm. Can we take it on the wall?'

He made coffee, she scraped the ice cream off the sides of the container, licked the spoon one last time and put it in the dishwasher, and they headed to the sea wall with Saffy in tow.

'So what are you wearing tomorrow night?' he asked, trying not to think too hard about the flimsy thing in his dream and failing dismally. That kiss had been such a bad idea.

She slurped the froth off her coffee and licked her lips. 'Dunno. Define pretty in this part of the world. What do your dates wear?'

He laughed at that. 'I have no idea, Connie. You're asking the wrong person. I thought I'd told you that. I don't date, I never go out except for dinner with friends occasionally. I have absolutely no idea what women wear these days.'

She turned and studied him curiously. 'You don't date at all?' Not even for sex, she nearly asked, but shut her mouth in the nick of time.

'Not any more. After Cathy died I went a bit crazy, sort of tried to lay her ghost, but I just ended up feeling dirty and disappointed and even more unhappy, so I gave up. So, no, I don't date. Not even for that, before you ask. I was just scratching an itch, and frankly I can do that myself and it's a lot less hassle.'

Wow. She thought about that. Thought about his candid statement, and felt herself colouring slightly. It wasn't the fact, it was his frankness that had—well, not shocked her, exactly, but taken her by surprise. Which was silly, because Joe had never been coy and she'd never blushed before. Maybe it was because it was James and his sex life they were suddenly and inexplicably talking about. She changed the subject hastily.

'So—dress? Long linen skirt and top? Jeans and a

pretty top? Or I've got a floaty little dress that's rather lovely, but it might be too dressy.'

Gauze. Pale, oyster pink gauze, almost the colour of your skin, with dusky highlights over the nipples and a darker shadow—

He cleared his throat. 'I don't know. It's an art exhibition. Something arty, maybe? Molly will probably wear some vintage creation.'

Please don't wear gauze.

'So who will be there?'

'Oh, all sorts of people. David's family and the people he works with, his old friends, some of the doctors. They asked me to spread the word and gave me some invitations to hand out, but how many of them will come I don't know. Andy and Lucy Gallagher probably won't, with a three day old baby, but they might because they were seriously interested, and Ben and Daisy wanted to come because they've done up their house and they're looking for artwork for it. Otherwise I'm not sure. The movers and shakers of Yoxburgh society, I imagine.'

She gave a little splutter of laughter. 'Does Yoxburgh society have movers and shakers?' she asked, slightly incredulously.

'Oh, yeah. David's probably one of them. His family own that hotel and spa on the way in, near the hospital site. The big one with the Victorian facade.'

'Wow. That's pretty smart.'

'It is. Ben and Daisy got married there and it was lovely.'

'Is that the Ben I met today?'

'Yes. Daisy's an obstetrician, too, but I think she's pretty much on permanent maternity leave and she's loving every minute of it, apparently. They've got two little ones and Ben's got an older daughter.'

Another happy family twisting the knife. Yet it was interesting, she thought, that all of his friends seemed to be family-orientated. To replace his own family? He had no one. Like her, he was an only child, and he'd lost both his parents in his twenties, and then he'd lost Cathy and the baby. And if that wasn't enough, he'd lost Joe, his closest friend. He must be so *lonely*, she thought. She knew she was. It was why she'd brought Saffy home, and part of the reason she wanted a baby, to have someone of her own to love.

'Why are you frowning? You look as if you disapprove.'

'No. Not at all. I was thinking about my clothes,' she lied glibly.

But Saffy was lying propped against him, her head on his lap, and he was fondling her ears absently as he sipped his coffee and stared out over the darkening sea. Maybe she should give Saffy to him? She seemed to adore him. At least that way he wouldn't be alone. Or she could stay with him, and they could live together and have a family and all live happily ever after.

And she was in fantasy land again.

'I could sit here all night,' she said to fill the silence, and he gave a slightly hollow laugh.

'Sometimes I do. You know, on those nights when you can't sleep and things keep going round and round your head? I don't know what it is—the sound of the sea, maybe. It just seems to empty out all the irrelevancies, like when you clean up your computer and get rid of all the temporary files and other clutter, the cookies and all that rubbish, and everything seems to run faster then, more efficiently. Only the stuff that really matters is left.'

She wondered what that was, the stuff that was left, the stuff that really mattered to him now.

'Interesting theory. I might have to try it.'

'Do. Be my guest.'

She laughed softly. 'Nice idea, but I'll take a rain check. If I'm going to look pretty tomorrow night, I need my beauty sleep or I'll look like a hag and frighten off all the potential buyers. Molly wouldn't like that.'

He chuckled and stood up, shifting Saffy out of the way, and the dog shambled to her feet and stretched, yawning and wagging her tail and looking lovingly up at him.

'No way,' he said firmly. 'I'm not sharing my bed with a dog. I've done enough of that in my time.'

'Are you sure? I'm happy to lend her to you.'

Her voice was wry and made him chuckle. 'No, thanks. Although I did wonder about her being shut in the crate all day.'

'It's not all day. And I don't like it, either, but what else can I do?'

'I could build her a kennel outside, and a run,' he suggested. 'She'd have access to water, then, and she wouldn't have to cross her legs till you get home.'

'She might bark.'

'But she doesn't, does she? I've never heard her bark.'

'No, but I can't guarantee it, and I wouldn't want to annoy your neighbours,' she said, but she was seriously tempted to take him up on it. 'I could buy a kennel if you didn't mind making her some kind of run. It would have to be pretty strong.'

'I know that. Leave it with me. I'll think about it.'

They paused at the foot of the veranda steps and he stared down at her, his eyes in shadow. 'Are your cuts really all right?'

'Why, are you offering to dress them?'

Why on earth had she said that?

He frowned. 'Do they need it?'

'No. Really, James, I'm all right. They're just little nicks. Tracy had a look for me.'

He nodded, looking relieved. 'OK. Well, keep an eye on them. I'll see you tomorrow. Come in at nine again. It seems to work.'

'OK. Thanks.'

'You're welcome.'

His face was still in shadow, so she couldn't read his expression, but she could feel his eyes on her, and for a moment she wondered if he was going to kiss her again. Apparently not.

'Goodnight, Connie,' he said eventually, his voice soft and a little gravelly. 'Sleep tight.'

'And you. 'Night, James.'

She took Saffy into the cabin. By the time she'd finished in the bathroom, Saffy was ensconced on the bed, so she turned out the light and stood at the window for a minute, watching the house through a gap in the curtains.

He was in the kitchen. Every now and then he walked past the window and she could see him. Then the light went off, and she watched the progress of the lights—the landing, then a thin sliver of light across the roof from his bathroom. Then that went off, leaving a soft glow—from his bedroom?

After a few minutes that, too, went off, plunging the house into darkness. She pressed her fingers to her lips and softly blew him a kiss.

'Goodnight, James,' she whispered. 'Sleep tight.'

And pushing Saffy out of the way she crawled into bed, curled on her side and tried to sleep.

It was a long time coming.

CHAPTER SEVEN

HE SPENT HALF the night wondering why the hell he'd kissed her again and the other half dreaming about her flitting around in the garden in that scrap of gauze he couldn't get out of his mind.

He really, really wasn't thrilled when the alarm went off, but by the time he'd washed and dressed and gone down to the kitchen, Saffy was waiting for him on the veranda, tail wagging, and there was a little plume of steam coming from the kettle.

He stuck his head out of the door and found Connie with her feet up on the veranda rail, dressed in another pair of those crazy pyjamas, her nose buried in a mug.

'More tea?' he asked, and she shook her head, so he made himself a lethal coffee and took it out and sat himself on the bench beside her. Her feet were in sun, the bright clear sun of an early summer's morning, slanting across the corner of the house and bathing them in gold.

Her toenails had changed colour. They were greeny-blue today, and pearly, the colour changing according to the angle of the light, and the sun made them sparkle dazzlingly bright.

'Interesting nail varnish.'

'Mmm. I thought I'd go arty, for tonight,' she said, grinning at her toes. 'Cool, aren't they?'

'I don't think they'd suit me.'

'Well, we've already established I do pretty better than you.'

Their eyes locked for a moment, something—an invitation?—glimmering in hers for the briefest instant. Surely not. Really, he needed more sleep. He grunted and stretched his legs out, turning his attention to his coffee as a potential means of keeping his sanity. 'So, about this dog run.'

'Really? It's a lot of effort, and where would you put it?'

'I've been thinking about that. There's a little store room under here. I could divide it off so there was a kennel one side and a store the other, and build a run off it against the fence. What do you think?'

'Are you sure? Because I do worry about her and that would be amazing. I'd pay for all the materials.'

'OK. It shouldn't take much. We'll have a look at it after work.'

'No we won't, because we're going out. You hadn't forgotten, had you?'

Fat chance. How could he forget, with 'pretty' haunting his every waking moment and tantalising him in his sleep? Never mind those kisses he couldn't seem to stop giving her.

'Of course I haven't forgotten.' He downed his coffee and went back into the kitchen, grabbed a banana, slung his jacket on and headed out of the door.

'I'll see you later,' he muttered, running down the steps, and she dropped her feet to the veranda floor and wriggled them back into her flip-flops as she watched him go. He looked hunted, for some reason. Because of the private view?

She had no idea, but it was the last thing they'd talked about and he'd taken off like a scalded cat.

'Fancy a run, Saffy?' she asked, and Saffy leapt to her feet, tail lashing. 'That's a yes, then,' she said, and pulled her clothes on, locked up the cabin and the house and headed off.

She went on the sea wall for a change, and ran along to the end of the sea defences, then up a long set of steps to the top of the cliff and back down towards the harbour through the quiet residential streets.

She'd never been along them before, but it was obviously where the movers and shakers lived, she thought with a smile, and she wondered how many of them would be coming tonight.

She felt a tingle of anticipation, and realised she was actually looking forward to it. It was ages since she'd been out, ages since she'd had an occasion to dress up for, and she was determined to enjoy herself. And if she had anything to do with it, James would enjoy himself, too.

He felt ridiculously nervous.

He didn't know what to wear, so in the end he wore a lightweight suit with a silk shirt. No tie, because that would be overdoing it, but a decent silk shirt, open at the neck because it was a warm night.

Maybe not as warm as he felt it was, though. That was probably because he was waiting for Connie to come out of her cabin, and he was on edge.

She'd left him out something to eat, and he hadn't seen her since he'd got home. Saffy was in the garden, though, so he sat on the veranda and watched the cabin door and waited.

* * *

Was it all right?

She'd settled on a knee-length dress with a flirty hem in a range of sea colours from palest turquoise to deep, deep green, and it was soft and floaty and fitted like a dream. She'd bought it last year for a friend's wedding and she'd thought it would be perfect for tonight, but now she wasn't sure.

What if she'd overdone it? There was no long mirror in the cabin, so she'd had to make do with peering at the one in the shower room and trying to angle her head to see herself, but she couldn't. Not adequately.

And it was five to seven, and James was on the veranda, watching her door and tapping his fingers on the bench.

She took a steadying breath, slipped her feet into her favourite strappy sandals with killer heels, because, damn it, why not, and opened the door.

'Does this count as pretty?'

He felt his jaw drop.

He'd seen her looking beautiful before, lots of times, when she'd been with Joe. At their engagement party. On her wedding day. At a ball they'd all attended. Hell, sitting on the deck in her pyjamas this morning she'd nearly pushed him over the edge.

But this...

'I think you'll do,' he said, his voice sounding strangled.

Her face fell. 'Do?'

He got up and went to the top of the steps, looking down at her as she walked towards him and climbed the steps on incredibly sexy, utterly ridiculous heels that showed off her legs to perfection, and stopped just beneath him.

'Connie, you look—' He closed his eyes, then opened them again and tried to smile. 'You look beautiful,' he said, and his voice had handfuls of gravel in it.

'Oh.' She laughed, and her whole body relaxed as the laugh went through her. 'I thought, for a minute—you looked so—I don't know. Shocked.'

'Shocked?'

Try stunned. Try captivated. Try completely, utterly blown away.

'I'm not shocked,' he said. 'I just—'

He didn't like it. Damn. He was just being nice. 'Look, I can go and change. There isn't a mirror in there, but it's probably a bit much. A bit too dressy. I just don't have a lot to choose from, and—well, Molly did make a point—'

'Connie, you look fine,' he said firmly. 'Utterly gorgeous. Believe me. There's nothing wrong with the way you look. You're lovely. Very, very lovely.'

'Really?'

Her eyes were soft and wide, and he so badly wanted to kiss her again. 'Really,' he said, even more firmly. 'Let me just put Saffy away and then we'd better go.'

He called the dog, put her in her crate in the cabin and breathed in the scent of Connie. It had been diluted in the garden, drifting away on the light sea breeze, but in the confined space of the cabin the perfume nearly blew his mind.

'Good girl, Saff,' he said, closing the door on her. She whined, and he promised her he'd make her a run, then closed the cabin door and braced himself for an evening in Connie's company.

Torture had never smelt so sweet.

* * *

It was already buzzing by the time they got there.

She'd heard lots of cars going past on the gravel road, and so she wasn't surprised. And she wasn't over-dressed, either, she realised with relief. All the women were in their designer best, diamonds sparkling on their fingers, and the men wore expensive, well cut suits.

None of them looked as good as him, though, and she felt a shiver of something she hadn't felt for years.

'Connie, James, welcome!' David said, pressing glasses of champagne into their hands. 'Just mingle and enjoy—the pictures are all over the place, and there's a pile of catalogues lying around somewhere on a table. Just help yourselves. And there are some canapés coming round.'

'Wow,' she said softly as he moved away, and James raised an eyebrow.

'Indeed. The movers and shakers,' he murmured.

She suppressed a giggle, the bubbles of the cham-pagne already tickling her nose. 'I ran past some pretty smart houses this morning up on the clifftop. I guess they're here.'

'Undoubtedly. His friends are pretty well connected. Ah—Andy and Lucy *are* here. Come and say hello.'

Not only were they there, she realised as he made the introductions, they had the baby with them, snug in the crook of Andy's arm, and her heart turned over.

James leant over and kissed Lucy's cheek, his smile looking entirely genuine if you ignored the tiny tic in his cheek. 'Congratulations. How are you? I didn't really expect to see you here so soon.'

'Oh, I'm fine,' Lucy said, positively glowing. 'My parents are here helping us out for a few days, and we really wanted to come, so we thought we'd sneak out while the going was good. And I'm really glad, because I get to meet Connie and say thank you for stepping in like that so I can have Andy at home.'

'Oh, you're welcome,' Connie said with a laugh, liking Lucy instantly. 'It's nice to be back at work. I've had a sabbatical and I was beginning to feel a bit redundant.'

'Oh, well, glad to be of service,' Lucy said with a chuckle. 'And this is Daniel, the cause of all the trouble.'

'Oh, he's so beautiful,' she whispered, and she felt her eyes fill with tears. 'Sorry. Babies always do that to me,' she said with a light laugh, but she could feel James watching her.

'Oh, good,' Andy said. 'You can hold him while I dig out my chequebook. Lucy's found a picture and I need to pay for it. Here.'

And he reached over and gave her little Daniel. Just like that, her arms were full of new baby, closing round him automatically and cradling him close, and she felt the threatening tears well again. 'Hello, little guy,' she crooned softly, breathing that wonderful new baby smell and welling up again. It just felt so *right*. 'Aren't you gorgeous?'

James felt his heart squeeze just looking at them together. *She should be a mother,* he thought suddenly. *She's born for it. It could be my child, but if I stop her, it'll be someone else's, and how will that feel?*

'So how do you two know each other?' Lucy asked, and James dragged his eyes off Connie and the baby before he went crazy.

'We worked together nine years ago, and we've kept in touch.'

He noticed Lucy's eyes flick to Connie's wedding ring, and winced inwardly, but he didn't say any more, and neither did Connie. She was absorbed by the baby, utterly focused, and she just looked so damned *right* holding him that he could hardly think straight, never mind make small talk or fend off gossip. Not that Lucy was a gossip, but he didn't feel it was up to him to broadcast Connie's personal circumstances.

'All done.'

Connie looked up at Andy and smiled ruefully. 'Does that mean you want him back?'

'Afraid so, having gone to all that trouble to get him.'

So she handed him back, releasing him reluctantly, her arms feeling suddenly desperately empty and unfulfilled.

And then she glanced at James and saw a muscle clench in his jaw, and she thought, *I'm not alone. He feels it, too. The ache. The need. The emptiness. Only how much worse is it for him?*

'So what do you think of the exhibition?' Lucy asked.

James shrugged. 'I don't know, we've only just arrived.'

'Well, you'd better go and look, the red dots are going on faster than a measles epidemic,' Andy said with a grin.

'Oh, I don't do pictures. It would require finding a hammer and a nail to put it on the wall, and that would mean unpacking the boxes.'

Andy laughed, and James was still smiling, but it was lingering there in his eyes, she thought. The emptiness.

He still wants a child, she realised with sudden clarity. *He wants one, but he doesn't know how to move on.* But maybe, once he'd got to know her—maybe she'd be able to do something about that...

'Well, hi.'

'Ben! Nice to see you. How's our patient?'

'Fine. Doing well.'

'Are you two going to talk shop?' Lucy asked pointedly, but Connie just grinned.

'No, we three are. Sorry. So how is she? How's the head injury?'

'A nice shade of purple, and so's her knee, but she's fine. This is Daisy, by the way.'

She was scintillating.

She mingled with everyone with the confidence of someone totally at ease with herself, smiling and laughing and waving her hands all over the place to illustrate what she was saying. Which was great, because it meant he didn't need to stand right next to her all night, breathing in that intoxicating perfume and threatening to disgrace himself.

'So, what do you think?'

He turned round to Molly. 'Great exhibition. Really good.'

'I meant of Connie.'

'Connie?'

'Oh, James, come on, you haven't taken your eyes off her. Doesn't she look beautiful?'

Well, he could lie, or make some excuse, or drop his drink.

Or he could just be honest.

'Yes. She does. It's the first time I've seen her look happy in ages. Thanks for inviting her. She's really enjoyed dressing up, I think. She's even got crazy matching nail varnish on her toes.'

Molly chuckled. 'Not that you noticed, of course.'

'Of course not. Why would I? I'd better go and rescue her, that guy's getting a bit pushy.'

'He's harmless, James. I'm sure she can cope,' Molly murmured, but *he* couldn't. Couldn't cope at all with the good-looking bastard oozing charm all over her like some kind of vile slime, and the words she'd said to him less than a week ago were echoing in his head. Words about pulling some random stranger in a club. Or at an art exhibition?

Fighting off the red mist, he made his way over to her, smiling grimly.

'There you are,' he said, slipping his hand through her arm, and he stuck his hand out. 'James Slater.'

The man blinked, introduced himself as Tony and made himself scarce. Excellent.

Connie turned slowly and looked up at him. Not that far up, not now, because she was teetering on those sky-scrapers that messed with his head and they brought her up almost to eye level with him.

'So what was that all about?' she asked, laughter dancing in her eyes.

'He was flirting outrageously.'

'Yes. He was. And I was perfectly happy letting him make a fool of himself. It was quite fun, actually.'

At which point James began to wonder if he was making a fool of his own self. Very probably. He tried not to grind his teeth. 'I thought he might be annoying you.'

'In which case I would have told him where to go. James, I've lived on an army base for years,' she said patiently, her eyes laughing at him. 'Several of them. And in every one there was someone like that. I can deal with it.'

He nodded. Of course she could. He'd seen her doing it years ago, for God's sake, handling the drunks on a Friday night in the ED. Tony whoever was nothing. 'Sorry. I didn't mean to come over all heavy, I just...'

He shrugged, and she shook her head slowly and smiled at him.

'You're crazy. Come with me. There's a picture I want to show you.'

She tucked a hand in his arm and led him through to another room. It was quieter in there, and she pulled him to one side and then turned him.

And there, on the wall opposite them, was a blur of vibrant colour. It radiated energy, and for a second he couldn't work out what it was. And then the mist seemed to clear and he could make out the figure of a runner, smudged with speed, the power almost palpable, and at the bottom was a fine, curved line.

'It's called Blade Runner,' she said softly. 'Isn't it amazing? As if she's tapped into his soul.'

'Amazing,' he echoed. 'It's incredible. It must be David.'

'I would think so. It's not for sale.' Connie let him stand there for a minute, then she tugged his arm. 'Come on. There are others. Have you looked at them?'

He shook his head. 'No. No, not really.' *Because he'd been watching her. Picturing her with a baby in her arms. Picturing her pregnant. Fantasising about getting her that way—*

'You should. Your walls are crying out for colour, for movement. And these are fantastic.'

He stopped thinking about Connie then and started to look at them, really look at them, and he was blown away.

'Wow. I love this one,' Connie said, pausing in front of a very familiar scene. At least he thought it was familiar, but Molly's work was blurred and suggestive rather than figurative, and he wasn't entirely sure.

'It looks like the marshes from my veranda.'

'Gosh, yes. I think you're right—what does it say?'

'"Mist over the ferry marshes",' he told her. 'I'm sure it is. I recognise the pattern of the landscape.'

'It's the view out the back here, she paints it all the time. She loves it,' David said in passing, and gave him another drink. He took it without thinking. So did Connie, and by the time they'd worked their way round the exhibition again, they'd had another two. At least.

Realising he'd lost count, he took a closer look at Connie and sighed inwardly. She was tiddly. Not drunk, certainly not that, but gently, mildly inebriated. At the moment. And frankly, so was he.

'I think it's time to go home,' he murmured.

'Really?'

'Really.' The crowd was thinning out, Andy and Lucy with their tiny baby were long gone, and he figured that he just about had time to get Connie home before the last glass entered her system and pushed her over the edge.

'Fabulous exhibition. I love every single one,' she told Molly fervently. 'I want them all, but I haven't got any money, and more importantly I haven't got any walls or I might have to start saving.'

Molly laughed. 'Thank you. I'm glad you like them. And you'll have walls one day.'

'I've got walls right now that need pictures,' James said, surprised to realise that he meant it. 'Can I come and see you tomorrow?'

'Sure. We're opening the door at ten. Come before then. Both of you, come for coffee.'

'That'll be lovely. Thanks.' He kissed her cheek, shook David's hand and ushered Connie out of the door.

'Can we walk by the sea?' she asked, so he led her up onto the sea wall, her hand firmly anchored in his.

'Oooh. That's a bit steep. When did that happen?' she asked, eyes rounded, and giggled.

'When you had all that champagne,' he told her wryly, and she laughed and tucked her arm in his and they walked arm in arm along the sea wall until they reached his house. Then she looked down at the bank.

'Hmm. We walked along the road before, didn't we?'

'We did.'

'Oh.'

If it was anybody else, he would have thought it was staged, but Connie wasn't that artful. He shook his head and hoisted her up into his arms, and she gave a little shriek and wrapped her arms around his neck.

'What are you doing?'

'Carrying you down the bank so you don't break your ankle in those crazy shoes.'

'Don't you like my shoes?' she asked, lifting one foot up and examining it thoughtfully, and he turned his head and looked at her leg and groaned softly.

'Your shoes are fine,' he said a little abruptly, and put her down. She slid down his front, ending up toe to toe with him, their bodies in contact from chest to knee.

Dear God.

'James?' she whispered.

She was so close her breath teased his cheek, and it would take only the tiniest movement of his head to bring their lips into contact.

He moved, brushed his mouth against hers. Pulled back, then went in again for more, his hands tunnelling into her hair, his tongue tracing her lips, feeling them part for him. He delved, and she delved back, duelling with him, driving him crazy.

She whimpered softly, and he pulled away, resting

his head on hers and breathing hard, stopping now while
he still could.

'More,' she said, and he shook his head.

'Connie, no. This is a bad, bad idea.'

'Is it?'

'Uh-huh.'

'What a shame.' She hiccupped, and looked up at
him, her eyes wide in the moonlight. 'Do you think we
might be just a teeny, tiny bit drunk?' she asked, and
then giggled.

He closed his eyes, the imprint of her body against
his burning like flames, the touch of her lips branding
him forever. 'Just a teeny, tiny bit,' he agreed. 'Come
on, Connie, it's time you went to bed.'

And he turned her and pointed her in the direction of
the cabin, unlocked the door and pushed her in.

Quickly, before he did something that couldn't be
undone, something he'd regret for the rest of his life.

Something like cup that beautiful, laughing face in
his hands once more and bend his head and kiss her
again, only this time, he knew, he wouldn't stop...

How ironic. And what a brilliant way to find out that
he was ready to move on.

With his best friend's widow.

Great move, Slater, he told himself in disgust. He
picked up a pebble off the sea wall and hurled it into
the water. Or tried to. The tide was too far out, and he
missed by miles.

That was champagne for you.

Or the distracting realisation that you were about to
make a real idiot of yourself.

Even more disgusted, he threw another one, and this
time he was angry enough that it made its mark.

Better.

So he did it again.

She was woken by Saffy scratching at the door.

'Saff, no, it's too early, come and lie down,' she pleaded, her head thrashing, but Saffy wanted out, and she wasn't giving up. She whined, then gave a soft bark, and Connie stumbled out of bed and opened the door.

James was on the veranda, sitting there in the pre-dawn light, a mug cradled in his hands.

'Is that tea?' she asked, her throat parched and her head pounding.

'You need water,' he told her, and dropped his feet to the deck and stood up. 'Gallons of it.'

She walked barefoot across the dewy grass and climbed the steps gingerly. 'I want tea.'

'Water first,' he insisted, handing her a glass.

'I wasn't that bad,' she protested, but a sceptical eyebrow flickered and she scowled at him. 'I wasn't!'

'No. To quote you, you were only a teeny, tiny bit drunk.'

'Oh, God,' she moaned, and slumped down onto the bench and put her head in her hands. 'Did I disgrace myself?'

'No. You were lovely,' he said, his internal editor clearly on holiday, and she dropped her hands from her face and straightened up, turning slowly to look at him.

'I was?'

'Well, of course you were.'

She smiled and leant back, picking up the glass. 'Phew. For a moment there I thought I might have made a fool of myself.'

He chuckled. 'You didn't, but probably only because I got you out of there in time.'

'You didn't *have* to carry me home,' she pointed out, which answered the question of how much she remembered. More than he'd expected, probably. The kiss?

'I didn't. I just carried you down the bank.'

'Yeah. Crazy shoes. I bought them after Joe died. He was only three inches taller than me, and they're five inch heels. And I love them soooo much.'

'I don't know how the hell you walk in them.'

'Carefully,' she said with a little laugh. 'So—I've drunk the water. Can I please have tea now? Because I do have a teensy little headache.'

'I'll just bet you do,' he grumbled, getting to his feet again. 'What did your last servant die of?'

And then he stopped in his tracks, swore viciously and turned back to her. Her eyes were wide with shock, all laughter gone, and he could have kicked himself.

'Ah, hell, Connie, I'm sorry—I didn't mean—' He swore again, and dropped his head against the doorframe, banging it gently. OK, maybe not so gently. 'I'm really sorry. That was inexcusable. I can't believe I said it.'

'Hey. It's all right,' she said softly. 'It was just a silly remark. We all do it. And it's exactly the sort of thing Joe used to say to me. I'll forgive you if you get me tea and stop making wisecracks about my hangover. Done?'

'Done,' he said, sending her a wry, apologetic smile. 'Do you want anything to eat?'

'It's a bit early.'

'Not if you've been up all night.'

'Survivors' breakfast?' she said, and there it was again, the spectre of Joe between them, and this time it was her fault.

I can't do this, he thought. *I can't just be with her feeling like this with Joe hanging over us. And I'm not*

*sure I can cope with the idea of giving her a baby. Ever.
I can't even cope with thinking about it because I want
it so much. How did I get myself in this mess?*

Easy. He'd been forced into a corner by the staffing
crisis, and he'd been so desperate for help that Connie had seemed like the answer to his prayers, so he
hadn't let himself think about it too hard. The trouble
was, she was hoping he'd be the answer to hers, or at
least give her the answer to her prayers in the form of
a baby, and he really wasn't sure he could. Not in the
way she wanted, anyway, just a clinical donation of his
DNA. Not when the real alternative was growing more
and more compelling by the second—

'Something like that,' he said mildly. 'Bacon sandwich?'

'Oh, amazing! That would be so good.'

'Coming up.'

And he retreated to the kitchen, dragging the task
out far longer than necessary while he tried to work out
if she'd remembered the kiss or if she was just avoiding
the subject like him.

'Are you growing that tea?' she asked, appearing
in the doorway in those inadequate pyjamas, and he
slid the mug towards her, fished the bacon out of the
pan and dropped it on the bread and hesitated, sauce
bottle in hand.

'Ketchup or brown sauce?'

'Neither. As it comes. Unless you've got fresh tomato?'

He gave an exaggerated sigh, got a tomato out of
the fridge and sliced it, and handed her the sandwich.
'Right. I'm going for a run,' he said, and left the kitchen
before his body gave him away. He was going to cut
those pyjamas up, he vowed, plodding up the stairs

and turned the corner into his bedroom, to come to a dead halt.

'Connie! Your dog's up here, in my bed, and she's eating my trainers!'

Saffy was in disgrace.

They'd been his favourite running trainers, he said, and she felt racked with guilt.

'I'm really sorry—I'll buy you a new pair,' she promised, but of course that didn't help him, he wanted to go for a run there and then, and so he wore his old ones and came back with blisters. He had, however, taken Saffy with him, and she came back panting, as if the run had been further and harder than she was used to.

'Poor Saffy. Did he wear you out, darling?' she crooned, and he laughed.

'Poor Saffy?' he said with studied sarcasm. 'She's had a great time. She chased the seagulls, and played on the beach with a Labrador, and she's had brilliant fun.'

'You let her off the lead?' she squawked.

'Don't sound so horrified, she was fine.'

But she was horrified, because the only time she'd tried it, it had taken her all day to find the wretch. But that was her, and this was James, and Saffy worshipped him. Even to the point of wanting to eat his smelly old trainers.

'I'm going to shower. Try and make sure she doesn't eat anything else while I'm gone,' he said drily, and so just to be on the safe side she took Saffy back into the cabin with her and put her in the crate while she had a shower herself.

'So, jeans and a T, or my blue dress, Saffy?' She looked at the options, debated for a second and then grinned at Saffy. 'Blue dress. Excellent choice. It's going to be a hotty.'

She pulled on the sundress, found some flip-flops and slid her feet into them, and went out to find James with his head in the store under the veranda. The kennel?

Oops, she thought. Poor old Saffy really was in trouble!

'Is this a work party? Because if so I probably ought to change, only I thought we were going up to Molly and David's this morning.'

He pulled his head back out of the doorway and thumped it on the head of the frame. 'Ouch. No, it's not a work party,' he said, and then looked at her stupidly for a moment.

She looked—well, she'd been beautiful last night, elegant and sophisticated and downright stunning. Now, she just looked plain lovely, the dress that barely brushed the top of her knees leaving those gorgeous legs exposed to taunt him again, and he wanted to walk over to her, scoop her up in his arms and carry her up to bed.

Which was *so* not going to happen!

'I thought I'd investigate the possibilities before she eats anything else of mine,' he said, trying not to sniff the air to see if she'd used that same shampoo. She didn't have the perfume on, he was sure of that, because even in the garden he would have been able to smell it.

'And?'

And? And what? 'Um—yes, it'll work,' he said hastily, retuning. 'We'll do it later. So, are you ready to go?'

CHAPTER EIGHT

THE PICTURES WERE every bit as good in the cold, sober light of day as they had been last night with the clever lighting, but there was nothing there that just said, Buy me.

'There are some others,' David said. 'We ran out of wall space. Come and have a look.'

He took him through into Molly's studio, and immediately he was captivated by a canvas propped up on the easel.

'Oh, wow.'

It was a view across the harbour mouth, painted from the vantage point of the sea wall, he thought, looking out. The sea was a flat, oily calm, the skies threatening, and it was called 'Eye of the Storm'.

He loved it. Loved everything about it. The menace. The barely leashed power. The colours in the lowering sky.

'She got drenched doing the sketches for that,' David said with a chuckle.

'It was worth it.'

'What was worth what?'

He turned and smiled at Connie. 'Getting drenched.'

'Wow. I can see why. That sky looks pretty full.'

'It was a lot emptier a few minutes later,' Molly said

drily. 'I had to retreat to the bedroom to carry on. I painted it standing at the window in the attic bedroom at your house, James, and I never finished it because I couldn't seem to get the sea right. I got it out again the other day and it sort of fell into place. Do you want another coffee?'

'No, thanks. I think I want to buy this picture. Kind of poetic, taking it home. I might even hang it in the bedroom, since my sitting room is still a work in progress. I know it's not in the exhibition, but is it for sale?'

He found the hammer and some picture hooks, buried in the back of the tool shed under the veranda, and he took Connie inside to help him hang it.

'So, where?'

'Sitting room?'

He looked around, but there wasn't anywhere obviously right for it. The books were still in boxes and he wasn't sure if the furniture worked where it was, and just then sorting it out and unpacking the books and getting to grips with it seemed too big a task.

'No. Bedroom. Come and help me place it.'

So not a good idea, he thought the moment they were in there. The walls seem to close in, the air was sucked out of the room and the bed grew until it filled all the available space.

'So—' He cleared his throat and looked around a trifle desperately. 'Whereabouts would you put it?'

'I don't know. You want to be able to see it from the bed, don't you?'

'Probably.'

And before he could breathe she was there, sitting cross-legged at the top of the bed, bossing him about.

'Try there.'

Try what where? The only thing he wanted to do was crawl onto the bed beside her and kiss her. Drag her into his arms and slide that blue dress off over her head and kiss her from top to toe—

Focus!

'Here?'

'No. Angle's wrong. Try that side—that's better. Down a bit. Perfect.'

And she scrambled off the bed and took the picture from him. 'You look at it. Go and lie on the bed and look at it.'

Really? Right there, where she'd just been? Where he'd been fantasising about kissing her?

'Is it really necessary—? OK, OK,' he grumbled, defeated by that challenging stare, and he threw himself down on the bed, propped himself up on the pillows and was immediately swamped by the scent of her. Had she *bathed* in the perfume? Sprayed it on her legs? Sheesh!

'Well? My arms are aching.'

'Um—yeah, that's really good.' He swung his legs off the side, found a pencil and went over to mark the top of the picture so he could put a hook in the wall, but she was just there, so close, and the urge to lean into her, to take the picture from her and put it down and kiss her nearly—so nearly—overwhelmed him.

He reached past her and marked the wall before he lost it completely. 'OK,' he said, and she stepped back so he could put the hook in, then she settled the picture on it.

'Great,' she said. 'One down, however many more to go.'

'What?'

Connie turned to look back at him; she was already heading down the stairs to get away from the image of him lying sprawled on his bed where she'd imagined him so many times. She simply hadn't done him justice.

'The rest of the house,' she explained. 'The sitting room needs at least three pictures—unless you have one huge one.'

'I can't afford a huge one. This one was bad enough.'

'I'm sure she'd do a bulk discount. There was that fabulous one of the marshes. It would go really well in there.'

She left him standing there staring at her, and ran down the stairs and out onto the veranda. She needed fresh air. The window had been open in his room but—well, clearly on a hot day the heat rose to the top of the house. There couldn't be any other explanation, or not one she wanted to consider.

Not James! she told herself. *You can't fall for James! You'll just break your heart. You can't just have a trivial affair with him, and you know he doesn't want more than that! Hell, he doesn't even want that, and especially not with you. If he did, he wouldn't have stopped after that kiss. So, keep out of his bedroom, keep out of his way, just—keep out of his life! It's not safe, not at all. He's not in the market for anything permanent, and if you mess this up he won't even be your friend. Don't do it!*

'Coffee?'

'Mmm. Flat white, if you've got the milk, please. And good and strong.'

'Coming up.'

She spent the next few minutes lecturing herself along the same lines, until James appeared on the veranda again with her coffee. Interesting, she thought as he put it down in front of her a few moments later. The rosetta was a mess.

'Losing your touch?' she teased, trying to introduce a light note, but he avoided her eyes.

'I knocked my hand on the kettle,' he said, but he sounded evasive and she just—wondered...

He was a man, after all, and she knew she wasn't exactly ugly, and she'd been sitting on his bed. And he'd already admitted that he didn't have a woman in his life and hadn't for ages. And he'd kissed her.

Was it mutual, this insane and crazy attraction?

Surely not. It wasn't her. Probably any half-decent woman with a pulse would make him think twice if she was sitting on his bed. It hadn't even occurred to her, and it probably should have, but it wasn't happening again. No, no, no, no, no!

She drank her coffee without a murmur and got out of his hair the moment it was done.

'Wow. What are you doing?'

'Making the kennel—what does it look like?'

Like he'd emptied the shed out all over the garden, was what, but she had the sense not to say so. 'Want a hand?'

He hesitated, then nodded. 'It might be useful. Steadying things, you know.'

'I'll put Saffy in her crate out here so she can watch us. I don't think she needs to get involved with this lot.'

'Probably not. Do you want a cold drink before we start?'

'That would be good. I wouldn't mind a sandwich, either. Have you eaten?'

'No. I've got some ham and salad, and a few cartons of soup in the fridge. Want to make us something?'

'Sure.'

She changed into her scruffiest clothes, because there

was no way this was going to be anything other than a hot, dirty, sweaty job, and then threw together some lunch before they started.

'In your own time, Slater,' she said, carrying it all out to the table in the garden next to Saffy, and he washed his hands and joined her.

'Looks good. It's a long time since we had breakfast.'

'Yeah. Bacon and tomato sandwich, ham salad sandwich with tomato soup—do you see a pattern emerging? Maybe I need to go shopping later this afternoon and stock up the fridge.'

'Only when this run's made. I'm not having anything else chewed up. I loved those trainers.'

'Oh, Saffy,' she said slowly. 'Are we in trouble?'

'Too right.' He swiped the tail end of his sandwich around his empty soup bowl and sat back with a sigh. 'That was good. Thanks.'

'Tea?'

'If you insist.'

'I do. You need liquids.'

'Says she, the queen of dehydration.'

'I was not dehydrated.'

He snorted softly and got up. 'Call me when it's made. I want to see if I've got enough wood to make a doorframe.'

It took them ages. Far longer than he'd anticipated, and he'd had to go shopping twice for materials, but finally Saffy had a kennel with a run, and his possessions were safe.

The only downside was that he'd had to spend the afternoon with Connie, and every second of it had been exquisite torture. She might have changed, but she was still wearing that perfume, and working in the confined space of the kennel had been enough to push him over the brink.

He'd kept bumping into her, her firm-yet-soft body close enough to him that he could feel the warmth coming off it, and then every now and then he'd shift or she'd reach up and they'd bump. Just gently. Just enough to keep his hormones simmering on the brink of meltdown.

He banged in the last nail and threw the hammer down. 'Right, that's it, I'm calling it a day. If that's not good enough, I give up.'

'What are you talking about? It's fantastic. Brilliant. Saffy, come on, come and have a look at what James has made you.'

She was wary, but with a little coaxing she went inside and had a sniff around. 'She might feel happier if her crate was in there, with the door open,' Connie suggested, so he wrestled it through the narrow doorway and set it down at the back, and Saffy went straight in it and lay down, wagging her tail.

'Excellent. Job done,' Connie said, and gave him a high five. She was laughing, her whole face lit up, and he felt a huge ache in the centre of his chest.

'Great. Let's clear up the tools and have a drink.'

'How about something fizzy?'

'Didn't you have enough of that last night?' he asked mildly, and she gave him a level look.

'I meant fizzy water, or cola or something. Not champagne.'

'Ah. Well, I have spring water.'

'Perfect.' She emerged from the kennel, he put the last of the tools away and then she remembered the parlous state of the fridge. 'Damn.'

'What?'

'I forgot to go shopping.'

He shrugged. 'We can go to the pub. It'll be a good test for Saffy. We'll leave her in here, sit outside at the pub and listen. If she barks or howls continuously, I'm sure we'll hear her.'

'I'm not sure I want to know,' Connie said drily, feeling a twinge of apprehension.

'Oh, man up. She'll be fine. She'd better be, after all we've done for her.'

Connie just raised a brow. 'Man up?' she said, trying not to laugh. 'Really?'

'Technical term.'

'I have met it.'

He grinned and threw her one of Saffy's toys. 'Here. I'll get her water bowl.'

She was fine.

They had a peaceful, undisturbed meal at the pub.

Undisturbed, that was, by Saffy. Connie, though, was ridiculously aware of James the entire time. His soft, husky laugh, the crinkles round his eyes, the bones of his wrist—there didn't seem to be a thing about him that didn't interest or absorb her.

And that was deeply distracting.

It was such a shame, she thought as she went to bed that night after shutting Saffy outside in her new quarters, that if she eventually had a child it wouldn't be his.

But the sudden ache of longing at the thought, low down in her abdomen, nearly took her breath away. She pressed one hand to her mouth, the other to the hollow, empty ache inside, and blinked away the tears that inexplicably stung her eyes.

No! She couldn't fall in love with him! Not really, truly in love with him, and that's what it was suddenly beginning to feel like. She couldn't let herself, she had far too much to lose. He would never be in it for the long haul, and she'd lose her heart, lose a friend she treasured, and lose her only chance to have a child. Because if she fell in love with him, truly, deeply in love with him, how could she ever consider having any other man's child inside her body, when all she longed for was his?

Far, far too late for common sense to intervene, she realised just what an incredibly stupid mistake this all was. She ought to cut her losses and go. But she couldn't leave, she thought desperately. Not while there was still hope. Maybe if she stayed, if they got to know each other better, explored this attraction, then at some point in the future maybe—

She was clutching at straws, dreaming up a happy-ever-after that could never be! She was deluding herself, and she really, really should know better.

She turned over, thumped the pillow into shape and made herself relax. She ached all over, not just in that hollow place inside that craved his child, and tomorrow was going to be hard enough without a sleepless night, so she slowed her breathing, tensed and relaxed all her muscles in turn, and finally fell asleep, only to dream of James.

He ended up on the sea wall again at stupid o'clock in the morning.

He'd crept out the front so he didn't disturb Saffy, and he was sitting there staring blindly out over the water and wondering what had happened to the amazing, relaxing properties of the waves because frankly they didn't seem to be working any longer.

Mostly because when he'd gone to bed, he could still

smell the lingering essence of Connie's perfume on the pillows, and his mind was in chaos.

He couldn't believe how much he wanted her. He told himself it was lust. He told himself it was just physical, she was a beautiful woman, it had been so long that frankly any half-decent-looking woman would have the same effect.

He knew he was lying.

It was Connie. He'd felt it for years, off and on, but because Joe had been there he'd managed to keep it down, keep it under control. Not now. Now, it was driving him crazy, and tomorrow he was going to go into work and change the rota so they didn't have to work together so much.

Or, more to the point, be at home together so much.

But first, he was going to see David and Molly about that picture of the marshes for the blank wall in his sitting room. At least clearing the room up ready for it would give him something to do for the day, even if he couldn't have the picture till the exhibition closed.

He got stiffly to his feet, stretched his arms out and groaned softly. He ached all over from the unaccustomed physical exertion of building Saffy's run.

He wondered if Connie ached, and immediately an image of him massaging her long, sleek limbs filled his mind, running his oiled hands up her back and round over those slender but surprisingly strong shoulders and then down, round her ribs, under her breasts—

He swore, quietly and viciously, stabbed a hand through his hair and headed back to the house. Sleep wasn't an option, he realised, so he went into the sitting room, unearthed the boxes of books and unpacked them, putting them on the empty shelves that had mocked him for the last two and a bit years.

Better, he thought, and it had only taken him a little over an hour. They weren't sorted, but they looked a lot better than they had, and he could always move them. And it was pointless spending a small fortune on a picture to hang it up in a room that was so obviously unloved.

He debated cleaning the room properly, but tomorrow would do. He'd dusted the shelves, put the books on. That would do for tonight. And anyway, he needed something to do tomorrow to keep him out of Connie's way.

Connie. Always it came back to Connie.

He gave in to the urge and went back up to his bedroom, lay down in the cloud-soft bedding and went to sleep, wrapped around in Connie's perfume. It was almost like lying in her arms...

'Wow, that looks amazing!'

She stood in the opening between the kitchen and the living space and stared in astonishment at the transformation. There were books on the shelves, he'd rearranged the sofas and it actually looked lived-in rather than as if the removal men had just walked out the door. 'What time did you get up?'

'Two,' he said, trying to ignore the pyjamas. 'I've been back to sleep since for a while.'

'I'm glad to hear it. Want a cup of tea?'

'Yeah, why not? Have I got time for a shower?'

'Sure. You won't be long, will you? I'll make it now.'

He'd like to be long. He'd like to be long enough that she went and got dressed into something he was less excruciatingly conscious of, but that clearly wasn't going to happen. He paused in the doorway. 'How was Saffy last night, by the way?'

'Fine. I've let her out, she's sniffing round the garden at the moment. Thank you so much, James. I actually had room to stretch my legs out.'

He laughed. 'Happy to oblige,' he said, and hit the stairs. 'Don't make it too strong, I've already had a lot.'

He had. There were three teabags lying on the side, and she picked them up and put them in the bin. He always did that. So idle. No. Not idle, she corrected herself, remembering how hard he'd worked yesterday. He just had odd little habits. She made the tea, wiped the worktop down and went into the sitting room to study it.

Saffy followed her, looked at the sofas and then at her, and lay down on the floor.

'Wise move,' she said, and Saffy's tail banged the floor.

'What's a wise move?'

'Saffy. She eyed the sofas.'

'Did you?' The tail thumped again.

'So where are you putting the picture?' she asked him.

'I don't know. I'm not sure yet. I can't have it till after the exhibition, so I thought I'd work out where I want everything else. The first thing I'm going to do is give the place a thorough clean, now I've got it more or less straight.'

'I'll give you a hand.'

He almost groaned with frustration. 'You don't need to—'

'Oh, come on, you spent all day yesterday making the run for Saffy. It's the least I can do. Here, drink your tea while I get dressed, and we'll get started.'

So much for his escape plan.

* * *

He went to the hospital in the afternoon, and savaged the rota.

He had to leave most of the coming week alone, but the following week onwards he chopped to shreds. He spoke to the other key people who would be affected, shifted whatever he could and managed to minimise their contact really quite successfully.

And if it all got too much at home, there was always a massive stack of admin with his name on it. He could always come back in. If necessary he could invent a few meetings.

He gave his desk a jaundiced look. Locked in the drawers for confidentiality were a stack of files.

So—Connie, or admin?

Admin won, which was testament to his desperation, and it only kept him going till six that evening, at which point he gave up. Six on a Sunday, when he wasn't even supposed to be working, was more than late enough.

He locked the files away, headed home and walked in to the smell of roasting chicken.

'Hey, smells good.'

'Saffy thinks so.'

She unravelled herself from the sofa and wandered through to the kitchen looking sun-kissed and delectable, and he had to forcibly stop himself from kissing her. 'So how's your day been?'

'Tedious. I had to rework the rota and do some admin. I've moved us around—we're really short of suitably qualified people in the next few weeks, so I've split us up a bit so one or other of us is there. I know it's not ideal, but I'll only be here or doing admin in the department, and it'll be better for Saffy.'

She nodded. 'OK. And if the offer's still open, I

might go and collect all the stuff that's in store and sort it out. You've only got me down part-time on the rota, haven't you?'

'Yes.'

'So when you aren't here and I am, I can go through it all. And I can have the kettle and toaster in the cabin, so that if it's raining I can make tea without coming over here.'

Except in practice she'd been over here all the time, and it had never been an issue—well, not for her. Still, it was an excuse to get the things and start to go through them, and maybe it was because of James dealing with his boxes, but she suddenly just wanted to clear up all the loose ends and get it sorted out.

'Are you sure?' he asked, watching her closely. 'I just remember going through Cathy's stuff. It can be a bit gut-wrenching.'

'I'm sure it can, but it has to be done, and I'm ready now.'

'Well, go for it. You can always stop and put it all away if it gets too much. And I won't charge you storage.'

He smiled, a wry quirk of his lips that said so much, and she felt warmed inside. He was such a good friend. She had to protect that friendship at all costs.

'Thank you,' she said humbly. 'So—roast, mashed, boiled or jacket?'

'Excuse me?'

'Potatoes. With the chicken.'

'Um—roast. Always.'

She smiled. 'Thought you'd say that. I'll put them in.'

It worked well.

He did a little more shuffling that week, and it ended

up panning out nicely, so that Saffy wasn't shut away for too many hours in her run, both of them had some personal time alone and there was enough company to make the place feel homely.

Actually, he realised, it was great. She'd got the stuff out of storage and started working through it, and everything was going fine. And since he'd washed his sheets, the hormones weren't such an issue, either. She didn't wear perfume at work or if they weren't going out anywhere, and life settled down into a regular and almost cosy routine.

And then he had a job application in from someone who sounded perfect. A woman with two children whose husband had taken himself off to another country with his second wife and left her literally holding the babies.

He phoned her, and she came in that afternoon to look round and impressed his socks off.

She wanted part time, her mother was in Yoxburgh, and she was going nowhere. She was young, younger than Connie, and it would be her first consultancy, but her CV and references were stunning. And she could start whenever he pressed the button. He just had to put it to the hospital board, get her a formal interview and it would all be set in motion.

It was like a dream come true—but it meant that he didn't really need Connie beyond the end of Andy Gallagher's paternity leave, and a bit of him felt gutted because he loved working with her.

But she wasn't there forever, he knew that. She wanted to go off and have her baby and start her new life somewhere else, and there was nothing here to keep her now.

Nothing except him, and he knew that didn't count.

He went home and found her sitting in a welter of Joe's possessions with Saffy snoozing on the floor at her side.

'How are you doing?' he asked, sitting down cross-legged on the floor opposite her and scratching behind Saffy's ears.

'OK. There's a lot of rubbish—paperwork that's meaningless now, irrelevant stuff about our army accommodation and so forth. I'll never need it, but it's got personal information on it.'

'Want to borrow my shredder?'

'Oh, please.'

He went and got it, and they spent an hour shredding documents. Then finally he called a halt.

'Stop now. I need to talk to you.'

She stopped, her heart hitching for some reason. He sounded so—serious? 'About?'

'I've had a suitable applicant for the job.'

'Wow.' She stood up on legs that trembled slightly, picked up the bag of shreddings and followed him downstairs, Saffy trailing after them. 'What's he like?'

'She. Very good. Divorced, two kids—twins. Dad walked. I interviewed her today.'

'And?'

'She's nice. Really nice. Open, friendly, efficient—little bit nervous, but that's to be expected. I need to get it rubber stamped, but we've been looking for someone for three months now without success, so I'm sure it won't be an issue.'

She nodded, trying to be practical, trying not to cry for some crazy reason. 'Good. Well, for you. For Andy, too. Takes away the guilt.'

'And you?'

She shrugged. 'I knew it was short term. I guess it's

just going to be shorter than I'd expected. I had hoped I'd have a bit longer to find a permanent job and somewhere to live, but I'm sure I'll find something. When can she start?'

'Now. She's free, so as soon as the formal interview's taken place and she's officially accepted, she can start.'

She stared at him across the kitchen, feeling the bottom drop out of her stomach. 'Oh. Right. So I haven't got time.'

'Well, you don't have to leave here, you know that, but the job will go. I'm really sorry. I honestly thought it would take months and I'm really grateful to you for what you've done.'

She shrugged, her shoulders lifting a little helplessly, and he felt a complete heel, but what could he do? It was only the truth. The job was taken, he didn't need her.

Not in that way, and he wasn't even going to think about the other.

'Don't worry about it. I'll be fine. I'll find a job, I always do. And I'll get out of your hair, just as soon as it's all rubber stamped and she's ready to go.'

'If you find something else you want to go to, if there's a job that comes up with your name on it, I don't expect you to give me any notice, Connie. You can leave whenever you like,' he said, and she felt her heart break a little more.

'Oh. Right. Well, I'll start packing.'

'But you haven't got anywhere to go to! I'm just saying, do it in your own time, don't worry about fitting in with me.'

'But you're right, there's nothing here, I might as well get myself out into the job market.'

'Connie, there's no rush. Sleep on it, give yourself time to work out what to do next.'

What's to sleep on? You want me out! Out of your home, out of your department, out of your life!

'Good idea. I'm tired. We'll talk tomorrow. Saffy, come on, James is going to bed.'

And she all but dragged the reluctant dog out of the door and down the steps and into her cabin. She got the door shut—just—before the little sob broke free, but it had a friend, and then a whole posse of them, and she shut herself in the shower room, turned all the taps on and sobbed her heart out.

Then she blew her nose, washed her face and put her pyjamas on.

She didn't need James. She could do this. She could still have a baby, still have her dream without the complication of knowing the father.

Simpler all round—except her dream had changed, and she'd realised that she didn't just want a baby, any baby. She wanted James's baby. And she wanted James.

God, what a mess.

She put Saffy out for a moment, and when she ran back in, she jumped straight up onto the bed, circled round and lay down in a perfect pattern of earthy footprints on the immaculate white bedding.

Tough.

Connie got into bed, shunted Saffy over a little and curled on her side, the dog behind her knees, and wondered what on earth she was going to do and where she was going to go.

She had no idea. She was out of options. The tenant in her house was there for the next six months, at least, and there was nobody else she could ask. Not with Saffy.

She'd have to get onto it first thing in the morning, try and find somewhere to go, somewhere to rent.

And a job?

God, it was all so complicated. It had been complicated since the day she'd agreed to have Saffy, and it just got worse. She needed a job, she needed a home and she didn't need James telling her she didn't need to work any kind of nominal notice period because he wanted her out of the house.

He hadn't said that, to be fair, but it felt like that.

And then she had a brilliant idea.

She'd apply for the job. Formally, properly. She'd find herself somewhere to live nearby, somewhere she could keep Saffy, and she'd go down the anonymous donor route, and then James would be close enough to help out if necessary, and she wouldn't lose his friendship, and it would be fine.

She just had to get him to agree.

There was no sign of her in the morning, and Saffy's run was hanging open.

Unlike Connie's curtains, which were unusually firmly shut.

He stood on the veranda and hated himself. It wasn't his fault that this woman had turned up when she had. It was nobody's fault. But it was his fault that they'd reached this point, that he hadn't given Connie a flat-out no right at the beginning so that she'd moved on with her life already.

And now she'd retreated into a cocoon, and he felt like the worst person in the world.

He made tea and took it over to the cabin.

'Connie?'

No reply, just a scuffle and the sound of Saffy's toe-nails clattering on the wooden floor as she came to the door.

'Connie? I've made you tea.'

He knocked and opened the door, to find her sitting up in bed, huddled in the quilt and watching him warily. She had her phone in her hands. Looking for a job?

'Are you OK?'

'Of course I'm OK. Put the tea down, I'll get it in a minute.'

Go away, in other words.

'Has Saffy been out?'

'Yes. I'm afraid she trashed the quilt cover.'

He glanced down and saw a crazy pattern of muddy pawprints all over it. 'It'll wash,' he said, although he doubted it, but the quilt cover was the least of his worries. Connie looked awful.

Tired, strained, her eyes red-rimmed, her back ramrod straight.

He put the tea down and left her to it, plagued by guilt and unable to change anything for the better.

He'd gone.

She'd hoped to catch him before he left for work, but he'd been too quick off the mark. Damn. She hadn't wanted him going to the hospital board before she had a chance to talk to him about it, so she took Saffy for a quick run, showered and dressed in work clothes and drove to the hospital.

'Anyone seen James?' she asked.

'He's not in the ED but he's around somewhere—want me to page him?'

'Please. Tell him I'm in the ED.' And hopefully it wasn't already too late.

The phone didn't ring. Had he not taken his pager? No, that wasn't like him. Just ignored it? Maybe he was in a meeting—with the chief exec?

He walked in, just as she was ready to give up.

'Connie. Hi. I gather you're looking for me.'

'Have you got a minute?'

'Sure. I'll just make sure Kazia's all right. We've got a patient with a head injury waiting for a scan but he's stable.'

He stuck his head into Resus. 'You all OK for a few more minutes?'

'Sure. No change.'

'Thanks, Kaz. Page me if you need me.'

He turned to Connie. 'My office, or do you want to get a coffee and sit outside?'

'Your office,' she said. She wanted this to be formal, in a way. A little bit official. And an office seemed the place to do that.

'OK.'

He led her in, shut the door and offered her a chair, then sat down opposite her. 'So. Talk to me.'

'I want the job.'

He felt his jaw sag slightly.

'Job?'

'Yes. The part-time consultant post in the department. I want to make an official application, and I want you to interview me.'

He sat back in his chair, fiddling with a pen to give him time, straightening the notepad, lining up the small ring-stained mat he used to protect the top of the desk.

'No,' he said in the end, because it was the only word that came to mind that wasn't unprintable.

'No?' She sat forward, her face shocked. 'Why no? I'm good, James. Whatever this other woman's got, I've got more, and I've thought it through. This is a sensible decision. I want a child, I have a dog already, I can't work full-time. You said you'd support me in my decision about the baby, and if I'm here in Yoxburgh, that makes it easy for all of us. I understand you don't want the fatherhood thing, that's fine, but I've thought it all through. I'll sell the house and buy one here, and I'll have a stable base, friends in the area—this is just the perfect answer.'

'No, Connie. I can't do it. I can't offer you the job because I've already offered it to the other woman. I offered it to her yesterday and I can't retract it. And anyway, I've spoken to the board and they've agreed. They're interviewing her now, as we speak. I'm really, really sorry.'

So was she. If only she'd thought this through sooner, mentioned it earlier—but she'd thought she'd had time, and she hadn't. Her time had run out, and it was over.

Just as well, perhaps. She'd get away, leave him behind her, start again. Good idea. Maybe one day it would feel like it.

She got to her feet, her legs like rubber, her eyes stinging.

'It's OK. It's not your fault. I understand. I hope it works out well. Goodbye, James.'

And she walked out of his office, through the department—why hadn't she agreed to coffee outside in the park?—and out of the doors.

Her frustration and anger at herself for not doing this in time sustained her all the way back to his house, and then she opened the gate to be greeted by Saffy wagging her tail, waiting to be let out of her run.

The run James had made for her out of the kindness of his heart.

Damn.

She let Saffy out, went into the cabin and started packing. There wasn't much, and it didn't take her long.

She took the kettle and the toaster, because she'd need them, and all her clothes and bits and pieces, and she stacked them as tightly as she could in the car.

Saffy's crate went in next, packed around with as much as possible, until she was left only with a box or two of things in the spare bedroom. She'd got rid of a lot of the stuff, and this was all that was left that was still unsorted.

Well, she wasn't doing it now. She was getting the hell out of here before James came home, because she really didn't think she'd be able to hold it together when she saw him again.

She'd been doing so well, and now she felt lost again.

Don't think about it!

She scooped up the last two boxes, carried them downstairs and out to the car, and with a little repacking she even got them in. She could hardly see out of the car, but that was fine. She had wing mirrors. She'd manage.

Wherever she was going.

Where *was* she going? She had no idea, none at all, and it was already lunchtime.

Back towards Nottingham?

She had friends down in Cornwall, but that was too far and she couldn't expect them to help. But there was nobody in the world who'd tolerate Saffy in the way that James had.

Nobody else who'd build her a run and not mind when she stole the fillet steak or trashed the sheets with her muddy paws or ate his favourite trainers.

There was only one option open to her, and it broke her heart, but in many ways it was the right answer.

She'd leave Saffy with James.

CHAPTER NINE

HE HAD THE day from hell.

He couldn't leave, but Connie's face was etched on his mind and he was hardly able to concentrate.

What had he done? He could have told her about the other applicant, could have offered her the chance, but he'd wanted her out of his life because she was upsetting it, messing it all up, untidying it. He'd been trying to make life easier for himself, because the thought of having her working there with him indefinitely, driving him mad on a daily basis with her crazy pyjamas and her lace underwear, was unthinkable.

And now she was going, and he realised he didn't want her to. He didn't want her to go at all. And she'd said goodbye.

Hell. He had to go home to her.

He pulled his phone out of his pocket, called Andy and drummed his fingers until he answered.

'I need a favour. Is there any way you can cover for me? I need to go home urgently.'

'What, now? No, that's OK, I think. Lucy's here.' He heard him talking to Lucy, then he came back. 'That's fine. I'll come now. Give me ten minutes.'

'Thank you,' he said, but Andy had gone, without prevaricating or asking any awkward questions. Still, ten minutes was a long time and he just hoped to God nothing kicked off in the meantime which meant he couldn't leave.

He was there in five.

'I'll be as quick as I can,' he promised.

'Don't worry. Just go.'

'Thank you.'

He drove home on the back roads because there was less traffic, his heart in his mouth.

'Please be there, please be there, please be there—'

She was, her car on the drive, the door hanging open. He pulled up beside it and swore. It was packed to the roof with all her worldly possessions. Except Saffy. There was a crate-shaped hole in the back, but no crate, no dog, no sign of her.

She must be taking her for a last walk, he thought, but her keys were in the ignition, and his heart started to race.

Where was she?

The cabin was locked, the curtains open, the bed stripped. The house was unlocked, though, so he searched it from top to bottom, but there was nothing. No clue, no sign, no hint of what was going on. He even looked under the beds and had to stop himself from being ridiculous, but where had she gone?

'Connie?'

He yelled her name, again and again as he raced through the house, but all that greeted him was silence. So he rang her, and her phone rang from the car. From her handbag, lying there in the gap between the two front seats, squashed in.

Had Saffy run off at the last minute? Unsure what to do, where else to look, he locked her car, pocketed the keys and went up onto the sea wall. Nothing. He could see for miles, and there was nothing, nobody.

Nobody with a sandy-coloured, leggy dog with dangling ears and a penchant for stealing, anyway.

He looked the other way, went up to his attic for a higher view of the river wall, but there was nothing there, either. All he could do was wait.

So he did. He made himself a cup of tea that he felt too sick to drink, took it out onto the veranda and waited.

And then he heard it.

A sob.

Faint but unmistakeable, from under him.

The kennel. Idiot! He hadn't searched the kennel!

He took the steps in one, crossed the run in a single stride and ducked his head through the entrance. 'Connie?'

'I couldn't leave her,' she said brokenly, and she started to sob again.

'Oh, Connie. Leave who? Why?'

'Saffy. James, where can I take her? How can I? I don't even have a home—'

Her voice cracked on the last word, and he squashed himself into the crowded kennel, dragged Connie into his arms and wrapped her firmly against his chest.

'Crazy girl. You don't have to go anywhere.'

'Yes, I do. I have to make a life. I have to start again, make something of my future, but I can't do it with this stupid great lump of a dog, so I was going to leave her here, because I thought, you promised Joe you'd take care of me, and he loved Saffy too, and I know you do, so I thought maybe you could look after her instead, but I can't leave her—'

The sobs overwhelmed her again, and he pressed his

lips to her hair and held on tight. His eyes were stinging, and he squeezed them shut, rocking her gently, shushing her, and all the time Saffy was licking his arm frantically and trying to get closer.

He freed a hand and stroked her. 'It's OK, Saffy, it's all right,' he said, his voice cracking, and Connie snuggled closer, her arms creeping round him and hanging on.

'Oh, Connie, I'm sorry,' he said raggedly. 'So, so sorry. I don't want you to go, and if I'd only known you wanted the job I could have done something, but I'm not letting you go anywhere like this. Come on, come out of here and blow your nose and have a cup of tea and we'll talk, because this is crazy.'

'I can't just stay here,' she said, still hanging on to him and not going anywhere. 'You don't need me, you don't want me...'

Oh, hell.

'Actually, that's not true,' he admitted quietly. 'I do.'

'You do?' She lifted her head, dragging an arm out from behind him to swipe a hand over her face. 'I don't understand.'

'Neither do I, but I know I can't let you go. I can't do what you came here to ask me. I've dug deep on this one, and one of the reasons I just can't give you a baby and then step back is because my feelings for you are very far from clear.'

She went utterly still. 'I don't understand.'

His smile felt twisted, so he gave up on it. 'Nor do I. I don't know how I feel about you, Connie. I know I want you. You have to know that, up front, but you're a beautiful woman and it's not exactly a hardship. But whether that has the capacity to turn into anything else, I don't know. We've both got so much emotional bag-

gage and Joe may be an obstacle that neither of us can
get over, but I just know I can't lose you forever without giving it a try, seeing where it takes us.'

She said nothing. She didn't move, didn't speak, just
clung on to him, her eyes fixed on his face, but her
breathing steadied and gradually some of the tension
went out of her.

'Connie?'

She tilted her head up further, and in the dim light
he could see the tear tracks smudged across her face.

'Can we start by getting out of here?' she said. 'It's
all a little bit cosy and I'm not sure about the spiders.'

He gave a hollow chuckle and unravelled himself,
standing up as far as he could and ducking through the
doorway, and she followed him out, Saffy squashing
herself between them, her eyes anxious.

Poor dog. She felt racked with guilt.

She put her hand down to Saffy and found his there
already. He turned it, and their fingers met and clung.

'Did you say something about tea?' she said lightly,
and he tried to smile but it was a pretty shaky effort.
She didn't suppose hers was a whole lot better.

'If you like.'

'I like.'

'I'll make it. You go and wash your face. I'll see you
in a minute.'

She looked awful. Her eyes were so red and puffy
they were nearly shut, and her cheeks were streaked
with tears and dirt from being in the kennel, and her
clothes were filthy.

What on earth did he see in her? He must be mad.
Or desperate.

No. He was single by choice. A man with as much

going for him as James wouldn't lack opportunity. And he wanted to explore their relationship?

She closed her eyes and sucked in a shaky breath. This was about so much more than just giving her a baby. This was everything—marriage, a family, growing old together—all the things she might have had with Joe, but had lost. The things he might have had with Cathy and their baby.

He was right, they had a hell of a lot of emotional baggage, but if they could make it work—

She let herself out of the cloakroom and went back to the kitchen.

'Out here,' he called, and she went and sat next to him, exactly over the spot where he'd held her while she'd cried, and Saffy leaned against their legs and trapped them there.

'Do you think she's telling us we can't go anywhere until this is sorted?' she asked, a little hitch in her voice, and James gave a quiet laugh.

'Maybe. Seems like a sensible idea.'

'Mmm.' She sniffed, still clogged with tears. 'So—what now?'

'Now? Now I suggest we unpack your car, settle Saffy back in and then I go back to work. I called Andy in, but I can't really leave him there for hours. Just—promise me you'll be here when I get back.'

'I'll be here. Where else can I go?'

'If you really want to, I'm sure there's somewhere. And for the record, I would have had Saffy for you. Not because of Joe, or you. Just for herself.'

Her eyes filled again and she blinked hard and cleared her throat. 'Will you please stop making me cry?' she said, and he hugged her, his arm slipping naturally around her shoulders and easing her up against his side.

'Oh, Connie, what are we going to do?'

'I don't know. I'm totally confused now. I thought you didn't want a relationship, I thought you were happy on your own.'

'Not happy,' he corrected softly. 'Just—accepting. I couldn't imagine falling in love like that again, and maybe I never will, but maybe it doesn't have to be like that. Maybe we're both so damaged that we can't ever love like that again, but it doesn't mean we can't be happy with someone else, someone who doesn't expect that level of emotion, someone who can accept our scars and limitations. Maybe it would only work with someone equally as hurt, someone who could understand.'

Which would make them ideal for each other.

Would it work? Could it work?

She took a deep breath. 'I guess there's only one way to find out.'

'Shall we unpack your car?'

'I'll do it,' she said. 'You go back to work. I won't go anywhere, I promise.'

He went—reluctantly—and she sat a little while longer, trying to make some kind of sense of the developments of the day.

She didn't even know how she felt about a relationship with him. It had seemed so unlikely she hadn't ever really let herself consider it, but—a couple? Not just an affair, but a real relationship?

She tried to get her head around it, and failed. Unrequited lust she could understand, but happy ever after? Could he do it? What would he be like as a partner? People who'd been single a very long time found it hard to be part of a couple, to give and take and compromise.

Could she? Joe had been away so much she'd been pretty self-sufficient. Could she cope with someone having a say in her life?

'I don't know,' she said out loud. Saffy lifted her head and stared up at her, and she rubbed her chest gently. 'It's OK, Saff. We'll be all right. We'll find a way.'

She wasn't sure how, if this thing with James didn't work, but it seemed they were still friends, at the very least, and she wanted to make sure that continued. It had to. Friends, she'd learned over the years, were infinitely precious. She only had a few, and James, it seemed, was one of them. The best.

She eyed her car. She ought to unpack it, really, but she'd stripped her bed and put the sheets in the washing machine; they were done, so perhaps she should hang them on the line before she started?

'Oh, Saffy, we're OK, the pawprints came out. That's a good job, isn't it?' Saffy wagged her tail, tongue lolling, and Connie shut her back in the run and emptied the car.

There was no point putting the stuff that had been in storage back in James's spare bedroom. There was so little left—had only ever been so little of any consequence, really—that she put it into the cabin with everything else.

And all the time there was a little niggle of—what? Anticipation? Apprehension? Excitement?—fizzing away inside her. Should she cook for him? If there even was anything in the fridge. She wasn't sure. She'd look later, she decided, after she'd sorted herself out, but by the time she'd unpacked her things, hung up her clothes, found her washbag and had a shower, he was home.

And the butterflies in her stomach felt like the images she'd seen of bats leaving a cave in their thousands.

* * *

She'd put her stuff in the cabin.

All of it, by the looks of things, because the car was empty and there was no trace of her possessions in the house. He went up to his bedroom to check, and it was untouched since he'd changed his clothes before he'd gone back to work.

He stood there, staring at it, and tried to analyse his feelings. Mixed, he decided. A mixture of disappointment—physical, that one, mostly—and relief.

His common sense, overruling the physical disappointment, pointed out that it was just as well. Too early in their relationship to fall straight into bed, too easy, too fast, too simple. Because it wasn't that simple, sleeping with Connie. Not after Joe.

Inevitably there would be comparisons. He knew that. He wasn't unrealistic. And he wasn't sure he wanted to be compared to his best friend. He didn't want to be better in bed, but he sure as hell didn't want to be worse.

He swore softly, sat down on the edge of the bed and stared at the picture of the estuary that Molly had painted here in this room.

The Eye of the Storm.

Was that what this was? The eye of the storm? The lull before all hell broke loose again in his life?

'James?'

He heard her footsteps on the landing, and went to his bedroom door. She was wearing jeans and a pretty top, and from where he was standing he had a perfect view of her cleavage. 'Hi. I'm just going to change, and then I thought we could go out for dinner if you like.'

'That would be lovely,' she said with a wry smile.

'I've just looked in the fridge and it's none too promising.'

He chuckled. 'Give me ten minutes. I'll have a quick shower and I'll be with you.'

A cold one. He retreated, the updraught through the stairwell wafting the scent of her perfume after him, so that it followed him back into the room. He swallowed hard. Damn his common sense. Just then, the other side of the coin looked a lot more appealing.

Dinner?

As in, supper at the pub, or dinner? Formal, dressy, elegant? Because jeans and a floaty little cotton top wouldn't do, in that case.

But he came down the stairs bang on time in jeans and a crisp white cotton shirt open at the neck with the cuffs turned back, and she relaxed. She didn't feel ready for a formal dinner. Not yet. Too   what? Romantic? Laden with sexual expectation?

'So—Chinese, Indian, Thai, Tex-Mex, English gastro pub or fish and chips out of the paper? You choose.'

She laughed, feeling another layer of tension peel away. 'Gastro pub?' she suggested. 'It's a lovely evening. It would be nice to eat outside, if we can. And if you want to drink, I don't mind driving, or we could go to the Harbour Inn and sit outside so we can walk.'

'We've done that, and I don't need more than one glass. I'll drive. There's a lovely pub just a few miles up the river. We'll go there. Have you fed Saffy?'

'Yes. She's ready to go in her run.'

He rubbed the dog's head. 'How is she? Has she settled down?'

'I think so. She was a bit clingy until I'd unpacked everything and put it all away in the cabin but then she was fine. Oh, by the way, I put the rest of the stuff from storage in the cabin, too, so your spare bedroom's yours again. There wasn't much, and it'll make it easier to sort out. I can pick at it, then.'

'Good idea,' he said, stifling the regret. 'Right, shall we?'

It was a lovely pub, as he'd said.

The setting was wonderful, down on the edge of the river bank and miles from anywhere, or so it seemed. The river was wide at that point, and there were lots of boats moored on the water.

'It's buzzing, isn't it?' she said, slightly surprised, and he smiled.

'Wait till you taste the food. It'll all make sense then,' he said.

'It makes sense now,' she pointed out. 'Look at it. It's gorgeous here.'

They sat outside at a picnic table, side by side, and watched the boats come and go, sipping their drinks and reading the menu and just chilling out. It had been a gruelling day for both of them, and the quiet moment by the river was just what they needed, she thought.

She scanned the menu again, her mind slightly numb with all that had happened, her concentration shot. 'I can't decide.'

'We can come again. It's not life or death, it's just food and it's all good.'

'But I'll just get food envy,' she said, and he thought instantly of the time he'd watched her eat that hog roast roll, the apple sauce squeezing out and dribbling down her chin.

'We could always share.'

'Dangerous.' Hell, had he really said that? He hoped

she hadn't heard—or caught the tiny eye roll he'd done at his impulsive comment.

Both.

She scrunched her lips up and gave him a wry grin. 'You're right. You might come off worst.'

'Never. I fight for my food.'

She smiled and put her menu down. 'Me, too. I'll go for the sea bream fillet on samphire.'

He put his menu down. 'I'll have the same. That way you won't be tempted.'

She pouted, and he chuckled softly, hailed the waitress and placed their order.

'Wine?'

'Oh—I'll have a small glass of whatever.'

'Two of the sauvignon blanc, then,' he said, handing back the menus, and he cradled his mineral water, propped his elbows on the table and leant against her.

She leant back, resting her head against his, and sighed.

'You OK?' he asked quietly. He felt her nod.

'Yup. You?'

'I'm OK.'

'Good.'

They sat there until their food arrived, in contact from shoulder to knee, feeling the way forward. From where he was sitting, it felt pretty good.

More than good.

And it smelt amazing—or, rather, she did. She'd put that perfume on again, and it had been teasing his senses ever since he'd got in the car.

He would have joined in, for once, but the only cologne he had was some Joe had given him for Christmas the year before he'd died. He hadn't opened it until now and it didn't seem like the time to break it out, when he was contemplating seducing his widow. She'd have to make do with clean skin.

'That was amazing.'

He smiled, his eyes crinkling at the corners. Funny how she'd never really registered just how gorgeous his eyes were. Not just the colour, that striking ice-blue with the navy rim, but the shape of them, the heavy, dark lashes, the creases at the corners, the eloquent brows.

They said so much, those eyebrows. She could often tell exactly what he thought of something just from the tiny twitch that gave him away. She'd seen it in the ED, when someone had been trying to lie about how they'd injured themselves. She could always tell if he thought it was a pile of steaming manure.

And if he was troubled, or concentrating, they crunched together, but in a different way.

So complex, the facial muscles. So revealing.

He glanced across at her as he fastened his seat belt. 'Will that still go round you?'

'Cheeky,' she said without rancour. 'It would have been rude not to have a pudding. Anyway, I was starving. I hadn't eaten all day.'

'Really?' He shot her a quick glance, surprised, but then realised he hadn't had much, either. And nothing since he'd spoken to her in his office that morning.

He drove her home, parked the car and looked at her. 'Coffee?'

'Is that *coffee* coffee, or go upstairs with you?' she asked, hoping he'd say no.

Something happened to his brows, but she couldn't quite work out what. 'That's *coffee* coffee,' he said, firmly, and she felt her shoulders drop because all the way home she'd been beginning to get tense.

She smiled, the tension sliding out of her like a receding tide. 'Yes, please. Can we have it on the sea wall?'

'Sure.'

They took Saffy, and as usual she sat in between them, her head on her front paws, hanging slightly over the edge of the wall. He lifted one of her ears and laid it across his thigh and stroked it rhythmically, and Connie chuckled.

'I swear, if a dog could purr,' she murmured, and he laughed softly.

'She's just a hussy. No wonder you couldn't leave her.'

'No. I wanted to burn my boats with you, but I just couldn't. Even if I'd left her, I couldn't have walked away. Not completely.'

'No. I'm glad you didn't.' He stopped stroking Saffy's ear and held out his hand, and she placed hers in it. His hard, warm fingers closed around it gently and he lifted it to his lips and kissed the back of it, drifting his lips over her knuckles.

It sent a shiver through her, a tingle of something electric and rather beautiful. Something she'd almost forgotten.

He turned his head slowly and she met his eyes, holding his gaze for an age. Their hands fell softly to his lap, and he straightened her fingers out over Saffy's ear, so she wasn't really touching him, but she was.

It was utterly harmless, totally innocent, and yet not, and the air seemed trapped in her chest so she could only breathe with the very top of it, just very lightly, a little fast.

His eyes fell to her cleavage, watching the rapid rise and fall, and then they dragged back up to meet her eyes again.

Even in the darkness, with only the soft light from the front of the cottage to illuminate them, she could see that his pupils had gone black. His mouth was slightly open, his chest moving in time with hers, and the tension was coming off him in waves.

She eased her hand out from under his and turned away, breaking the spell, and they sat there in silence, the heat simmering between them, and gradually their breathing returned to normal.

'So am I coming to work tomorrow?'

'You're down on the rota.'

'What time?'

He cursed himself inwardly for changing the rota so they never saw each other, but maybe, with the sizzle he'd just felt between them, that was just as well.

'Eight o'clock. I'm on from one till nine.'

'OK. Will you take Saffy for a run for me?'

'Of course I will.'

'Thanks.' She picked up her cup and turned her head to face him. 'I'm going to turn in now. Don't bother to get up. You take your time. I'll see you tomorrow. And thank you for a lovely evening.'

'My pleasure. Sleep well, Connie.'

And then, to his surprise, she leant over and kissed him. Just the lightest brush of her lips, not like the last kiss they'd shared but the first, and then she was gone, walking away, leaving his mouth tingling and tasting of regret.

She did sleep, to her surprise. She slept like a log, and woke in the morning feeling refreshed and ready for the day.

He greeted her on the veranda with a cup of tea and a slice of hot, buttered toast, and she ate it, said goodbye to Saffy and at the last minute leant over and kissed his cheek.

He hadn't shaved, and the stubble grazed her skin deliciously. 'See you later,' she murmured, and he nodded.

'Call me if you need to, if it gets too chaotic.'

'Are you implying I can't cope?' she asked cheekily as she went through the gate.

'I wouldn't dare,' he said, laughing, and watched her go.

Gorgeous, he thought, as she flicked her hair back over her shoulder and stuck her sunglasses on her head to anchor it. Utterly, unaffectedly gorgeous.

And if he'd thought that this was in any way going to be easier than ignoring his feelings, he was finding out just how wrong he was.

He sighed heavily. If only she hadn't been Joe's woman, he would have kissed her last night. She'd been all but hyperventilating when he'd brushed her knuckles with his lips, and if it hadn't been for Joe he would have slid his hand around the back of her neck and eased her closer and kissed her till she whimpered. And that would have been it, because this time they were stone cold sober and knew exactly where it was leading.

He sighed again.

So near, and yet so far.

They passed in Reception at lunchtime, him on the way in, her on the way out.

'Good shift?'

'Yes, fine. No problems.'

'Good. I'll see you later. Don't wait for me to eat, I won't be back till after nine.'

'OK. I'll have something ready for you.'

'Star.'

He winked. No kisses here, not in front of the others, she realised, and she was glad, really. This was all too new, too precious, too fragile. It could so easily go wrong.

She drove home, changed into her running gear and took Saffy out. Not for long, because James had taken her once already, but just for a gentle lope along the sea wall as a reward for being good shut up in her run.

Then she showered and made herself a sandwich and a cup of tea and went back into the cabin. Those last two boxes of stuff were all that was left, and she had time now to deal with them.

She put the tea down on the bedside table, took a bite of the sandwich and opened the first box.

Correspondence. All sorts of stuff, out of the top drawer of Joe's desk. She'd just emptied it out, stacked it all together and packed it, and she had no idea what it was.

A will, for one thing, she realised.

There had been a copy with the solicitors who'd done the conveyancing on their house, so in many ways it was redundant. She checked it, and it was the same, leaving everything to her.

Letters. Letters from his sisters, from his mother, from her, grouped together in elastic bands, kept out of sentiment. There had been more of those that had been sent home to her when he'd died, but she'd never looked at them. And then, leafing through them, she found two others she'd never seen before.

One to her, one to James.

To be opened in the event of his death.

Trembling, her fingers not quite brave enough to do this, she slit the envelope open, pulled out the single handwritten sheet and spread it out on her lap.

My darling Connie,

If you're reading this, then I guess it's caught up with me at last. I'm so sorry. I've been waiting for it for a long time now, dreading it, expecting it, hoping I was wrong, and I know you have, too.

I hope you're OK, that my family are taking care of you and making sure you're all right. I'm sure you're not, not really, but you will be. It takes time, but you'll get there, and when you do, I want you to go out and grab life with both hands.

You've been an amazing wife, a wonderful partner and a really good friend, loyal and supportive and understanding, even when you didn't agree with my choices. I'm just so sad that we've never had a family, that the baby I know you've longed for has never come, that I've let you down, but you'll have a chance now to find that happiness with someone else, and I want you to take it. Don't hold back because of me. I want you to be happy, to be a mother, if that's what you'd like, but I can't bear to think of you all alone without me, so don't be. Don't be sad, don't be lonely. If the chance for happiness arises, take it.

I've left a letter for James. Make sure he gets it. He promised me, the last time I saw him, that he'd take care of you when I died, and I know that whatever happens, he'll do that because he's that kind of person. I've always wondered, though, what would have happened to you two if he'd never introduced us. I know Cathy's death tore him apart. I don't know the details, but he's shut himself down and I know he's lonely, but I'm sure he could love again if the right person came along, and maybe you're the right person for him, have been all along.

There's always been something between you, some spark. I've noticed it sometimes and been jealous, but why should I be, because I've been the one privileged to share my life with you, and I always trusted you both implicitly.

I know I shouldn't meddle, shouldn't match-make, but I can't think of a single person more worthy of you, no one I'd entrust your happiness to the way I would to James, and maybe this would give you both a chance at happiness, a chance to be parents, to have the family I know you've both longed for.

I love you, my darling. Completely, unreservedly, to the depths of my soul, and I always will. But life moves on, and time heals, and I want you to be happy.

Goodbye, sweetheart.
All my love,
Joe x

She closed her eyes, the tears spilling down her cheeks, and she let them fall. She didn't sob. She just sat there while the tears flowed, his voice echoing in her head as he said goodbye.

She was still sitting there motionless when James got home, the sandwich long gone, stolen by Saffy when supper didn't seem to be forthcoming.

CHAPTER TEN

SHE WAS IN the cabin. He walked in and saw her, and something about her stillness alarmed him. He went over to her and sat down on the bed beside her, taking her lifeless hand in his.

'Connie?'

'I found a letter,' she said, her voice hollow. 'From Joe. There's one for you.'

She handed him the envelope.

'If it's anything like mine, you might want to read it on your own,' she said, and she folded the closely written sheet that was lying on her lap. It was smudged with tears, creased from the pressure of her hands, and she laid it gently down on the bedside table and got up and walked away.

Not sure at all that he wanted to read it, James slit the envelope.

Dear James,
I know you won't want to hear a load of sentimental crap, but there are times when it's necessary and this is one of them.
I asked you to take care of Connie for me when I died. If you're reading this, it's happened, and I hope she's giving you a chance to do that.

*Whether she is or not, I know you'll be keeping
an eye on her if only from a distance.*

*You've been the best friend a man could ask
for. Too good to me, I've thought from time to
time. You gave me Connie, for a start, and she's
filled my life with joy, but I sometimes wonder if
you cheated yourself when you did that. There's
always been something there between you. I've
seen you watching her, but I know I've always
been able to trust you to do the decent thing, and
I trust you now. I trust you not to use her, but I
also trust you to love her if that's the way it goes.*

*I know you won't hurt her deliberately. I never
have, but my choice of career and my inability to
give her the family she's longed for have both hurt
her deeply and it grieves me.*

*I know Cathy's death hurt you, too, very deeply,
but maybe together you can find happiness. If not
together, then I hope you both find it another way,
because of all the people in the world, I love you
two the most and I want you to be happy.*

*If it's right for you, then please feel free to love
her as she deserves, as you deserve. You have
my blessing.*
Your friend
Joe

Hell.

He put the letter down, folding it carefully and putting it with Connie's, and then he got to his feet and
went to find her.

She was on the sea wall, and she was waiting for
him. He sat beside her, on the other side of Saffy, and
she looked up at him searchingly.

'Are you all right?'

He closed his eyes because it hurt simply to look at her. 'I'll live,' he said, hoping it was true, because for the first time since Cathy had died, he really wanted to. 'How about you?'

She smiled a little wanly. 'Me too. What did he say?'

'I've left it on your bedside table.'

She turned to look at him again, her eyes searching in the dim light. 'Did you read mine?'

'No—God, no, Connie. Of course not.'

No. Of course he hadn't. It simply wasn't like him to do that.

'He wants me to be happy,' she said. 'And I think he's matchmaking.'

Beside her, she heard James huff softly. Not a laugh, not a sigh, something in between, a recognition of the character of the man they'd both loved and lost.

'I know he's matchmaking—or at least facilitating. He gave us his blessing, Connie.'

She nodded slowly. 'It makes a difference.'

'It does. It makes a hell of a difference. I've been feeling guilty, thinking of you as Joe's woman, but it's what he wants, if it's right for us. He wants us to be together. He's given us permission, Connie, handed us to each other and bowed out. I don't think I'd be that bloody noble.'

She laughed, the same little noise he'd made, something closer to a sob. She heard him sigh softly.

'Or maybe I was. When Cathy died I felt as if my life had ended. There was nothing in it, nothing worth having, and chasing round the world for God knows how long didn't seem to make it any better, so I came home and still there was nothing.

'And then you came into my life, bright and funny,

clever, quick-witted and warm—so warm. In another life, I would have grabbed the chance, but it was then, and I was broken, and so I introduced you to Joe. And I've never regretted it, before you ask. I loved seeing you together. You made him happy, and for that I'm truly grateful, because at the end of the day we're still alive and he isn't, and he deserved that happiness and so did you.'

She didn't say anything. She couldn't speak. She just sat there beside him, and their hands found each other over the top of Saffy's shoulders and clung.

It was pitch dark by the time they moved.

The sky had clouded over, the moon obscured, and he made her wait there while he went back to the house and turned on the lights.

She heard him stumble, heard the dog yelp and him swear softly, and then the lights were on and he was back there, holding out his hand to help her up.

She got stiffly to her feet, her body cold with lack of food and movement, and he led her back to the house, his arm slung loosely round her shoulders, holding her by his side.

'You're freezing. When did you last eat?' he asked, and she shrugged.

'I made a sandwich about three. I had a bite or two, then I opened the letter. I guess Saffy had the rest. I haven't fed her.'

He made a soft sound with his tongue and fed the dog, fed them both some toast slathered with butter and honey, and poured two glasses of wine.

'What's that for?' she asked, and he laughed, if you could call it that.

'Dutch courage?'

She blinked. 'Am I so scary?'

'You are when I'm going to ask you to come to bed with me.'

She felt her jaw sag slightly, and then she laughed. Softly at first, and then a little hysterically, and then finally she stopped, pressing her fingers to her mouth, tears welling, unbearably touched by his nervousness.

'Are you sure?' she asked.

'As sure as I can be. I don't know if I can love you like Joe wants me to, I have to tell you that, but, my God, I want to try, Connie. I've wanted you for so long, and you've been out of reach in every conceivable way, but now you're not, maybe, and I want you so much it hurts.'

She nodded. 'Me, too. I've always liked you, always felt I could trust you, known that you were decent to your bones, but just recently my body's woken up again and it's like I've seen you for the first time, only I haven't. I've always known you oozed sex appeal, it just wasn't aimed at me so it didn't register. But now...'

'Is that a yes, then?'

'It could be. Just—talking of conceivable...'

'Don't worry. I'm not going to get you pregnant, Connie. Not by accident. If and when we reach that point, it'll be by choice.' He smiled wryly. 'I went shopping yesterday, after I left work. Just in case.'

He drained his wine glass, stood up and held his hand out to her.

'Coming?'

She smiled. Not coquettishly, not the smile of a siren, but gently, with warmth. 'I hope so.'

Heat flared in his eyes, and he gathered her against his chest with a ragged sigh. 'Ah, Connie,' he whispered, and his lips found hers and he kissed her. Tentatively at first, and then more confidently, probing the inner recesses, his tongue duelling with hers, searching, coaxing until her legs buckled and she staggered slightly.

'Bed,' he said gruffly. 'Now.'

'Saffy,' she said, and he stopped, swore, shut the dog away with an extra biscuit and was back to her in seconds.

'The cabin's unlocked.'

He ran back and locked it.

It was closer, but the letters were in there, and this first time together they needed to be alone without the ghost of Joe smiling over them.

However graciously.

They ran upstairs hand in hand, right to the top, and then he stopped and turned her towards him and undressed her. He would have done it slowly but she was wearing that blue dress again and he lifted it over her head, leaving her standing there in that lace bra and the tiny, fragile little cobweb shorts that had tantalised him so much. He'd put on the bedside light, and its soft glow gilded her body and nearly brought him to his knees.

'You're wearing that raspberry red lace again,' he groaned, and she smiled, a little uncertain this time.

'It's comfortable.'

'I don't care. I think you've worn it long enough,' he said, and turning her away from him, he unfastened the catch of her bra and slid the straps off her shoulders, catching her soft, firm breasts in his hands as they spilled free.

He dropped his head against hers, his mouth raining kisses down the arch of her neck, over her collar bone, under her ear—anywhere he could reach. It didn't matter. Every brush of his lips, every touch of his tongue made her gasp and shudder. He slid his hands down her sides, but she pushed him away and turned, her mouth finding his as her fingers searched his shirt for buttons.

He was still in his work clothes, she realised. The shirt was nothing special, just a normal shirt, so she grasped the front of it and tore it open, buttons pinging in all directions. And then she giggled mischievously.

'I've always wanted to do that.'

'Have you?' he said, and took his trousers off himself, just to be on the safe side.

'Spoilsport.'

'Vandal.'

He kicked off his shoes, stripped off his boxers and socks and trousers in one movement and held out his hand.

'Come to bed with me, Connie,' he said, his eyes suddenly serious. 'I need to make love to you and I don't think I can wait any longer.'

She went with him, toppling into the bed in a tangle of arms and legs, hungry mouths and searching hands. So hungry. So searching.

So knowing. Knowing, clever hands that explored her body inch by inch. She'd thought he was in a hurry, but there was nothing hurried about his thorough exploration.

'James—please,' she begged, and he lifted his head and touched her lips with his fingers. She could taste herself on him, and she moaned softly, rocking against him.

'Please—now, please…'

He left her briefly, then he was back, his eyes glittering with fire and ice, his body vibrating with need.

'James,' she begged, and then he was there, filling her, stroking her, pushing her higher, higher, his body more urgent, his touch more demanding, until finally he took her over the brink into glorious, Technicolor freefall.

His body stiffened, pulsing deep within her, and then as the shockwaves ebbed away he dropped his head into the hollow of her shoulder and gathered her gently against his chest, rolling them to the side.

They lay there in silence for a moment, scarcely moving, and then he turned his head and kissed her.

'You OK, Connie?' he murmured, and she lifted her head and met his eyes and smiled.

'I'm fine. More than fine. You?'

He smiled back. 'Oh, I'm fine, too. I'm so fine I think I must be dreaming.'

'Not unless it's the same dream.'

He hugged her, then let her go and vanished to the bathroom and left her lying there staring out of the roof window at the night sky. The clouds had cleared, she thought. There was moonlight on the side of the reveal that had been in shadow.

He came back to bed and turned off the light, pulling her into his arms, and they lay together staring at the stars and watching the moon track across the sky, and they talked.

They talked about Joe, and Cathy, but about other things, too. How he'd lost his parents, how she had, what he should do with the garden, and about her career.

'I'm sorry I put you in a difficult position,' she said quietly. 'I know you didn't have a choice, not if you'd offered her the job. I just didn't want to hear it. I can't afford to hear it, if the truth be told, because my money's running out fast and I need to work.'

'Not necessarily. Not yet, at any rate. If this works

for us, if we don't get sick of each other and decide we can't tolerate the other one's appalling habits—'

'What, like leaving a little heap of teabags on the side?' she teased, and he laid a finger over her mouth and smiled.

'If we don't get sick of each other, then it's not an issue. If we do, if one of us thinks it isn't working for them, then I'll support you until you find a job. Don't worry about the money, Connie. I promised Joe I'd look after you, and one way or the other, you're stuck with me.'

'Thank you.' She smiled tenderly, and leant over and kissed him, her lips gentle. 'I can think of worse fates.'

They both had irritating habits, it turned out.

He left the teabags in a heap, she was bordering on OCD with the arrangement of the mugs in the cupboard. Handles on the left, and God help anyone who put them away wrong.

She squashed the toothpaste in the middle, he didn't put the lid on.

But they muddled through, and the nights took away any of the little frustrations encountered along the road to adjustment.

Work was going well, too. Annie Brooks, the new doctor, had started, and Connie was doing only occasional shifts and researching career options and training Saffy in her free time.

The career thing was a bit difficult, because she didn't really know where she should be looking for a job.

Living with James was great, the sex was amazing, they seemed to get on fine at work—but emotionally he still hadn't given her a hint of his feelings, of how he thought it was going, of how their relationship might pan out long-term.

And she wanted to know. Needed to know, because she was falling in love with him, she was sure, and she didn't want to fall too far if he was going to pull the plug on them. She'd tried to hold back some of herself from Joe, but it hadn't worked. She thought it had, but then he died and she realised she'd been fooling herself. She wasn't going to let herself do the same thing with James.

And then one day towards the end of August they were down at the little jetty, and James was pointing out things on the other side of the river. Saffy was at his side, patiently waiting for him to throw her stick again, and then it happened.

One minute they were standing on the dock, the next a boat went past and sent up a wave that knocked Saffy off her feet.

She fell into the churning water and was swept out, right into the middle of the current.

'Saffy!' she screamed, and then to her horror James kicked off his shoes and dived in after her. 'Noooo!' she screamed. 'James, no, come back! What are you doing?'

He went under briefly, then re-emerged a little further downstream.

'He'll be all right, love. Tide's going out, and Bob's gone to fetch them.'

'Bob?'

'The harbourmaster. Don't worry. It'll be all right.'

Would it? She didn't think so. He went under again, and then came up, dragging Saffy by the collar, just as Bob got to him. Terrified, still unable to believe her eyes, she watched as Bob pulled Saffy's body into the boat.

20% OFF*

with code **THANKSJUN**

Visit www.millsandboon.co.uk today to get this exclusive offer!

Ordering online is easy:

- 1000s of stories converted to eBook
- Big savings on titles you may have missed in store

Visit today and enter the code **THANKSJUN** at the checkout today to receive **20% OFF** your next purchase of books and eBooks*. You could be settling down with your favourite authors in no time!

MILLS & BOON

JUN13

'That's a goner,' someone said, and her breath hitched on a sob.

'Get him out,' she pleaded silently. 'Please, get him out.'

'He'll be all right now. He's got a rope wrapped round his wrist. Don't you fret.'

Fret? She was beside herself as the boat pulled up at the jetty and someone dragged James out of the water.

'Get the dog out of the boat,' he snapped, and hauling her onto the wet boards of the jetty, he pumped down hard on her chest. Connie fell to her knees beside him, numb with shock.

'What can I do?' she asked, and he met her eyes, his own despairing.

'Nothing. I'm going to swing her.'

And grabbing the big dog by the back legs, he lifted her up and swung her over the side of the jetty to drain her lungs.

Nothing happened for a moment, and then water poured out.

He dropped her back on the jetty, clamped her mouth shut and breathed hard down her nose. Her chest inflated, and he blew again, and then again, and suddenly she coughed and struggled up, and his face crumpled briefly.

'It's OK, Saffy,' he said gently, holding on to her for dear life. 'It's OK.'

But it was too much for Connie.

'No, it's not OK,' she yelled, losing it at last now she knew they were both safe. 'That could have been you lying there with filthy water pouring out of your lungs, scarcely breathing! I've lost one man with a death wish, I'm not going to lose another one. You could have told me you were an idiot before I let myself fall in love with you!'

And spinning on her heel, she ran back towards the cottage, tears of rage and fear and relief pouring down her face, blinding her so that she ran smack into something.

Someone?

'Connie?'

David. It was Molly's David, her blade runner, gripping her shoulders and holding her upright, and she fell sobbing into his arms.

'Connie, whatever's happened? I heard all the commotion—what is it? Where's James?'

'He went in the river,' she said raggedly. 'Saffy was swept in, and he went in after her.'

'Where is he?' he asked, starting to run.

'He's out, David. He's out of the water. He's fine. I'm just—so angry.'

'And Saffy?' he asked, coming back.

'I think she'll be all right. She didn't breathe. She had water in her lungs, and he got it out, but his stupid heroics—'

She broke off and clamped her mouth shut so she didn't make an even bigger fool of herself, but it was too late, apparently, because James was coming now, Saffy walking unsteadily at his side, and at the sight of him she started to cry again.

'Did you mean it?' he asked, stopping right in front of her. In front of everyone.

'Mean what? That I'm angry with you? You'd better believe it.'

'That you love me.'

The crowd went utterly silent.

'Well, of course I love you, you idiot,' she ranted. 'Why else would I put up with your teabags?'

He laughed, his face crumpling after a second. 'God knows, but I love you, too,' he said, then reached for her, dragging her up against his sodden chest and kissing her as if his life depended on it.

Against her leg she could feel Saffy shivering, and in the cheering crowd someone said, 'What was that about teabags?'

'Time to go home,' he said firmly, and tucking her under his arm, he walked slowly back, Saffy on one side, the woman he hoped to spend the rest of his life with on the other.

'We need to rub her dry and keep her warm,' he said, bringing towels for Saffy into the kitchen.

'Let me do that,' Connie said, taking a towel. 'You need a shower and some dry clothes on before you catch your death.'

'I'm fine. Call the vet. She'll need antibiotics after that.'

Saffy staggered to her feet again and went out onto the veranda and retched, bringing up more of the murky water, and then she came back, lay down beside them and licked his hand.

His eyes filled, and he blinked hard and rubbed her with a towel until she stopped shivering.

Connie was kneeling beside Saffy, keying a number into the phone and muttering about him catching his death of cold, and he sat back on his heels and looked at her. 'Can I ask you something?'

'What?' she said, holding the phone to her ear.

'Will you marry me?'

She stared at him, her jaw sagging slightly, and put

the phone down on the floor before she dropped it. 'Marry you?'

'Yes. You know, big dress, diamond ring, honeymoon, babies—'

Her heart started beating harder, so loud now it almost deafened her. 'Babies?' she asked, just to be sure she'd heard it right.

'Absolutely. Definitely babies. I can't wait.'

Her breath left her in a rush. 'Neither can I.'

'So—is that a yes?'

She laughed—or was it a sob? He wasn't sure, but she was in his arms, saying, 'Yes, yes, yes,' over and over again until he actually began to believe it.

'Good. We'll talk in a minute.' And he picked up the handset from the floor.

She stared at him, listening to someone saying, 'Hello? This is the vet surgery. Did you call?'

Oh, no! Had they heard? She felt hot colour surge into her cheeks, and he smiled at her, his eyes laughing. 'Yes. Sorry about that, we got a little distracted. Can you come out on a house visit, please? We've got a rather large dog who nearly drowned in the river. I think she needs looking at urgently.'

He gave them the details, hung up and tucked her in closer beside him. 'I'm sorry I scared you. Tell me you've forgiven me.'

'No, I won't,' she said, snuggling up to his side and ignoring the rank smell of river water that clung to his sodden clothes. 'I don't know if I ever will. I thought I was going to lose you, James. I was so scared.'

'I'm sorry. I didn't think. I just saw her go in, and I couldn't let her die. Not Saffy, not after all she's been through, all she means to you, to Joe. You would have been devastated. She's our family, Connie. And I knew the tide was going out. It's when it's coming in it's so dangerous, because the denser sea water sinks under the river water where they meet and it drags you under.'

'And if you hadn't known that? Would you still have dived in?'

He shrugged. 'I don't know. Probably not. I might have nicked a boat and gone after her, but even on an outgoing tide, the current's really strong. I do know it's dangerous. I'm not an adrenaline junkie, Connie, not like Joe. I want to grow old with you, and see our children graduate and have babies of their own. I have no intention of dying. Not now. Not now I've got something worth living for. Some*one* worth living for.'

Saffy lifted her head and laid it on his lap, and he stroked her gently. 'Poor old girl. Two someones.'

Connie leant over and pressed a kiss to the dog's now warm flank. 'Thank you for rescuing her. You're right, I would have been devastated if we'd lost her.'

'I know that. I'm sorry I frightened you.'

'Don't do it again. Ever.'

'I won't.'

'Good.'

Two hours later, after the vet had been and Saffy was declared fit enough to stay at home to recover from her experience, they were all upstairs in his bedroom.

Saffy was snuggled up on an old quilt on the sofa by the window, snoring softly, and James and Connie were in bed, emotionally exhausted but happy. They'd showered to get rid of the smell of the river water which by then had been clinging to both of them, and now they were lying propped up on the pillows watching Saffy's chest rise and fall and letting the drama of the day subside.

'I love you,' she murmured, and he bent his head and pressed a warm, gentle kiss to her hair.

'I love you, too. I've loved you for years.'

She turned her head then and looked up at him. 'Really?'

'Really. I didn't let myself think about it before but you've always been more to me than just a friend. That was one of the reasons I couldn't just say yes to giving you a baby the way you asked, because I wanted so much more. I wanted to do it properly, like this, in the context of a permanent loving relationship, and anything less just seemed wrong, as if it would cheat all of us.'

'Oh, James…'

She lifted her hand and cradled his cheek, touching her lips to his, and he eased her closer, deepening the kiss, feeling the warmth of her soothing him.

It was like coming home, and he couldn't quite believe it.

'So—about these babies,' he murmured against her lips, trailing a daisy chain of kisses over her cheek and down towards the hollow of her throat.

She arched her head back, the soft sigh whispering in his hair. 'Mmm—want to make a start?'

She felt his smile against her skin.

'You read my mind,' he said softly, and kissed her all over again.

* * * * *

THE ER'S
NEWEST DAD

BY
JANICE LYNN

First published in Great Britain 2013
by Mills & Boon, an imprint of Harlequin (UK) Limited.
Harlequin (UK) Limited, Eton House, 18-24 Paradise Road,
Richmond, Surrey TW9 1SR

© Janice Lynn 2013

ISBN: 978 0 263 89897 2

Harlequin (UK) policy is to use papers that are natural, renewable and recyclable products and made from wood grown in sustainable forests. The logging and manufacturing process conform to the legal environmental regulations of the country of origin.

Printed and bound in Spain
by Blackprint CPI, Barcelona

Dear Reader

Sometimes a person comes into our lives that we just can't forget, no matter how long or hard we try. For Dr Ross Lane that person is Nurse Brielle Winton. Brielle was Ross's girlfriend for several years, but when their relationship turned rocky and he was offered a prestigious internship in another state he ended things and took off for greener pastures.

But sometimes there's no leaving the past behind. Five years later Ross needs to know once and for all if Brielle is all that his memory makes her out to be and if he made a mistake in walking away.

Despite the chemistry still alive between them, apparently she isn't haunted by the past the way he is. But, having seen her again, Ross knows she is the one for him, and he's determined to win her forgiveness and give her the happily-ever-after she deserves.

I hope you enjoy Ross and Brielle's story, and the return to Bean's Creek, North Carolina. You can visit me at www.janicelynn.net or on Facebook to catch up on my latest news.

Happy reading!

Janice

I wrote this book while my mentor, dear friend,
and the greatest doctor I've ever known battled cancer.
While I was working on revisions he lost that battle.
My very first Medical Romance™ was in dedication to
him, because he was a real-life hero
and someone I loved like a second father.

This book is in loving memory
of Dr Leon Lovon Reuhland. I will miss you.

CHAPTER ONE

Ross Lane had messed up big-time.

Every time his gaze settled on the petite blonde nurse in Bay Two the message reverberated louder and louder through his skull, pounding like the worst of headaches.

Idiot.

Fool.

Stupid.

Oh, yeah, he'd messed up big time five years ago.

Lately, not a day went by that he didn't wonder what his life would be like had he stuck around and been the man Brielle Winton had wanted him to be.

Funny how time changed one's perspective, one's priorities.

He leaned back against the emergency room nurses' station, pretending to read the hospital newsletter someone had handed him moments before. In actuality, he soaked in every detail of the woman he had never been able to forget.

Beautiful as ever, she smiled at the elderly gentleman she was hooking to telemetry. Dimples dotted the corners of her lush mouth, tugging at past memories and something deep in his chest. She went about her job efficiently, smiling often, speaking in a soft, soothing tone, completely unaware that he couldn't drag his gaze from her, that tension crackled from his every pore.

She was so close.

Yet never had she felt so far away.

How could he have walked away and broken her heart?

How could he have believed that out of sight would mean out of mind?

How could he have believed she would forgive him if he showed up out of the blue five years down the road from when they'd once been inseparable and he'd stupidly thrown away what they'd shared?

She looked up, her brown gaze meeting his with an intensity that jackhammered the pounding in his head.

Her friendly smile morphed into an agitated scowl. Shooting a quick glare that told him exactly where she wanted him to go, she turned her attention back to the frail gentleman lying on the emergency room hospital bed. Her expression was immediately pleasant for her patient's benefit, her smile so potent he was shocked the man's heart monitor didn't go haywire.

Brielle had no smiles for *him*.

Not a single one.

She barely spoke to him and never when it wasn't patient related.

He didn't blame her. He couldn't. Not when almost everything that had gone wrong in their relationship had been his fault.

Almost everything, but not all.

They'd both made mistakes. His had just been bigger.

Much bigger.

Huge.

Super-sized.

Pulsating pain stabbed his temple, making him wince.

Letting Brielle go really was his biggest regret. The one thing he couldn't get over no matter how many successes he achieved, no matter how much time passed. When he closed his eyes, she was who filled his mind, who he longed to wrap his arms around and hold close, who he wanted to share those successes with.

Five years had passed since he'd touched Brielle, but he hadn't forgotten one thing. Not the sound of her laughter or the feel of her hand clasped within his. Not the way she looked upon first waking or the way that no matter how tired she'd been she'd always had a special smile just for him.

If he'd been haunted before, his memories had escalated to torment when he'd bumped into her older brother at a medical convention. He'd known within minutes of seeing Vann that he would go to Brielle. He'd had to know if his memory played tricks on him, making the recollection of her more than the reality had ever been.

Although he had brought her up a couple of times during conversations, his former friend had barely commented on his sister, had managed to change the subject each and every time Ross had mentioned her.

Actually, Vann hadn't said much of anything about Brielle since the night he'd broken Ross's nose. That night Vann had said plenty. Lots. Mostly about how Ross had better never set foot near his sister again or he would do more than bloody his nose.

Ross hadn't fought back. He'd taken Vann's punch,

figured he deserved the pain, and he'd walked away from his best friend and the woman he'd been crazy about.

The one woman who had enough of a hold over him that once he'd learned where she was living—had Vann let that slip intentionally or on purpose?—he'd taken leave from his thriving family practice to accept a temporary emergency room position just to be near her, to work side by side with her as they once had. For the next three months he'd cover for the emergency room physician who was on maternity leave.

Then what?

Would three months be enough to finish whatever unresolved business existed between Brielle and himself?

Would three months be enough for him to know if all those years ago she had stolen his heart and he'd been too blind to realize it? Too young and stupid to know what he was losing? Or was guilt over what he'd done to her the culprit for why she haunted his dreams? Why his mind couldn't let her go?

Either way, he had to know.

He'd reached a point where he was ready to find someone to share his life with, to settle down, marry, have a few kids, and experience all the craziness that went along with being married with children.

Back in Boston, he'd been dating a beautiful, talented hospitalist, had even considered asking Gwen to marry him, but hadn't been able to bring himself to do so. Something kept holding him back.

Or someone.

So, instead of a proposal, he'd come back from his conference, broken things off with her and put his current life on hold so he could reconcile his past with his future.

The pretty little blonde, once again glaring at him from beside her patient's bed, was the starting point for him to achieve that next phase in his life.

One way or the other, his future started with Brielle Winton.

If only she'd co-operate.

Surely she needed resolution too?

Or maybe she had gotten all the resolution she needed when he'd left. Maybe she already knew that his leaving had been the right thing and that her feelings for him hadn't been real after all. Her antagonistic attitude toward him sure gave testimony to the fact she didn't want him here.

Then again, she always had been a stubborn little thing, but that had never presented a problem before.

In the past they'd always wanted the same thing.

Almost always.

When she'd started talking marriage almost non-stop, even to the point they'd argued more often than not, he'd flown the coop.

Figuratively and literally.

He'd already been considering the internship in Boston. Not everyone got offered such a great opportunity. He'd have been a fool to turn the chance down. But he had hesitated, and he'd known why. Brielle. Part of him had resented that their relationship was holding him back, keeping him from fulfilling all his career dreams. Crazy, immature, but he'd suddenly felt a noose tightening around his neck.

Still, he regretted the panicked tailspin he'd nose-dived into.

Thinking she could forgive him was pure foolishness.

Yet forgiveness was why he was here.

Brielle was why he was here, why he wouldn't leave until he had the answers he needed, why he wouldn't let her animosity get to him.

To prove his point, he winked at her, not one bit surprised when her scowl deepened.

"Dr. Lane, there's a UTI in Bay Four if you want to have a look." Cindy Whited's words interrupted his thoughts, causing him to glance at the buxomly nurse. "Her urinalysis results are in the computer for your review."

"Thanks. I'll be right there," he assured her, his attention immediately shifting back to Brielle. Their gazes collided again, causing a rumble in his chest, the same rumble he got every time he looked at her.

Love? Shame? Guilt? Regret about the past?

It was high time he knew exactly what role Brielle would play in his future. The sooner he knew, the better.

The stirring below his belt every time he looked at her left no doubt at the role he wanted her to play in his present.

His memory hadn't overplayed the reality at all. Brielle was all that he remembered and more.

He wanted her. In his life and in his bed.

She evoked his senses as no other woman ever had. Just looking at her left him wanting to drag her into the doctors' lounge and have his way with her delectable, curvy little body.

He wouldn't, of course. Bay Four was waiting. Not to mention that she would bite his head off if he tried.

Once upon a time she'd worshipped the ground he'd walked on, but that had been years ago. Now she looked at him as if she wanted to bury him six feet under the ground he walked on.

He wanted Brielle to look at him with the light that had once shone in her eyes just for him. He wanted her to want him as much as he wanted her, for them to burn up the sheets and see if there was anything left beyond the phenomenal chemistry they'd always shared.

With the way she regarded him these days he may as well wish for the moon.

He straightened his shoulders, stared at her with renewed determination. He'd never backed away from a challenge.

Well, perhaps once, and hadn't he lived to regret that mistake?

"Forget McDreamy and McSteamy. If that man were a television doctor, he'd be McHottie." Cindy fanned her busty chest to emphasize her point.

Brielle ignored her friend's antics, as she'd grown accustomed to doing since *McHottie*'s arrival earlier that week. If only her friend knew what evils lurked beneath Ross's beautiful façade she wouldn't constantly harp on about his royal hotness.

No, he hadn't been evil, she admitted. He'd just… No, she wasn't going to let her mind go to the past. Not again.

"Too bad he only has eyes for you," Cindy continued, unfazed by Brielle's lack of response. "Because I wouldn't mind feeling the heat."

Brielle fought to keep from looking up from the computer monitor where she was entering a patient's latest assessment data. She would not react to Cindy's comment. She couldn't. Her friend would have her shoved into a supply closet with Ross and bar the door. Cindy was constantly trying to get her to date, to splurge on life's niceties, as she called the opposite sex. Brielle had other priorities.

"Take now, for instance," Cindy said with a hint of amusement in her voice.

Brielle wasn't going to look up. She wasn't. Ross seemed to have eyes for her a lot these days, but she didn't care. *She didn't.*

"Here I am practically having hot flushes over those sultry blue eyes and that chiseled body, and does he even notice?" Her friend sighed dramatically. "No, he just keeps looking at you as if you're a fascinating puzzle he has to solve, as if you're a dessert he has to taste, as if—"

"You can have him," Brielle interrupted before Cindy could elaborate further, before her face could grow any hotter.

"Because?"

They'd been friends too long for Brielle not to know exactly what her friend's expression looked like without having to glance her way. Cindy's brow was arched high in question and a smile toyed on her lips.

Wasn't that the thing she'd loved most about Bean's Creek? That no one knew Ross other than Samantha and Vann? That she'd been able to move home without anyone feeling sorry for her because the man who'd been her world had abandoned her when she'd needed him most? Granted, he hadn't known the full story, but she had tried to tell him more than once and he'd refused to listen.

"He's not my type."

"Honey," her friend scoffed with another wave of her hand, "that man is every straight woman's type."

Brielle hit the "enter" key, then leaned back in her chair. "Not mine."

"Because?" Cindy persisted.

Been there, done that, have the scars and the kid to prove it.

"He just isn't."

A short silence followed and when Cindy spoke her tone was softer, more serious. "Because he reminds you of Justice's dad?"

Hello. Had Cindy read her mind? Brielle's gaze jerked up.

She shouldn't have looked. Really, she shouldn't have. Yet her gaze had instantly gone to Cindy. A very curious Cindy, who was watching her way too closely. No wonder. She probably looked like a deer caught in headlight beams. Maybe her friend really had read her mind. Or maybe she'd just thought she was talking in her head and really she'd mumbled her sarcastic remark out loud? No, she knew she hadn't.

"Why would you ask that?" Had her voice squeaked? Had the racket her mouth had emitted even been actual words or pleas to not push?

"I am your best friend," Cindy reminded her, sounding slightly offended. "Plus, I'm not blind. Dr. Lane's eyes are a fantastic blue, just like Justice's."

"Lots of people have blue eyes." She did her best to look bored with the conversation, to look as if she thought Cindy was crazy.

Cindy *was* crazy if she thought Brielle was going to have this conversation while entering patient data at the emergency room nurses' station. Especially when Ross could step up at any time.

"True." Cindy shrugged. "I just thought—"

"Quit thinking."

Cindy's brow rose, and she shook her head. "Oh, yeah, comments like that one from my way-too-serious, too logical, always-overthinks-things friend doesn't raise questions in my mind. Not at all."

Was that how her friend saw her? Fine. She'd earned the right to be logical and serious. Brielle winced. She had to get her act together. To quit being so jumpy where Ross was concerned. Three months. Less than three months now. She could keep her cool for that long. Then he'd be gone and hopefully never come near her again.

That gave her pause.

Never see Ross again?

Not that she'd thought she ever would. Not after he'd told her he didn't want anything to do with her ever again, that she was holding him back, and he planned to get on with his life. Without her.

And he had. All too quickly he'd moved on.

Yet, here he was, back in her life, creating emotional havoc.

Just as Cindy was, waiting for an explanation. Any moment her friend would start with the hands-on-hips foot-tapping.

"Look," Brielle said slowly, hoping to put off the interrogation, "the man annoys me and isn't someone I'd be interested in. Let's just leave it at that. Please."

Cindy considered her a moment, then shrugged. "Okay, for now, but only because your annoyance factor is about to skyrocket anyway."

Brielle took a deep breath, turned slightly to see Ross headed their way. Great. Her annoyance factor shot into orbit.

"Hey, Brielle, can I talk to you a moment?"

One one thousand. Two one thousand. Three one thousand. If she counted to infinity it wouldn't calm her Ross-ified nerves.

She could do this. She could be calm, professional. He meant nothing to her. Nothing but a pesky fly she'd like to swat away.

Swat.

"Obviously, you can."

Perhaps she shouldn't be so snappy with a physician who was her superior, but she couldn't help herself. Not so close on the heels of Cindy's question about Justice.

Her son's eyes were the exact shade of blue of Ross's. He had the same strong chin and facial structure. Made expressions that were so similar to Ross's that at times Brielle's breath caught and memories pierced her heart.

Justice looked a great deal as Ross must have looked at a similar age. Except that her son had arrived into the world two months early and was small for his age. She couldn't imagine six-foot-two-inch Ross ever having been anything but big.

"I'm going to go clean Bay One," Cindy told no one in particular as she fanned her hand over her chest one last time and grinned at Brielle while mouthing, "Hot."

When they were alone at the nurses' station, Ross sighed. "Is this how it's going to be the entire time I'm here?"

"This?" She pretended to have no clue what he referred to.

"You hating me."

"I don't hate you." She didn't, did she? She just wanted him to go away without disrupting her life further, without disrupting Justice's life. No way would she let Ross hurt their son the way he'd hurt her.

"Good to know."

"Don't let the knowledge go to your head," she advised, not wanting to encourage him in any way as keeping an emotional distance was difficult enough already. "I may not hate you, but I don't like you."

Not looking one bit nonplussed, he grinned. "Let me take you to dinner tonight so we can work on that. Once upon a time there were a lot of things you liked about me. Let me remind you."

An invisible hand jerked at Brielle's throat, choking the breath from her. No sound would come out so she shook her head.

"Why not?"

Did he really not know?

"Should I give you a thesis on the reasons? Or just the top-ten list?" she snapped, her voice freeing itself from the mute clutches of shock.

"No," he said, leaning against the nurses' station and crossing his legs at the ankles in a casual pose, too casual really. "What you should do is say yes."

"No."

"Brielle."

"Don't Brielle me, Dr. Lane. There is no reason why I should say yes. No reason why I ever would. This is a wasted conversation because there's no point to us going to dinner. Ever."

"Sure there is." There was an undercurrent to his voice that caused her head to jerk up, for her eyes to study him closely. He looked casual, relaxed, but there was a steely, determined set to his jaw.

Did he know? Had he somehow learned of Justice? Had she been wrong to believe he didn't have a clue? Really, why else would he be there?

"What reason would that be? Because I sure can't think of a single one." It wasn't as if he'd woken up one morning and thought, Hey I miss Brielle Winton. Wonder what she's been up to. Maybe I should move hundreds of miles away for a few months so I can find out. *Right*. But, then, why else would he have chosen to work here?

Unless he'd discovered her five-year-old secret.

"Because I like you," he answered without hesitation, as if his reasons were logical and she shouldn't have had to ask.

Her heart pounded in her chest and she grabbed hold of the edge of the nurses' station, grounding herself. "You don't even know me."

"Sure I do." He sounded so self-confident, so cocky that she wanted to scream with frustration. Did he think her life had just stood still since he'd walked away? That she had been in limbo, waiting for him to come back to pick up where they'd left off?

"You may have known me better than anyone once upon a time, but not any more. Five years changes a person. I've changed."

His gaze skimmed over her, dragging slowly across each of her facial features, lower till he reached where the nurses'-station hid her body. "Not that much. You're still the same Brielle."

She fought the urge to cross her arms over her chest, her belly, her hips. "Don't act as if you know me when you don't. I have changed." Oh, how pregnancy and be-coming a mother had changed her. Her body. Her mind-set. Everything. Justice had changed her for the good. Unlike his father. "I'm a completely different person, have different priorities, different dreams."

He moved round the desk, stood close, quietly re-garding her, seeming to consider her comment. "What do you dream now, Brielle?" His question came out soft, curious, almost a plea to know her inner desires.

As if she'd tell him anything about her dreams.

"Not so long ago all your dreams featured me," he reminded her softly, no trace of his cocky arrogance to be heard in his voice for once.

There went that jerk to her throat again, but this time she held onto her ability to speak.

"Long enough." For ever ago. "Like I said, I've changed. For however long you are here, I will treat you with professional courtesy, but I will not cater to you beyond that limited role. Anything else between us ended long ago." Five long, horrible years ago when he'd changed the course of her life by ending their re-lationship and moving far away. "At your bidding, I might add."

Had that been bitterness in her tone? She wanted in-difference, not the slightest hint that he'd hurt her, that he still held the power to hurt her.

"Brielle—"

"Unless what you have to say is regarding a patient, please don't speak to me," she interrupted, unwilling to listen to more. "Just leave me alone."

His brows drawn together, he sighed. "If that's how you want things."

"It is." With that she turned back to her computer

monitor and pretended he wasn't standing so close, pretended that he didn't mean a thing to her.

Not pretended. He didn't mean a thing to her. Not really.

Not for a long time.

Not ever again.

CHAPTER TWO

GLAD HER SHIFT was almost over, a tired Brielle handed an elderly gentleman an emesis pan. "Use this if you need to throw up. Dr. Lane will be in momentarily to order something to ease the nausea." A noise caught her attention as someone entered the room. She didn't have to look to know who it was. The quickening of her pulse gave all the indication she needed. "Here he is now."

"Hello, Mr. Gardner, I'm Dr. Lane," Ross introduced himself as he washed his hands. "I've looked over your labs. The good news is that your chest pain doesn't appear to be cardiac in nature."

"The bad news?" the slightly balding, white-haired man asked, his expression pinched. His frail hands clasped the white cotton blanket covering his thin body tightly.

Brielle fought the urge to take his trembling hand in hers while he awaited whatever news Ross had come to deliver.

"Your liver enzymes are through the roof, as are your amylase and lipase levels," Ross explained, elaborating on the details of the patient's labs and how they related to his symptoms. "I'm going to admit you to the medical floor for acute pancreatitis."

Ross spoke calmly to the man, taking time to explain

the diagnosis and the medical implications. Despite the fact that she should probably go and check to see if there were any new patients to triage, Brielle found herself fascinated by Ross interacting with his patient.

She'd always known he was going to be a phenomenal doctor. He'd had such a reassuring manner about him, an aura that promised his patients everything would be okay so long as their lives were in his hands, that he'd always do his best.

When it came to his patients, perhaps that was true. In the short time he'd been at Bean's Creek, he'd certainly earned the respect of his colleagues. No one could say enough good things about the gorgeous new doctor filling in for Cassidy Jenkins.

"Brielle, will you call the medical floor and have a nurse prepare a bed for Mr. Gardner? I'll get admission orders written." He looked up from where he listened to Mr. Gardner's chest yet again. "Oh, and one more thing, go ahead and give an anti-emetic prior to his transfer, please."

He named the medication, dosage, and route he wanted it administered.

Please. No wonder all her co-workers thought he was God's gift to the emergency department. Forget the man's extraordinary good looks, which made a girl willing to overlook most flaws, but, seriously, how many doctors said please and thank you routinely? As well loved as Cassidy was, even the lovely doctor on maternity leave wasn't known for pleases and thank yous.

Brielle didn't want to like him, this older version of the man she'd once loved with all her heart. Didn't want to have positive thoughts in any way, shape, or form regarding Ross.

She didn't want to have thoughts of Ross, period. Not good. Not bad. Not any.

Forcing him from her mind yet again, she nodded at the source of her annoyance and left the emergency room bay to carry out his orders. She'd just finished drawing up the injection when he stepped up behind her. Close. Too close.

She turned to tell him to back away, to leave her alone, but facing Ross was a mistake.

He was standing closer than she'd realized. So close that they practically touched. So close that when she looked up at him, she could see the flare of desire darkening the blue of his eyes.

She remembered that flare, that look that said he wanted her. Before he'd baled out on her, that look would have had her smiling, nodding, and them getting alone as quickly as possible.

A lump clogged her throat. She choked back a fresh wave of annoyance at how she remembered everything about him, how her body remembered every look and caress he'd ever bestowed on her. *Stupid body!*

He looked good, smelled good. It was all she could do to keep from deeply inhaling the musky scent of him. If she leaned just slightly towards him, she bet he'd feel good too. His lean body was as toned and fit as ever. Perhaps more so than when he'd been finishing his degree.

But Brielle didn't lean. Instead, she focused on the image of the last time she'd seen him when she'd gone to Boston a few months after he'd left.

An image of that wonderfully built body of his pressed against a woman Brielle hadn't known, but obviously Ross had, filled her mind. His lips had been firmly attached to the blonde stranger's. When he'd pulled back, he'd smiled at the woman, slid his arm to her lower back and whispered something in the woman's ear that had made her laugh and slap his upper arm.

Brielle hadn't laughed, but she had felt like slapping Ross. And herself for being so stupid as to think going to Boston to tell him about her pregnancy had been the right thing for her to do.

He'd told her he wanted nothing to do with her or anything that had to do with her ever again. Why hadn't she believed him?

She'd left somewhere between numb, angry, and so hurt that the airline stewardess had asked more than once if she was okay. Less than a month later she'd given birth to Justice, her obstetrician citing stress as the cause of her premature labor.

The memory of her Boston trip still held the power to almost bring her to her knees with pain, nausea, and weakness. It also gave her the power to resist the man standing before her, who was as sinfully tempting as the devil himself. Yes, she'd loved him once upon a time, but the flip side of the coin held her in its grasp much more firmly these days.

"Brielle," he began, his voice low, his eyes searching as if he knew her thoughts had gone somewhere dark. He reached for her shoulders.

"Don't!" She jerked back, clenching the medication-filled syringe between shaking fingers. "Don't you dare touch me, Ross Lane. Don't you ever touch me!"

She'd been louder than she should have been and Cindy glanced her way, frowning in confusion.

"Brielle." Her name came out as a sigh. He said something more, but the roaring in her ears prevented her

from understanding his words. Had he really thought
he could just show up and step back into her life? Was
that what he wanted?

Who cared what he wanted?

As far as she was concerned, Cassidy couldn't come
off maternity leave soon enough so that Ross could
pitchfork his way back to the fiery gates that had spat
him out.

She closed her eyes, squeezed them tight, hoping he
would be gone when she opened them.

No such luck.

She sighed. "Please go away."

He stared at her for long moments. "Is that what you
want? For me to leave and just stay gone?"

Was it?

She swallowed the lump in her throat. "The emergency room would be chaos if you left."

His lips twisted. "That wasn't what I meant, and you
know it. Go to dinner with me at the end of your shift
so we can talk."

"We've already been through this. I don't want anything to do with you." She fought back the bile rising
up her throat. Had she purposely flung his words back
at him? "What would be the point?"

"We could catch up on old times."

"Aren't you listening?" She glared up at him as if he
wasn't nearly as bright as she knew him to be. "I don't
want to catch up on old times with you."

He shrugged. "I'm flexible. Go to dinner with me so
we can make new times."

She started to shoot him down again, but thought of
Justice. This was her precious son's father. A father he'd
never met. Didn't she owe it to Justice to see if Ross

was man enough to do right by his son should she tell him of the miracle they'd created?

Was there really any choice a good mother could make other than to see what he had to say and then make any necessary decisions regarding her son's future?

Ross watched the play of emotions dance across Brielle's face. She'd never been good at hiding her thoughts. Time hadn't changed that.

She was considering saying yes. He wanted her to say yes. More than any sane man should, he wanted her to go to dinner with him, to spend time with him, regardless of what they were doing.

"Please, Brielle. Say yes." He didn't like pleading with her, but with their past he figured he owed her that much. Hell, he probably owed her a lot more than that, but he wasn't quite ready to grovel yet. "I want to spend time with you. Outside work."

Emotions continued to battle for dominance across her face. She didn't want to say yes. Not really. But he wasn't blind. There was still something between them, a heat, an inner connection that time, or his foolishness, hadn't eradicated.

"Let me take you to dinner. No pressure for anything more, I promise. I'll grovel if necessary."

Okay, so maybe he was ready to grovel. Groveling would be a new experience, but he'd learn to grovel with the best of them if it won him the chance of getting back in her good graces.

Her brown gaze lowered then lifted to his. "Okay, fine, I will go to dinner with you. But this means nothing, Ross. Nothing at all. I am not interested in rekindling a relationship with you or making new memories or anything of the sort. I'm focused on my future. You are part of my past that I would have preferred stayed part of my past."

Ouch. She wasn't mincing her words, but he didn't deserve any sugar-coating. Still, if she'd give him a chance he'd get there, would remind her how sweet their lovemaking had been. Sweet seemed too tame a word for what they'd shared.

As simple a thing as it was, she'd called him Ross again rather than Dr. Lane. Hearing his name on her lips pleased him way too much.

"Tonight? After your shift?" A wise man would get a commitment on a date and time. Ross was no fool.

"Tonight is as good a time as any," she sighed, her face pale as if she was battling nausea. "I want to get this over with."

Her tone made going to dinner with him sound worse than having root-canal treatment. Did she dislike him so much?

"Not that I'm not grateful you said yes, albeit with less enthusiasm than one would hope for, but why did you?"

"A glutton for punishment, obviously." She laughed a laugh he recognized as one full of irony. "But we both know you weren't going to let up until I said yes. Meet me at Julian's just down the street about thirty minutes after my shift change. A quick dinner. Nothing else."

She wasn't happy about agreeing to go but at least she'd said yes and that was a start. He'd take whatever crumbs she tossed his way until he convinced her he had seriously missed her.

Clinging to the fact that he was having dinner with

her, he smiled. "You need my number in case you get stuck working late?"

"No, Dr. Lane." Deep furrows cut into her forehead with her glare. "I figured out your number a long time ago."

Brielle was late arriving to Julian's, but she didn't call or text Ross to let him know. Despite her claim, she didn't have his number, not his cellular phone number at any rate.

Sheer stubbornness had prevented her from taking it earlier when he'd offered. That and her need to put him in his place even if it had only been a short-lived balm on the mega-blows he had delivered her way.

Maybe he'd have left already.

No such luck. She paused in the entrance of the restaurant, easily spotting where he sat in a back booth. A waitress stood next to the table, her pretty face bright with interest in whatever Ross was saying, her gaze eating him up.

Some things never changed.

Not that Brielle blamed the young girl. There was no denying that he was a beautiful man. He was. Yet Ross's appeal went so much further than the deep blue of his eyes, the coal-black allure of his soft, thick hair, the strong lines of his tanned face, the width of his broad shoulders or the taper of his narrow hips. His appeal came from the sharp intelligence that quickly became apparent when in his presence, from the witty humor that was always just beneath the surface, the charm that bubbled over without him even trying, the smile that dug dimples into his cheeks and made a woman need to smile back.

Based on the waitress's high-pitched laughter and flushed cheeks, Brielle guessed Ross's charm was bubbling. Although he was probably just being friendly, the sight brought her back to when she'd gone to Boston.

Just as now, he hadn't known she was there, watching him. What had been the point? He'd told her he wanted nothing else to do with her. He'd meant his words when he'd told her he was done. Some crazy part of her had clung to the belief that he'd realize he made a mistake, that they were good together, meant to be together always and for ever. Seeing him kiss the blonde when she'd still thought of him as hers had driven his words home as perhaps nothing else could have.

She'd fled heartbroken, pregnant, and uncertain about her future.

Perhaps she should have told him about her pregnancy anyway, but she hadn't been thinking clearly, had only wanted to get far away.

Later, when her emotions had settled somewhat, she'd made the decision to take him at his word, to let him have the life he'd said he wanted and had chosen over her.

Ross had no idea he had a son.

Or did he?

Nausea hit her. Hard. The room spun. Clamminess coated her skin with hot moisture. She dropped onto a bench meant for waiting customers. Wave after wave of fear slammed into her and she thought she was going to throw up.

"Brielle? Are you okay?" Concern poured from Ross, his expression worried and his voice gentle.

She blinked at him, shocked to see him so close. Obviously he'd noticed her and had left the table to check on her. He sat on the bench next to her, his hand on her face as if checking for a fever.

"Brielle?" he repeated, but she couldn't speak, couldn't respond other than to stare at him.

Had Ross come to Bean's Creek to claim his son?

CHAPTER THREE

HIS HEART POUNDING, Ross put his hand on Brielle's forehead. Red stained her cheeks, but otherwise her face was devoid of color. Although it wasn't overly warm, dampness clung to her pale skin.

"Honey, are you all right?" He shook her shoulder lightly, trying to get her to snap out of whatever had hold of her. Not once when he'd imagined finally feeling her skin against his again had he imagined it like this.

Face pinched with pain, she shook her head in denial.

What the hell was wrong with her? Why wouldn't she look at him?

"Brielle?"

Her body trembled within his grasp, making him want to take her into his arms and make whatever was wrong better.

Fine hairs along his neck prickled. "Talk to me. Tell me what's going on so I can help you."

She closed her eyes, swallowed then took a ragged breath.

"I need to get out of here," she mumbled, so low he barely made out what she said. "I don't feel well."

"Sir, is everything okay?" the hostess asked, the young girl's wide eyes glued to where Brielle dropped her head to between her knees.

"My friend isn't feeling well. Which unfortunately means we won't be staying." He pulled out his wallet, handed the girl a twenty. "Please give that to our waitress to cover my drink and her trouble."

His gaze went back to Brielle. She still leaned forward, rocked slightly back and forth.

"Let's go, honey." He helped her sit up, but one glance at her ashen face was more than enough to prompt him to make a quick decision.

He scooped her into his arms, waited while the hostess opened the restaurant door, and then carried her to his car, with her protesting the entire time that she could walk.

"Can you stand long enough for me to open the door?"

Still trembling, she nodded against his chest. "Put me down. I'm so embarrassed."

She felt good in his arms. What kind of cad was he anyway to notice how good she felt against him when she was ill? Still, he wanted nothing more than to keep holding her, to keep breathing in the scent that was uniquely hers. To keep feeling her warm body against his.

He'd missed her so much.

More than he'd admitted even to himself until that very moment.

"I said put me down," she said, with more gusto than he would have thought possible based on how pale she'd looked inside the restaurant. "You should never have picked me up like that!"

He didn't point out that she'd looked too weak to stand. Now didn't seem the time to start an argument. Instead, he gently put her on her feet, keeping his hand

on her, ready to steady her if she swayed, ready to sweep
her back into his arms if she stumbled.

He unlocked his door, helped her into his passenger
seat, then got into the driver's side of the car. Rather
than start the engine, he turned to her, watched her stare
straight ahead, wishing he could know what was running through her head.

"You okay?" Crazy question when she obviously
wasn't, but he didn't know what else to say to break the
silence stretching between them.

"Fine. Couldn't be better." Sarcasm didn't become
her, but her color was beginning to look a little brighter,
not so ghostly.

"What's going on? You coming down with something?"

"I'm not ill, just embarrassed at the spectacle we
just made."

She attempted to make light of his question, but he'd
have to be a fool not to realize her laugh was forced.

"Nothing contagious, at any rate," she continued,
still staring straight out the window.

He stared at her miserable profile, at how her shoulders sagged, at how her hand rested on her abdomen,
and a possible explanation of her symptoms, of her re-
jection of him, hit so hard that he thought he might be
ill, too.

Acid burned the back of his throat, searing him
straight through.

"You're pregnant?" He hated the words, hated asking, but he had to know. Had to know if he was too late.
If he'd stayed in denial of his feelings for too long, let
someone else move in and steal Brielle's heart. Claim
her body.

Her jaw fell. She turned to him, her eyes round and her expression aghast. "No," she denied so forcefully he couldn't doubt her. "I'm not pregnant. Why would you think that?"

"Because you were nauseated and looked like you were going to pass out." Relief washed through Ross but didn't fully ease his suspicions. "You're holding your stomach." He grimaced, wanting to hold his own nauseated stomach. "You're sure you aren't pregnant?"

Her hand fell to her side. She closed her eyes and laughed, though it sounded bitter-sweet. "I'm not pregnant."

Something about her answer struck him as odd, as not quite the whole story. "How can you be positive?"

"I'm not pregnant. Let's leave it at that." Sarcasm bit into her words.

"Maybe you are and don't know it." Why he persisted he wasn't sure. Maybe because the thought that she might be bothered him so greatly that he wanted to be one hundred per cent certain that she wasn't.

"I am not pregnant. End of story." She blew out an exasperated breath, dropped her head against his dashboard and rolled it back and forth slowly, before sitting back up to stare blankly ahead. "Men are so dense."

Wondering at her actions, he frowned. "What's that supposed to mean?"

"Just that you were oblivious when you should have…" She trailed off, closed her eyes and put her hand to her head, wincing as if in pain again.

"Headache?" he guessed, wondering why breathing suddenly felt easier at her assurance she wasn't pregnant, wondering at her comment and wishing she'd finished it.

She nodded. "I think one is coming on. If you'll take me somewhere to where I can lie down for a minute, I'm sure it'll pass."

She was looking pale again and as if she'd like to bring up anything in her stomach. "You need a bag or something to barf in?"

"Very technical term there, Dr. Lane, and, no, I don't need a barf bag. I haven't eaten anything since early this morning."

Why hadn't she eaten? Sure, they had been busy at the hospital, but she was supposed to have had a lunch-break. How had he not noticed that she hadn't taken one?

"That's probably why you feel so poorly and is likely what triggered your headache. Hypoglycemia is serious business, Brielle. You shouldn't play around with your health. You know better."

Eyes closed, face squished, she shook her head and pointed towards the road. "It's not hypoglycemia. My blood sugar is fine. I'm fine. Just drive."

Ross wasn't sure where he was supposed to take her, but a place to lie down was a requirement he didn't have a lot of choices on. He took her to the furnished apartment he'd leased for the three months he'd be in Bean's Creek.

Despite her protests that she was fine to walk, he carried her inside, laid her on his sofa, pulled her tennis shoes off and propped her feet on one of the throw pillows that had come with the apartment.

"I'll be back in just a minute," he promised. "Don't move."

Eyes closed, she grunted in acknowledgement of

his comment. He fetched a glass of orange juice and a couple of tablets to knock out her pain.

"I don't recall you having issues with headaches. How often do you get these?" he asked when she'd settled back on the sofa. He placed a cold, damp cloth on her forehead and stroked loose hairs away from her face.

"Almost never." Hating that his touch felt so good, Brielle closed her eyes, willed her body not to respond to the gentle strokes of his fingers brushing over her face, her hair.

"Sometimes hormonal changes can trigger headaches."

"Stop it, Ross. I am not pregnant," she repeated, enunciating each word with emphasis.

Really, could the situation be any more ironic? When she'd been pregnant with his child, he'd failed to notice the changes to her routine, to her body. Tonight, when she'd merely felt ill, he'd immediately jumped to that conclusion. Men.

"Are you dating anyone, Brielle?"

Grateful that her eyes were closed and he couldn't read the truth in her eyes, she held her tongue in check.

"I suppose you're not answering because you think the answer isn't any of my business. Maybe you're right that it's not. But what you do feels as if it's my business." He sighed and it sounded so weary that she opened her eyes, her gaze instantly colliding with his intense blue one.

"I want what you do to be my business, Brielle."

His admission surprised her.

"Tell me how to make that happen."

Oh, how sweetly seductive his words were to her

heart and yet… "Because you're here, I'm here, and you have three months to kill?"

"I'm here because of you," he owned up, his gaze not wavering from hers. "You have to know you're why I'm here. The only reason I'm here."

She knew that. On some level she had known. Yet her heart did a jiggly dance in her chest all the same.

"I sought you out, took this job just to be near you, and my sole purpose for being in Bean's Creek is you."

Thud. Thud. Thud. Her heart pounded against her ribs. "Why?"

"You know why."

He was wrong. She didn't know.

"Sex?" she guessed. Their chemistry seemed to zap as strongly as ever, promising just as volcanic a ride. They'd had a great sex life. A great life period, but physically they'd have won Olympic gold once upon a time. If she were honest with herself, she'd admit that she couldn't be near him without wanting to rip his clothes off, without wanting to touch him and re-familiarize herself with every aspect of his body.

"If all I wanted was sex, I wouldn't have had to leave Boston."

That she didn't doubt. Of course a gorgeous successful doctor with his looks, charm, and sex appeal would have women falling at his feet. No doubt he'd had many women during the time they'd been apart. Her heart clenched into a tight, painful ball.

"I want *you*."

"You want sex with me?"

"Not just sex." He paused, looked torn. "At least, I don't think so." He ran his fingers through his hair then squatted down next to the sofa, met her gaze with his usual confidence. "I want you, Brielle. I want you to look at me the way you used to look at me. I want you to beg me to make love to you over and over until we both collapse in exhaustion and then I want you to tell me you want me again."

Barely breathing, she shook her head. "Impossible. You can't have that. Those feelings are gone."

Yet even as she said the words the urge to beg him to do all those things drummed louder and louder through her head. Lord help her, she wanted that sweet exhaustion he spoke of, that sweet exhaustion she knew he had the power to deliver.

"Are they?" He traced his finger over her lips as if to pound home his question. "I think the attraction is as strong as ever between us."

That she couldn't deny. Just his lightest touch had her entire body tingling as if every cell had suddenly woken up after a long hibernation.

"That's just physical." Please, let it just be physical. "I'm a grown woman now and know better than acting on just physical."

Hadn't she learned that lesson? He'd been a good teacher. So why did recalling all the other things he'd taught her seem so much easier at the moment?

"There was a lot more than just physical between us."

"Was there?" she asked perversely. "I remember things differently."

His gaze settled on her mouth. His finger toyed with her lower lip, barely grazing the inner moisture of her mouth. "Tell me what you remember, Brielle. Tell me you remember how your body came alive when I kissed you, how you responded to my slightest touch." He lifted his finger to his mouth, supped off the taste of her lips. "Tell me you want me to kiss you right now because I see how your pulse is racing, how your breathing is ragged, and how your eyes are eating me up."

"I don't want you to kiss me." She closed her eyes and held her breath, but she couldn't do a thing about her crazy racing pulse. "Even if I did, all you've done is proved my point. Physical. Physical. Physical. Nothing more."

Ross laughed. A sweet, relaxed, real laugh that sounded so familiar to her aching heart that everything in her went a little haywire.

Or maybe it was the light sweep of his mouth over hers that caused everything to go haywire.

"You taste of heaven, Brielle," he whispered against her lips. "Sweet, sweet heaven."

If she tasted of heaven, then he tasted of hell.

His lips were full, sure, full of temptation, *hot*.

Every cell in her body buzzed alive as if a direct connection had been made to where his lips met hers and he'd taken control of her nerve endings and demanded they deliver ultimate pleasure.

When he pushed his tongue into her mouth, for the briefest moment she considered biting him. But what purpose would that serve? If she wanted him to stop, she'd have stopped him. Instead, she'd parted her lips, let him have his blasted way.

He was right. She wanted this kiss. Had wanted his kiss from the first moment she'd spotted him in the emergency room on his first day at Bean's Creek.

Who was she kidding?

She'd never stopped wanting him. Not from their very first kiss years ago.

It's only curiosity, she assured herself as she opened

her mouth to his exploration. She just wanted to know if his kisses still set her on fire, if he still pushed her body beyond pleasure and into ecstasy.

The sensual movement of his mouth over hers assured that he did. And more.

His hands threaded into her hair. His fingers caressed her scalp, holding her to him. His touch was gentle, not forcing the embrace, allowing her the freedom to stop him if she desired. He was probably gloating that she wasn't, that she was so weak that the first time they were alone she was flat on her back, making love to him with her mouth.

Then again, one could argue that it was his mouth loving hers.

That it was his hands moving over her shoulders, down her arms, caressing her as if she were the most prized treasure.

His body that had leaned to hover just above hers.

Kissing her, he stared directly into her eyes. When his mouth lifted from hers, his breath came hard and fast against her lips. "I missed you, Brielle. So much."

She didn't answer, because what could she say? He'd been the one to leave, the one to be in the arms of another woman when she'd gone after him mere months later.

Memories of the last time she'd seen him, of his lips on the other woman's, of how quickly he'd moved on, gave her the strength to push against his chest.

"Stop," she ordered, wriggling to sit up on his sofa. "That wasn't appropriate."

He wiped his finger across his lips. Whether he was savoring their kiss or wiping it away, she wasn't sure. "You were as curious as I was. Admit it."

Curious? He had no idea.

"No."

"Not admitting to the attraction between us doesn't make it any less real," he pointed out, with way too much logic when her head was spinning.

"Doesn't matter." Why could she still feel his kiss? Taste him? She didn't want to remember. Didn't want to have new memories of him. "None of this matters. There are others involved."

His brows formed a V. "I'm not seeing anyone."

Wondering if she'd said too much, she closed her eyes. "That's not what I meant."

"There is someone in your life?"

She took a deep breath, knowing the truth was the best policy even if she'd rather not admit it. "There is."

He swore under his breath, seemed to consider his options and make a decision all in under ten seconds. His face serious, his expression pure dominant male in warrior mode, he met her gaze. "Then he is in for the fight of his life because I want what's mine."

Taken aback, she gulped. "What's yours?"

"You. You're mine, Brielle. You always have been. You always will be."

"No." She shook her head in denial. "That's where you're wrong. I'm not yours." Needing movement, distance between them, she rose from the sofa, straightened her uniform. "I haven't been from the moment you left me for Boston. Take me home."

Ross drove in silence, trying to decipher what had happened between him and Brielle. Had he taken her to his apartment in the hope of luring her into his bed?

He certainly wanted her enough that subconsciously

perhaps he had hoped the evening would end with her realizing how right the chemistry between them was. Either way, he'd failed miserably. One hot, explosive kiss that had filled his head with fantasies and she'd pushed him away, demanding to be driven home.

"You wanted that kiss as much as I did."

"Do we have to talk about that again?" At his nod, she sighed as if needing lots of patience. "Fine. If your ego needs to believe that, you go right ahead and believe that I've done nothing but pine away for your kisses since you walked out."

His ego wasn't what needed to believe that she wanted his kisses. He daren't name what body part needed to believe.

Surprisingly, it wasn't the one she'd probably guess.

"What happened between us was a long time ago, Brielle. We were younger, still had a lot to learn about life. I had a lot to learn about life, about who I was and what I wanted out of a relationship. Don't you think you owe it to us to let go of your anger at me for leaving?"

"Fine."

Was that her favorite word these days or what?

"You're right. What happened between us was a long time ago, best forgotten. We'll just be professional colleagues, nothing more."

If their discussion wasn't so serious, he could laugh at that. "You and I can never be just professional colleagues. Our kiss was proof enough of that."

"That kiss was a mistake."

"Why? Because of this man you're involved with?" His fingers gripped the steering-wheel tighter at the thought of another man touching Brielle, of another man kissing her lips or holding her affections. "Whatever is between you can't be serious because no one at the hospital is aware he exists. I asked your friend Cindy if you were dating anyone. She said no. I asked Samantha, too, and she also denied that you were involved with anyone." He paused, thinking of Vann's girlfriend, whom he and Brielle had often double dated with during their heyday. "After she told me where I could go, of course."

Brielle's face pinched and she opened her mouth as if to say something then clamped her lips closed. "This is crazy. Why are you here? Why are you doing this after all this time? Just tell me and be done with it."

He didn't understand the strain to her voice. Yes, he'd ended their relationship, but it wasn't as if he'd done her wrong. He hadn't cheated or bad-mouthed her or abused her in any way that he knew of. When he'd moved out, he'd even paid the rent on their apartment for three months to give her time to find a new roommate to help with expenses.

"I told you I want you in my life," he reminded her. "I've missed you."

She clenched her hands in her lap, shook her head as if to shake his words away. "Once upon a time I'd have given anything to hear you say that."

He didn't miss her use of past tense. "But not any more?"

The skin pulled tight over her pale face. She shook her head again. "Surely you didn't believe I've spent the last five years waiting for you to grow up?"

"My growing up wasn't the issue." Wanting to expand his learning experiences hadn't been childish or immature. He'd been a man given an amazing opportunity and he'd taken it. Their relationship had been strained with her sudden desire to walk down the aisle and him knowing he wasn't ready for that, not at that point in his career and life. "I know you've gone on with your life, just as I have. That doesn't mean what is between us is finished. It's not."

After kissing her tonight, being swamped with all the old feelings but also new stronger emotions too, he was beginning to believe what was between Brielle and himself would never be finished.

"Don't bring up this man you're involved with," he warned, before she could toss that in his face. "Because you don't love him."

Twisting in her car seat to stare more fully at him, her gaze narrowed to tiny slits. "How could you possibly know that I don't love him?"

He pulled to a stop at a red traffic light then faced her, daring her to deny the truth of what he was about to say. "Because if you were in love with him you wouldn't have kissed me. Not at all and certainly not with that passion."

"You're wrong," she countered, her smile scaring him. "I love him more than I've ever loved any man, anyone. He's my whole world."

Truth echoed from each word she spoke.

Ross stared at her, unable to label the crushing sensation in his chest. Denial shot through him. Strong denial. "No, you don't. Maybe you think you do, but you don't. You've not changed that much. You wouldn't kiss me if you were in love with another man. You aren't the type of woman to do that."

A need as potent as any as he'd ever felt hit him. A need to feel her lips against his, to reassure himself of exactly what he'd felt when he'd kissed her. No way had he imagined the emotion zapping back and forth between them when their bodies had touched.

That hadn't been just physical. He'd felt...more.

He leaned forward, intent on reminding her of those emotions, but she put her hand up, shook her head.

"Don't."

"Scared?"

"Of you?" She laughed but without any humor. "You won't hurt me, Ross. Not ever again, because I won't let you."

Was that what she thought he wanted?

"I'm not here to hurt you."

"I doubt you meant to hurt me last time either."

Her barb stuck deep. "But I did hurt you."

It wasn't really a question, but she answered anyway, her expression holding steady except for the slightest quiver of her lower lip. He hated that he'd caused the pain that lay behind that quiver.

"What do you think?"

That he'd been an idiot to leave this woman when she'd loved him with all her heart and had made him happier than he recalled being at any other time during his life.

"I loved you, Ross." Her voice was loaded with emotion. "And I believed you felt the same about me, that we would be spending the rest of our lives together. Of course it hurt when you left."

She'd loved him. His ribcage clamped down around his lungs at her heartfelt admission. He'd known she had, had heard her say the words in the past, but that had been in the past. He hadn't heard those words from her lips in five long years. She'd thought they were going to spend the rest of their lives together? She'd been ready for that then? In the midst of whatever relationship crisis they'd been going through she'd thought wedding bells would fix everything?

"Is that why you went crazy with bridal magazines and talking about getting married all the time?" he mused.

Shock dawned into realization in her golden-brown gaze. "That's why you left? Because I started talking about getting married and you had cold feet because you weren't in love with me and didn't want to marry me?"

"Regardless of how we felt about each other, we weren't ready for marriage."

"You never said you loved me," she reminded him, her voice catching. "Not a single time during the two years we were together did you ever say you loved me."

She had him there. He hadn't ever told any woman that he loved her, not even Brielle.

"They're just words. Saying labels out loud doesn't make emotions any more or less true."

But hadn't his own chest just done funny things at hearing her say the words, even in past tense?

"True." She turned to stare through the windshield, her face blank, withdrawn. When she next spoke, she sounded more defeated than he recalled ever hearing her. "The light's green. It's been a long day. I'm tired. Just drive me back to my car, please."

He did as she asked, drove them back to the restaurant in silence. He pulled into the vacant spot next to the place she'd pointed out where she'd parked her car. Funny, he hadn't even known what kind of vehicle she drove these days. When had she traded in the sporty little hatchback she'd driven for the efficient but nice four-door sedan?

He turned off the ignition, faced her, knowing he couldn't let things end where they had. "For the record, I cared more about you than any woman I've ever been involved with, Brielle."

She closed her eyes again, as if praying for patience or shielding her emotions. She toyed with the keys she'd taken out of her scrub top pocket. "That's nice, but it wasn't enough. Not then and not now. Have a nice life, Ross."

CHAPTER FOUR

ALTHOUGH PHYSICALLY, mentally, and emotionally exhausted from her workday and her ordeal with Ross, Brielle smiled at the image that greeted her when she stepped into her living room.

Toy building blocks were everywhere. In the midst of all the colorful blocks the two most important men in her life concentrated diligently on their efforts.

Justice added a block-bottomed flag to what appeared to be a bridge connecting two towering structures. He leaned back to survey his work.

"What do you think, Uncle Vann?"

The lean six-foot cardiologist, who was too serious for most of the world but who turned into a great big kid himself around his nephew, grinned and gave a thumbs-up. "Perfect touch, kiddo. Wish I'd thought of it myself."

Brielle loved her brother. A better man had never existed. How his long-time girlfriend could constantly turn down his marriage proposals, Brielle didn't begin to understand. She just hoped that whatever was holding Samantha back from grabbing hold of happily-ever-after with Vann would work out soon. Her brother deserved every happiness.

Then again, did anyone ever really get happily-ever-after outside fairy-tales?

Certainly no one in her life ever had.

"I see you two have been busy," she said softly, causing both males to glance up from where they worked on the floor.

"Mommy!" Justice's face lit up with excitement. He leapt to his feet and wrapped his tiny arms around her upper legs.

Heart swelling with joy and her eyes tearing just a little, she laughed and basked in her son's love. Soon enough he'd outgrow showering his affections on her, but for now she was the center of his world. She cherished each moment of his precious life.

She dropped to her knees and hugged her son to her, kissing the top of his shiny blond head. "I missed you today!"

She always missed him when they were apart. She loved her job, but nothing compared to the time she spent with Justice. Their son looked so much like Ross. Seeing him only reinforced how much Justice favored him. Same eyes, same mouth, same smile, same ability to twist her heart into a million pieces.

"Come look at what Uncle Vann and I made. A whole kingdom." Just as quickly as his attention had turned to her, his focus was once again on what he and his uncle had been building. He tugged on her hand and led her to where Vann sat on the floor. "This is my castle and this is Uncle Vann's. Mine's stronger and has a magic force field."

"A magic force field, eh? I didn't even know they made magic force field building blocks," Brielle mused, checking out their handiwork.

"Obviously you've been buying your blocks at the

wrong stores," Vann promptly informed her with a wink. "I did inform him that my castle has more heart."

"Just 'cos he's a heart doctor," Justice explained, eyeing his uncle's castle critically. "My castle has lotsa heart, too, plus the magic force field."

As he had been much of Brielle's life, her brother had been a godsend where Justice was concerned. Could she have survived those first few months of Justice's life, helplessly watching her tiny premature son fight for every breath, every milestone without her brother's unwavering support and love?

"Obviously," Brielle agreed, her gaze falling on the new toy packaging on her sofa. She smiled, more grateful to her brother than words could ever convey. "You'll have to let me in on the secret to knowing which packages contain the magic blocks."

Vann and Justice exchanged glances. "Think we should train her on the secret ancient methods of sensing special powers?"

Justice considered his uncle's question a moment then nodded. "She is my mom, you know."

"I know…" Vann ruffled Justice's hair "…but she's also a girl. Sometimes we guys have to stick together, you know, look out for one another when it comes to womenfolk."

"Moms aren't real girls, Uncle Vann," Justice explained with a "duh" expression, taking Brielle's hand and pointing out different aspects of their handiwork. "'Mantha isn't a real girl either. She's nice."

"Nice. Right," Vann said with a touch of sarcasm, making Brielle wonder if he and Samantha were arguing again. After fifteen years of dating, you'd think they'd have worked out the kinks by now, but perhaps some couples never worked out all the kinks.

Brielle sat down on the floor cross-legged and pulled her son into her lap, hugging his wiggling, giggling body close to her, breathing in the scent of his shampoo. Happiness filled her. Life was good. She didn't need anything more. Not a relationship with Ross or whatever he'd come to Bean's Creek to accomplish. She didn't need anything he could give her.

Not anything beyond what he'd already unknowingly given.

A big twinge twisted her heart like a dishrag.

She couldn't imagine not knowing her son, not being a part of his daily life, all the firsts, all the adventures, all the day-to-day miracles of watching him grow. Just the thought of not having experienced those things with her son made her chest ache.

Made her question long-ago decisions.

Never had she meant to keep Justice from Ross. She'd repeatedly tried to tell him once she'd realized he wasn't going to jump on board with getting married. Silly, but she'd hoped he'd take her hints and sweep her off her feet without her telling him her birth control had failed. She'd wanted him to propose because it was what he wanted, because she was the woman he wanted to spend his life with, not because they were going to be parents.

Instead, he'd balked.

Still, she'd meant to tell him, would have told him had he not kept interrupting her, telling her that they were finished and he wanted nothing more to do with her, and had she not been so devastated by what she'd seen when she'd gone to Boston to finally tell him.

She closed her eyes, breathed Justice in again, and reminded herself that she'd only given Ross exactly what he'd told her he wanted. She'd left him alone, let him live his life the way he wanted, and she hadn't interfered with his dreams.

When she opened her eyes, her gaze met her brother's. Something about how he watched her struck Brielle as odd. She couldn't quite label the expression on his face, just knew something was going on in that brilliant mind of his besides which plastic block castle was his and which one was Justice's.

Then again, they hadn't had a chance to talk about Ross's appearance. Vann had texted her the day before to tell her he'd pick Justice up from preschool so he could spend some time with his nephew and that he'd see her when she got home.

"Thanks for staying late," she told him. "Sorry I called so last minute to make sure it was okay."

"No problem. There's leftover pizza in the kitchen," her brother told her, watching her with an intensity she imagined he used while assessing his patients.

"Pizza!" Justice jumped up from her lap and grabbed hold of her hand, tugging her up. "Uncle Vann let me order whatever I wanted on our pizza. I don't like black, uh—leaves."

Brielle laughed at her son's wrinkled nose and disgusted expression.

"He ordered one with everything and one with just the things you like. Go figure."

Realizing that despite meeting Ross at Julian's and their discussion at his place about her skipping meals, she'd actually ended up not eating a thing. Neither did she feel hungry, but she knew she needed to eat. She put a few slices on a paper plate and ate in the living room while her brother and Justice took toy bulldozers and demolished each other's castles with a lot of sound effects. They visited and laughed until Justice's bedtime. Brielle gave her son his bath, tucked him into bed with a story, lots of kisses, and a prayer. Within minutes he was sound asleep and with one last kiss to his forehead she went to find her brother.

He'd completely cleared away all traces of their building/demolition spree and now reclined, flipping through the television channels with the outstretched remote.

"Nothing's on," he commented, setting the controller on the chair arm. "He down for the night?"

Nodding, Brielle sank onto the sofa. "Thanks for clearing up the blocks, but that doesn't get you off the hook."

"You're welcome, and I didn't know I was on the hook."

"You didn't return my calls earlier this week," she reminded him, nervous energy keeping at bay the fatigue she should be feeling after her long day.

He shrugged. "You said there wasn't an emergency. I knew I'd see you today. Tell me about why you were late coming home tonight."

She eyed her brother closely. If Vann Winton was the type of man to squirm, he'd be wiggling against the leather recliner. He didn't, of course, not her big, brave older brother, but he may as well have.

"You know exactly why I was late coming home tonight, don't you? You knew he was coming." She couldn't bring herself to say Ross's name out loud.

Not bothering to pretend he didn't know exactly what

and who she meant, Vann sighed. "Samantha told me as soon as she learned who was filling in for Dr. Jenkins. I can't say I was surprised."

Brielle's heart rate picked up. "Why? How could his showing up to work at the hospital where I work not be a surprise after all this time? Do you two stay in touch?"

"No." Vann's expression pinched and Brielle had another twinge of guilt, one triggered by how her relationship with Ross had affected his relationship with her brother. Vann shifted in the recliner, shrugged. "I ran into him a few weeks ago."

"Ran into him?" Panic replaced her guilt. Had Vann mentioned Justice?

"At the medical conference I spoke at in Philadelphia. He was also one of the presenters and our paths crossed a couple of times."

"That was almost two months ago," she accused, feeling as if her chest was caving in around her lungs. "Knowing what you know, you didn't bother to mention running into him?" Her heart beat wildly against her ribcage. Had Ross known all along and just been faking not knowing about their son? Had he been waiting for her to tell him?

"Why would I mention him to you?" Vann's eyes narrowed suspiciously. "You're over the man, right?"

"Right, but…" She trailed off, took a deep breath, and reminded herself to remain calm. "You know the reasons you should have mentioned seeing him to me."

His face tightened. "Justice?"

Brielle didn't answer. There was no point in answering. Not when he already knew the answer. He'd never asked if Justice was Ross's child. He hadn't had to.

"That doesn't explain why you thought he might come here."

"He asked me about you a dozen times in Philly."

Her heart quickened. "Asked what?"

"How you were, if you were married, if you were seeing anyone, if you ever mentioned him, where you lived. Those kinds of questions. He couldn't seem to get enough information about you."

Panic hit afresh. "What did you tell him?"

"I didn't tell him about Justice, if that's what you're wondering."

No, that was her job and what weighed on her mind.

"You need to tell him."

Her brother's words crashed into her thoughts.

"Why do you say that?"

Vann just stared straight into her soul, the same way he had at any point in her life when he was waiting for her to do what he considered the "right thing".

"This isn't taking a tube of lipstick back to a department store, Vann."

He didn't say a word. He didn't have to. Just as he hadn't had to when she'd gotten mixed up with the wrong crowd back in the ninth grade and had made a stupid mistake. He'd been right then. Yes, returning the make-up she'd taken had been a horribly humiliating experience, but the right action. However, this was her son's life they were talking about. Her life.

"I tried to tell him," she reminded him, hating it that her voice whined, that she sounded so defensive.

Vann didn't blink.

"He said he didn't want anything to do with me." Saying the words out loud ripped scabs off wounds best left untouched. "I tried to tell him, and he wouldn't listen."

"Maybe he wasn't ready to hear what you had to say."

Brielle's jaw dropped at her brother's calm tone. "You're defending him? Really? Why would you do that?"

Vann took a deep breath, ran his fingers through his dark hair, which was graying slightly at the temples. "All I'm saying is that maybe he's ready now to hear what you have to say. Maybe that's why he's here."

Brielle's chest swelled with—was that frustration? Anger? Hurt? "What about me? Who says I was ready to have an unplanned pregnancy thrust on me? To sit week after week in NICU, praying my premature son lived while he went off to build his career? To chase other women?"

"He didn't know about Justice, Brielle. If he had, he would have married you."

"Oh, yes, every girl's happily-ever-after dream. To know the man she loves is only with her because she got knocked up." Oh how the thought of that hurt. Like mother, like daughter. "That's so not what I wanted and you of all people should understand that."

"Don't be crude and don't compare yourself to our mother," Vann scolded, then drew his brows together in a slight scowl. "Loves? As in present tense?"

Brielle rolled her eyes. "I was speaking about in the past. Until this week I hadn't seen the man in five years."

"Yet in the few days he's been here he's put you in a major whirlwind."

"Of course he has. I'd be foolish if I wasn't upset. What if he tries to take Justice away from me?"

Vann's expression darkened. "He wouldn't do that. You're a good mother."

She stared at her brother. "Can you guarantee that? Because I'm not willing to risk losing my son to that man."

"*That man* is his father."

"Yes, but…" Oh, how she hated it when Vann made sense, when he was logical, when his voice remained calm but his words delivered thunderous blows, *when he was right*.

She collapsed back into the fluffy cushions on her sofa, closed her eyes, and faced the inevitable.

She had to tell Ross about their son.

As if the devil heard her thought and mocked the decision she'd been going back and forth on from the moment she'd first seen Ross in Bean's Creek, Brielle's doorbell rang.

When she opened the door, a distraught Ross stood on her doorstep.

CHAPTER FIVE

ROSS STARED AT Brielle's shocked expression and tried to recall what argument he'd given himself on why he had a right to follow her home, to drive around aimlessly mulling over all the things they'd said, on why he now stood on her doorstep.

"Can we talk?"

"I…" She glanced over her shoulder, as if looking at someone, then glanced back at him. "We can." She closed her eyes. "We need to." She swallowed hard. "But now isn't a good time."

Ross glanced at the expensive luxury sedan in her driveway, realization dawning. "You have a man here?"

The man? The one she claimed to love? His stomach clenched. Sweat prickled his skin.

"Yes, she does," a deep male voice answered. "What about it?"

"Vann." A myriad of emotions struck Ross. Initially, relief that Brielle hadn't gone from his arms to another man's, then overwhelming regret. This man had been his college roommate, his best friend. Why had he not fought to repair the friendship after his and Brielle's break-up? Why had he let their friendship end too? He'd lost his two best friends when he'd left North Carolina. No wonder he'd been so bone-aching miserable and lonely when he'd first arrived in Boston that he'd gone on a social whirl, trying to fill the void.

"Good to see you," he said with brute honesty.

His former friend eyed him for long moments, then surprised him by turning to Brielle.

"I've got to head to Samantha's." He bent and kissed her cheek. To Ross he only nodded then walked past him out the door.

"Don't go!" Brielle practically begged her brother. "Please, don't go."

Vann paused, turned, looked directly at her. "I figure you two have things to talk about that I'd just be a third wheel for, but..." his gaze cut to Ross and his expression hardened "...I'm only a phone call away if I'm needed."

Yeah, Ross knew exactly what Vann meant. Hurt his sister again and he'd do more than bloody his nose. That had been Vann's promise.

Brielle was staring at her brother in shock. No doubt she'd never heard the dark threat in Vann's tone before. Vann didn't do dark, but when it came to Brielle he'd hold his own with anyone.

Ross nodded his understanding at the man glaring at him.

"You don't have to go, Vann," Brielle began again, obviously not wanting her brother to leave. Did she think she needed protection from Ross?

Recalling how hot the fires burned between them, perhaps they both needed protection.

"You know I do, sis." Vann's expression seemed to be saying a lot more than his words. "You're going to be fine. Regardless, you will be fine."

Swallowing, she nodded.

"Call if you need anything. I'll be at Samantha's all weekend." He winced. "Unless we argue again."

Ross couldn't help but wonder at Vann's comment. Were he and Samantha having problems? They'd been together so long he just assumed they got along. Maybe more had changed over the past five years than just his relationship with Brielle.

He and Brielle stood on her porch, watching her brother get into his car and drive away until the tail-lights had disappeared down the street.

Crickets chirped in the distance. The smell of some-one's barbecue floated on the night air. Ross cleared his throat.

"I suppose we could go in." She didn't sound thrilled at the prospect.

"If you don't want to, we could sit in your porch swing and talk," he offered, trying to ease her discom-fort and perhaps even his own.

Her gaze went to the porch swing built for two. He watched the emotions flash across her face, knew ex-actly what she was thinking. The porch swing was made for two without extra space for avoiding touching each other.

"No, come inside. We just have to keep it down be-cause Justice is asleep."

"Justice?"

Brielle's face paled. Her mouth dropped open. She grasped the doorjamb as if to steady herself.

"I can explain," she said, but she didn't. She couldn't do more than just stare at him, her eyes filled with what? Horror? Shock? Fear?

"Who is Justice?" he asked, knowing he wasn't going

to like the answer. "The man you mentioned earlier? He's here? Asleep in your house?"

She winced, shook her head. "No."

"Then who is sleeping in your house? Who is Justice?"

She swallowed. Hard. "My son."

Shock reverberated through him with the force of an earthquake.

"You have a son?" Ross was certain that it was his eyes, his very soul that were filled with horror, shock, fear. An odd, extremely painful tug ripped at his heart. Brielle had a son. "Why didn't Vann tell me you had a kid? Why didn't you tell me?" He knew his words were accusing, but he didn't care. Brielle had a child. How could she have done that to him? The thought of her having a child felt like the ultimate betrayal. Had he really expected her to have just been waiting for him the past five years? Perhaps, arrogantly, he had. He raked his fingers through his hair then grimaced, took a deep breath. "You really have a child?"

Still gripping the doorjamb for dear life, she nodded.

"A son." He took an even deeper breath, needing oxygen in his aching lungs, needing clarity for his racing mind. "Is his father still in the picture? Is he the man you claim to love?"

"His fath— No," Brielle shook her head, not meeting his eyes. "I did love him, but he isn't in the picture. He hasn't been for some time."

Ross's brows came together in a deep V, digging almost painfully into his forehead. "Not at all? Not you or your son's?"

"He hasn't been a part of my life for a long time. Or Justice's."

Justice. Her son. That odd tug yanked at his chest again. He just couldn't believe Brielle had a child. He tried to picture her pregnant, to imagine her belly swollen with child, and he just couldn't. Curvier through her hips and breasts, her body was even better than it had been five years ago.

"Justice..." Ross said the name slowly, letting the boy's name roll off his tongue. Brielle was a mother. His Brielle. None of his fantasies of her had featured discovering that she was a mother. He didn't like the ragged emotion jagging through his mind and body. Jealousy that some man had shared that with Brielle. Red-hot, raging jealousy. She'd given birth to another man's child. Only the idiot hadn't stuck around. Disappointment that she had that strong a connection to another man, to a child who depended on her for all his needs, hit Ross in the solar plexus.

Selfishly he wanted her to himself, wanted time to explore remaining feelings between them. Instead, she really had moved on, had another life that was far beyond anything he'd imagined.

"I'm not sure what to say. I wasn't prepared for this."

"I..." She grimaced, closed her eyes then met his gaze with steely determination shining in her gaze. "Let's go inside."

Ramming his trembling fingers into his pants pockets, he followed her into the house, processing the idea of Brielle as a mother, taking in everything around him.

Unlike the apartment they'd shared, Brielle's house oozed warmth and hominess. Their apartment had been efficient and minimalist. Pictures lined these walls. Pictures of a little boy who looked remarkably like his mother with his pale hair and big eyes. They were blue rather than brown, but those eyes were so similar to

Brielle's that he stopped to stare at a photo of the boy sitting in his mother's lap. Rather than facing the camera directly, they'd been looking at each other, Brielle smiling, the boy laughing up at her.

"How old is he in this one?"

Brielle paused, took a deep breath then gazed at the photo he was referring to. "He's two there."

Two. He realized he didn't even know how old Brielle's son was. "And now?"

She stared at the photo long moments, inhaled sharply. "Is there a particular reason you're here, Ross? I've had a long day."

"I wanted…" His gaze went back to the photo, stared at the boy, at the pure love and joy shining in Brielle's eyes and expression as she gazed at her son. "You're a good mother, aren't you?"

Her mouth opened then closed. Her face unreadable, she continued to look at the photo then shrugged. "I love my son. He's my whole world. I try to do what's right for him, but I'm human and make a lot of mistakes along the way."

"He's lucky to have you for a mother."

"I hope you feel that way after…" Her voice trailed off. She closed her eyes, shifted her feet, filled her chest with air then blew it out slowly.

"After…?" he prompted, instinctively knowing that whatever she'd been going to say, it had been monumental.

"Let's go and sit down."

Odd. She'd never been one to avoid conflict in the past. If anything, she'd wanted to discuss everything right then and there. Then again, there really hadn't been a lot for them to discuss. They'd rarely fought until those last few weeks.

"What changed at the end of our relationship?"

Her brow lifted. "What do you mean?"

"You were different. Why?"

"You're right. I did change." She sighed. "That's one of the things we need to talk about."

"'One of'?"

"First, tell me why you are here."

It was his turn to take that deep breath and slowly release it from his uncooperative lungs.

"Because all I could think about was you," he admittedly truthfully, knowing tonight he had to set pride aside and be straightforward with her. "I wanted to be sure you made it home okay after you felt bad, so I followed you. I just wanted to be sure you made it okay, so I drove on past and just kept driving and driving. This evening was running through my mind and I just kept coming back to the fact that I've missed you."

"You said that earlier," she reminded him. "Why come here to say it again?"

"Because I felt like things were left wrong between us when I dropped you at your car. As if, instead of settling anything, we'd just muddied the water even more."

She flexed her fingers at her sides, curled them tightly into her fists. "You're here to clear the water?"

"I'm here because I couldn't stay away." Which was the truth, whether he wanted to admit it or not. He reached for her then stopped himself. "I want you, Brielle. The fact that you have a child doesn't change that." He raked his fingers through his hair. "Not really. Even now, I just want to take you into my arms and kiss you until you forget every man you've ever been with other than me. Until my name is the only one leaving your lips."

* * *

Brielle hadn't been prepared for this conversation. Not tonight. Sure, she'd imagined it hundreds of times in her mind, but never quite this way.

She closed her eyes, searching for the right words. Whatever words she chose, her life was going to be changed for ever. Once she told Ross about Justice their relationship would be changed for ever.

Not that she thought he'd want marriage, not now. Just as well, she'd never marry a man just because of a child.

If she'd learned nothing else from her mother's mistakes, she'd learned that lesson. Twice her mother had gotten pregnant by men who hadn't been her husband. Both times the men had married her "for the baby's sake". Both times the marriages had been dismal failures because, really, how could a marriage be a success when it wasn't based on love and knowing that person was *the one*?

Her mother, a sad, bitter, and lonely woman, had died during Brielle's senior year of high school.

"Does the turmoil on your face mean you're struggling because you want me too?" He sounded hopeful. "Tell me you want me to touch you as much as I want to touch you."

Part of her was still startled that Ross was admitting he wanted her. Then again, physical attraction wasn't enough. If it was, she'd be doing a lot more than telling him she wanted his touch. She'd be touching and kissing and dragging him into her bedroom.

Curling her fingers into her palms, she sighed, walked into her living room and sat on her sofa. "Touching isn't a good idea for a zillion reasons and that isn't what I need to talk to you about."

Joining her on the sofa, he regarded her for seconds that seemed to drag out much longer. "I could give you a zillion reasons why touching is a very good idea, but we'll do this your way. What is it you want to talk to me about?"

"Justice."

"What is it about Justice—" his face pinched as he said the name "—that you want to talk about?"

"Like I told you before, he's my whole world. I'd do anything to protect him."

He nodded. "I wouldn't expect less from you, Brielle. I've no doubt that you really are a great mother. Surely you don't think I'd do anything to interfere with your relationship with your son?"

Despite her current stress level, his praise pleased her. "No, I don't think you would interfere with my relationship with Justice." Or did she? "At least, I hope you won't." But the reality was that Ross *would* interfere with her relationship with her son. Just his very presence in their lives would shake up their whole world. "The thing is, well, Justice is—"

"Mommy?"

Both Brielle and Ross turned toward the sound as Justice padded into the living room in his superhero pajamas, well-loved stuffed frog in his hand. Why the kid had latched onto the long, skinny, stuffed frog she wasn't sure, but Ribbets was his favorite must-have sleeping companion.

"I need a drink of water," Justice continued, rubbing his sleep-swollen eyes then staring directly at Ross. "Who is that man?"

Your daddy.

The only man I've ever loved.

The man I'm trying to confess a five-year-old secret to.

"This is Dr. Ross Lane. He works at the hospital with Mommy and he's…" She searched for the right description of Ross for their son since she wouldn't be using any of her previous thoughts. "He's a friend of Uncle Vann's. They went to school together when they were in college."

"Uncle Vann is awesome," her son said with conviction, giving Ross a closer look. He wasn't used to waking up to find a strange man in their house. Curiosity and uncertainty creased his forehead.

"That he is," Ross said, seeming to finally find his tongue as he'd not spoken since Justice had interrupted their conversation.

Brielle scooped Justice up in her arms, knowing she wouldn't be able to do so for much longer as he was growing like a weed. She loved the feel of her son in her arms, of his freshly washed hair and warm little body. Her heart swelled at how much he meant to her, how much he'd blessed her life.

"Come on, Bruce," she said gently, kissing the top of his head. "Let's get you that water so you can get back to bed."

"Bruce?" Ross asked, looking confused and a bit overwhelmed. She'd felt his gaze on her and Justice while she held him, had sensed his curiosity and even awkwardness, as if he felt he was watching something private, just between them, that he shouldn't be witnessing yet couldn't bring himself to look away.

Brielle pointed to her son's superhero-covered pajamas.

"Oh, right." He laughed low, unnatural sounding almost. "Bruce."

Justice found his comment or something about it funny and began to laugh, too.

Curious about how strong, confident Ross looked and sounded awkward, Brielle hugged the giggling boy to her, kissed his brow. "Come on, giggle box. Water, then back to bed for you."

Knowing exactly how to wrap his mother around his precious little fingers, Justice put his hands on her cheeks, palms flat, and kissed her. Normally, she might have given in, held him in her lap, and just enjoyed the moment. Not tonight. Not with the past waiting to engulf her.

"That was a great kiss," she informed her son. "But you still have to go back to bed."

Frowning, Justice shook his head, his fine blond hair flying away from his head with the movement. "Uncle Vann's friend is here and I should take care of Uncle Vann's friend for him." He spoke so fast, making his argument, Brielle couldn't help but appreciate her son's sharp little mind. "He would want me to."

Fighting the squeezing motion gripping her heart, Brielle stared at her son and was curious about where his thoughts had gone. "Just how would you take care of Uncle Vann's friend?"

"I'd teach him how to build a castle like me and Uncle Vann did. You'd like that, wouldn't you?" Her son turned wide blue eyes to Ross and, just as everyone else was, Ross seemed instantly charmed by their son.

Looking directly at Justice, his face intent, he nodded. "I'm an expert castle builder. The best in the state."

Justice's eyes got huge then he shook his head, sending his hair flying again. "Nope. Uncle Vann is the best. I know he is."

Brielle's heart caught in mid-beat.

"Not biased, are you, champ?"

Justice's big blue eyes lifted to her at Ross's question.

Knowing her son didn't understand Ross's comment, she clarified. "Dr. Lane just means that you love Uncle Vann very much and sometimes when you love someone, that makes you think they are the best."

Justice, sharp as ever, seized the moment. "Like you are the best mommy ever?"

Brielle couldn't keep from kissing her son's downy head. "Exactly. Now, let's get you that water and back to bed."

Ross followed her and Justice to the kitchen, watched as she got her son's water, watched the little boy take a sip and hand the cup back to his mother with a big smile.

"Thank you," Justice said automatically, reaching for her to pick him up again. Brielle did so, letting him wrap his legs around her waist and his arms around her neck. "Love you."

"Love you, too, Bruce."

Justice giggled at her pet name for him and buried his face against her chest, yawning.

Unable to look towards Ross, she walked past him to carry her son to his bed, tucked him in, and told him a quick story while lightly scratching his back until he fell asleep.

For long moments she watched him in the low light given off from his superhero nightlight.

The safe little existence she'd made for them was about to change for ever.

Her heart beat so loudly she couldn't believe it didn't awaken her precious child.

Tonight she'd tell Justice's father that he had a son.

Ross stood in the doorway of the little boy's bedroom, watching as Brielle went through the ritual of getting her son back to sleep. The soft, soothing tone of her voice as she told Justice a story about saying good-night to the moon did little to ease the very real agitation moving through him.

Agitation he didn't understand.

Not at first.

But as he watched the motion of her hands moving gently back and forth across the sleeping boy's back, the unease that had gripped him from the moment he'd realized she had a child began to make perfect sense.

"He's mine."

Brielle's head shot up at his low words, staring at him across the dimly lit room.

Despite the truth written all over her guilty face, he needed to hear her say the words.

"He is my son, isn't he?"

Her hand stilled, flattened against the sleeping boy's back almost protectively. "I…" She stopped then stood slowly, taking care not to disturb Justice. "Let's go talk."

She wasn't denying it.

Brielle wasn't telling him that he was crazy, that he'd lost his mind.

She wasn't telling him that she'd met someone, gotten pregnant on the rebound, and had had that man's child.

She'd been pregnant when he'd left for Boston.

She'd given birth to his son and had never bothered to tell him.

As she walked past him to head back into the living room, he wanted to grab her shoulders, shake her, demand to know why she hadn't told him, why she would have done something so cruel. Had she hated him so much when he'd left?

She didn't look at him, just waited for him to move out of the doorway then gently pushed the door closed.

Without a word, she turned to go to the living room. He supposed it made sense to move away from the boy's room so they didn't wake him again, but he couldn't wait another second.

"Say the words, Brielle. Tell me what we both know is the truth." He spat out the demand, knowing in his soul what was coming, what seemed impossible yet blared through his being as the truth.

The truth that it seemed imperative to have confirmed verbally.

"Justice is your son." Her tone was deadpan, as if her words didn't have the effect of a tornado ripping through his mind and chest, leaving everything within him in turmoil.

She stood there, not looking at him, hands at her sides, body slightly trembling, and waited.

Ross was waiting himself.

Waiting for an explanation of why she hadn't told him about his child.

CHAPTER SIX

BRIELLE'S ENTIRE INSIDES shook. Her tongue swelled to where it stuck to the roof of her mouth. Her brain spun like a child's toy top. She felt so dizzy she thought she might fall. Her head pounded as if her eardrums had taken up a jungle beat. But she stood firm, not looking at Ross but waiting for a reaction from him.

She half expected him to turn, leave her house, and never darken her doorstep again.

Another part of her expected him to rush into Justice's room, wake him up and tell him he was his daddy.

His daddy.

Justice's father.

Tears burned her eyes, blurring her vision. Not that it mattered that she couldn't see. It didn't because she refused to look at Ross, refused to see whatever was on his face.

Her mind was doing a bang-up job of filling in the blanks anyway. Anger. Hurt. Betrayal. Disgust. Disbelief.

"You have a lot of explaining to do." His voice broke into her imaginary cocoon. He grabbed her hand. His grip didn't hurt, but he wasn't gentle either as he pulled her towards the living room, away from where their son slept.

Tension bubbled so hot she was amazed the paint didn't peel from the walls as they passed by.

"When is my son's birthday?"

His angry tone triggered a hundred old hurts, a thousand wishes of Ross being there to share Justice's birth and each year's celebration of that special day, a thousand moments of feeling so abandoned without the man she'd given her heart to without reserve. Every protective wall she had flew up.

"Perhaps if you'd stuck around you'd know the answer to that question." Sarcasm was so thick on her tongue that it left a bitter taste in her mouth, but she dug her feet in, putting a halt to their trip down the hallway. She jutted her chin and glared straight into Ross's vivid blue eyes.

Eyes that were so like her son's.

His gaze narrowed. His jaw tightened then worked back and forth once. "When was he born? How long after I left was it before my son was born?"

She told him Justice's birth date.

She watched him do the math in his head. "That's just…" His gaze grew darker, more accusing. "You knew you were pregnant when I left, didn't you?"

"He was a couple of months early." Her chin went up another notch. "But so what if I knew? What difference does that make? Either way, you left."

His jaw dropped as if he couldn't believe what she was saying. "You were pregnant with my child and didn't tell me? Don't you think that's something I had a right to know?"

Anger and hurt swelled her chest. Lifting her shoulders, she repeated words that had haunted her time and again over the years since he'd carelessly tossed them at her. "You gave up your rights when you told me you didn't want anything to do with me or anything that involved me. My son involves me. I took you at your word."

His jaw began working back and forth again, then he tugged on her arm, pulling her the rest of the way into the living room. She let him for the sole reason of hoping they didn't wake Justice.

Again without hurting her but with some force, he pushed her toward the sofa. "Sit."

With pleasure, she thought, flopping onto the sofa. Much better to sit than to end up falling on her face because of her wobbly, nervous legs.

Ross didn't sit. He stood next to the sofa, staring at her as if he were looking at a stranger. "Let me get this straight. You think my saying I wanted our relationship to end gave you the right to keep my son from me?"

I wanted our relationship to end.

Hearing him say the words sliced way too deep for five years to have passed. Maybe some blows never stopped wounding no matter how many times they'd pierced your soul.

Then again, Ross sounded pierced as well. Would he really have wanted her to tell him? To have interfered in his life?

"It's not as if I hid him, Ross." She went for flippant, but knew her attempt fell flat. "You were the one who left us."

"I didn't leave *him*," he thundered. "I didn't even know he existed."

She flinched at his harshness, at the searing truth of his claim. "Fine. You left me and he was a part of me. Same difference."

"Wrong!" As if he could no longer stand still, he paced across the room, turning and meeting her gaze. "I wouldn't have left if I'd known you were pregnant. You know I wouldn't have."

There it was. The truth she'd known and avoided so thoroughly because a man staying with her because she'd been pregnant had been the last thing she'd wanted. She'd wanted him to stay because of her, because he'd loved her and wanted her in his life for ever. She'd believed Ross had, but she'd been wrong. Never would she have trapped him into staying. She wasn't her mother.

"You think I would have let you stay if the only reason you were staying was because I was pregnant? Hardly."

"That wouldn't have been the only reason and you know it."

"I know nothing. You left so whatever the other reasons were, they weren't enough."

"I didn't know," he repeated.

"Lucky you," she seethed, going on the offensive because she didn't like being defensive, didn't like any of the feelings swirling around in her chest. "Nothing to stand in the way of your career aspirations."

"Lucky me?" He resumed his pacing, his hands thrust deep in his pockets as if he didn't know what else to do with them. Or perhaps it was to keep him from wrapping them round her neck because he looked as if he'd like to do that and more. "I've missed out on almost five years of my son's life and you call me lucky?"

When he put it like that…

"You don't even like kids," she accused, guilt punching a hole in her argument.

He stopped, turned to face her, his cheeks blotched red. "Who said I don't like kids?"

Brielle slid her hands under her thighs, feeling restless just sitting on the sofa. "I saw how you reacted earlier when I said I had a son, how you clammed up when you discovered I was a mother."

"Exactly. I discovered you were a mother." He made his claim sound like a dirty accusation. "You should have told me, Brielle. You had no right to keep that to yourself. No right whatsoever."

"I had every right." But she hadn't. Hadn't she already admitted that to herself?

"No, you didn't. He is mine. Just as much mine as yours."

Fear replaced guilt and she jumped to her feet, started pacing herself.

"What is that supposed to mean? Justice is my son." If she'd been close enough to Ross she'd have poked her finger in his face to emphasize her point. "I wanted him when you very plainly told me that you no longer wanted anything to do with me or anything that was even slightly involved with me. You told me you didn't want me in your life. Well, Justice has to do with me, is more than slightly involved with me. I carried him in my body, loved him from the moment I found out about him and more and more every day since. He is mine. You didn't want him."

"Have you not heard a word I've said? I didn't know he existed." He enunciated each word slowly, emphasizing his point.

She crossed her arms over her chest. "If you'd stuck around, you would have known."

"I shouldn't have had to stick around to know I'd

fathered a child. You should have told me the moment you discovered you were pregnant." Confusion lit his face. Sincere, real confusion. And hurt. Hurt that ran so deep he looked gutted. "Why didn't you?"

The emotional damn she'd erected to hold in over five years worth of doubt and pain burst. Tears flowed down her face and she swatted at the hot moisture. She hated this. Hated having to admit to how she'd felt when she'd discovered she was pregnant, hated it that all those same fears and insecurities were swamping her present.

"Because I loved you." She mumbled the words but couldn't manage anything clearer.

"Speak up. I couldn't understand you."

After a deep breath, she repeated herself.

He laughed. An ironic laugh, not humorous at all, that grated along her raw nerves. "You loved me? How can you say that?" He gazed at her with contempt. "You stole something from me that I can never get back."

"I…" She wrapped her arms tighter around herself, wishing she could find a glimmer of comfort. What could she say? He was right. He couldn't ever get the time back with Justice that she'd denied him. "I didn't think you wanted to be in his life."

"A decision you made without consulting me," he pointed out, his expression terse. "You were wrong."

"I tried to tell you," she retorted defensively, reminding herself that she had attempted to tell him at their apartment and again when she'd gone to Boston.

"Right. You're a smart woman, Brielle. If you tried, I'd have known." He paced across the room, his gaze bouncing around the room, taking in every photo, every knick-knack.

Unsure what she should do, Brielle sat down again,

tucking her palms up under her legs, wishing she could just snuggle down into the cushions and forget any of this had happened.

"That's what changed, wasn't it? Those last few weeks when I couldn't figure out what had happened to the amazing, wonderful woman I'd been sharing my life with? You kept acting so strange and I couldn't figure out what was different. You knew you were pregnant that whole time and, rather than tell me, you..." He stopped walking, his eyes grew round, his face reddened so much she thought he might blow his top. "That's what the sudden urge to get married was all about. Brielle, all you had to do was tell me you were pregnant and I'd have married you."

Brielle cringed. Deep and all the way through her body she cringed. "I didn't want you to marry me because I was pregnant."

"But you *were* pregnant," he pointed out, missing her point.

Bile burned her throat and she swallowed. "Pregnancy was not going to be the reason I got married. Not then. Not now. Not ever."

Ross regarded her snidely. "How'd that work out for you? You are still single? Or perhaps there's something else you need to tell me?"

His harsh question had her head jerking towards him again. "What is that supposed to mean? You know exactly how it worked out for me. You left me. And, no, I am not married."

"I didn't leave," he corrected in a treacherous tone. "You drove me away."

She gasped, jumped back up from the sofa and glared at him. He was going to blame her for his decision to leave? Hardly. She had made mistakes, lots of them, but she hadn't wanted him to leave, far far from it. "I did no such thing."

"Sure you did. With the sudden constant tolling of wedding bells and the bridal magazines left on every flat surface in our apartment, you wouldn't stop going on about marriage and weddings. You stopped talking to me about anything but marriage and weddings and then you stopped talking to me altogether, Brielle. You were too busy being angry at me to talk to me. Say what you will, but you drove me away."

She shook her head, not willing to accept the blame. "I was trying to give you a hint."

"If you'd wanted to get married perhaps you should have been leaving baby rattles and packs of diapers around instead of bridal magazines. I might have picked up on what you were really trying to tell me."

Acid hit the back of her throat. "I told you that I didn't want to get married because I was pregnant." She knew first hand what those marriages usually led to. An unhappy life together and eventual divorce. "I wanted to get married because I was loved."

"I did love you!"

Brielle's legs gave way and she flopped onto the sofa. She'd never heard him say those words. He never had.

She'd believed he'd loved her but never had he said them.

Until just now. In the past tense. Perhaps it would have been better to have never heard them than to feel the aching sense of loss that now swamped her. She dropped her head into her hands, feeling lost and over-whelmed.

"You never told me that," she reminded him. "Not ever."

"Like I told you earlier, I shouldn't have had to say the words." He sounded annoyed, but at least he had lowered his voice again. "Words weren't necessary. Not between us. I showed you every day how I felt about you."

"You did. You left me."

"Because you drove me away."

"Because you wanted to go to Boston. Tell me, Ross, how long before another woman was warming your bed? Because we both know it wasn't long."

"What is that supposed to mean?"

When she didn't answer he walked over to the sofa and sat down beside her, not touching her but close enough that she felt his body heat, felt the anger emanating from his every pore.

"Explain that comment, Brielle."

Hadn't she already said too much? But realistically she might as well tell him everything at this point. "I came there."

That took the wind out of his sails. "What?"

"I bought a ticket and I flew to Boston. I came to tell you about our baby, that I missed you more than I knew how to say." Her voice broke and she hated her weakness, hated how much he affected her, especially hated how much her next words hurt. "I was almost seven months pregnant and I came to tell you everything, but I saw you with another woman."

She couldn't keep the pain from her voice. She tried, but failed miserably.

"And then what? You judged me unworthy and left without telling me because I'd moved on? I dated other

women, Brielle. That didn't give you the right to leave
without telling me I was going to be a father."

His words hurt. Hurt deep. Deep down she'd wanted
a movie moment, one of those where he cleared up what
had really been happening that night, that the woman
had been a long-lost cousin, that what she'd thought
had looked like a romantic embrace hadn't really been
anything of the sort.

"I left because when I saw you with her, I knew I'd
been foolish to come there, that you'd meant what you'd
said. I left because you put to rest any doubt I had about
us and I had to move on with my life, too, without you."

His gaze narrowed. "I didn't have all the facts when
I said what I said. You know that."

"You had enough facts that you made the decision
to leave."

"I came back, Brielle. For you. I'm here right now.
We've been working together this week and you've said
nothing. Not a word about the fact that we have a son
together." He drove his point home. "Why haven't you
told me?"

"Over five years have passed since you left. I didn't
know why you were here."

"You knew I didn't randomly decide to work in
your hometown. I was here for you, but why I was here
doesn't matter. What matters is that I was here and you
didn't tell me that you'd given birth to my son. My son!"
His anger rolled across the room, shaking her to her
very core. "You continued to deceive me."

"I wasn't deceiving you," she said. "I never lied to
you."

"Same difference. You didn't tell me the truth."

"Fine. Now you know."

"Now I know," he replied, suddenly seeming dazed. "I have a son. Justice is my son."

"*We* have a son," she corrected him, not liking his possessive tone.

His blue gaze shifted to hers, bored into her, dared her to defy him in any way. "I plan to see him, to spend time with my son."

She wasn't sure if he was talking to her or just thinking out loud, but she nodded. After how he'd reacted to learning about his connection to Justice, she'd figured that. "I have no problem with you seeing him. You can visit him here some evenings."

He shook his head. "Not good enough. I want to get to know my son. A few hours in the evenings here and there aren't going to allow me to do that. I want more. Lots more."

More? Her ribcage tightened around her lungs. "What are you saying?"

He considered her question for a few seconds then made one of those quick, confident decisions that made him the excellent emergency room doctor he was. "I'm moving in."

"Pardon?" Brielle shook her head, sure she hadn't heard him correctly.

"You heard me, and it's not up for debate."

"You're not moving in here."

"Yes, I am." He looked quite pleased with his plan, quite the arrogant, self-assured man, quite the man whose brain was making plans faster than she could thwart them. "If you don't have a spare bedroom, yours will do just fine."

"I am not having sex with you!"

His eyes were cold when they turned to her. "Oh, you

don't have to worry about that any more, Brielle. Something about knowing that you kept my son from me has completely put out any flame that still burned for you."

His words stabbed deep into her chest and twisted the blade of regret painfully back and forth.

"If I stayed in your room, you could sleep on the bed, the floor, the living-room sofa." He patted the cushion for emphasis. "Or with Justice." He shrugged as if he didn't want to waste another moment even considering her. "Makes no difference because, regardless, I won't be touching you."

When she started to argue, he stopped her. "I'd suggest I sleep with Justice, but I figure it might traumatize the boy for a stranger to move into his room. Even if that stranger is his father that his mother failed to inform him of."

He meant the last to make her feel guilty again but she refused to allow him to pull that stunt with her. She'd worked hard, taken good care of her son. Ross had left on his own. He had no one to blame but himself.

"You can't just move into my house, Ross. I don't want you living here."

"This isn't about what you want. This is about what is right for Justice."

He had a point, but…

"You moving in here is right for him how?"

"He will get to know me, really know me, and I will get to know him—that is what's right. Perhaps you missed the memo, but boys need their fathers every bit as much as they need their mothers."

She couldn't argue with him. Not on that. Boys did need their fathers. Didn't Justice latch onto every second with Vann?

"There's a spare room where Vann stays sometimes. I'll clean it for you."

His haughty expression said he'd never doubted that he'd get his way, that he planned to get his way on a lot of other things too. He'd taken control of this situation and felt it within his rights to correct what he saw as major wrongs.

"Are you working tomorrow?"

She shook her head.

"I'll be by in the morning with my things." He headed to the front door. "And, Brielle?"

She met his gaze.

"Don't even think of running with my son," he warned, his voice icy. "Now that I know about Justice, I'd spend every breath I have left tracking you down, and when I found you, there would be hell to pay."

Ross paced back and forth across the living room of his leased apartment.

Nervous energy burned through him, singeing every nerve ending.

A son. He had a son. He and Brielle had a son.

An almost five-year-old son.

He'd missed nearly five years of his child's life.

He thought back to the end of their relationship, searching for some hint that she had been pregnant. Some hint that she had been trying to tell him more was going on than met the eye.

The truth was, with her erratic behavior he'd been in a claustrophobic frame of mind and he'd probably have even missed her clues if she had set baby rattles and diapers throughout their apartment.

All he'd known had been that he'd been offered that

great opportunity in Boston and he'd been torn about accepting it. Right up until he'd had enough of the bridal magazines, Brielle shutting him out, the awkwardness that had developed between them, her being mad at him more often than not, them arguing over nothing at all, and he'd called it quits.

Had he been looking for an out?

Tonight, in the heat of the moment, he'd told her he'd loved her. Words he'd never said out loud to any woman. He had cared more for Brielle than any other woman he'd ever known, but had he loved her?

He must have because the words had come from deep within him.

He had loved Brielle.

She'd deceived him in the worst way.

She'd given birth to his child and kept knowledge of that child from him.

He had an almost five-year-old son he knew nothing about.

Except that he looked like his mother and liked caped superheros.

And that the boy loved his mother.

Regardless of what he considered her wrongs, Brielle had obviously done a good job of raising their son. She was a good, loving mother, and their son adored her.

Which made things complicated.

Because Ross's gut instinct was to pursue custody, as much custody as a judge would grant him, and if that wasn't enough he'd take the case to a higher level, even if it cost him every dime he had. He would be in his son's life. But the logic that saw him through medical school and beyond warned that he had to proceed cautiously or he'd alienate his son before they ever had a chance to bond. Or traumatize him in ways therapists would warn would take him a lifetime to get over.

Ross had enough medical training to know the psychological impact his coming into his son's life could have, especially if he pulled the boy away from his mother in any shape, form, or fashion.

So he'd move in with them and Brielle would foster his relationship with Justice. Whether she wanted to or not. She owed him that much.

She owed him much more.

Once he had developed a relationship with his son, once he had all this sorted in his head about what was best for his son, then he'd decide what he was going to do about custody of his child.

Because he was going to be a part of his son's life.

An active, see-him-every-day part.

If Brielle didn't like that, it was too bad.

She'd had their son for five years, now was his turn.

CHAPTER SEVEN

THE NEXT MORNING, Brielle felt sick.

How in the world was she going to explain to Justice that Ross was moving into their house with them? Could she just say that Uncle Vann's friend was going to sleep over for a few nights and Justice not question why?

Worse, how was she going to explain to him that Ross was his father?

That one Justice would question, and big time.

Rightly so.

Her son was as sharp as a tack and was going to question everything. If not immediately then very quickly as his brain started adding up the facts and coming up without answers.

She leaned forward, banged her head against the refrigerator door. Justice had woken her as usual on her days off work by climbing into bed with her and snuggling up next to her with a bright "Time to wake up!"

She'd lain there, holding him, chatting with him about whatever popped into his brain, which was a plethora of topics ranging from dinosaurs to where rain came from to where Vann's friend was. That last one she'd dodged by starting a tickle-fest because she had no idea how to tell Justice about Ross's role in their lives.

When they'd gotten out of bed, she'd been intent

on maintaining her normal routine with her son, was currently in the kitchen to make breakfast for them both, but she wasn't getting much done. She kept getting distracted.

Because Ross would be there at some point.

To move in with them.

Or would he?

Why did her belly quicken at the thought that perhaps, instead of carrying through his threats of the night before, he'd high-tail it, just as he had five years ago?

To be fair, he hadn't known about their son.

As nervous as she was about the ramifications of Ross knowing about their son, she also admitted that she was glad he knew. She had never meant to keep Justice a secret from him.

She'd not told him immediately but had started hinting at marriage because in her mind she'd believed that's where they'd been heading anyway and, call her old-fashioned, but she'd wanted a proposal, a real one, not a shotgun wedding because she was "knocked up". In the end, she'd gotten neither and the longer she'd gone without telling him, the harder the thought of contacting him and telling him had become.

He'd been right. She had robbed him of something he couldn't get back. Five precious years of their son's life.

Yes, she was glad he knew.

She was also terrified.

"Mommy," Justice asked, stepping into the kitchen, fully dressed and teeth brushed, as she'd instructed him to do when she'd headed to the kitchen to start their breakfast. "Why are you head-butting the refrigerator?"

Without lifting her forehead from the refrigerator

door, she turned to glance at her son, who stared at her with big, curious eyes.

"You look funny," he informed her matter-of-factly, then turned towards the doorway. "I think Mommy is knocking some sense into the refrigerator, but I don't know why. Sometimes mommies do silly things, but we kids love them anyway."

Her heart beating fast, forehead still pressed against the refrigerator, Brielle shifted her gaze to see who her son was talking to.

"Morning," Ross greeted her, looking way too handsome and relaxed compared to the restless night she'd spent. What had happened to the scowling, angry man who'd left her house only hours before?

"Having a bad day?" he asked, gesturing to the refrigerator.

She straightened, brushed her fingers through her hair, wished she'd taken time to actually dress, brush her hair and teeth, and throw on some mascara. Instead, she wore faded old pajama bottoms sporting cartoon penguins and a cotton-candy-pink T-shirt that had seen better days but was so comfy she kept wearing it anyway. She'd twisted her hair, haphazardly clipped it back, and wore stained fuzzy white slippers on her feet.

Ross looked like he'd stepped out of the pages of a magazine advertising the perfect man. His T-shirt stretched perfectly over his chest and appeared to be of the softest cotton. His jeans fit so well they could have been custom made for his body. His hair was perfectly groomed, his eyes bright, and his smile relaxed and natural looking.

Shouldn't he look a bit harried? At least a little? Life could be so unfair.

Oh, yeah, she was having a bad day.

She forced a smile to her face. "Couldn't be better."

"Denting refrigerators a part of your new usual morning wake-up ritual? Guess that'll take me a while to get used to."

"Or not," she countered with a glare.

Ross gave her one sharp look, glanced toward their son who watched them closely, then smiled at her. A smile that was no more real than hers had been. His served as a warning that she somehow read just as clearly as she'd read him all those years ago, back before her pregnancy and their relationship had fallen apart.

A smile that was for Justice's benefit and to let her know he expected her to mind her Ps and Qs. Their son was watching with sharp little eyes, taking in every detail of their interaction.

As contrary as she felt towards him, Ross was right.

She had to put on a positive front for Justice's benefit because how she interacted with Ross would influence how their son viewed him.

Despite her many flaws, if Ross wanted to be a part of Justice's life, she wanted that for her son's sake. She knew the statistics of children who grew up without fathers. Yes, she did her best and Justice didn't go without material needs or love and attention, but there were some things that, no matter how much she tried, she couldn't do or be for her son.

She pasted a very bright smile on her face and focused on what was most important in her life, her son. "You hungry, Bruce?"

His confused expression relaxing, Justice nodded. He climbed up on the barstool next to the kitchen counter that extended from the sink and was open on both sides of the eat-in kitchen/dining area combo room. He usually perched at the counter, coloring, drawing, or working on a jigsaw puzzle while chatting to her as she prepared their meals. Sometimes he helped.

Ignoring that Ross walked over and sat in the second barstool next to Justice, Brielle began taking items out of the fridge and setting them on the countertop.

"My daddy is hungry, too," Justice said matter-of-factly. "He's been away working for a very long time, but he's back now and he's very hungry so he needs breakfast too."

My daddy?

Brielle dropped the carton of eggs she was holding.

She'd wondered how they'd tell Justice, how they'd explain who Ross was and why he was living with them. She'd planned to talk to him about letting Justice get to know him before springing something so huge on the boy.

Obviously, Ross had taken matters into his own hands and dropped the bomb on their son.

Shaking, not wanting Justice to see her face, she stooped to clean up the eggs, paused when Ross's hand covered hers. Tumultuous emotions swirling all through her, she lifted her gaze to his. Could he see how upset she was that he'd taken the liberty of telling Justice? She hoped so. She hoped a lot of things.

"Why don't you take a morning off?" Ross's eyes darkened to a blue so deep she felt she might topple in and drown. Was that concern or mockery shining back at her? "Go and shower while Bruce and I cook breakfast for you."

Could he tell she was seething at his use of the pet name, at him having told Justice rather than allowing her to? Had he worried about what she would have said to their son or had he just arrogantly taken control without ever considering that she might have wanted to tell Justice herself?

"That's not really my name," Justice pointed out, still watching them closely enough that Brielle knew he was trying to figure out the tension in the room.

His father had been missing for the first five years of his life. Of course something wasn't right between his parents. But he wasn't quite five so he didn't understand the complexities of adult relationships. Then again, neither did she.

"I know, Justice." Ross emphasized the name, turning to look at their son for a brief moment, before returning his gaze to Brielle. "I think your mommy needs a few minutes to herself this morning. Sometimes mommies need to pull themselves together before facing their day. We guys just have to let them do their thing."

Ross remained squatting next to her, his hand covering hers and causing all kinds of electrical zig-zags and criss-crosses that annoyed her. His gaze was intent and full of…she wasn't sure. He was angry at her. Although he was pleasant, that harsh emotion was there, just beneath the surface, waiting to raise its ugly head if she didn't co-operate and do things his way. That she knew. But there was something different in his gaze, too, something more empathetic perhaps. And desire. Possibly the chemistry would always burn between them despite his claim the night before that he no longer wanted her. A claim that had hurt but which had just been another blow in an entire battlefield of injuries.

"I'm fine," she said, hoping to convince her son, if not herself. "But I do need a shower and to get dressed."

Because maybe if she wasn't in her pajamas she wouldn't feel so vulnerable.

"I'm dressed." Justice pointed to his shorts and T-shirt, then glanced at Ross and proudly announced, "I picked out my clothes myself and can tie my shoes."

"That's great," Ross praised, smiling at the boy with a raw look to his eyes that Brielle had never seen. Her heart squeezed at the monumental events happening around her.

Ross was there. Justice was there. Ross knew he was Justice's father. Justice knew Ross was his father. How many times had she imagined this moment?

"I'm pretty sure you and I can rustle up something edible that'll pass for breakfast for us all while your mom does her thing."

"I can make my own cereal," Justice announced proudly, puffing out his little chest. "I can pour my favorites without making a mess. Mommy doesn't like me eating sweet cereals too often, but she's so proud of me being a big boy and making my own."

Her son, always a talker, prattled on about his favorite breakfast cereal while Brielle could do no more than stare at Ross. He was going to make her breakfast? What, and add strychnine? Because she sure hadn't expected him to be nice to her. Was it all for Justice's sake?

"What do you think?" Ross asked, removing his hand from hers and immediately filling her with a sense of loss. "Hungry, Mommy?"

She missed his touch already.

Which was crazy.

This was not about her and Ross.

That wasn't why he was here. Whatever had been there or might have been between them had ended last night when he'd learned of Justice. Justice was their only real connection now.

She wasn't her mother.

She'd do well to remember that.

"You shouldn't call me that."

"What would you like me to call you?"

Yours.

No, she didn't want him to call her that.

Not any more. She'd just established that, hadn't she?

"You are a mommy and he's the daddy, so it's okay if he calls you that," Justice helpfully pointed out, pulling his basket of coloring books and crayons over in front of him. When he found the book he wanted, one full of his favorite caped crusader, he took out a crayon and held the box out towards Ross.

Ross Lane coloring? Brielle just couldn't picture it, but Ross took the box, selected a color and began to help Justice fill in between the lines as if he did the same thing every morning, as if he'd do whatever his son wanted of him.

Brielle stared at her son in amazement. Oh, the resilience of a four-year-old. Brielle stood, ignoring Ross's outstretched hand, and pulled out a mixing bowl.

"No."

She stopped, turned toward Ross, startled at his harsh word.

"Justice and I are going to make breakfast for you," he clarified in a more normal tone. He glanced at his son's expectant face. "Right after we finish coloring this page, right, buddy?" His blue gaze went back to Brielle. "Go, take a bath, relax, do your hair, whatever it is you women do. We'll take care of this and when you're ready, we'll eat."

Brielle hesitated.

Dared she leave Justice alone with Ross?

"We'll be fine."

That wasn't what she was worried about.

He must have read her mind because his gaze narrowed and his face darkened. "We'll still be here when you come out. I'm not like you."

He didn't have to say more. She knew what he meant. He meant that he wouldn't leave with their son and hide him away from her.

Like she'd done to him.

But that wasn't what she'd done and she wanted to argue that point, but although Justice was busily coloring a winged car, she knew he wasn't missing a single word of the conversation. He never did. So she bit back all the things she wanted to say and smiled politely at the man who was invading her home and her life.

She'd play his game. For now.

"Fine. I'll go take a shower and be back out in about twenty minutes."

Less. Because even though she didn't really believe Ross would run with Justice, she couldn't quite get past how nervous it made her to leave her son alone with his father.

Heart slamming against his rib cage at all the morning's events, Ross glanced down at the top of his son's shiny blond head. Justice's tongue stuck out the corner of his mouth as he concentrated intently on the picture he was working on.

"You're very good at coloring," Ross offered, suddenly nervous about the prospect of being alone with Justice until Brielle returned. When he'd knocked on the front door and Justice's voice had asked who was there, he'd not been able to stop the words that had left his mouth.

Your daddy.

Without unlatching the safety chain, Justice had cracked the door, peered out at him.

"I thought you were Uncle Vann's friend?"

"I am," he'd answered. "Can I come in?"

"Mommy says I'm not supposed to let anyone into the house without her knowing."

"I'm not just anyone."

Justice's little face had twisted with thought then without a word he'd shut the door.

Ross's heart had pounded, fearful that his over-eager announcement had shocked the boy. But within seconds he'd heard the chain rattle, seen the door open.

"Since Mommy said you were Uncle Vann's friend, that makes you not a stranger, right?" Justice had asked, still blocking the door with his tiny body, as if he'd been protecting his home and was still withholding house-entering privileges.

"Right."

"Then I guess you better come in because I'm not supposed to stand with the door wide open. Lets bugs into the house. I think that's cool, Mommy doesn't." Justice's face squished up with another thought. "Are you really my daddy?"

Ross had wanted to wrap his arms around his son, to hug him close, to breathe in his scent, and never let go. Instead, he'd stepped into the house, closed the front door, and bent to one knee to put him almost at eye level with Justice.

"I am really your daddy."

Justice seemed to digest that. "Where have you been for so long?"

A thousand answers ran through Ross's mind and as much as part of him wanted to lay all the truth on his son, a more logical part of him knew that pointing fingers wouldn't do Justice any good.

"I've been working in Boston, but I'm home now and want to be a part of your life."

"Do you have to go back to Boston?"

Did he? He hadn't really made the decision that he wasn't going back to Boston, but in that moment Ross knew.

"No, Bean's Creek is my home now, here with you and your mom."

"That's cool. I've missed you."

Ross's chest tightened and he wondered how his son had missed him when he hadn't known him, but he knew what his son meant. Justice hadn't missed him but had missed having a father. Another flare of anger erupted within him at what Brielle had robbed him of, what she'd robbed their son of. How could she have done that?

"Mommy gets sad sometimes and cries at night. She thinks I don't know, but I hear her. I think she was missing you, too."

His son's words put him right back in the middle of the emotional tug of war he'd waged all night. As angry as he was at Brielle, he also admired the way she'd taken responsibility for their son, at what a good job she'd done, caring for him.

"I've missed her, too." Seeing his son's frown, he corrected himself. "I've missed you both. Very much. But I'm here now and not ever going to leave again."

Staring at the boy coloring at the kitchen counter, Ross knew he'd told his son the truth earlier when he'd made that claim. He wasn't leaving Justice, not now that he knew about him.

"I know I'm a good colorer. Mommy tells me all the time how awesome I am at staying between the lines," Justice said, so matter-of-factly that Ross laughed at the boy's nonchalance at his praise.

"Does she, now?"

Not looking up, the boy nodded. "She tells me how good I am at lots of things. Mommies are like that. It's their job."

Curious, Ross couldn't keep his next question in. "What's a daddy's job?"

That had Justice looking up at him with a "duh" expression. "To work and take care of the mommy and the kids."

Smart kid. Ross nodded. "Yep, that's the daddy's job."

"Are you going to take care of my mommy and me now that you're my daddy?"

Justice's eyes were so intent, so eager for Ross's answer that he struggled to form words. Struggled to keep from promising him the world.

"Yeah, I'm going to take care of you and your mommy now that I'm your daddy."

What he really wanted to explain was that he had always been Justice's daddy, that he would have been there taking care of them all along had he but known about him.

He should have been there.

Brielle had been pregnant, given birth to his child.

To this adorable little boy.

Somehow he should have known, should have sensed that something monumental was happening.

His throat threatened to clog up and he cleared it just to be able to keep his lungs from collapsing from lack of air. "The first order of business on taking care of you and your mommy is for us to cook breakfast so we don't starve to death."

Justice gave him a not so sure look. "I just know how to make cereal."

"Then it's time you learn to make a good omelet. Chicks love omelets."

"Chicks?" Setting his crayon down, Justice giggled as he repeated the word.

Ross ruffled the boy's hair in what was supposed to be a light gesture. Instead, it was the first time he'd ever touched his son and his fingers lingered at the softness of his hair, at the innocence in the eyes staring up at him.

This child was his flesh and blood.

His.

Suddenly he understood the fierceness with which Brielle spoke of their son. He understood the love she felt for the boy. He felt it too, knew that he'd spend the rest of his life seeing to it that his son had a good life and knew that he was wanted, loved. By both of his parents.

As much as he wanted to take the boy into his arms and hold him close, he knew Justice wasn't ready for that, neither would he understand Ross's emotional overload. So, wishing he could somehow have the past five years to live over so he could experience every moment of this child's life, he kept the mood light by giving Justice a meaningful look. "You know, girls."

Eyes wide, Justice wrinkled his nose and went back to coloring his picture. "What do we care if they love omelets or not?"

Ross gave his son an I-can't-believe-you-said-that look. "Obviously you haven't met the right girl yet."

Justice's eyes crinkled with delight. True to the blood flowing through his little veins, Ross's son set down his crayons and regarded him with a confident expression. "I've met lots of girls. There are bunches in my preschool class." He said this as if revealing top-secret information. "Emma Beth has a dog even." Justice's attention turned toward the items Brielle had set out on the counter. "I want a dog, but Mommy says they are a lot of work. I bet I'm good at making omelets."

Ross grinned, ruffled the boy's downy soft hair again just for another touch of his son's warmth. "I bet you are, too."

In the end, neither was good at making omelets that particular morning. Usually Ross had no problems mustering up simple dishes in the kitchen. As a long-term bachelor, he was a decent cook. But whether it was knowing that he was cooking with his son, that he was cooking for Brielle, or the constant fear that Justice was going to topple out of the chair he stood on, fall off the countertop Ross kept repositioning him on, burn himself by getting too close to the oven, or some other situation that four-year-old boys got themselves into, Ross wasn't sure. Just that his kitchen skills were lacking that day.

When Brielle stepped into the kitchen, she was confronted by a mess the likes of which her kitchen had most likely never seen.

"Um, I see you boys have been busy." Her gaze traveled over the countertops, which were covered with various bowls, pans, and measuring utensils.

Ross just stared at her, wondering what had happened to his ability to breathe. Brielle took his breath away.

She'd changed into shorts and a T-shirt that hugged her breasts and accentuated her tiny waist. He longed to wrap his arms around that waist, to hold her to him, to see if their bodies fit together the way they once had.

So much for his claim of the night before.

Not that he hadn't meant it. At the time he had. But he'd been blinded by anger and betrayal.

Perhaps the same anger and betrayal Brielle had felt when she'd come to Boston, pregnant with his child, and seen him with another woman.

He had dated. He'd had to do something to occupy his mind, his lonely heart, because as bad as things had gotten between them, he'd missed Brielle like crazy when he'd gone north. He'd serial-dated those first few months, searching for but never finding what he'd once had with Brielle. Not ever even coming close.

"We're making omelets for chicks," Justice announced proudly, obviously not realizing what a disaster their attempt was. Then again, one had to appreciate a kid who looked on the bright side of things.

"Do what?" Her gaze jerking to Ross, Brielle frowned, obviously seeing nothing bright in the current disaster she surveyed or their son's comment.

"Uh, yeah," Ross interrupted before Justice elaborated. "Omelets for chicks. One in particular. You. Unfortunately, we ran into a few problems."

Glancing around the cluttered countertops, Brielle's brow rose. "Just a few?"

Justice surveyed their mess and wrinkled his nose. "My daddy and I aren't very good at getting chicks."

"Obviously you don't know your dad," Brielle said with the sarcasm that seemed to accompany most of what she said to or about him these days. Then, realizing what she'd said, she popped her hand over her mouth, wincing at her blunder. "Sorry," she mouthed at him, her eyes softening and holding real regret. "I didn't mean that the way…well, you know."

He did know. He'd seen his son for the first time the night before. Of course the boy didn't know him, and that was Brielle's fault.

And his own. Somewhere during the long night he'd admitted to himself that he hadn't been blameless in the events that had played out.

Rather than call her on her comment, he just shrugged as if her barb hadn't stung. "How about I take you both out for breakfast this morning?"

With one last look around the disaster they'd made of her kitchen, she accepted his olive branch. "That sounds like a good idea. On the way you can explain to me why my son has mentioned 'chicks' twice."

"Our son mentioned chicks because that's where eggs come from and we were making omelets, right?" Ross glanced at Justice for confirmation.

Being the sharp little munchkin he was, he nodded as if he were in on the biggest of secrets. He slipped his hand into Ross's and grinned. "Right."

Ross's gaze went from where his son's hand held his to Brielle's pale face. If she expected him to apologize for trying to form a bond with their son, for telling him the truth, she'd be sorely disappointed. The kitchen was another matter altogether. That he'd make up to her later by cleaning up the mess.

"Let's go before we both end up in the doghouse," he warned his son, holding onto the boy's hand loosely yet so emotionally tight that he'd never let go.

Coming to Bean's Creek had been the right thing.

Without even realizing it, he'd been coming home.

CHAPTER EIGHT

DISINFECTING HER HANDS at the nurses' station, Brielle frowned at her friend. "No, I do not want to talk about why Dr. Lane said he enjoyed the breakfast I cooked this morning."

What she wanted was to strangle Ross for saying such a thing in front of Cindy. Why did he think she insisted on taking separate vehicles to work? Was he trying to make her life as complicated as possible? Probably, as he seemed to go back and forth between being so angry at her that she could feel the almost hatred rolling off him to other softer, pleasant emotions that were too similar to the way they had once been for her liking.

"I'm not blind, you know."

"I know." Brielle sighed. "Do we have to talk about this at work, though?"

"Well, you've been busy every night this week," Cindy reminded her. She glanced towards where Ross was talking to a patient in Bay One. "Not that I haven't known why."

"It's not what you think," Brielle quickly assured her, punching a code into the medication cart.

"Oh?" Cindy's brow rose. "It's not that Dr. Lane is really your long-lost love returned from the past to sweep you off your feet?"

"Not even close."

"No?" Cindy's gaze narrowed. "Then my second guess must be the right one."

"What would that be?" Brielle asked, knowing she probably shouldn't but doing so all the same.

"That he's Justice's father and realized that he screwed up big time by not being part of that kid's life and he's here to do right by you both."

"Mostly right."

Both women jumped and spun toward Ross.

"Don't do that," Brielle hissed.

He shrugged. "What? Walk up to the two best nurses in the hospital so I can ask one of them to get Radiology to do a chest X-ray on Mrs. Jones? Also, I'd like a comprehensive metabolic profile, a complete blood count, and a BNP to assess for congestive heart failure."

"Uh, yeah." Heat flushed Brielle's face. "I'll get right on that."

Glancing back and forth between them, Cindy shook her head. "Nope, Mrs. Jones is my patient. I've got this." Her gaze met Brielle's. "You stay and find out why my second guess is only mostly right."

Brielle and Ross watched Cindy go over to Mrs. Jones, say something to her, then draw blood from her patient's left arm.

"I should help her," Brielle said, to fill the silence that stretched between them and as an excuse to escape his always overwhelming presence.

"Scared?" He took a step closer to her, leaving only inches between them.

"Of?" She didn't budge, hating the way her feet itched to run and how his nearness affected her.

"Doing what Cindy suggested."

She lifted her chin despite how it put their faces closer together. "I'm not scared of you."

"No?"

"No." But she took off to help her friend, who didn't really need help, to the sound of Ross's laughter behind her.

The emergency department had been crazily busy in spurts and almost dead at other times. Now was one of those crazy times. Everybody available was busy but no matter how busy they were Ross was aware of where Brielle was at all times. Starting an intravenous line, giving an injection, doing an assessment, she always managed to be busy to the extent that she didn't have to spend any downtime with him.

Which should be just fine, but wasn't.

They'd been living together almost a week now and she kept him at arm's length. What was up with that? He was the one who'd been done wrong by her. He should be the one to keep distance between them. Instead...instead, he just felt confused. He'd come to Bean's Creek for her, to reconcile his unresolved emotions for Brielle. He'd not resolved a thing and was more confused than ever about the frustrating woman.

What he wasn't confused about was his son. Justice was an amazing child. Smart, funny, full of spunk. Ross was in awe of the boy's thought processes and how quickly his little mind worked. Being a constant part of Justice's life was the one certainty throughout the week's craziness. Doing what was right for his son would be his priority and if Brielle wished he'd just disappear, that was too bad.

"Dr. Lane, we have a problem." Cindy interrupted

his thoughts. "Brielle just brought back a thirty-seven-week gestation female who is dilated to ten. The patient had been brought in because she was involved in a minor road traffic accident, but the shock must have sped up her labor. Brielle wanted me to get you now."

"Call Delivery and see if we can get her transferred." Ross went to the bay he'd seen Brielle go into a few minutes before while he'd been finishing up the notes on his previous patient.

"I know you want to push but try not to," Brielle encouraged the woman, propping another pillow behind her. "Is that better?"

"I have to push," the woman cried, sweat dripping down her brow. "I hurt so bad."

The woman's husband noticed Ross. "Are you the doctor? Can't you do something? She's hurting really bad. I think something's wrong because she shouldn't be hurting this bad. Is it because of the accident? It's my fault for driving too fast; I was so scared about getting here on time."

"We'll take good care of you." Ross cleaned his hands then gloved up. "I need to see how far along you are."

The woman nodded her permission, her hands clamped tightly to the bed rail. Her husband was rubbing her arm, trying to soothe her.

"She's at ten," Brielle warned, glancing at the fetal monitor as she continued to talk. "The baby's head is crowning and another contraction is about to start."

Ross gently pulled back the covers to where he could check the woman and immediately his gaze went to Brielle's. One more big contraction and they'd be delivering a baby.

"Labor and Delivery won't have a bed available for about half an hour," Cindy informed them from where she peeked her head around the curtain.

"We don't have half an hour." Even as Ross said the words the woman's abdomen began to pull tightly with the contraction that Brielle had seen coming on the monitor.

The woman began whimpering and her husband reminded her to breathe.

"I need to push. I really need to push."

"Cindy, get some towels and everything else I'm going to need." He glanced at Brielle, who stood at the head of the bed, keeping close tabs on the woman.

"I have to push," the woman cried. "I have to."

"Try to make it to your next contraction before pushing."

"I can't." Obviously she couldn't because she began pushing and grunting with pain.

"Breathe, honey. Don't forget to breathe."

The woman's eyes cut towards her husband and she growled something about his breathing, then she closed her eyes and cried out.

"The head's out," Ross told them as he cleared the baby's airway. "Stop pushing."

The contraction was coming to an end. The woman whimpered. Her husband moved to the end of the bed to where he could see what Ross saw. His face paled and he plopped down into the sole chair in the room.

"Put your head between your knees and breathe," Brielle told the man from where she was still attending her patient. "Don't forget to breathe."

Ross glanced up just long enough to meet her eyes and grin at her comment. She started to smile back, caught herself, and glanced away, leaving him yet again feeling as if he had been the one to wrong her rather than the other way round.

She'd denied him this. Seeing his child come into the world. Getting to be there during those first few moments of Justice's life. Being there for the first five years of his life.

"I want to push again. Please tell me I can push," the woman begged.

Ross glanced at the monitor, watched for the right time during her contraction for her pushing to be most effective. "Now. Push."

The woman bore down, pushing, crying, breathing in deep gasps.

Ross caught the baby as the shoulders appeared then the remainder of the body rushed out of the birth canal. He did a quick visual assessment of the crying baby. "Apgar is ten. Perfect. Congratulations. You have a beautiful baby girl."

Ross put the baby on the woman's stomach, clamped the umbilical cord, reached for the sterile scissors Brielle was offering him, and glanced towards the baby's father. "Do you want to cut the cord?"

The pale man shook his head. "You do it."

Ross had delivered quite a few babies during his residency, had cut the cord numerous times. But since he'd discovered he was a father, that a baby he'd help create had entered the world, he'd done neither.

Who had been in the delivery room with Brielle? Who had coached her and comforted her? Who had cut Justice's cord?

Most likely her brother had, but it should have been

him. He should have been at her side, feeding her ice chips, wiping her brow, reminding her to breathe.

Justice had been two months premature. Had his birth been a complicated one? Had he been delivered vaginally or by Cesarean section?

Had Brielle wished that he had been there or had she been grateful that he was out of her life?

Brielle watched Ross snip the umbilical cord and tried not to think about the fact that she'd just helped deliver a baby with him. Who would have believed that they'd work together to help bring a baby into the world? That she'd share the miracle of birth with him?

The miracle of birth that she'd wanted to share with him when Justice had been born.

That miracle she'd endured alone. The plan had been for Vann to be with her, but she'd gone into labor early at seven months and had needed to have an emergency Cesarean section.

Cindy came into the room with warm towels, took one and swaddled the baby in it then handed the baby girl to her mother.

"She's so precious," the woman said, obviously still in a great deal of pain but no longer caring. "Look, she's beautiful."

The man had moved to the head of the bed and gazed down at his little girl in awe, then at his wife with more awe. "You were amazing, honey. Absolutely amazing." He bent and kissed his wife's cheek. "I love you."

Feeling as if she was intruding on a very private moment, Brielle's eyes watered and she fought sniffling. This was how it should have been.

Ross should have been at her side, holding her hand, helping her bring Justice into the world.

He shouldn't have been in Boston, living it up with some other woman, while she'd brought their son into the world alone, while she'd lain in the hospital bed watching her son be whisked away for immediate medical treatment because of his premature lungs.

All the emotions she'd felt during those moments—the loneliness, the fear, the hatred—came rushing back, making her feel weak.

She glanced toward where Ross worked, delivering the placenta. As if sensing her gaze, he glanced up, met her eyes, and seemed shocked by the animosity she aimed at him.

"You should have been there," she mouthed, unable to completely fight back the words. The new parents were so caught up in their new baby they failed to notice, but Cindy did.

"Sorry to do this, but I have to get her to the nursery for her to get a thorough once-over," Cindy said, gently taking the baby.

"Do you mind if I do that and you stay and help Dr. Lane?" Brielle asked, her eyes pleading with her friend to co-operate. She couldn't explain it, but she had to get out of this room, had to get away from Ross.

"Sure," Cindy agreed, glancing back and forth between her and Ross as if expecting to see something tangible. She wouldn't, of course. The only thing tangible between Ross and herself was the wonderful little boy who was at preschool while his parents worked.

Ross congratulated the couple once more as Cindy rolled the woman's bed out of the emergency department. Labor and Delivery had a bed available and she was being transferred for the obstetrician to examine her and to take over her care.

He glanced around the emergency department, spotting Brielle at the nurses' station, charting. He was glad that things had once again calmed down to a lull. It was only about an hour until shift change and he hoped things remained slow. Usually he did just fine, but today he felt exhausted. Perhaps not so much physically as emotionally.

Brielle's mouthed "You should have been there" had continually played through his head.

He should have been there.

He would have been there.

Had he known.

She didn't glance up as he dropped into the chair next to hers. Neither did she acknowledge him in any way. Which was an acknowledgement of its own. One that said, Go away.

"Tell me about Justice's birth."

She didn't look up, just closed her eyes and swallowed.

"Please," he added, when she didn't say anything.

"What would you like to know?"

"Everything."

"I went into labor at seven months and had to have a Cesarean section when Justice got into trouble. He was in the hospital for six weeks after his birth but other than being a little small for his age he's fully recovered."

To look at his son one would never know that he'd once fought for life.

Ross pictured what Justice must have looked like, a premature infant hooked to multiple tubes and wires, and the image gutted him. How much worse it must have been for Brielle to have lived each day with their son's life teetering on the edge. How much worse that she had to endure that alone.

"Was Vann with you?"

"He'd meant to be in the delivery room, but everything happened so fast that I delivered alone. He stayed with me afterwards, helped me keep focused on what was important—Justice. I couldn't have made it through that time without him."

"You could have, but I'm glad you didn't have to, that he was there for you."

He didn't say it was because he hadn't been there. He didn't have to. They both finished the sentence in their heads.

Brielle swallowed, then stood. "I can't do this. Not right now." She glanced around the emergency room as if searching for something to do, but there weren't any new patients and the ones currently in bays had more than sufficient nursing care already. "I...I need to go to the bathroom."

"Or anywhere I'm not," he added for her, as she rushed away from him.

Ross couldn't say coming to Bean's Creek was a mistake. It hadn't been. But coming here, thinking that Brielle could ever forgive him, had been foolish.

Perhaps too much had happened for them to ever be able to forgive each other, but somehow for Justice's sake they had to at least try.

A week later Brielle stared across the breakfast table at a local diner where Ross and Justice sat. Much as he had since Ross had entered his life, Justice had insisted on sitting beside Ross. He couldn't seem to get enough of his father and thus far Ross hadn't seemed to mind. Actually, he seemed to soak up every morsel of Justice's attention and want more.

When Justice struggled to cut up his pancakes, Brielle automatically reached for his plate, meaning to cut them into bite-sized pieces, as she usually did.

"No, my daddy will do it."

Brielle froze, her gaze going to Ross's then lowering because she didn't want him to see how her son's words had affected her. She wasn't quite sure how to label her emotions, but for Justice's sake she just smiled and nodded.

"That's fine, Justice. Your dad can cut your pancakes for you."

For the most part she may as well not even be at the table and they wouldn't miss her. Although her son knew she was there, he was all over his new-found father. With the dogged persistence of a curious four-year-old he drilled Ross with question after question, although some of them he'd asked Ross more than a dozen times since his arrival in their lives.

Ross patiently answered each one, never seeming to tire of Justice's boundless energy and curiosity.

Where have you been?

Where's Boston?

Do you have other kids?

Brielle's heart stopped on that one. Never had she considered the possibility that Ross might have had other children along the way.

"No other kids, just you." Ross's gaze met Brielle's. "At least, no other kids that I know of."

If he expected her to crawl under the table in shame,

he would be sadly disappointed. She wouldn't. She'd done the best she could given the circumstances at the time. She'd done what she'd thought had been right.

No one was perfect.

But watching Justice soak up every morsel of attention Ross gave him, Brielle had to concede that her son did need a father. Had needed one all along.

Something that she'd denied him by omission. For that, she was sorry.

"Justice, Ross can barely eat for talking. Let him finish his meal, baby, then you can ask him more questions."

Justice nodded, was quiet for almost an entire thirty seconds, staring at Ross expectantly as he took a bite then another. After three bites Ross set his fork down, probably to have a drink, but Justice started back with more questions.

"What are we going to do today?"

It was their first full day off work and preschool together since the morning Ross had moved into her house.

"What would you like to do today?" Ross countered, grinning at his son. Ross always had smiles for Justice, and patience. Had she ever allowed herself to think about what kind of father Ross would be, she'd have fallen short on the reality. Then again, all this was still new to him and perhaps he'd get bored before long.

"Mommy and I like to go fishing."

Casting a look toward her, Ross's eyes grew wide. "Fishing?"

Justice nodded.

At Ross's shock, Brielle lifted her chin. "You didn't

think I was taking my son to ballet and baking classes, did you?"

"I would like to think you were keeping our son well rounded and that if he was interested in the arts or baking classes you'd be open-minded."

That surprised her. She would have taken Ross as a man's man who wouldn't want his son doing anything girly.

"What's well rounded?" Justice asked, glancing back and forth between them.

"It means you get to try a lot of different things in life."

"Like cinnamon pancakes?" Justice gestured to his plate, not something Brielle would regularly have wanted him to order as she encouraged him to eat healthily, but she'd given in to Ross's insistence that today was a special occasion. She supposed in some ways it was. Their first full family day with no work, no school, no moving into her house. Ross was there and seemingly settled in for...for how long?

No, she wouldn't think about that right now. She'd focus on Justice. His happiness and well-being was what mattered most.

"Yes, like cinnamon pancakes," she answered her son, smiling at his cherubic face, which had a smudge of syrup on his cheek.

"And fishing?"

Brielle nodded, reaching across the table to clean the smudge with her napkin.

Clean faced, Justice turned big, imploring eyes on Brielle. "Is my daddy going to take us fishing? That's what daddies do. April from preschool said so."

To hear how quickly Justice had taken to calling Ross

Daddy, to thinking of him as his daddy told Brielle how hungry her son had been for a father. That made her feel sad, as if she'd somehow not been enough.

How eager he was to spend every waking moment with Ross rather than her also made her feel a little sad.

She knew that was silly, wrong even, but she couldn't help the feeling. Even though she knew she'd done a good job raising Justice, she hadn't been enough. Not really.

Yes, part of the fascination was new-toy syndrome, but part of it was that thus far Ross had taken his role in Justice's life seriously, dedicating himself one hundred percent to the little boy when he wasn't at work. No wonder Justice was enthralled. Who wouldn't be at having all Ross's attention focused on them?

"Daddy—" the word felt so foreign on her lips, for so many reasons "—probably has other things to do."

"No, I don't," Ross quickly corrected her, eyeing her curiously and probably seeing a lot more than she wished. "My whole day is clear to spend with my family."

"We're not your family," she said automatically, without thinking. The immediate darkening of his expression told her that she'd made a mistake.

"Yes." His voice was firm, direct, offering no room for argument. "You are. Justice is my flesh and blood. My son, my family."

She clamped her mouth closed, uncertain what more to say yet wanting to say a lot, but really what could she say? He was right. Justice was as much his as he was hers and for her son's sake she foresaw a lot of tongue-biting in her future to prevent him from hearing things best left unheard by little ears.

CHAPTER NINE

WHISTLING A TUNE from a cartoon he'd watched one evening with Justice, Ross threaded line through an eye of the fishing pole he'd bought less than an hour before. He'd also bought a tackle box, lures, and a few other items he'd thought they might need to go along with the simple kiddy poles Justice and Brielle already owned and used.

Someday soon he'd buy his son a real pole and tackle, but for now the black superhero one with its emblem on the float would do. After all, the kid was only four.

"You look as if you know what you're doing, but do you actually know how to fish?" Brielle asked from where she was perched on a rock, watching him rather than baiting her hook. Then again, she'd already informed him that they usually used plastic bait rather than live crickets or earthworms.

What was the fun in that for a little boy?

He'd bought both, but after a few minutes of watching the crickets and letting the earthworms crawl around in his palm, Justice had lost interest. Right now he was stooped over just out of earshot, more interested in searching through the rocks, looking for dinosaur fossils, than in fishing. Apparently dinosaurs were starting to give Justice's favorite superhero a run for his billions.

"I grew up just a few hours away, Brielle. Of course I know how to fish. My dad and I went fishing several times a month during school breaks. Those times are some of my favorite memories of my childhood. The last time he and my mom came up to Boston we chartered a boat and went out for a day of fishing." He smiled at the memory. "It was a good day."

A slight frown marred her forehead. "How come I never knew that about you?"

Not sure how to answer her question, he shrugged. "You never asked. When I was with you I had other things on my mind besides fishing."

When he and Brielle had been together, she'd occupied way too many of his thoughts. Ultimately, when their relationship had become stressed, he'd resented the distraction. Obviously, out of sight was not out of mind when it had come to Brielle Winton, though. Far far from it. He'd never forgotten her, never gotten over her. Now that he knew she was the mother of his child he accepted that she was part of his life. For ever. Even with how strained their relationship currently was, he couldn't say he resented her effect on him. Not this time. He was older, wiser, had learned a lot of life lessons.

"*We* never went fishing," she pointed out, almost sounding accusatory, and he grinned at the near pouty expression on her pretty face.

"I was in medical school and pouring my heart and soul into becoming the best doctor I could be," he reminded her. "What little free time I had to spend with you, well, I didn't want to spend that time fishing."

She blushed bright red and Ross bit back a smile. If she recalled, she wouldn't have wanted to spend their limited free time fishing either, unless it had been fishing in the dark for each other.

"No, I guess we didn't have a lot of spare time for things like fishing..." Her voice trailed off, then she lifted needy eyes to him. "We did have a lot of good times, didn't we, Ross? I didn't imagine that, did I?"

He tied the line around the hook, knotted it, then secured it to the pole by looping the tip around an eye. He stood the pole next to him, propping it against the tackle box and holding it loosely in his grip just to have something to do with his hand.

"We had a lot of good times together." He looked at her, at the nostalgic expression on her face, and he mentally kicked himself yet again. How could he have tossed away their relationship without fighting for her? Without trying to correct the things that had gone wrong? He knew the answers, of course, but he couldn't help but think that if he had his life to live over from that point, he wouldn't have left Brielle behind. He'd have convinced her to go with him, have put effort into repairing their relationship. And that was even without the knowledge that she'd been pregnant. "You know we did."

Memories of chasing her around their apartment, both of them laughing so hard they could barely breathe, of catching her and tickling her while she squirmed, trying to escape, of his touches soon going from playful torture to sexually charged. Of her lips going from teasing to moaning with pleasure. Of her squirming morphing into needy gyrations as his body took control of hers.

But not just the sex. Memories of holding her while she'd cried after her first code where the patient had died, letting her fall asleep in his arms, and lying there breathing her in, feeling as if she had been right where she'd belonged, feeling as if he'd been right where he'd belonged.

With Brielle.

That same feeling hit him, making him grip the fishing pole tighter. For the first time in five years he was where he belonged. With Brielle.

"Great times," Ross rasped, then cleared his throat, hoping to ease the tightness clamping down on his vocal cords. "We were great. The best."

His gaze met Brielle's and the tightness took hold of his whole body. He'd often heard the expression "tension so thick you could cut it with a knife." This was one of those moments. A moment so intense that emotions were almost palpable around them. Sexual tension. Physical tension. Emotional tension. Mental tension. Tensions he couldn't label pulsed between them.

The past. The present. The future.

All pulsated alive and real between them.

Her chest rose and fell in rapid, shallow breaths. Her lips parted.

He fought kissing her. He wanted to kiss her, to hold her, to chase her around until they collapsed together in laughter and kisses. And more. He wanted so much more with this woman.

If Justice wasn't a few yards away, he would kiss her.

He missed kissing her. Missed the feel of her plump lips pressed to his, the feel of her warm breath against his mouth, the taste of her sweetness.

They had been great together, the best.

No other woman even compared to the one sitting a few feet from him, staring at him with a hundred emotions shining in her eyes, not the least of which was desire matching his own.

And anger that was just as strong as his. She rollercoastered back and forth between the positive and negative between them, just as he had for the past two weeks.

He'd come to Bean's Creek for her, to rekindle any sparks that remained between them. The reality was that wildfire burned any time they were near each other. Then he'd discovered she'd had his child.

A child she'd kept from him and would have continued to keep from him had he not come looking for her.

He could so easily hate her for depriving him of his son. Just as she could so easily hate him for not being there for her during her pregnancy, during her delivery, during all the days, weeks, months, and years that had followed while she'd cared for their son alone.

"They were great times." Brielle finally spoke from her perch on the small boulder. She pulled her knees up close to her body, wrapped her arms around her bare legs. "Then you left so perhaps they weren't so great after all or you would have stayed."

He was the one who was supposed to be angry, not her. He was the one who had been cheated out of five years of his precious son's life. She had done that to him.

So why did her softly spoken words gut him? Make him want to beg for forgiveness for leaving her when she'd needed him? For letting her give birth to their son alone when he should have been at her side? Ever since they'd shared the delivery earlier that week, he'd been haunted by the image of her bringing their son into the world alone. Yes, he blamed her, but he also blamed himself. A lot.

He should have been there, should have helped ease

her financial burden, her physical and emotional load as she'd struggled with the trauma of a premature baby who had required weeks of hospital care. How had she managed the medical bills? Had Vann lightened her load? Not that she seemed to mind raising their child by herself, otherwise she would have asked for child support.

If only she had.

He'd been such a fool to leave her, but perhaps if he'd stayed his resentment would have festered. He'd like to think not, but he'd been immature in some ways, had had a lot of growing up to do. He wasn't the same man who'd left her. Not by a long stretch.

He glanced at where she hugged her legs. From his position he had a perfect view up her shorts leg to see the hint of the curvature of her creamy thigh. Nothing more, just a glimpse up her shorts, a cheap thrill really, but that was all it took to make him want to push her back on that rock and rediscover her body, to search out and cherish the changes carrying their son had added to it, knowing that those changes were honored badges of her motherhood.

Noticing his gaze, she glanced down, tugged on her shorts. "Sorry."

"Brielle, I…" He paused, trying to figure out what it was he wanted to say to this complex woman who held so much power over him. Did she even realize? "I wasn't telling the truth last week when I said I could sleep in the same bed with you without wanting to touch you. This week has been strained with us in the same house, but, no matter how upset or angry I am with you, I can't be within ten feet of you without wanting to touch you."

She tugged on her shorts again, as if she was trying to stretch them over every piece of exposed skin to keep his prying eyes away.

"Why are you telling me this? I don't want you to touch me." But she was lying and they both knew it. He could see the truth in her eyes. In the way her nipples puckered through her bra and T-shirt to declare just how much he affected her, just how much she wanted to be touched.

"But it's not just the wanting that is between us," he continued. "You make me feel more than any other person I've ever known. In a single minute you can take me through every emotion. No one else can do that. Just you."

She quit tugging on her shorts, stared at him as if trying to decide if he was serious or if he was setting her up some way just so he could knock her down. He hated the mistrust with which she gazed at him, but he supposed only time would heal some wounds.

"You think you don't affect me just as strongly?" she asked, adjusting her gaze to stare out at the sparkles from the sun on the lake water. "I don't want you here and yet…" Her voice trailed off and she shrugged.

"You don't want me to leave?"

She turned, smiled softly, sadly. "No, Ross, I don't want you to go. I never wanted you to leave. Despite what you may believe, I always wanted you in Justice's life." When he started to speak, she lifted her hand to stop him. "Maybe you find that hard to believe since I didn't tell you. All I can say is that I did want you there and I missed that you weren't there. Always. More than you will ever know or believe. Let's leave it at that, okay?"

He didn't want to leave anything. He wanted her to

explain, to make him understand how she'd made the decisions she had and had thought they had been the right decisions when they had meant keeping his son from him. But at the moment he wanted to have a truce with her more than anything else.

"For Justice's sake," he said, knowing that at some point they would have to discuss the very things she'd just asked him to leave alone.

"And although we both feel this heat between us, Ross, we have to ignore it," she continued, her gaze going to where their son was studying a rock he held in his palm. "Justice wouldn't understand."

Did she think he was going to do her up against the kitchen counters with their son around? Hardly.

"If we opted to become sexually involved with each other again," Ross began, "he wouldn't have to know. Neither should he know, really."

Shaking her head, she laughed at his comment. "You'll quickly learn that there is no keeping things from Justice. He'd know something was happening between us. Just as he knows there are negative feelings between us regardless of the fact we pretend otherwise in front of him."

On that she was right and he agreed one hundred percent. Justice might be just under five and Ross had just met him, but he could tell the boy was very perceptive.

He glanced at their son, watched the boy intently examining the rock. That was his child, his flesh and blood. Amazing how quickly the boy had stolen his heart. Then again, Justice was also half Brielle.

He took a deep breath, blew it out, and felt a great deal of tension leave his body along with the air. "Which is why, despite how betrayed I feel by the choices you made five years ago and every day since, I am going to let that hurt go and move forward, because from this point on we have to focus on the future, on what is right for our son."

"I... Yes, you're right." Brielle nodded in agreement. "I agree. Justice is what's most important. His well-being. Thank you for understanding that."

He understood much more than she gave him credit for. He wondered just how agreeable she was going to be when he pressed forward. Probably not nearly so accommodating as her current smiling face.

"On that same token," he told her, watching her closely, "you have to let go that I left, Brielle."

Her amicable expression paled.

"You can't keep bringing it up," he continued, determined to see this through. Not only for Justice but for both their sakes, too. They needed peace, for the past to be in the past, for the present to be clear so they could figure out the future. "You can't keep throwing the past between us as a barrier to us starting over and forging a new relationship, whatever that relationship might be."

Her eyes widened.

"It's time you forgave me." Past time as far as he was concerned. "Do you think you can do that?"

Ross waited, but she just sat on the rock, knees held to her chest, skin pale.

When she still didn't speak, he continued. "If I can put the fact that I lost five years of my son's life behind me and forgive you..." which he wasn't sure he had, but he could either dwell on the past or embrace the future. He preferred to embrace the future "...then it really isn't too much to expect you to do the same in regard to me having accepted the position in Boston."

The fact that he couldn't say "leaving you" should tell him that she was right to blame him in some ways, because it had been about much more than just accepting the position.

His gaze met hers and he saw tears shimmering in her big eyes, saw regret and so many other things blazing in those golden-brown depths.

"Ross, I—"

"I found one!" Justice came running towards them, his hand outstretched with a rock gripped in his tiny fingers. "Look!"

"Be careful," Brielle warned, her attention completely off Ross and focused solely on their son. Her face pinched as she stood to reach for Justice right as he lost his footing on a loose rock and tumbled forward, falling just a few feet away.

Brielle moved quicker than Ross, getting to the crying boy and lifting him into her arms. "You have to be careful on the rocks, baby. Let me check you. What hurts?"

But even before the boy sobbed out an answer Ross was already taking in the red soaking into Brielle's shirt, taking in the red that ran down Justice's leg and dripped from his hand.

The sight of blood had never bothered him. He was a doctor, for goodness' sake. But the sight of his son's blood leaving his tiny body, of blood staining Brielle's clothing, made him feel light-headed, and if he hadn't known better he'd say that was nausea welling in his stomach.

"Oh, Justice, sweetie." Cradling him in her arms, kissing the top of his head and offering tender words of comfort, Brielle examined his bleeding hand then his knee while Ross tried to pull himself together.

What was wrong with him? His knees didn't threaten to buckle at a little blood. Or a lot of blood even. At various points during his medical career he'd dealt with nasty motor vehicle accidents, amputations, and hemorrhages that had looked like a massacre had taken place. None had twisted his stomach inside out the way the site of his son's lifeblood on the wrong side of his tiny body did.

"The cut on his hand is pretty deep, but the one on his knee is worse," Brielle said above the sound of Justice's crying. She stared at Ross as if wondering what was up with his frozen-statue routine. "What do you think? He's going to need stitches in both, isn't he?"

"I don't want 'titches." Justice's crying picked up a notch and Brielle's gaze dropped to the sobbing little boy in her lap.

"Shh, baby. It's okay," she comforted him, holding the boy even more tightly in her arms. "Mommy's got you." When Ross didn't answer her question or move, she glanced up at him and frowned. "I'll hold him while you check him, Ross. We've got to get some pressure on to stop the bleeding. Now," she said, the last word in a raised voice, her tone warning him that he needed to get his act together.

Ross kicked into doctor mode and bent to check Justice. First his hand, which had an avulsion tear in the center of his palm where he'd tried to save himself from his fall. The jagged edge of a rock had torn into his tender flesh, lifting the skin back in a V shape. Next he checked the wide cut on his knee.

"Both are deep enough that they need sutures," he

said, hating that Justice was feeling pain, would have to be anesthetized and sutured.

"That's what I thought," Brielle agreed, her eyes widening as Ross took off his T-shirt. "What are you doing?"

"Making Justice bandages. You can apply pressure while I drive him to the hospital where I can suture him. Plus, he won't be so upset if we stop the bleeding and he's not seeing blood."

Neither would Ross because the sight of blood all over Justice and Brielle was upsetting him too. These were the two most important people in his life and one of them was hurt and there was little he could do.

He needed to be doing something, anything.

"You're going to suture him?" Brielle sounded surprised.

Surely she hadn't thought he'd let someone else do what he was more than capable of doing? Then again, after he'd been frozen for those first several seconds, perhaps she'd been justified.

"I am a medical doctor who works in the emergency room at the hospital where we will be going," he reminded them both as he ripped his T-shirt, making a rough strip of the piece he'd torn from around the hem. "I don't see a reason for someone else to suture my son, do you?"

"I don't want sutures," Justice cried pitifully between sobs, although Ross wasn't sure if the boy even knew what stitches or sutures meant. Or maybe he did. Had his son ever had sutures? There were so many things he didn't know. So many things he wanted to learn about his son.

For the rest of their lives he'd be there, would know all the things there were to know about his child.

"I just thought…" Brielle began, then stopped, closed her eyes. "Whatever you want to do is fine. He is on my health insurance from the hospital so if you don't want to suture him, that's fine. My insurance will cover the emergency room visit."

Only after her out-of-pocket maximum and deductible were met. Or had she already met her deductible? Had Justice had other accidents? Other medical expenses earlier in the year?

Medical expenses. Expenses period. Brielle had been carrying the financial load from the beginning. Five years she'd carried the burden of being a parent alone. Lord only knew what Justice's birth and preemie care had cost. Many women would have told him, a doctor with a great income, about their pregnancy just to have him pay child support and share in the expenses. Not Brielle. Leave it to her to be one who'd bear the challenges silently, never complaining, never asking for help even if she struggled to make ends meet.

That would change.

He made a makeshift bandage and tied it round Justice's knee, putting constant pressure on the wound. "For the record, I will give you back child support. Five years' worth. More. You tell me how much and it's yours."

"Where did that come from?" Brielle's mouth fell open and she stared at him aghast. "I don't want back child support. Justice and I get along just fine by ourselves." Sensing that her tone was upsetting their son further, she softened her voice. "Now is not the time for us to be having this discussion."

She was right.

Justice was still crying in her arms, but with a lot less fervor. His decreased agitation had helped to slow the bleeding as well.

Ross took Justice's small hand in his, hating the feel of the sticky blood covering his skin. He made a bandage of sorts from the remainder of his shirt and pressed it to the wound.

"Ouch. Ouch. Ouch," Justice cried anew, jerking his hand away from Ross's, not wanting anything to touch his wound. "Mommy, make him stop."

"Here, buddy," Ross said, trying not to flinch at the pain in his son's voice, or at how he'd felt at Justice jerking away from him. "I need you to be super-brave and hold this tight against your hand. Put it right here on the wound. Squeeze it tight in your fist."

"Shh, baby, your daddy is just trying to bandage your hand." Brielle rubbed Justice's arm, trying to comfort him and trying not to look at Ross.

Would he please put his shirt back on?

Not that he could even if he wanted to. Not with it being in tatters and soaking up Justice's blood.

Her son was bleeding, albeit a lot less at this point, and all she could think about was that Ross's chiseled chest was beautiful.

What was wrong with her?

Sure, she'd dealt with children's cuts and scrapes in the past and as an emergency room nurse she knew that Justice wasn't in any real danger. But at this moment her son was hurt and she was distracted by a gorgeous display of man-flesh. Shame on her.

And what had been up with the look they'd exchanged moments before Justice had tripped?

When it came to Ross, she really was pathetic.

She hugged her son closer to her, kissed the top of his head and wished she could take his pain on herself rather than have him suffer even the tiniest amount.

"Help him hold this on the place on his hand. I think his knee has stopped bleeding because it hasn't soaked through the material yet." He gestured to where he'd wrapped the material round Justice's knee and tied it in place using the T-shirt hem.

"I think you're right," she agreed, brushing her lips across Justice's head again. "It's gonna be okay, baby," she assured him. "I promise. We're going to take good care of you."

He'd twisted in her lap and had his head buried against her chest and his hand tucked between them. He still cried but only a little.

"Justice, son, your mother is going to carry you to the car while I pack our stuff up super-quick," Ross said, already gathering their supplies.

"Batman-quick?" Justice asked from between quivering lips.

"Faster," Ross assured him, setting everything down in a pile and reaching for Brielle's hand. "Here, let me help you to your feet."

She could stand from a sitting position while holding Justice, but doing so was becoming more and more difficult the older he got. Thinking Ross deserved bonus points for being so considerate, she took his hand while holding securely to Justice with the other. Not that her son was going anywhere anyway. Not with the tight grip he had around her neck with his arms and her waist with his legs.

Her belly flip-flopped at the skin-to-skin contact of her hand gripped tightly in Ross's firm grasp. The man exuded more electrical current than a power plant. Had to.

His fingers lingered longer than necessary, his gaze meeting hers, making her wonder what he felt when they touched. Was he bombarded with tiny zaps of excitement or drowned with memories? Or perhaps he felt nothing at all.

"I'll take Justice to the car and get him in his seat."

He still didn't let go of her hand.

"I'll meet you there," he said, his voice soft, steady, full of promises she didn't understand. Why did it sound as if he meant so much more than meeting her at the car?

She wiggled her fingers within his. His gaze dropped to their hands, as if he'd forgotten he held her. So much for her causing an electrical storm within him, the way he did her.

He let go and looked as if he was about to say something, but stopped, shook his head, and gathered up their gear.

Without another glance at him she headed towards the car with Justice. When she reached the vehicle, opened the back seat door and started to put him into his safety seat, Justice tightened his hold.

"No."

"No? Baby, I have to put you into the car so we can get your knee and hand taken care of where Mommy works."

Justice pulled his hand protectively close to his belly. "I don't want to go."

"We have to, sweetheart."

"I don't want us to leave my daddy. He might not find us again."

Brielle's heart constricted at the sincerity and concern in her son's voice, at his four-year-old logic, at what she'd deprived both Ross and her son of—each other. "Honey, we're not going to leave your daddy. He's just gathering our fishing gear so we can go fishing again some time. Together."

Despite her cajoling, Justice wouldn't let her go until Ross joined them.

"Everything okay?" he asked, eyeing them curiously as he popped the trunk with her key fob, which he'd stuck in his pocket after driving them to the lake.

"Fine," she answered, not wanting to repeat what Justice had said. At least, not until later when she and Ross could talk in private.

They needed to talk. They had a lot to say to each other. She had a lot to say to him.

Ross didn't look completely convinced, but he loaded the gear and put on a spare shirt he always carried in his hospital bag, which was stowed in her trunk, while she strapped a mostly co-operative Justice into his car seat.

Rather than get into the front seat beside Ross, she climbed into the back seat next to Justice so she could attend to him better should the bleeding worsen. Blood still hadn't soaked through the makeshift bandage on his knee, but the material held in his hand was quite messy.

Ross didn't say anything, just drove them to the hospital while she talked softly to Justice the entire ride, reassuring him about what would happen when they got to Mommy's work.

When they got to the ER, Brielle went to get Justice out of his car seat.

"I'll carry him in."

Arguing with Ross would only cause another scene in front of Justice and, really, what would be the point?

Justice was already reaching for his father to get him anyway. The sight of Justice in Ross's arms about undid her, making her legs feel weak, but she forced one foot in front of the other.

"Brielle? Dr. Lane?" Cindy's eyes were huge as they took in Brielle's bloodstained clothes and Justice wrapped around Ross. "What happened?"

"He fell. His hand and knee are cut. Not too badly but he's going to need stitches. Can you get me set up in Bay…" he glanced around the ER to see which bay was empty "…Two?"

"Don't you think he should see the doctor on duty?" Cindy asked, eyeing them all curiously.

Ross ignored her. "After you get Bay Two set up, bring a clean scrub top for Brielle to change into."

"Right," Cindy answered, her gaze telling Brielle there was no way she was going to be put off this time.

Yeah, yeah, she got the message. All week she'd put off Cindy's questions about Ross being Justice's father, but there would be no more delay in giving an explanation.

Ross motioned for Brielle to sit on the hospital bed then he handed Justice to her.

"Son, I'm going to wash my hands, glove up, then clean your leg and hand. I need you to be very brave like I know you are, okay?"

"Like—" He named his favorite superhero.

"Exactly like him."

Determined to make his father proud, Justice sat very still in Brielle's lap, taking in everything Ross did.

Cindy tossed a clean scrub top onto the hospital bed beside them then gloved up also. "I have everything I thought you might need set out on the tray."

"Thanks," Ross said, sliding his hands into his gloves. "If you need to go and take care of your patients, I think Brielle and I have this."

Cindy gave them a reluctant look. "You're sure?"

He nodded. "We'll be fine, but if we need you, I'll call. I know you have other patients as this was the only open bay."

She nodded, her gaze going back and forth between them. "I do, but...okay, call if you need me."

"Is he allergic to anything?" Ross asked Brielle.

"Penicillin is his only allergy."

"You're not allergic to anything," Ross remembered. "He gets that from me. I'm allergic to penicillin."

Ross sounded a bit incredulous, in awe that his son had one of his traits. Ha, Justice had a lot more of his father than just an antibiotic allergy.

He removed the bandage from Justice's hand. The bleeding had stopped and the torn skin had lifted away from the palm.

"Ouch," Justice whimpered, then seemed to recall that he was being brave and sucked his lower lip into his mouth.

Ross rinsed the wound out with saline solution, making sure there was no foreign debris. Next he swirled iodine solution from the center of the wound outwards so as not to drag any bacteria into the wound. He picked up the anesthetic-filled syringe to numb the area prior to suturing the skin back together.

"I don't want a shot." Justice forgot about being brave and began scooting back against Brielle as tightly as his little body would go. "Mommy, don't let him give me a shot."

"I'm just going to squirt a few drops into the tear to begin with. It'll sting a little, but won't be too bad," Ross promised.

Justice still didn't want any part of the needle and Brielle had to forcibly hold his palm out while he squirmed, saying "Ouch" over and over.

Ross squirted a generous amount of anesthetic into the open wound, waited a few seconds then injected the area to the sounds of his son screaming.

Brielle cringed at her son's pain, wishing yet again she could take his pain for him.

"No. Stop! I don't like you. No. Ouch. Ouch. Daddy, stop!"

She winced at him calling Ross "Daddy" in the middle of their workplace. No way had all their co-workers not heard his cries. Then again, they all suspected something was going on between her and Ross. May as well have it all out in the open so they could move on to some new tidbit of gossip.

"You need help?" Cindy asked, poking her head into the bay, her dark gaze going straight to Brielle.

"We're fine," Brielle and Ross said at the same time.

Ross finished injecting the area and set the syringe down. Justice had already calmed down somewhat.

"Alrighty, then," the nurse said, disappearing again. "Justice, sweetie, if you need anything, you yell for me, okay?"

Justice nodded, wiping his face on Brielle's shirt. "I don't want 'titches."

"Justice, does your hand still hurt?" Ross asked.

Not looking at Ross, he nodded again.

"It does? You're sure? The magic potion medicine I put in should have put a spell on your hand and made it stop hurting completely."

Justice seemed to consider that. "Maybe it worked a little."

"That's good, son. I want you to tell me if your hand starts hurting again because the magic potion is to protect you so your hand doesn't hurt at all, okay?"

Justice eyed his hand as if expecting a glow or puff of smoke to be emitted from the wound.

Ross began to do his magic for real. He pulled the skin flap down, lining up the wound edges as perfectly as possible then began putting in suture after suture.

On the first suture Brielle distracted Justice's attention to something elsewhere in the room rather than at what Ross was doing, and he was halfway into the second one when Justice noticed the needle.

"No." Justice tried to pull his hand away, but Brielle kept a firm grasp on it.

"You've got to hold very still, son. Remember the magic potion," Ross urged in a gentle but firm voice. He didn't stop what he was doing. "You didn't feel the first suture and you won't feel this one either. You're under the protection of magic, remember?"

Justice didn't look completely convinced but he let Ross finish, his tiny body relaxing against Brielle's. During the eighth suture his eyes closed.

"He's exhausted," she informed Ross as he tied off the last stitch and cut the Ethilon.

"No wonder. Fishing and this."

"He never even cast his line."

"Fossil hunting can be exhausting, too," he said, obviously trying to go for lightness.

Something about them being alone with their son sleeping between them made Brielle feel nervous.

Moving gently so as not to wake Justice, Brielle repositioned herself so Ross would have easy access to the cut on Justice's knee. He cut the knot, releasing the material of the makeshift bandage. The knee had bled enough to stick the fabric to the wound and he poured saline over the area to re-wet it so he could remove the fabric more easily from the area without tugging on the wound.

He repeated the steps he'd taken on Justice's palm, first cleaning the wound, then disinfecting it, then squirting anesthetic into the open wound to provide some numbness before he anesthetized the area properly by injecting anesthetic around the wound.

Justice sighed in his sleep, but Brielle comforted him, singing softly and rubbing his back as she'd done his entire life when holding him, and he didn't wake up completely.

Ross sutured the knee while Brielle watched, still singing softly to Justice.

"You're very good with him," Ross praised when he'd trimmed the Ethilon on all the sutures.

Something warm and gooey moved in her chest. "I was thinking that about you. That was brilliant with the magic potion."

"He likes magic. Almost everything we played this week ended up involving some type of spell or magic force field."

"Most children are fascinated by such things."

Ross's gaze dropped to their sleeping son nestled against her chest. "You've done a really good job with him, Brielle. A man couldn't ask for a better mother for his child."

Heat infused Brielle's face. Whether from his praise or from the way he was looking at her, she wasn't sure, just that she was getting the warm fuzzies inside and Ross was causing them.

Then again, this man had always caused her to get warm fuzzies of one kind or another.

"It was nice having you here today to help me with him," she admitted, stroking her fingers along Justice's back to occupy her hands. "Much easier than if I'd had to deal with his cuts on my own."

"I should've been there every time you needed help with him, Brielle." He grimaced, sighed, then stared directly into her eyes. "I would have been there from the beginning if I'd known."

"I know."

She did know. Only she'd wanted him to be there because he'd wanted to be there, not because he'd felt obligated to be there.

Men who stayed because they felt obligated ended up leaving and the ones left behind were all the more devastated for having believed in for ever and always.

CHAPTER TEN

Ross carried his son's limp body to his bedroom, waited while Brielle pulled back his bed covers, then gently laid the boy down. Brielle helped to position him in the bed, fluffing his pillow beneath him, adjusting the comforter that Ross had pulled up over the boy.

His son.

It was crazy that just two weeks before he hadn't known he had a son. Already he couldn't imagine going back to an existence without Justice. The child had won his heart completely.

He couldn't imagine going back to an existence without Brielle either.

His gaze lifted to her, caught her watching him. Her eyes were glassy, as if she fought tears. Then she lost the battle and a wet streak slid down her cheek.

"Don't cry, Brielle. He's okay." He wanted to take her into his arms, but she'd only push him away. Despite their moment of peace at the hospital, she'd clammed back up, sliding the walls she held between them back into place.

"I know." She nodded, swatting at her tears. "It's not that. It's…"

"It's…?" he prompted.

She glanced toward their sleeping son, shook her

head, then quickly slipped past Ross without looking at him.

Ross watched her go, realized that more than anything he didn't want her to go, so he went after her.

"Brielle?" he said, knocking on her bedroom door.

Not having been properly latched, the door fell open. She sat on the edge of her bed, her face buried in her hands as she sobbed silently.

Ross gave in to the need to hold her.

He gave in to the need to feel her in his arms and breathe in her scent.

He gave in to everything that was inside him that said this was the woman he wanted.

Without waiting for permission, he crossed the floor, sat beside her on the bed and pulled her into his arms.

Her gaze lifted to his, startled as if she hadn't realized he was there until he held her. Had she been so lost in her misery?

"Don't cry, Brielle. I can't stand to see you cry," he said gently, brushing his fingers lighttly across her cheeks to dry her tears. "I never could."

"Don't be nice to me," she surprised him by ordering in a low but firm voice.

"Why wouldn't I be?"

"I don't deserve your kindness."

He held her tighter to him. "Sure you do."

She huffed, not meeting his eyes.

He put his hand beneath her chin, lifted it. "Look at me." When she didn't, he repeated, "Look at me, Brielle."

She looked up, meeting his gaze and wincing.

"You deserve my kindness because you are the mother of my son, because when I chose to walk away rather than to fight for us, you didn't make the wrong choice. You gave our son life and you have done an amazing job of raising him by yourself without any help from me when I should have been by your side the whole way."

"You would have been if I'd told you. I know you would have."

"But that isn't how you wanted me, was it, Brielle?"

She shook her head. "No, I wanted…" Her voice trailed off and she averted her gaze.

"You wanted what?" he prompted, tilting her chin, realizing that the distance between their mouths was closing. He could feel her breath teasing his lips, could feel the warmness of her mouth beckoning him.

"You," she answered simply, closing her eyes and looking as if she was in agony.

Agony that Ross understood. He was feeling pretty agonized himself.

"I wanted you," she whispered, eyes still shut.

He leaned forward the slightest amount, putting his lips in direct contact with hers, and ended his agony.

Her lips felt amazing against his.

Her eyes shot open, searched his for answers that he doubted she'd find because he didn't have answers, not to any of the questions shining in her eyes.

All he knew was that he had never stopped wanting this woman. That for five years he'd wanted her but had been too stubborn to admit that he'd needed her all those years before.

He needed her now.

Her mouth remained perfectly still and he couldn't stand it. He wanted to taste her, to put his tongue into the sweet recesses of her mouth and conquer all.

As if sensing his need, she parted her lips and Ross growled his pleasure.

"You taste so good," he groaned, supping on her lower lip. "So perfect."

"Don't talk," she ordered low against his mouth. "Please, just don't say anything. Just…just kiss me."

Ross might have stopped to analyze her comment had he been thinking straight. But he hadn't been thinking straight from the moment he'd taken her into his arms.

No, longer than that. He hadn't been thinking straight for years, since the first time he'd laid eyes on his roommate's kid sister who had just been finishing nursing school and had literally taken his breath away. What had happened to make him forget that?

To forget how she'd affected him? How he'd instantly known he'd have her? Yet he'd been the one to walk away, and for what?

At the moment nothing seemed as pressing as loving this woman, familiarizing himself again with everything about her.

Her lips. Her mouth. Her face. Her neck.

Oh, her neck. How he'd always loved her neck.

What a sweet arch she had.

When he kissed her collar bone, slid his hands under the borrowed hospital scrub top to push the material out of his way, he groaned. Brielle had more curves and slopes than a geometry textbook.

Her fingers tangled in his hair as he breathed in the lovely scent between her breasts.

Fuller, he thought. Her breasts were fuller than when they'd been together before. Had time or childbirth done that?

Either way, he was going to reap their bounty.

His fingers found the clasp to her bra and freed her beautiful breasts. He stared in appreciation. "You're beautiful, Brielle. So beautiful."

"No talking," she reminded him, pulling his mouth back to hers and kissing him so thoroughly, so hungrily that the constriction of his shorts grew painful and he had to adjust himself.

He pushed her back on her bed, leaned forward and kissed her belly, then lifted his T-shirt over his head, wanting to feel his skin against hers, his body against hers with nothing between them.

"You're the one who is beautiful," she murmured, tracing her fingers down his chest. "You always were so beautiful, Ross."

He started to correct her, to tell her he was a man and far far from beautiful. Then her fingers found their way to his waist. All he could do was suck in his breath in eager anticipation of what she'd do next.

No, he thought. This wasn't about him. It was about Brielle. About how much he wanted to make her feel good, about how much he wanted to give her pleasure. He wanted Brielle so caught up in him that she was as hungry for him as he was for her.

Hungrier. Starved.

His hand covered hers just as she slid his zipper down and he shook his head.

Her brow lifted in question.

By way of answer he tugged on her elastic-waisted shorts, sliding them over the curve of her hips, down her toned thighs and calves, and tossed them onto her floor.

Lying on the bed in only her bright pink cotton panties, Brielle was easily the most beautiful sight his eyes had ever been lucky enough to behold.

Beautiful.

His.

He may have been stupid enough not to acknowledge the connection between them when he'd been younger, but now he knew. He and Brielle were meant to be together. Always and for ever.

This time he was wise enough to embrace that fact rather than try to run from something so powerful.

Love.

He loved Brielle.

Always had. Always would.

He slipped his fingers beneath her panties and slid them down the same path as her shorts.

Immediately, he realized he'd been wrong.

Looking at her, completely naked, lying on the bed waiting for his touch, that was the most beautiful sight he'd ever been lucky enough to behold.

She watched him, her skin flushed with desire, her eyes half-lidded and her lips parted.

So beautiful.

He ran his hands over her legs, going slowly, enjoying every glide of his skin across hers, growing more and more excited with the goose-bumps that prickled her skin at his touch, at the way her nipples puckered and strained upwards, eager to touch him, to be touched by him.

As much as he wanted to explore every inch of her body, slowly and surely, kissing her breasts, bringing her to the brink of pleasure and then toppling her over time and again, he couldn't do it.

Because he couldn't resist the tantalizing pull of between her legs.

He bent, dipped his tongue between her pretty pink lips, and suckled the swollen flesh.

"Ross," she murmured, her fingers back in his hair, working across his scalp as her hips writhed against the thrust of his tongue.

He laved her most sensitive part until her breath came in short pants and she said his name over and over as if chanting a magic spell all her own.

Perhaps she had because certainly he felt enchanted, under her spell, as if some magical force was at work making him completely and totally hers.

She arched off the bed, curled her fingers tightly into his hair then cried out softly with her orgasm.

Hearing her pleasure, seeing her reaction to his touch, feeling her, tasting her overwhelmed Ross's senses and he lost control.

Lost control of his mind and his body.

He finished the job she'd started, shucking his shorts off in record time and moving over her, positioning his body, then without hesitation slid home to where he'd always belonged.

With Brielle.

Brielle closed her eyes at the sheer pleasure moving through her body.

Every touch of Ross's hand against her lit fires that had burned low for too many years. Every brush of his mouth against her body started infernos only he could quench.

Now, feeling him stretching her, filling her up with

him, she wanted to cry from the joy of it. Then again, crying was what had started this.

No, she wouldn't think about the emotions that had assuaged her when she'd gone to her room and given in to the tears. For the moment she was just going to be greedy, to take what his body was giving, to feel all the things she'd had denied her for five years.

Five long, lonely years since she'd made love to this man. To any man. Five long, forlorn years when she'd loved him, missed him, wanted him to miraculously reappear in her life, sweep her off her feet and tell her he felt exactly the same way about her.

Never had she actually believed he would.

Not really.

Or had she?

Sure, there had been a part of her that had dreamed, hoped, but she'd kept that part buried so she could survive day by day with a big chunk of her heart missing.

She'd focused on Justice, Vann, her job. She'd been happy, even if she'd always known something was missing. Someone. Ross.

But here he was. Buried deep inside her, his gorgeous body moving against hers, thrusting deeper and deeper until rational thought was becoming more and more difficult, until all she wanted was to lose herself in him.

His lips marauded hers, as if her mouth provided him with the necessities of life itself and he was a dying man in need of sustenance.

His hands caressed her, then supported his body above hers where he angled himself, driving even deeper into her, but where he could watch her beneath him.

From her vantage point she admired the chiseled

lushness of his chest, of his cut abdomen. She wanted to reach out and touch him as she had earlier, but her insides began to melt and she could only curl her fingers into tight fists. First she melted only at the very core of her, but then she liquefied in a spiraling outward motion that built in momentum until every nerve cell was rocked with the force of a tornado turning her insides out in a pleasurable explosion.

She gripped her bed covers. Her fingers clenched and unclenched. Wave after wave of glorious spasms shook her body. She arched into Ross, then bit her tongue to keep from crying out with the enormity of the orgasm that hit her.

Total. Orgasmic. Meltdown.

But he wasn't through. Oh, no. Just as she crashed over the pinnacle of her pleasurable ride, he jetted her right back up by taking her nipple in his mouth and giving her a hard suckle, all the while imprinting her body over and over with him.

She lost count of how many times he brought her up, let her fall just a little so she could appreciate the next ascent to an even higher crest. Over and over until she was positive her brain would never function again. That all of her body had completely short-circuited from the lightning running through her and she would remain a sizzled, spent gob of ooey-gooey goop.

When she felt the change in his pace, the tightening of his abdominal muscles, the tension pouring from every pore of his body, she arched into his thrust, meeting his rhythm, welcoming the rush of pleasure filling her body as, that time, it was her name crossing his lips in a possessive growl.

His body glistening with sweat, he virtually collapsed onto her, kissing her cheek. "Perfect."

Not perfect, but his words and the way he hugged her to him, rolled them over to where she was lying on him rather than vice versa, holding her close and managing to keep their bodies joined throughout the maneuver as if he couldn't bear to part from her yet, warmed a part of her that had been cold for a long time. A part she'd buried in the icy recesses of the past to keep the pain from destroying her.

Their bodies stuck together and she hid her face in the groove of his neck, breathing hard. Her heart pounded so forcefully that every finger and toe throbbed in pulsating cadence. Her entire body throbbed, ebbed, flowed.

The intensity began to recede and her brain began to reboot itself, to register the impact of what they'd just done. Her sweaty, spent body was stretched out over Ross's long, hard body, both of them out of breath, both of them clinging to the other.

Crack after crack she heard the thaw, felt the reality of her vulnerability to Ross become more and more exposed.

Barely here two weeks and she'd already spread her legs and welcomed him inside her body. Did that make her easy?

Perhaps, but if so, she was only easy for this one man because he was the only one with the power to move her so. The only man she'd ever wanted.

Was she wrong to have taken what he'd offered? To have given in to the need within her to be with him?

She hadn't planned on this. Had planned just the opposite, especially with him living with her and Justice. They didn't need to be doing this or touching at all. There were too many obstacles between them as it was. Sex would just end up being one more.

Sex?

Was that what they'd just done? Had sex?

Never in the past when she'd been with Ross had she questioned that they were making love. Never.

But then he'd left her and that had changed everything, had changed her. He may have been irresistible, he may have exposed her vulnerable heart, but no longer was she the naive girl who'd fallen in love with him and given him her heart and body.

This time she knew that Ross wasn't playing for keeps and the good thing was that even if he was, she wasn't.

He'd permanently cured her of that.

She refused to be like her mother and that one thing would keep her safe from Ross, even if nothing else would.

Despite his tight hold, she rolled off him, lay flat on her back and stared at the ceiling, each breath still coming hard and fast. Ross's breathing was coming even harder, faster from his position next to her.

He took her hand, squeezed, dropped their clasped fingers to the bed, and took several deep breaths, before blowing everything she'd just thought right out of the water.

"We should get married."

Ross didn't have to turn his head to know Brielle was staring at him as if he'd lost his mind. He felt her horrified glare. Felt the shock pouring from her every pore as she gawked at him.

Not exactly the reaction a man hoped for when discussing marriage with a woman.

"We have sex once and you say we should get married?" She sounded incredulous, as if he'd spoken in a foreign tongue about something impossible and far-fetched.

"Not just once," he reminded her, expecting her to point out that it had only been once in the past five years.

A deep V cut into her forehead and she just continued to stare at him as if he'd lost his mind. "All those times that we did so much more years ago, when I loved you with all my heart, and none of the previous times inspired you to want to walk down the aisle with me. Am I so good now that after a single time you feel the need to shroud me in white and listen to wedding bells peal? Pardon me if I don't buy it."

He rolled onto his side so he could see her more easily. "Sarcasm? Really? After what we just shared you give me sarcasm when I ask you a serious question?"

She didn't so much as flinch. "You asked nothing."

Ross frowned. Hadn't he?

"You want me to get down on my knee and propose, Brielle? Would that put a nice smile on your face? Would that make you happy? Because if that's what you want, I will."

"No." Her gaze narrowed and he regretted his snappy comment. Only hadn't she just been right there with him, experiencing the same things he'd experienced? Sex between them had always been good, but that had been… He searched for a word and still failed to define what he'd just shared with Brielle.

"I don't want to marry you." Her words sliced into his thoughts.

"What?" He sat up, stared down into her stubborn face, not quite believing she was serious. She'd loved him, was the mother of his child, had practically beat him over the head with bridal magazines just a few years before, and now she didn't want to marry him?

"You heard me."

He glared at her, trying to read her expression, trying to decipher what was really going on behind her words. "Is this your idea of retribution because I didn't jump on board five years ago when you were trying to shotgun me down the aisle?"

She sat up too, glared much more fiercely than anything he could pull off. "No, this is me not wanting to marry you and saying so."

"You used to want to marry me," he reminded her, not liking how his euphoria of just moments before had completely dissipated and was being replaced with something dark and ugly.

She shrugged. "What I used to want is irrelevant to what I want today. I don't want to be your wife."

He eyed her, noting the slight quiver to her lower lip, the rapid pulse at her throat. "People don't change that much."

"Exactly," she agreed, although he didn't understand what she was agreeing to. She crossed her arms over her breasts then, seeming to realize she was naked, she yanked her bed covers over her body. "You are the one man I won't ever marry. Got it?"

What the…?

"Why not?" He didn't bother keeping his voice low because…well, just because, although he remembered too late that his son was just down the hall and the last thing he wanted was Justice to hear them arguing. "Why not?" he repeated much more softly, hoping she'd take his cue and keep her voice down too.

"Justice."

"Now I really don't understand. Our son is why you won't marry me? Perhaps you didn't notice but the boy likes me and needs his father, me, in his life."

"I never said he doesn't need you or that you shouldn't be in his life. And of course he likes you. You've showered him with attention and gifts. Why wouldn't he like you?"

"You make the fact that I bought my son a few things this week sound as if I was trying to bribe him. Thanks to you, I have five years to make up for so forgive me if I go a little crazy here at the beginning and want to see my kid's face light up a few times. I've only been a father, that I knew of, for a little over a week. Forgive me if I don't get everything just perfect. I'm learning as I go. I think I'm owed a little slack there, don't you?"

Gaze downward cast and pulling her comforter over her body, she nodded. "I'm sure you are. I can't change the past any more than you can. What's done is done. If I'd known you'd have wanted to be a part of Justice's life, I'd—"

"Oh, spare me your sob story," he interrupted, frustrated, angry, pulling on his underwear and shorts. "We both know the truth. You didn't tell me to punish me for leaving."

"I didn't," she gasped, sounding horrified.

"You did. Did it give you satisfaction to know that you'd given birth to my child, were raising my son all without me being any the wiser? Did you feel as if retribution had been served every time you looked at him and knew my eyes had never even seen him?"

Her mouth fell open, her gaze narrowed, and her eyes flickered with anger. "Get out!" she ordered, pointing toward her bedroom door.

"The truth hurts, doesn't it?"

"Get out!" she repeated, grabbing her clothes and dressing in haste then tossing his T-shirt at him. "Get out of my bedroom, out of my house, and out of my life! You aren't wanted here. Do you hear me? We did just fine without you and don't need you here. I don't want you here!"

"As if you could make me stay," he countered, sliding on his T-shirt, wondering how the magic of moments before had morphed into something so ugly, wondering why he wasn't stopping this because deep down he knew he didn't want to go.

"You'll be hearing from my lawyers," he said, instead of begging her to forgive him for his pride. "I tried to do this the nice way, even asked you to marry me, but you had to be difficult, didn't you?" Or was he the one being difficult? Had he rushed things? No, he wanted to marry the mother of his five-year-old child. If anything, he was behind the times. But she no longer wanted to marry him. A fresh pain stabbed his heart. "Have it your way. We won't get married, but my son will live with me. Not just every other weekend."

"No," she cried, her face paling to a pasty white as she dropped onto the edge of the bed as if her legs were no longer strong enough to support her. She sat, staring at him in horror. "You can't do that."

He wouldn't do that. She was a good mother. Justice needed her.

"Oh, yes, Brielle." He barely recognized his own voice, but defensive pain pushed him down a different path than the one he wanted to travel. No, he didn't need to feel sorry for her. He needed to remember what she'd done to him, to their son, and why? Because she'd had some misguided notion that he should have married her without knowing and since he hadn't agreed, she wouldn't marry him at all? She didn't deserve his consideration. She sure hadn't shown him any. "You had five years. I want what you stole from me. Five years."

Red splotched her pale cheeks. "No judge is going to give you that!"

"No?" He arched his brow, too hurt and angry to stop his bitter words. "You think you can provide that boy with a better life than I can? Think again."

"I have provided him with a good home, a good life. I give him everything he needs," she insisted.

"No." He shook his head with disdain. "You didn't. You didn't give him the father he obviously craves and needs. Me."

With that he gave her one last look of disgust then left her bedroom. He wanted to slam her door. Lord, how he wanted the satisfaction of slamming her bedroom door. Instead, in deference to their hopefully still sleeping son, he closed the door behind him with a resounding click that echoed through his mind as he walked down the hallway.

Away from Brielle.

Why did that feel so wrong?

CHAPTER ELEVEN

BRIELLE HAD DREADED going in to the hospital because she'd have to see Ross. There would be no way to avoid seeing him in the emergency department with them both working there.

Perhaps she shouldn't have bothered worrying.

He seemed as intent on ignoring her as she was on ignoring him.

She'd not seen him since he'd stormed out of her apartment three days before. A mere week at her house and everywhere she looked she saw him, had flashbacks of seeing him there with Justice, of hearing his laughter, of his scent filling her home, of just knowing he was there.

As much as she missed him, Justice missed him more.

The day after their argument Ross had called and very tersely asked to speak to Justice. She'd handed her son the phone, wanted to listen in, but had forced herself to go to the kitchen for a moment to give her son a minute of privacy. When she'd come back into the room, Justice had set the phone down and gone to his room. She'd picked the phone up but the line had been dead.

The silence at the end of the phone a harsh reminder of the void in her life.

Justice hadn't mentioned what Ross had said, but he'd been full of questions.

"Where's my daddy?

"Why did my daddy have to go far away?

"Is my daddy coming home soon?

"We need to go find my daddy."

Justice couldn't seem to focus on anything except the void Ross's disappearance from their house had left. Even Vann had commented on it when he'd come to visit them. Her brother hadn't said too much about Ross. He'd just listened to her give a glossed-over version of what had happened because she sure wasn't telling him she'd been stupid enough to have sex with Ross. Then Vann had told her to be patient and forgiving, that Ross was dealing with a lot and probably just needed some time.

That hadn't sat well and so they'd opted to not discuss Ross for the rest of her brother's visit.

Only Justice had grilled his uncle on Ross's whereabouts.

Her poor son. She'd wanted to protect him. Instead, she'd been stupid, given in to her own passion for Ross and ended up ruining everything.

Had they been destined to fail from the beginning? The past too painful for them to forge any kind of amicable relationship in the present?

For Justice's sake, she hoped not.

Part of her had been on edge, expecting to receive a court summons regarding custody. Probably she would as, realistically, those things took much longer than a few days to set into motion.

She wouldn't fight him regarding sharing their son. Justice needed both of his parents. But she would fight till her dying breath if he attempted to take Justice from her completely.

Maybe he did have the right since he'd missed five years of his son's life, but he'd destroy her if he denied her access to Justice.

Somehow she knew he wouldn't, that he'd only do what he thought was right for Justice. He himself had said that she was a good mother, that she'd done a good job with Justice. Despite their argument, she knew Ross wouldn't remove Justice completely from her life. Not for her sake but for Justice's.

"Bay Three needs vitals, to be hooked up to telemetry and cardiac enzymes drawn." Ross's order cut into her mind's meanderings. "His information says he has chest pain, so why isn't someone with him?"

Good point. She'd seen the nurse call him back immediately after he'd signed in to the emergency department, stating he had chest pain, but that had been a few minutes ago and the nurse had disappeared.

"Yes, sir." Brielle put down the clipboard she was making notes on, turning it upside down to prevent passersby from being able to see her patient's recorded information. She didn't bother to explain that Bay Three was another nurse's patient. If something was going on in the emergency room, whoever was available took care of it regardless of who'd been assigned to the patient.

She wasn't sure where the nurse had gone during the middle of triaging the patient, but Brielle would finish it and carry out Ross's orders.

When she stepped into the bay, she introduced herself to the fifty-three-year-old man, who was holding his chest.

Ross was right. The man shouldn't have been left alone. His face was ruddy, his skin clammy, and he had a nervous, wild-eyed appearance that set warning bells off in Brielle's head.

"Mr. Cook, do you have anyone with you?"

The man shook his head. "No, I drove myself here."

Scary thought for him to have been behind the wheel of a car, but she smiled, wanting to keep him calm and definitely not wanting to raise his anxiety level.

She assisted in removing his shirt, put an automatic blood-pressure cuff on his left upper arm, and began hooking the telemetry to him. He had a hairy body and the leads wouldn't stick. She quickly shaved the hair in the appropriate spots and stuck the leads on, getting good adherence.

She pressed the button, turning on the heart monitor. What she saw widened her eyes.

His erratic pulse was registering anywhere from one hundred and forty to two hundred beats per minute in a horribly irregular rhythm.

"Dr. Lane?" she called, keeping her voice calm. "I have Mr. Cook's heart monitor started if you'd like to check him."

Knowing she wouldn't have called him if he didn't need to come immediately, Ross stepped into the bay, saw what had concerned her and began taking action.

"Give him..." He named the appropriate medication and dosage. He rattled off more orders and Brielle made a mental note of each one, even as she began drawing up the medication to administer it.

As the man didn't have an intravenous line in yet, Ross sat down next to him and started the IV himself.

Again, Brielle had to question where the nurse assigned to the patient had disappeared to. Ross got the line started and she pushed the medication in.

"I want Cardiology here now," Ross told her, then turned to Mr. Cook. "At the minimum, you're going to need to be admitted so we can check you out really well to see what is going on. Right now your heart is out of rhythm. The medications the nurse gave you will help keep you from developing a blood clot and will help the heart not have to work quite so hard until the heart specialist gets here to evaluate you."

The man nodded as if he understood but rather than answer Ross, he closed his eyes.

The monitor's beeping became a constant steady drone.

A drone that caused adrenaline to surge in any medical professional's body.

Brielle's stomach fell and her own adrenaline skyrocketed.

Mr. Cook had flat-lined.

Beginning CPR, Ross called the code as Brielle grabbed the crash cart. She prepared the defibrillator and handed the paddles to Ross.

"All clear," he said, and immediately gave the man an electric shock with the paddles.

Nothing.

Hearing the code call, Cindy joined them and began giving the man breaths of air via a hand-held air bag as they performed two-man CPR. Brielle took over compressions while they waited for the defibrillator to recharge.

"Again," Ross said, the second the machine was ready to deliver another charge. "All clear."

Cindy and Brielle stepped back. Ross put the paddles to the man's chest. The man's body jerked from the jolt of electricity.

Brielle held her breath, waiting, hoping.

His heart gave a resounding beep on the monitor. Then another. And another.

"Thank God," she breathed, knowing that the man was far from out of danger as at any moment the tide could turn.

"Give him…" Ross named the medication and Brielle nodded, turning to grab the injectible medication from the crash cart. He turned to Cindy. "Get Cardiology here stat."

"Yes, sir. Dr. Heather Abellano is in the CCU. I saw her earlier." Cindy glanced toward Brielle then headed out of the partitioned exam room.

Brielle continued to monitor the patient, all too aware that Ross was watching her. Okay, so really he was observing the patient, but she could sense his gaze shift to her every few seconds.

But he didn't say a single word to her. Not one.

Within minutes, Dr. Abellano was in the room, examining Mr. Cook and having him transferred to the cardiac care unit for further evaluation and treatment.

Once Mr. Cook was on his way, Brielle sighed in relief, glad her shift was almost over and she could go home to Justice.

She glanced toward Ross. He was scribbling on Mr. Cook's emergency room encounter, no doubt documenting the man's code, stabilization, and transfer.

He glanced up, caught her staring at him. His brow lifted, but she only looked away. What did he expect? For her to say something? What was she supposed to say that they hadn't already said?

* * *

Ross signed his name at the bottom of the emergency room encounter, trying to focus on the task at hand and not on the woman across the room restocking the crash cart.

The woman who'd turned his life upside down.

He couldn't say that he regretted his decision to come to Bean's Creek. If he hadn't, he'd never have known about Justice. He'd done the right thing.

About coming here, if nothing else.

On everything else he just wasn't sure.

Everything had seemed so clear in his mind when he'd stormed out of her house.

He'd had to leave.

Yet hadn't he done exactly what she'd expected all along? Left when things got sticky?

He wasn't a quitter, or the type of man who walked away from a problem. He'd have labeled himself a problem-solver, not a runner.

Yet perhaps Brielle was justified to think that way of him, because with her he hadn't stuck around when things got muddled.

But unlike in the past, he hadn't left with no intention of returning. Over the past few days he'd made major life decisions. Decisions that he'd needed to make with a clear head.

Apparently, a clear head and being near Brielle didn't go hand in hand. Not for him. She made him crazy.

She made him alive.

More alive than at any other point in his life. Every emotion was more intense, more real, more vivid with Brielle back in his life, and that's where he wanted her, in his life.

He probably should have stayed, camped out on her sofa until they'd both cooled off. Instead, he'd flown to Boston, arranged to sell his practice to his partners, put his apartment on the market and tied up loose ends because he wouldn't be moving back at the end of his three months in Bean's Creek.

Regardless of what happened between him and Brielle, he was staying in North Carolina, was staying where his family was, Justice and Brielle.

What was happening between them?

What did he want to happen?

Hadn't that thought been foremost in his mind over the past few days? What was it he wanted more than anything?

Not what currently was, that was for sure.

His skin crawled every time he caught her looking at him with her big sad eyes. He wanted her eyes smiling, her lips laughing, her world a better place because he was in her life. What he didn't want was to cause her stress and grief.

But he was going to be a part of Justice's daily life.

He'd missed five years of his son's life. He wouldn't miss any more. He missed that kid.

He missed Brielle.

He glanced at where she was talking to the nurse who'd just returned from helping transport Mr. Cook. Brielle looked tired, stressed, as if she hadn't been sleeping well, and he knew he was to blame.

He wanted to wrap his arms around her and tell her he wanted to come home.

Home? Was that how he thought of her quaint little house? Home was where the heart was.

His heart was wherever Brielle and Justice were.

Yes, he wanted to go home.

Which meant he and Brielle needed to talk. No coercion or threats on his part regarding custody of Justice, though. He wanted her to invite him to come back. For her to tell him she'd missed him as much as he'd missed her.

He wanted her to love him as much as he loved her.

As much as she had loved him once upon a time.

If she'd loved him once, he'd win her love again. He knew Brielle. She wasn't the kind to love lightly. She'd given him her heart and he was going to stake his future happiness on the fact that she'd never gotten it back completely, otherwise she wouldn't have made love with him.

They had made love. Yes, the chemistry between them was phenomenal, but their connection went way beyond physical.

Love really was the most powerful thing in the world.

Why question himself?

He knew what he wanted.

The time apart had cleared that up for him and he had no doubts about the direction he wanted his future to take.

He glanced at his watch. Their shift was almost over. Thank God. Today had been a killer day. Or maybe it had been the tension between him and Brielle that had made him feel that way.

He'd known that at the end of their shift he'd talk to her, get down on his knees and beg her to open her heart to him.

Somehow he would convince her that he deserved a second chance, deserved her love, deserved the opportunity to love and cherish her and their son for the rest of their lives.

He put his hand in his scrub pocket. His fingers traced over a velvet box. Why had he brought the trinket with him? It wasn't as if he'd do anything with it at the hospital, yet he hadn't wanted to leave it at the apartment he'd returned to late last night either.

Brielle came over to the station where he sat and picked up a clipboard.

"I'd like to see Justice tonight."

"Fine."

Ross cringed. He really didn't like that word.

"Could I take you both to dinner?"

She hesitated only a second. "No, but you are welcome to spend time with Justice, either taking him to dinner or playing with him at my house."

"But I'm not welcome to spend time with you?"

She shook her head. "The less time we spend together, the better for Justice's sake."

"Why's that?"

"Because us being together is like mixing fire and gasoline. We can't coexist."

"We coexisted for years. Quite well," he reminded her.

"That was before."

"Before?"

"Justice."

"Justice is all the more reason for us to coexist."

Which was exactly why Brielle couldn't even try. She couldn't be her mother. Hadn't she seen the devastation that forcing a man into marriage caused?

"You are welcome to see him. He misses you."

"I miss him." Ross raked his fingers through his dark hair. "Look, Brielle…" he glanced around the for once almost empty emergency department "…we need to talk. Not here. Not at your place with Justice there. Just you and me."

"I don't see the point."

"Then give me the opportunity to show you the point."

She sighed. As much as she didn't want to have the conversation with him, she knew that eventually she'd have to. He was her son's father and would always be a part of her life.

"Fine. We'll talk, but I have to pick Justice up from his preschool after-care when I get off work, so not to-night."

He seemed ready to argue with her, but the vibration of her cellular phone in her pocket and her pulling the phone out to check the number stopped him.

She rarely got a phone call at work.

The preschool.

"Hello."

"Hey, Brielle, this is Rachel. I don't know how to tell you this, but…Justice is missing."

Brielle's heart stopped. "Missing? What do you mean, missing?"

"We've looked every where at the school and can't find him. He's gone."

Brielle couldn't say another word, could barely stand. Her gaze met Ross's concerned one and she held the phone out to him in a hand that visibly shook.

He took the phone. "This is Dr. Ross Lane. What's going on?"

Brielle moved in a daze as Ross had her get her purse

while he informed Administration that they were both leaving. Fortunately, it was close enough to shift change that their replacements were already at the hospital.

Wordlessly, she climbed into the passenger seat of his car, rode to the preschool with panic and fear foremost in her heart and mind.

Missing. Justice was missing.

Ross had called the police the moment he'd hung up from the preschool, reported what the preschool teacher had told him. Although not enough time had passed for them to file an official missing-person report, they were sending an officer to meet them at the preschool.

When Ross reached across the car seat and took her hand into his, she didn't pull away. Somewhere in the horror of the moment she registered that his hand trembled. Yet she drew great strength from knowing he was there, that he was with her and she didn't have to face this alone.

She acknowledged she was in shock.

She moved through the next thirty minutes without anything really registering except that she ached inside as she'd never ached before.

Ross stayed at her side, holding her, letting her cry, helping her when her hands shook too much for her to remove the photo of Justice from her wallet to give to the police.

"We'll have all units on the look out and give you folks a call if we hear anything. I suggest you go home and see if he's gone there."

Hope lit in Brielle's heart. Was it possible that Justice had gone home?

Had he run away from the preschool? Her mind had

gone in a hundred directions, all of which involved someone snatching her son.

But what if Justice had left on his own?

Why would he do that?

She glanced at Ross, the truth dawning and hope growing that Justice was okay. "He's not at home."

"How do you know that?"

"He's gone to find you."

Ross's brows lifted. "But I told him I'd come back, that I was only going to be in Boston for a few days."

He'd gone to Boston? Why?

"Obviously he didn't want to wait a moment longer to find you. He kept saying we needed to go find you."

She closed her eyes, remorse filling her.

Oh, Justice. She should have taken more notice of his questions, known that her brilliant son would be a person of action, not waiting around for something he wanted desperately.

"We'll check at local bus stops and contact the local taxi services to see if anyone remembers seeing him," the officer informed them, putting a call in to the communication center.

Brielle nodded then jumped as her phone started ringing. Oh, please, oh, please, oh, please, be Justice, she prayed.

Vann's number showed on the screen. She winced. She hadn't even thought to call her brother. Vann. Justice would have gone to Vann for help.

She hit the answer icon on her phone. "Is Justice with you?"

"Yeah, he just showed up. Alone. What's up?"

Her body sagged with relief. "Thank God. Oh, Vann, thank God."

"He's with Vann?" Ross asked, relief evident in his voice as well.

She nodded, listening to her brother explain how Justice had shown up at the hospital where he worked in a taxi, stating he needed Vann's help to find his daddy.

Brielle started crying and couldn't quit. Not silent tears but full-out, shaking-her-entire-body sobs.

Ross wrapped his arms around her. "Shh, baby, it's going to be okay. He's all right. He's with Vann and he's bringing him back to us."

After letting the police and the preschool know what had happened, they left and went to Brielle's house to wait for Vann to arrive.

"I won't stop him from seeing you. Ever," Brielle informed him when they were sitting on her kitchen bar stools. Ross had forced her to sit, and drink a glass of water. She knew he was just trying to distract her while they waited, anything to help pass the time.

"I know. I feel the same. He needs us both."

Swiping at her eyes, which were wet again, she nodded. "He does." She glanced at Ross, met his redrimmed eyes and realized that her eyes weren't the only ones that were wet. "Oh, Ross. I'm so sorry. For everything."

She stood, wrapped her arms around him, felt the comfort of his arms around her. How long they stood there she wasn't sure. Just that they clung to each other, comforting and being comforted.

"Forgive me, Ross. Forgive me for not telling you I was pregnant," she sobbed, needing to tell him everything. "I wanted you to want me for me, not because I was pregnant."

"I did want you."

"I mean for ever, Ross." She pulled back, stared at him and buried her pride. "Call me silly or old-fashioned or a hopeless romantic, but I wanted you to sweep me off my feet because you loved me and wanted to spend the rest of your life with me. What I didn't want was for you to feel obligated to marry me because I was pregnant and the kid sister of your best friend."

"I was an idiot, Brielle. I should have known that something was going on when you started acting so different." He put his hands on her shoulders, gripped her tight. "I didn't understand and rather than fight for you, for us, I panicked and ran."

"You didn't run. Boston was a great opportunity. You'd have been a fool to turn it down."

"Leaving you made me a bigger fool."

"No, you didn't want the same things I did so you staying would have been worse."

"Tell me, Brielle, when did you start wanting to get married? Before or after you found out you were pregnant?"

She thought back. "From the moment I first kissed you I knew I wanted to marry you."

"But there wasn't a rush until you found out you were pregnant, right?"

"I always figured we'd wait until you were finished with your residency program and were in practice. Honestly, I was so happy being with you I never put a time frame on when we'd take that next step."

"Until nature forced you to put a time frame on it."

"I was wrong to not tell you outright. I just…" Her voice trailed off.

"You just wanted me to do the right thing and give you your happily-ever-after. Only I didn't have all the facts, Brielle. Not like you did, and I didn't understand the sudden rush and the personality changes and you shutting me out when we'd always been so close and of the same mind."

"I should have told you."

He nodded. "Yes, you should have." He took a deep breath. "But having spent several hours earlier this week talking to your brother, I can understand why you didn't, why you wanted more from me."

"You talked to Vann?"

"Yesterday, when my flight landed, I went straight to him. We had dinner, talked."

"I always regretted that your friendship with him ended because of me."

"I regretted that our friendship ended, but that wasn't your fault, Brielle. It was mine, because I let it end without fighting to save it, just as I let my relationship with you end without fighting for it. I can only blame ignorance and youth and stupidity."

"You're not ignorant or stupid, Ross."

"Letting our relationship go wasn't wise, Brielle. Not when it meant losing the only woman I've ever loved."

She swallowed, waited for him to say more, desperate to hear his next words.

"I did date, Brielle. I went through a lot of women, fast, out of sheer desperation. None of them could hold my attention. None of them were you."

The thought of him with other women pained her, but she only bit her lip, keeping silent, knowing he had more to say.

"I met a woman, a doctor I worked with. Theoretically, she was ideal, the perfect mate, and I considered asking her to marry me."

Brielle's heart squeezed. There had been someone special in his life? Thinking of him with other women who were meaningless was one thing. Thinking of him with a woman he'd loved quite another.

"But I couldn't bring myself to do it. You were on my mind more often than not and I kept wondering what you were doing, if you'd ever married, if there was any chance the sparks would still fly between us. I'd wake up from dreaming of you, reach over to hold you, and you wouldn't be there. I'd convince myself that we'd had our chance and only a fool looked back."

He gave a low laugh. "Then I went to this conference in Philadelphia, saw Vann, and instantly knew that I couldn't move on to whatever my future was supposed to be until I saw you again."

He'd thought of her? Dreamed of her? Possibly in the same moments she'd been thinking and dreaming of him?

"Quite casually Vann mentioned that the hospital where you worked was going to have a temporary opening in the emergency room when one of the doctors went on maternity leave. I jumped on it, knowing that just seeing you wasn't going to be enough. The anticipation of seeing you again was eating me alive. You want to talk about silly, hopeless romantic?" He gave an ironic smirk. "When I saw you all I wanted was for you to drop everything and run across the ER, meet me halfway, and throw yourself into my arms."

She swallowed the lump forming in her throat, couldn't quite believe her ears. "You wanted that?"

"I wanted you. I've always wanted you. And before you launch into a tirade about sex, I don't just mean physically, Brielle. I mean you. When I lost you five years ago, I lost a part of myself, and I want that part back."

Her heartbeat thudded in her ears, making hearing difficult, making thinking difficult. "What are you saying?"

"That my heart is yours."

"And you want it back?"

"Asking for it back isn't really what I'm trying to say." He paused, sighed. "When I said we should get married the other night, I wasn't thinking of Justice, or even you."

"What were you thinking of?"

"Me," he answered simply. "I was thinking of me."

"You?"

"I wanted you always, Brielle. I wanted you to be mine for all time. Not because of our son but because I don't want to be without you ever again. I need you." He put his hands on her cheeks, stared straight into her eyes. "I love you, Brielle Winton. I always have. I always will."

Ross waited for Brielle to speak, for her to say anything in response to the outpouring of his heart. Her lips parted then she seemed to lose strength and leaned on him, resting against his chest.

"Oh, Ross."

He held her, kissing the top of her head, wondering what "Oh, Ross" meant.

"You don't have to marry me, you know. I'm yours anyway. I always have been."

"I know I don't have to marry you, Brielle. But you're not listening to what I'm saying. I *want* to marry you."

"You're just saying that because of Justice, because

we got so emotional over his disappearance. We can just date. You can live here. We don't have to marry to be a family."

He took her hand, squeezed it. "My wanting to marry you has nothing to do with the stunt our son pulled today. I asked Vann for your hand in marriage yesterday, Brielle."

Her jaw dropped. "You what?"

"You heard me."

"What did he say?"

Ross gave a low laugh. "That it was about time and good luck with convincing you to say yes."

A slow quivery smile curved her lips.

"So, tell me, Brielle, how does a man go about convincing the woman he loves that he wants to spend the rest of his life with her, that he wants her last name to be his last name, that he wants her children to be his children, to have his last name?"

Eyes wide and shining brightly, she shrugged. "I imagine he should just ask her and see what she says."

"I suppose if he were smart he'd get down on one knee and do it right, wouldn't he?"

"Or he could just ask."

Putting his hand in his scrub pocket and placing his fingers around the box there, he dropped to one knee and took Brielle's hand.

"Ross, you don't have to do this," she whispered, her voice cracking with emotion. "I'll marry you."

"Shh, haven't you read any fairy-tales? You're not supposed to answer until after I ask."

She bit her lower lip, but was smiling all the same as he continued.

"Brielle Winton, will you do me the honor of being my wife and the mother of my children?"

"I could point out that in all the fairy-tales I've read the hero didn't ask for the heroine to be the mother of his children five years after the fact."

He gave an exaggerated sigh. "Obviously you've been reading the wrong fairy-tales." He squeezed her hand. "Woman, you are killing me here with your logic when I'm doing my best to be romantic." Grinning, he pulled the box from his pocket, opened the velvet lid, watched her eyes grow huge and fill with tears. "Answer me, Brielle. Marry me and spend the rest of your life letting me love you."

"Yes." She put her hands on his cheeks, stooped and kissed him, his lips, his cheeks, his lips again. "Oh, yes, Ross. I will marry you. I want to marry you. If you're sure."

"I'm sure." His heart swelling so full that he half expected it to burst, he kissed her back. "I love you, Brielle."

"I love you, too. So much. I always have, you know."

"I know." He did know. Deep down he'd always known they belonged together, even when he'd been too stubborn and foolish to admit how much he needed her. "And you always will, Brielle, because I will spend the rest of my life giving you a million reasons to keep on loving me."

"Am I dreaming?" she asked several minutes later when they came up for air, their bodies sated, Brielle's finger sporting a huge diamond that marked her as Ross's woman for all time.

He shook his head. "Nope, this is reality. Our reality."

"Funny," she mused, snuggling closer to him. "It feels like a dream."

"Like I told you earlier, you've been reading the wrong fairy-tales."

"Hmm?"

"Never mind, I don't want you reading fairy-tales," he corrected himself, lacing his fingers with hers. "I want you living a fairy tale, one of our very own with the most amazing, passionate, love story ever."

She rolled over, stared down into his eyes. "I like the sound of that."

"Me, too." He kissed her, then grinned up at her. "I also like the sound of knocking at the front door because that means Vann is here with our son."

Brielle sat up, scrambled to quickly put her clothes back on, then paused to smile at him with love shining brightly in her eyes. "Let's go and tell him a very special fairy-tale, Ross. One where everyone lives happily ever after."

EPILOGUE

JUSTICE LEANED FORWARD and blew out the candles on his birthday cake. Six candles altogether, five for his current age and one to grow on.

Around him, his parents, his Uncle Vann and Samantha, and several of his preschool friends with their parents watched as all six candles flickered.

Had someone asked him what he wanted for his birthday a few months before, he'd have said a daddy, but he had one of those now.

A good one who made his mommy smile a lot. Justice liked that. He also liked all the presents that his daddy was always bringing home for both him and his mommy. Sometimes he didn't understand their giggles, but adults were like that sometimes. Kind of weird and not always as smart as they should be.

After all, he'd been the one to have to go to bring his daddy home. Something his parents had scolded him severely for. How was he supposed to have known that his daddy had already come home and wouldn't be leaving ever again?

Despite the fact that he'd been grounded from the computer—and it wasn't as if he was going to arrange for a taxi pickup at his school again anyway—and hadn't been allowed to play video games for a whole week, Justice didn't mind since he now had his daddy and mommy all the time.

Only they were so busy looking all googly-eyed at each other and kissing each other that sometimes a kid just needed someone his own size to commiserate with.

He blew a bit harder, pushing every last bit of air out of his lungs, watching the last candle go out and made his wish.

He grinned, rubbed his hands together, and looked up at his parents, and couldn't wait for his wish to come true.

Wonder if he'd have a brother or a sister?

He hoped for a brother, but a sister would be okay, too. Maybe.

"What did you wish for, son?" his daddy asked, his arm around his mom's waist as it usually was.

Justice rolled his eyes at his parents. Didn't they know anything? "I can't tell you or it won't come true, but that's okay, because you will find out anyway when the stork shows up."

"The stork?" Ross and Brielle asked at the same time, eyes wide, then looked at each other and smiled as his hand slid around to cup her belly.

Justice wrinkled his nose at the goofy way they were looking at each other and smiling.

His Uncle Vann and Samantha's gazes went to his mom's belly, their mouths dropping open as his mom just smiled and nodded.

Adults. They were so weird.

Justice dipped his finger in his cake, came up with a big dollop of icing, and stuck it in his mouth.

"Mmmmm," he said, grinning as a camera flash went off, then another. "Is it time for presents yet?"

Because he really couldn't wait to find out if storks made same day deliveries.

* * * * *

A sneaky peek at next month...

Medical Romance™

CAPTIVATING MEDICAL DRAMA—WITH HEART

My wish list for next month's titles...

In stores from 5th July 2013:

❏ Dr Dark and Far-Too Delicious – Carol Marinelli

& Secrets of a Career Girl – Carol Marinelli

❏ The Gift of a Child – Sue MacKay

& How to Resist a Heartbreaker – Louisa George

❏ A Date with the Ice Princess – Kate Hardy

& The Rebel Who Loved Her – Jennifer Taylor

Available at WHSmith, Tesco, Asda, Eason, Amazon and Apple

Just can't wait?

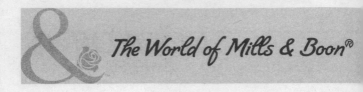
The World of Mills & Boon®

There's a Mills & Boon® series that's perfect for you. We publish ten series and, with new titles every month, you never have to wait long for your favourite to come along.

Blaze®

Scorching hot, sexy reads
4 new stories every month

By Request

Relive the romance with the best of the best
9 new stories every month

Cherish™

Romance to melt the heart every time
12 new stories every month

Desire™

Passionate and dramatic love stories
8 new stories every month

Join the Mills & Boon Book Club

Want to read more **Medical** books?
We're offering you **2 more** absolutely **FREE!**

We'll also treat you to these fabulous extras:

- 🌹 **Exclusive offers and much more!**

- 🌹 **FREE home delivery**

- 🌹 **FREE books and gifts with our special rewards scheme**

Get your free books now!

visit www.millsandboon.co.uk/bookclub
or call Customer Relations on 020 8288 2888